Praise for *Home So Far Away*

"Klara's voice is pitch-perfect, through wonderful dialogues and emotional reflections about belonging and gender in a nationally-bordered, male-dominated, and antisemitic fascist world. The diary form is a palette for Berlowitz's meticulous historical research, creating rich and vivid landscapes in which Klara forges a "freedom both from a homeland that does not recognize me as a citizen – as its child – and freedom to choose a home that resonates for me."

—Rina Benmayor, Professor Emerita, CSU Monterey Bay; Genealogies of Sepharad Research Group

"Captivating. On the eve of the Nazi rise to power, a German Jewish Communist finds the home she craves in Spain, where she becomes deeply involved in defending the Republic. Klara's passion for life and freedom and the pungent sensual details create an immersive experience. The kind of diary Anne Frank might have written if she had survived to adulthood."

—Kate Raphael, author of *Murder Under the Bridge, a Palestine mystery*

"Combining meticulous archival research with compelling literary creativity, Judith Berlowitz tells Klara's story in the form of a diary, from her first visit to Sevilla before the war to her involvement as a nurse and translator during the conflict. *Home So Far Away* not only brings history to us on a deeply personal level; it also offers a vital lesson for today and tomorrow about the threats to democracy and the critical role that commitment –ethical and ideological—can play in its defense."

—Anthony L. Geist, University of Washington; Abraham Lincoln Brigade Archives

"Judith Berlowitz's *Home So Far Away* is an absorbing tale: as her heroine Klara moves between a Germany where Jews are increasingly threatened, to Catholic Spain where Muslims & Jews once flourished, her Jewish identity becomes more central, just as it becomes more hidden. A fascinating historical adventure!"

—Penny Rosenwasser, author of *Hope into Practice*

"*Home So Far Away* is a tour de force of historical fiction. I walked in the shoes and saw through the eyes of the heroine, Klara, and for the first time, I felt the intensity of the struggle of the Spanish Civil War in my own bones —I lived the history through Klara's words. I couldn't leave the story behind, inspired by the strength and courage of those who fought for freedom at great expense and live on through our memory."

—Linda Joy Myers, President of National Association of Memoir Writers, author of *Don't Call Me Mother, Song of the Plains*, and the forthcoming novel *The Forger of Marseille*

"Set amid the travails of the Spanish Civil War, the Second Republic, and the Primo dictatorship before it, this book portrays one character's place in Spain's tumultuous early twentieth century. But it is more. Portraying a woman, who is a Jew, who is German, and who shuttles between Germany and Spain, Berlowitz also ruminates on one's place in history and the impact that large historical events have on all of us."

—Joshua Goode, Associate Professor of History and Cultural Studies; Chair, Department of History Claremont Graduate University

HOME SO FAR AWAY

HOME SO FAR AWAY

A Novel

JUDITH BERLOWITZ

SHE WRITES PRESS

Published 2022
Printed in the United States of America
Print ISBN: 978-1-64742-375-9
E-ISBN: 978-1-64742-376-6
Library of Congress Control Number: 2022901397

For information, address:
She Writes Press
1569 Solano Ave #546
Berkeley, CA 94707

She Writes Press is a division of SparkPoint Studio, LLC.

"Freiheit ist immer die freiheit des Andersdenkenden."

(Freedom is always the freedom of the one who thinks differently.)

—Rosa Luxemburg

"Die Heimat ist weit
doch wir sind bereit:
wir kämpfen und siegen für dich: Freiheit!"

(The homeland is far away
but we are ready:
we'll fight and win for thee, o Freedom!)

—Gudrun Kabisch,
refrain from the International Brigades'
hymn of the Thälmann Battalion

I

BERLIN, *Friday, 2 January 1925*

My mother's usually soft voice trumpeted through the apartment, interrupting Gerda's afternoon practice session, fortunately for me. I was beginning to wonder if my sister's soprano range would ever allow her to reach the low "A" in the Mozart aria she is learning.

"Klara! Gerda! A letter from Seville! From Onkel Julius!"

I was getting ready to leave for a meeting, but a letter from Mama's older brother is an important event in our home, so I gathered with everyone else at the kitchen table around steaming cups of tea as Mama read aloud from Onkel's thick missive, slowly deciphering his archaic, cursive German *kurrentschrift*.

What interested me most, of course, was the political intrigue: after a putsch in 1923, Spain now finds itself in the hands of General Miguel Primo de Rivera, right beside the king, who is referring to the dictator as his own Mussolini. And he evidently says that with pride! Onkel Julius does not offer his opinion, but it is possible that I will be able to hear it in person: Referring to the fact that Mama, Gerda, and I will all be having important birthdays this year (Gerda, thirty in April; Mama, sixty-five in August; and I, thirty-five in June), he insisted that we all come to Seville and spend a week—Holy Week, of all things—with him and his family.

Spain! Just saying the word, my breathing accelerates. Southern sunlight! Odors I have never experienced! Sounds I have yet to hear! Papa, of course, will need to stay here in Berlin, since that time of year represents major profits, and his customers will be flocking to buy their Easter outfits. And Artur and Gina cannot leave their psychology clinic or their home, especially with little Ellen just three and baby Renate not yet two years old. Liese will probably come, if she can be convinced to leave Heinzl and little Günthi with Moritz. Liese is a rarity among us: a true *hausfrau* and a devotee of the proverbial

1

three K's (*kinder, küche, kirche,* the designated domain of the woman—with her children, in the kitchen, and at church).

Onkel was born in Kassel and settled in Spain long ago, before I was born, as the representative of the very successful Brunner Mond chemical business. I think that he and his family are all Roman Catholics. So why is he still inviting us?

When we took down the calendar to determine the dates of Holy Week and our travel possibilities, Mama gasped, "*Gottenyu!* The first night of Passover is April eighth, right in the middle of the so-called Holy Week! So how can we go then?" She sighed, dropping the calendar as if it had just burned her fingers. "We certainly will not be able to make a Seder in Catholic Spain. And will they even know from *matzot?*"

Seder is dear to me as well. Communist that I am, this feast of liberation, of opening the door to others, is the best reason to be a Jew. "But when will we have such an opportunity to see the sights of Seville and to visit our uncle again, Mama?" I asked.

Gerda nodded her head, her tangled dark masses of curls a quivering cloud. "Yes, Mama, we may be able to make our own little private Seder."

My sister, taking my side! Rare and wonderful!

Mama took a few moments for another sip of tea, then set her cup delicately in its saucer and declared, "Well, all right, let's talk to Liese and write to Julius. Papa will be fine on his own here, with Birgit taking over."

With this settled, I dashed off to my meeting. I arrived very late, but as it broke up, I crossed the room to where Comrade D. had just separated herself from two people I did not know. She has spent time in Spain, and I think she is half Spanish herself. Her eyes, secret pools of dark water, and the animated way in which her body moves as she speaks are qualities alien to most Germans.

I asked Comrade D. about the status of the Party in Spain, and she informed me that it is now outlawed but that individual leftist groups may be allowed, if they qualify by turning in their records to the government.

She also mentioned local left-wing hubs scattered throughout Spanish cities, collectively called *La Casa del Pueblo.*

"So," she affirmed, briefly grasping my arm, "I have the address of the office in Sevilla, on the Alameda de Hércules. I will look for it and give it to you at next week's meeting."

Something more to look forward to with this trip besides family and maybe a bit of *Yiddishkeit*: political intrigue. And the dark and dismal streets of Berlin left behind, at least for a couple of weeks. And now that I have pressed its first pages into service, I shall definitely take along this *tagebuch*, just purchased from Benedict Lachmann's bookshop on Bayerischer Platz, to record my experiences abroad.

BERLIN, *Monday, 12 January 1925*

To prepare for our journey, Gerda and I have enrolled in a Spanish class at the Berlitz language school. Liese is busy at home, and Mama claims that she is too old to learn a new language. Yes, we will only be spending a little over a week in Seville, but we two younger sisters—for different reasons—like to be able to communicate with the people who live in the countries we visit.

No German is spoken in our class, but we somehow respond and are learning. We are very impressed with *el método*, by no means the way we learned French or English, and Señor Valenzuela makes learning enjoyable with his gestures, pictures, and even songs. He is most impressed with Gerda's voice, and the other students turn their heads to listen to her when we sing.

I love making these new sounds, doing new things with my mouth and with my whole face, new feelings in my whole body.

BERLIN, *Tuesday, 31 March 1925*

German election results have been tabulated. The German People's Party did not receive an absolute majority, so the election must be repeated at the end of April, according to the Weimar Constitution. The city is already covered with posters and handbills. Trucks roll through the streets, loaded with men and flags and broadcasting loud rhetoric along with their noxious fumes.

Hindenburg is receiving the support of many right-leaning groups, all in opposition to our fragile Weimar democracy. Opposing him will be the Social Democratic Party and the Centre Party. Both of these parties are committed to the Republic but don't seem to be able to overcome their differences in order to unite—a dismaying prospect.

I am feeling rather uneasy about Thälmann's role in the campaign. As Party chair, he has proposed ideas that I just don't think would be appropriate for Germany and that may not even be the best thing for Russia. I am reminded of the Italian expression "*più papista del papa*" and I dare say that Thälmann may be more Stalinist than Stalin.

The campaign will go on for nearly two weeks, but we will be in Spain. I am looking forward to the experience of a new culture, even as I wonder how we will be able to observe a Jewish holiday in the midst of the holiest time of the Christian calendar. I also wonder about Onkel Julius's feelings about living under a dictatorship. For us, being in Spain just might be a preparation for things to come in Germany. I now have the address of a Party office in Seville and just hope to be able to make contact there.

SEVILLE, *Thursday, 2 April 1925*

We finally arrived yesterday, after a long and exhausting journey. Liese's boys are staying at home with Ermengarde, their housekeeper, and of course Moritz. Heinz has just turned fourteen and is thinking seriously about studying medicine but must be reminded to stick to his studies. Little Günther (called "Putzi") is just four and is already trying to emulate anything his brother does. Luckily, Moritz knows how to be patient with his two boys.

Crossing the border into Spain at Cerbère was a rather enormous undertaking since the track gauges are of different sizes. We traveled across lovely, cultivated fields and past tiny towns to Andalusia, where I was almost hypnotized by the endless vistas of silvery olive trees. Just letting my eyes float across that expanse brought great peace to my mind.

At our final stop, an oriental palace rose up before us: the train station at the Plaza de Armas. An exotic welcome to Seville!

Onkel Julius met us alone at the station. Mama recognized him at once and began to sob, murmuring, "He is exactly like our father, Israël. The same neat goatee! The same graceful moustache!" She recoiled a bit, though, at the vigorous hugs he gave us all, kissing us noisily on both cheeks and calling out our names—"Ida! Klara! Elisabeth! Gerda!"

The porter loaded our valises into the boot of a spectacular Hispano-Suiza H6. In German squeezed out with much effort, Onkel explained proudly that the vehicle's engine was based on wartime aircraft engines. He also told us that France had bought up many shares of the company and so had acquired a great deal of control over design and production, putting many locals out of work. I was tempted to comment that if companies like this one were collectivized, the gap between workers and owners would be eliminated, but I held my tongue.

"I am going to take you on a circular route," began Onkel Julius (or "Tío Julio," as he asked us to call him). "I want to enter our street, probably the most *castiza*—echt, typical—street in Seville, Calle San Luis, by the most elegant way: through the Gate of La Macarena."

We were driving along the street called Torneo, separated from the train tracks by a low-lying wall that lent itself to political graffiti as well as posters and amateur works of art. On the other side of the street from the wall were large warehouses storing goods that had been imported or were about to be exported.

"You will occasionally be able to glimpse our river through the spaces in the *muro*, the wall," continued Tío. "Our river, the Guadalquivir, the big *wadi*—the only large navigable river in Spain. And that is the Arabic word. The Romans called it the Betis."

As he slowed down, I was able to make out some graffiti on the wall. I read one line aloud: "*Estibadores: Ni un paso atrás.*" I tapped Tío's shoulder: "What does it mean?"

"*Estibadores*," he said—"Workers of the docks—dock workers—Not one step back! These workers are very often *de huelga*—on strike."

"Ah, bravo!" I exclaimed and then fell silent, not certain of the impression I was making on him and sensing some disapproval from Mama and my sisters. I concentrated on peering out of the auto, and as I did, I noticed that the people of Seville are quite attractive, especially the women. They look more like us than does the typical German. I also saw beautiful posters announcing the springtime Holy Week and *Feria* (Fair) events all over the city.

After a pause, Tío haltingly broached a subject that seemed to cause him some discomfort. His German was even more difficult to understand than before as he said, "Now, dear sister and nieces, I must ask of you a grand favor. In my family, only my beloved wife, María Dolores, knows about my—our—*ascendencia*—our origins. None of our children know anything about this. We live in Spain as Catholics, and we belong to the parish of San Cipriano. I pray you that you not mention the word *Jew* to my children. This is not a thing that I want to associate with my family, *sobre todo*—especially—during this Holy Week. I hope you know what I mean and that you can understand my . . . circumstance."

None of us spoke a word for what felt like several minutes. Though we are not super-pious, what Papa would call *frum*, this was the first time any of us had been asked to actually deny our heritage. We sat silently, each of us in her own thoughts, and I considered the fact that we would be attempting to observe Passover next week. Then I decided to bargain a bit.

"All right, Tío," I finally offered, reaching again for his shoulder. "We won't tell anyone that we are Jewish—as long as you don't tell anyone that I'm a Communist!"

We all laughed a little, and with that, the ice was broken somewhat. Tío sighed and patted Mama's hand.

By then we had turned right onto Calle Resolana.

"This street is filled with sunlight, and that is how it received its name," Tío explained. "You will not recognize it when La Macarena shows herself next week."

"Julius, do you know the history of every street in Seville?" asked Mama in a somewhat chiding tone.

Tío's response was to launch into an eloquent description of the street on which the family home is located: "Calle San Luis has also been called Calle Real, or Royal Street, for a good reason. This street was the nerve center, the *Cardo Maximus*, of Roman times, as well as during the times of the *Moros*," he explained. "We are about to pass through the Gate of La Macarena, where kings and queens entered Sevilla."

As we emerged into the hub of the city, I suddenly felt sheltered within the embrace of the ancient wall.

"We are just passing by the *Parroquia*—Parish—of San Gil," Tío continued. "This is a very old church, probably built over a destroyed *mezquita*—mosque—at the time of the *Reconquista*, during the reign of Alfonso the Tenth, called *El Sabio*—The Wise. The church is built in the *gótico-mudéjar* style, that is, a mixture of Gothic and Mudéjar."

"What is Mudéjar?" piped up Gerda in a sleepy voice.

"It is a term from an Arabic word that means 'conquered.' It refers to the Muslims who lived in the areas newly occupied by Christians."

"So the Muslims were still permitted to produce their art," I commented. "Does that mean that the Christians were tolerant of other religions?"

"Well, for a limited time and in a limited way. Muslims were required to pay a fee to the Christian rulers in order to practice their religion. As the *Reconquista* advanced, religious intolerance grew. Ah, we are about to pass a street where we have one of our cork factories—but see? We have arrived at number forty-two!"

I was amazed to see how briskly Onkel Julius descended from the auto, opened the boot, removed all our luggage, and carried each piece to the polished wooden door, which opened directly onto the street.

Standing in the doorway of the two-story house and smiling at all of us, wearing a white apron with colorfully embroidered flowers, was a woman I assumed was the housemaid. Tío greeted her in quite rapid-fire Spanish. The first thing I noticed was the absence of the "S" sound in the phrase I caught: "*Aquí e'tamo'.*" Señor Valenzuela had mentioned in one of our Spanish classes that the Andalusian accent typically "eats" the "S," and now I am glad we attended that one.

The woman, Asun (Asunción), opened her arms and hugged and kissed us all in turn, on both cheeks, as Tío had done. She is small and solidly built, with ivory-pale skin and glossy black hair pulled tightly back into a bun. Without hesitating, she and Tío picked up our luggage, made their way down the hall, and led us up a staircase.

Asun informed us with gestures that our aunt was sleeping. She then directed us to our rooms, which are quite small compared to our bedrooms in Berlin. Each one contains two small beds. Gerda and I are sharing one and Mama is sharing the other with Liese. Our room overlooks a patio, and I opened the window to birds sweeping across the darkening sky, shrieking incomprehensible messages to each other or to some unknown audiences as they passed.

After we had all used the bathroom, a clattering of feet rose from the stairs, and I turned to receive the warm embrace of Cousin María Dolores—she has the same name as her mother—who exclaimed, "*Prima Clarita, soy Lolita* (Cousin Clarita, I am Lolita)!" Her two children followed closely behind their mother, along with Lolita's sister, another Clara. Each of them bestowed the double kisses on each of us.

On the way to dinner, I noticed a small room off the hallway filled with books, a world globe, and a desk. I shall have to ask about that!

Tante Lola was waiting for us in the dining room, which extended the full length of the house at the rear, with windows overlooking the patio. Her smile was welcoming as she hugged and kissed us all generously. She is a bit younger than Mama, whose hair is now completely gray. Tante's light brown hair waves softly around her face and her skin is also very soft. I would like to ask her if she uses any special product for her skin but will need more vocabulary.

Supper, served by Asun, was light: a Spanish omelet (called *tortilla Española*) made delicious and substantial with potatoes and onions. I was surprised to see the children having a bit of wine, albeit diluted with sparkling flavored water called *gaseosa*. Gerda and I soon became exhausted practicing our Spanish, while Mama and Liese spoke quietly in German with Tío.

Tomorrow evening, the solemn festivities begin with the *Viernes de Dolores* (Friday of Sorrows). We will be taking a walk southeastward, to observe the opening procession.

SEVILLE, *Friday, 3 April 1925*

We breakfasted this morning in an area of the patio covered with a canvas to keep us safe from the light rain. Asun brought us fragrant melon (eaten with knife and fork), sweet rolls, butter, marmalade, and incredibly strong coffee. The hot milk, added to the coffee from a silver pitcher, lingered on my tongue, rich and delicious.

After breakfast, I left the house alone to search for Party headquarters. I walked past Tío's cork factory and reached the Alameda de Hércules. Its spectacular entryway was flanked by two slim Roman columns topped with statues of Hercules and Julius Caesar, both considered founders of Seville. I imagined that the two were welcoming me to the Alameda, which is planted with white poplar trees (*álamos*) whose tender new leaves offered some shelter from the rain.

I finally located the office, a storefront marked with a small, hand-lettered sign reading *PCA*, which I assumed represented something like *Partei Comunista Andalucía*. I stepped inside and found two middle-aged men seated at a chessboard, cigarettes in hand. I did not wish to interrupt their game but one of the men, brown hair combed straight back, looked up and said, "*Buenos días.*"

I nodded and replied as well as I could, saying that I was from Berlin and from the Party of Rosa Luxemburg.

"*Ah, Rosa Luxemburgo,*" he responded. "*Bienvenida, camarada*—welcome, Comrade."

They both stood and shook my hand.

Hearing the sound of Rosa's name pronounced in Spanish, within the sheltering walls of Sevilla, was indeed welcoming. Her name, transformed in that moment, a magic formula, a key that had just opened a door for me. Rosa, now six years dead, returned to life in the warmth of the hands of these two strangers. Her name eliminated the need to explain the reason for my visit, the need to explain myself in a language I have not mastered.

"Please look around," added the other man, who had dark skin and hair and a generous smile, waving a hand toward the literature placed on shelves and on tables. I did just that, and after leafing through a few pamphlets, I purchased one that depicted Spain, and Andalusia in particular, as a feudal society, thanked the men, and left the building.

As I walked through the Alameda, I repeated to myself in a whisper the word *camarada* with a new sense of identity.

Nearing Calle San Luis, I became aware of a penetrating, dizzying fragrance that hung over everything, an odor at once of fresh, new life and rotting death. I approached an orange tree and plucked one tiny, waxy white blossom, the apparent source of the scent. A woman—one of the beautiful *sevillanas*—was passing by, and I asked her to tell me what it was that I held up between my fingers.

Her response sounded like "*aassah-áaah,*" and I repeated it, trying to imitate her facial expressions as well as the sound. Once back at the house, I presented my version of the word to Tía Lola. She laughed and wrote it out for me: "*azahar.*" Then Tío beckoned me over and we stepped into his library.

I was delighted to be let into his little sanctuary. "Azahar," he murmured, and pulled out a bulky dictionary that identified the word, of Arabic origin, to mean both "citrus blossom" and "luck." I now want to know more about the Arabic presence in this city and in Spain, and I hope the little blossom of azahar will indeed bring me luck.

We soon met all our cousins, as everyone had gathered at the house in preparation for our stroll. The eldest daughter, María Dolores ("Lolita"), whom we met yesterday, is about my age and widowed, with two children, ages nine and eight. They are very well-behaved, and they hugged and kissed all of us again. I am noticing the way people touch each other affectionately and in fact stand close to one another when conversing here, reminding me of Comrade D. I am not at all used to this but am trying to relax and not shrink back when someone touches me.

Carmen, Clara's twin, is married to Joaquín (who did not come) and they have a six-month-old baby girl (also called María del Carmen) who stayed at home with her nurse. Carmen and Clara look quite a bit like Gerda and me— the same broad forehead and coarse, curly hair, though Carmen apparently gets hers straightened.

We soon became well acquainted with Clara. She is pampered like a child, at the age of twenty-two. She is called "Clarita," and everything is done for her, though she is apparently perfectly strong and capable. We enjoyed a laugh today comparing the pronunciation of our name in our two languages. She executes the "A" sound with the tongue higher in the back of the mouth than we do, and the "R" with a flip of her tongue at the alveolar ridge, while her attempts at our "R" came out like growling or gargling. Later, I looked in the mirror while practicing the way it feels in my mouth to say my name in Spanish, and then I repeated the Sevillian pronunciation of "azahar" while holding the still-fragrant blossom. It made me feel like a Spanish woman, with a new name and a new vocal apparatus, and actually gave me a sense of freedom.

Gerda is rather blasé about this—her musical studies provide her with a wide palette of sounds, and she says that my name would be pronounced exactly the same in Italian as in Spanish. That may be so, but I am feeling something akin to a chemical change about my body. What I see in the mirror here is not the reflection my mirror in Berlin shows me. My breath quickens at the image of this wide-eyed woman sighing, "azahar."

SEVILLE, *Saturday, 4 April 1925*

I have never experienced anything like the events of last night. First, the concept of a religious brotherhood exclusively for Black people (called *La Hermandad de los Negritos*) struck me as a novelty in a country described as a melting pot by my German guidebook. The explanation that Africans were brought as slaves to Seville by the Portuguese and that the population ultimately "disappeared" makes me wonder how a people could "disappear."

We all boarded a tram eastward to the Calle de Recaredo (named for a Visigothic king—we can't escape them even here!) and dismounted near the entrance of the Chapel of the Angels, modestly constructed in Renaissance style. The rain had lessened somewhat, but the paving stones were quite slippery, and we clutched each other's arms and gripped the children's hands.

Through the open doors of the church, the glare of enormously tall candles struck me between the eyes. Clouds of incense poured out, and then a threatening blast of organ music was followed by the emergence of figures in white robes and grotesquely pointed hoods, brandishing crosses and standards and shuffling across the wet stones. Mama grabbed my arm and pointed downward. They were barefoot!

"*Penitencia* (Penance)," explained Tía Lola, who told us that these men were called *Nazarenos,* named for the town in which Jesus had spent a large part of his life.

After the last white robe had filtered out of the church, we stepped in to view the two figures that would participate in next Thursday's procession. Most spectacular was the Cristo de la Fundación, a crucifixion sculpted in 1622 by Andrés de Ocampo. This genius must have utilized cadavers as a model for a crucified Christ who continued to suffer in death—the wounds freshly inflicted, the diaphragm lifted for the last, agonized exhalation, the eyes recently closed. The cross was placed atop an elegantly carved platform, called a *paso*, made of mahogany and crowned with four ornate lanterns. On Holy or Maundy Thursday, the paso will be hoisted and borne on the shoulders of *costaleros*, volunteers from the community, and carried through the streets of Seville.

We made our way to a side chapel to view Our Lady of the Angels, sculpted in many colors. We approached the canopy that held the statue. Standing before it, surrounded by a multitude of blazing, scented candles, I gazed upon a young mother's grief, conveyed in wood and paint, including large teardrops and semi-parted lips. Then I looked into her eyes: they were making direct contact with mine. I had somehow been expecting glittering adornments, but I was surprised to see that Our Lady wore a plain, striped head wrap, with shawls draped around her shoulders and hips.

"Why is her clothing so simple?" I asked Tía Lola.

"She is dressed *de Hebrea*," she explained—that is, as a Jew.

Tío and I exchanged a sharp look, and I of course said nothing.

I think I am now more able to understand how religious devotion is reinforced, perhaps even created, by these images, which force one to actually make eye contact and to see blood dripping from the wounds of the Divine Being. It helps to combine these experiences with the concept of sacrifice and add the idea of resurrection, but it is the body that closes the circle and guarantees the allegiance.

Mama woke up sneezing this morning. I hope she is not getting ill, as she has a tendency to bronchitis and influenza and has a history of pneumonia. Whenever she sneezes, someone in Tío's family says, "*Jesús.*" I suppose that means that they want Jesus to watch over her health.

It was still raining, and I had planned with Cousin Clarita to visit the Reales Alcázares, which falls within walking distance. My guidebook describes the place simply as a "group of palaces surrounded by a wall," and I needed to see it for myself in order to interpret that description.

Sitting out on the patio under the awning and chatting with Clarita as we waited out the rain, I came to understand her a bit more and started to feel more comfortable conversing.

"So what do you do in Berlin, Prima Clarita?" She used the same diminutive form for me that her family used for her, and I found it very endearing.

"I work as a chemist, and Gerda and I worked as nursing sisters during the war."

"Oh my! I had a lot of medical problems when I was born." She nodded solemnly, her eyes opening wide.

"Not uncommon in twins," I remarked. "In what order were you born?"

"I was the second baby to be born, and I was much smaller than Carmen. The family hired a nurse just to care for me, and I was always given just a little more of everything."

"Oh, I see." I studied her face. "Did you think of yourself as different from your sisters?"

"Ah, yes. In a way I still do. I kept to myself a lot and read a lot."

"Interesting! What did you like to read?" I leaned forward, eager to hear and understand what she would tell me.

"Well," she answered, giggling a bit and also leaning closer, "I read a lot of my big brother's books. He tried to hide them from me. About knights and giants and wolves."

"Ah!" I laughed. "Did you think you wanted to be one of those things?"

"Yes, I thought I could be all of them!" She pushed back a lock of hair that had fallen across her cheek and said, lowering her voice, "I also drew pictures of myself as a knight, and even as a wolf!"

"Oh! Do you still have those pictures?"

"Ah, no." Her expression sagged a bit. "I was afraid to show them to anybody and I tore them up. My brother painted pictures *de fantasía*—but he could do that because he was a boy."

Had I really just heard what I thought I had? There was something still childlike about my twenty-two-year-old cousin, and I found myself almost lecturing her. "Clarita, dear, who told you that you could not be a . . . *mujer loba* (wolf woman)?"

"Nobody told me," she nodded, solemnly, sitting back against her chair. "I just knew it."

I do not think any Marxist readings could have come to my aid in those moments. I saw clearly the role of the family—in a sense, my own family!—as an instrument of capitalist society in quenching women's fires of imagination. And who knows where Church teachings fell in that sphere. But I decided to treat the matter lightly, rather than launching into an annoying lecture.

"Well, I hope that mujer loba is still alive somewhere inside you," I teased.

Clarita made a mock face of horror, eyebrows raised. "Won't you be afraid of her?"

I laughed. "I hope not." I noticed the rain had lightened, and I gestured toward the patio door. "Should we be leaving now?"

Clarita smiled and rose. "Yes, let's go."

We have just returned from the Reales Alcázares, and I would like to return there immediately, even live there, of course after emptying it of visitors. But what I am doing instead is staying in alone tonight, sipping a *fino* sherry from a delicate, hand-cut glass that Tía Lola handed me from her cupboard, and noting my impressions here in my diary about this unforgettable architectonic phenomenon.

The extension of the conglomerate is not merely horizontal or even spatial. It transports one up through time, from a deep space below, offering both dimensions from any one of the locations within the structure. Each of the areas, both tangible (visible) and invisible (disappeared . . . again, people who disappear!), constitutes a monument to the culture that chose this particular location to express its idea of beauty while proclaiming its power. The "original" structure was supposedly a Roman settlement, but why did the Romans choose this spot? Did Hercules the Phoenician set up camp there, and could one burrow down to view the temple—or fort—for which he selected that place?

The next occupying culture, the Muslims, placed its elegant stamp on the compound, delighting the senses of rulers, visiting dignitaries, and military leaders alike, as well as townsfolk. I purchased this card of the Patio del Yeso (courtyard of plaster), as I think it illustrates the surprise I felt at the discrepancy between the delicate working of the material and the military and political dominance of those who lived within these walls and the ideas that these institutions conjure up.

And when the Spanish Christians moved in to reconquer Spain, rather than destroying the symbols of the vanquished, they emulated the Islamic style known as Mudéjar to build their palaces within the compound, coexisting with the first Gothic palaces installed therein by King Alfonso the Tenth, "El Sabio." Clarita had brought a Spanish guidebook, and she pointed out two neighboring inscriptions adorning the palace of King Pedro I: one, in Gothic letters, declares, "King *Don* Pedro, by the grace of God." The other, in Arabic Kufic script, announces, "Only God is greater." The occasional Jewish star was also prominent. I was tempted to call Clarita's attention to that but hesitated—since, according to Tío, she is not aware of her own Jewish heritage.

Even the so-called Catholic Sovereigns, Ferdinand and Isabella, had no qualms about residing within walls designed by Muslims and Jews, despite their battles against the people of these religions and their apparent intolerance for them. But when their grandson, Charles I (Emperor Charles V), moves onto the grounds, we join in a sudden leap to the Renaissance of the West. Without destroying what had been laid down, the horseshoe arches spring open, embracing ancient Rome, while geometrical symmetry is offset by lively tapestries featuring figures of people and animals (depictions forbidden in Islamic art). Statues of gods, of lions, of nymphs and satyrs laugh at the unyielding monotheism of their predecessors—and their successors—and open the world to all possibilities and many deities—even to the *ba'alim* of Hebrew scriptures (Baal, the god from whom Sevilla itself takes its name!). At the same time—and in the same place—the ceilings cling to the Mudéjar style.

And then—the gardens! Viewing them in the rain from within the palaces and framed by the wrought iron grillwork of the windows (some featured calligraphic representations of Koranic scripture, at the same time graced by Jewish stars), I experienced a feeling similar to the comfort and pleasure caused by the olive groves we saw from our train windows, now enhanced with the music of fountains, the colors of the tiles, and of course, the heart-stimulating scent of azahar. . . .

I am now imagining myself reclining on a bed covered with embroidered silken cushions. I dwell in each layer of the cultures of Seville. The splash of the rain against my window reprises the music of the days of the ba'alim. I live compatibly with all of the "disappeared" inhabitants of the Alcázar. The thought is making me dizzy—or could it be the fino?

SEVILLE, *Domingo de Ramos, 5 April 1925*

Today's plan was to walk to the church of St. John the Baptist and follow the procession of its two pasos to the cathedral and back. The pasos represent "Jesus's Silence before Herod" followed by that of the Virgin of Bitterness (*de* la Amargura). Mama has indeed taken ill with a chest cold but insisted on accompanying us.

The church itself is modestly Gothic in appearance and crowned inside by a Mudéjar ceiling (somehow comforting to look at). The building sits atop what was an ancient mosque. I am beginning to expect such contrasts in this city.

The rain stopped for today, fortunately, and the mood of the crowd that clustered around the entrance of the church beginning at around seven o'clock was more animated than that of Friday night. People spoke loudly, and vendors hawked *roscos*, bagel-shaped pastries fried in orange-infused olive oil and dipped in sugar and cinnamon, and Coca-Cola, and a lemon-flavored beverage on blocks of ice.

At about ten minutes after the hour, the people began to shush each other, a solemn drumbeat issued, and from the church emerged the band, a high cornet squealing a sort of descant above a melody that sounded very exotic. Gerda informed me that the march music was in the Phrygian mode. The chief of the costaleros began bellowing encouraging commands to his burly crew, and then the paso itself came into view, step by rhythmic step, ornately gilded, with equally ornate candelabras illuminating the scene that represented Jesus's silence in the face of the challenges hurled at him by King Herod. Jesus, dressed in a white tunic with gold embroidery, faced the crowd. At the other extreme of the paso sat the king on his throne. Jesus's hands were tied before him, and his eyes gazed into a space low on the side, as if wishing to ignore the king's insults. His face was smoothly youthful despite its curly black beard, and nearly expressionless. Herod's features, on the other hand, displayed more character, more history, and he was garbed in more exotic robes. On either side of the king, two figures bent toward him, wearing what looked like Arabic headdress and striped tunics. "*Lo' judío*'!" burst a child's voice from the crowd—"The Jews!"—and then I understood who the figures represented and why my Tío had asked us not to reveal our ancestry. I wheeled to face him, and he cast his eyes downward, almost mirroring the expression on Jesus' face. I wanted to flee the scene, fear gripping my heart, but I forced myself to listen to the music and to follow the procession.

We finally reached the cathedral, which I shall try to describe at length another day, but then we returned directly home, as it was already eleven at night, and the procession seemed likely to continue until two in the morning. The children were exhausted, and Mama was coughing and running a slight fever.

SEVILLE, *Monday, 6 April 1925*

Tío's downcast eyes hovered all night over my uneasy sleep, and as soon as possible this morning, I headed for his little study. He was seated at his desk with a large volume open before him but stood when I tapped on the door-frame and opened his arms to me.

"Klärele, up so early!"

"Yes, Onkel." I took a chair and pulled it up to sit near his desk as he sat down again, clasped his hands on the desktop, and leaned over slightly to look deeply into my face. His smile exuded sweetness, and his balding head reflected the innocence of a baby. Mindful of his cautionary words in the auto on our way here, I began, uncertain of what his response would be but encouraged by the kindness he radiated—

"I was wondering if you realize that Pesach begins this Wednesday night." I hesitated. "We usually do something at home."

He lowered his head, then reached a hand out to grasp mine. "Frankly, Klara, it has been many years since I have marked the—holidays. Nevertheless"—his face brightened—"I think I can show you some Jewish sites that you will be able to connect with."

"I will be happy with anything you care to show us," I replied, relieved, and I squeezed his hand gratefully. "I also have not been very observant since I have become more involved in Party matters, but I think that Gerda and Liese, and especially Mama, would be very touched."

"I understand." Tío gazed for a moment off into the distance. "Well," he finally said, "I think I might be able to please all of you."

"Ah, lovely." I could not imagine what he meant, but I had decided to accept his response, no matter what. My heart warmed with gratitude.

"We will meet here on Wednesday at around seven o'clock," he said. "Let us hope for dry weather."

SEVILLE, *Tuesday, 7 April 1925*

This morning, Mama woke with a noisy cough and was very congested. I worry about her since she tries to take part in everything, and then her health suffers.

When Liese told Asun, with expressive gestures and sounds, that Mama had been coughing all night, Asun said, "*Hay que pone'le lo baho!*"

We looked quizzically at Tío, who interpreted: "*Los vahos.* Steam treatment! We have everything here."

"Except eucalyptus leaves!" offered Asun.

"Eucalyptus?" I echoed. "In Seville?"

"Get your coat. We're going to the street."

Once we were out the door, Asun took my arm and steered me up Calle San Luis to the Plaza Pumarejo. People of all ages sat on the sidewalk behind lines of baskets of herbs. Signs announced remedies for everything from acne to *impotencia*, and under "*Para la tos*"—"for cough"—I spotted a basket of aromatic eucalyptus leaves.

As we walked back to the house with our purchases, I was able to talk to Asun a bit about her life. She seems like a very strong woman, confident in herself and her role in the family. She made an effort to speak slowly and clearly to me. What I understood is that she has been working for the family for over twenty years, since the girls were little. There was also a boy, Julio, who died just three years ago, in circumstances that I simply did not understand. Asun told me that he was a skilled painter. Now I am curious to see his work and understand that this must be the brother Clarita described as painting pictures "*de fantasía.*"

I tried to ask Asun about her working conditions. When I asked if she was connected to other domestic workers, she smiled, patted my shoulder, and said something like, "God willing, that will happen someday."

As soon as we returned home, Asun set to boil a liter of water, peeled and chopped two onions and added them to the pot, dropped in two spoonfuls of honey, and finished by shaking in about a hundred grams of the eucalyptus leaves. Then she lowered the flame but didn't cover the pot and invited Mama to sit in the kitchen while the potion was simmering. Mama entertained herself looking at the delightful animal image tiles—which, Asun explained, had been made in Triana, across the river.

After about half an hour, Asun turned off the fire and let the mixture cool a bit; then she brought a towel and made a sort of tent over the pot, which she placed on the table. She motioned for Mama to lean forward and then covered her head with the towel. "*Re'pire de'pasio,*" she commanded, and modeled deep, slow breathing.

After about ten minutes, Mama was breathing more easily and said she wanted to go back to bed. Asun strained the infusion into a cup and instructed Mama to take sips of it throughout the day. She awoke in the afternoon, feeling much better. I have never seen a quicker-acting medication than this simple remedy.

SEVILLE, *Wednesday, April 8 1925*

Mama was still coughing this morning, though her fever had subsided. She insisted that she felt well enough in the afternoon to gather with us in the small front room to await Onkel Julius, whom we could hear talking to Asun behind the closed kitchen door. Soon, he strode down the hallway and into the front room, smiling and carrying a large woven shopping bag.

"We will take the car," he announced, with no more explanation. The Hispano-Suiza was parked in front of the house, and he maneuvered it until we were heading down Calle San Luis, toward the Alcázar.

As he drove southward, Tío began to hold forth in a way that has by now become familiar: "I assume you know about the Reconquista."

We all murmured some sort of assent, anticipating his explanation.

"The Christian king Fernando III, now called 'El Santo,' entered Seville with his army at the end of the year 1248, after a prolonged siege. He was recognized as the new ruler and was offered two keys to the city by his new subjects, one key from each group. Who do you think they were?"

"The Jews?"

"The Moors?"

"The Visigoths?"

"The Phoenicians?"

We were now making our way down a fairly broad and straight avenue called San José.

"Ha." Tío chuckled. "Not many *visigodos* and especially no *fenicios* lived here then. It was Jews and Muslims who lived within the walled enclaves. The keys that are held today in the *Tesoro* of the cathedral represent these two communities. The king invited descendants of Jews who had fled the invasion of the Almohades a century earlier and taken refuge in Toledo to return. Oh, the Almohades were fierce and religiously intolerant warriors. They were magnificent builders, responsible for the Gold Tower and *la Giralda*, among others, but they wanted no Jews in this city."

"That is a familiar situation for us," Liese said. "We have just come from people like that in Germany."

"*Nihil novi sub sole*," Tío said. "So Fernando settled more Jews in Seville, to serve him and prop up his regime. His son, Alfonso, 'El Sabio,' was even more supportive of the Jews."

"Where were the Jews settled?"

Tío stopped the car and turned to face us. "Right here. We are now within the area inhabited by the Jews of Seville, called the Aljama."

We all gasped and looked out of the window but saw nothing remarkable—no plaques, no walls, just a rather ordinary-looking, smallish church.

"When the Christian conquerors entered Sevilla in 1284, one of the city's many mosques stood on this spot," Tío explained. "Three of these mosques were converted to synagogues when Alfonso assumed the throne. All three monotheistic religions have worshipped in the spot we are looking at now. The relationship between Christians and Jews looked promising, but toward the end of the next century, Christians began to envy the financial power of the Jews."

I felt compelled to interrupt: "Onkel, did the Christians not think of money as something dirty, which is why they restricted the Jews to financial roles in their governments? So now they become enraged when Jews control the purses?"

"Yes, I suppose that is a valid explanation," he responded. "At any rate, what happened was that in 1391, a fanatical archdeacon, Ferrán Martínez, bellowed from the pulpit that his parishioners should kill every Jew within sight, destroy or occupy their homes, and confiscate all religious articles and send them to the Church. The king tried to stop these pogroms, but they spread like disease among the Christian population and infected all of Spain. I think the Christians believed they would be assigned a higher berth in heaven for every Jew they murdered or forced to convert."

"Gottenyu!" exclaimed Mama, coughing a few times. "That is why we want to observe Pesach: to keep the Angel of Death from returning to Seville."

Tío fell silent as he turned into increasingly narrow and uneven streets, negotiating ever-sharper turns, and finally parked the auto by a tree-lined plaza that featured a cross of delicate grillwork.

"We can get out now," he declared.

I wondered if this was some sort of cruel trick: nothing there in that large space except for that cross.

"This place also has a Christian title: La Plaza de Santa Cruz," Tío said. "But it was the location of the largest synagogue of Seville. We don't know its name, nor do we know the name of the mosque that it replaced. After the pogroms of 1391, the synagogue was transformed into a church. But the church was destroyed, by the French, in 1811. Of course, there were no longer Jews here by then. They and their crypto-Jewish and *converso* descendants had been expelled by *los Reyes Católicos*—the so-called Catholic Sovereigns—in 1492."

We all stood facing some benches, away from the cross, in silence, pondering Tío's words. Behind the benches, the fragrance of azahar drifted from the few orange trees.

"What we are standing on now, is the *solar*. We cannot actually set foot directly on any other Jewish site in Seville."

The solar. At first, I was not entirely sure of the meaning as Tío pronounced the word. But then I recalled having seen the word in the guidebooks. It means the soil, the foundation, the earth, but also the antecedents, the lineage, the heritage. *Home. Die heimat*. Standing there, I experienced a sensation similar to what I had felt in the Alcázar. Surging up through my feet and my legs pulsed the sanctity for which this location had been chosen. A sanctity recognized and shared by those early inhabitants—who knows how many millennia ago—even before Jews or Muslims reached Spain. It flowed up through my spine to my heart and my throat. But then, through this deep connection, I found myself witnessing the ripping away of our solar—the clubbings, the stabbings, the insults shouted by the intolerant, ignorant, misguided, murderous mobs. Sorrow overtook me, and the chaos of the past overwhelmed me, and I began to sob.

Awareness of anyone else vanished until Tío gently took my arm and we all moved to sit on the benches beneath the orange trees.

He began to pull things out of the shopping bag. First a plain white cloth that he placed on the bench, next a round brass plate, then a package wrapped in a large white napkin, which, when he unwrapped it, I realized was round, flat bread.

We all gasped, and I began to laugh, though tears still fell from my eyes. "Matzot!"

"Well, almost," Tío chortled. "*Pan ácimo*—unleavened bread, baked today by Asun. We call it *"pan de Jesús,"* and of course you all know that the bread taken as the host replicates the matzot that Jesus consumed with his disciples—at a Passover Seder."

Soon on the platter there appeared the other elements of the ritual: a hard-cooked egg, a roasted lamb bone, chopped dates with nuts, a few sprigs of parsley, and some dark green leaves I understood to represent *maror* (bitter herbs).

"I did not bring saltwater," Tío admitted apologetically. "But I think Klara has provided that with her authentic tears." He smiled, put his arm around my shoulders, and gave me a squeeze. Then he pulled out a gaseosa bottle filled with water, a bottle of red wine, and six simple glasses, each wrapped in a dish towel. The sixth glass was, of course, for Elijah, the Prophet. Would he show himself in Seville? Whose door would be open to him? Would he bring the Messiah?

"How about candles, Julius? Did you bring them?" asked Mama.

"I was afraid that would call undue attention to us," Tío said softly, looking around, even though there was no one about, and I don't think anyone would have understood what he was saying in any event—his German mixed with Spanish and Yiddish phrases. It made me realize that even there, atop our ancestral solar, in the twentieth century, we were not safe. "To the average Christian *sevillano* passerby, we are just people having a picnic in a plaza. But lacking the candles, let us pour the first cup of wine."

He poured the wine into each of our glasses, including Elijah's. Mama murmured the blessing over the wine, and I realized that Onkel was to be a sort of spectator at this ritual. He had provided this experience for us as his guests and as his family, but no longer as his people. It was we four women who were to enact this, our ancestral ritual. I wondered, *Is my uncle now an outsider? Or is he an ambassador, sent by Elijah, to watch over us?*

Onkel poured out a splash of the water for each of us to wash our hands. But it was Mama who gently touched my tear-streaked cheek with the parsley—the *karpas*—and Liese who broke the middle matzo in two and scurried furtively into the bushes to hide the broken half.

Then Tío's question responded to my doubts: "*Gerdele,* will you please ask *di fir kashes?*"

"But Onkel," Gerda protested, "I am the youngest daughter—the four questions are asked by the youngest son—"

"Gerda, you are the youngest person here," I insisted. "This is our solar. It is our day."

She nodded, gently cleared her throat, and began intoning the chant timidly, finally rising to full voice only when it was clear that we were truly alone.

With the final phrase, "we all recline," we made an effort to lean back on the hard benches.

"Let's now recite the ten plagues," I suggested, and dipped a finger into my wineglass to begin: "*Dam,*" I pronounced, spilling the drop of symbolic blood to the ground. As we alternated, naming the plagues and sprinkling the drops onto the ground, Tío remained silent and did not spill any of his wine. I am sure that some of us were wishing for our enemies to be visited by one, or even all, of the plagues. God knows I was. Was Tío also wishing it? Perhaps not. Did he forgive?

With the mention of the tenth plague, the death of the first-born son, he uttered a low moan. *Oy, his first-born!* I remembered. He died just three years ago. Julio. Did the Angel of Death take the son, mistaking him for the father with the same name? I knew I could not ask Onkel about this.

It began to get dark, and the air thickened with the threat of a light drizzle. We helped Tío replace all of the items in the bag.

"Who will find the *afikomen*—the hidden matzo?" asked Gerda.

"Some hungry creature, I hope," Tío said. "We will bring the rest of the bread home for tonight."

Does it matter if an animal eats the Passover matzo? Is that the meaning of "let all who are hungry. . . ."? Was this matzo just a piece of flatbread, baked by a Christian woman in her kitchen? Does matzo acquire meaning solely for the one who consumes it?

I think this holiday will never be the same to me again. No one uttered, "Next year in Jerusalem"—at least, not aloud. I had actually felt that I was in my own Jerusalem for a few moments.

Back home on Calle San Luis, we each ate a piece of matzo at the end of the evening meal. Tía Lola complimented Asun on the bread. I wondered if she knew what it meant to us—to her husband. And if the act of taking communion would change for him after this night, so different from all others.

SEVILLE, *Friday, 10 April 1925*

This day has shown me the strength of the religion of today's Seville. It actually began in the first, dark hours of the day, which the locals call "*la madrugá*," or the dawning. Tío and Tía had reserved seats for us all in a large plaza at the top of Calle Sierpes, called Campana. Around midnight, we dressed warmly—trousers and woolen overcoats, hats and scarves—and joined the throngs of people who were already on the street, heading toward Campana. Asun had prepared a warming, tasty batch of *pavías de bacalao*—codfish pieces dipped in batter and deep-fried in that wonderfully rich and tangy olive oil, all packed tightly in a lightweight metal container called an *hucha*.

We found our hard wooden seats and sat down to enjoy the pavías, wrapped in little tissue-like paper napkins. An urgent drumbeat and brassy fanfare issued from a band that made its way into the plaza. The public began shushing each other, and Liese pointed upward to a balcony. There stood a smallish woman of about my age, dressed in black and gesturing toward the paso. The murmuring ceased, leaving only the incessant, now muffled, drum-beat, and the woman's voice broke out in a tearful "*Ay, ay, ay!*" in what I now recognized as the Phrygian mode. Her voice embroidered around the tonic and returned to it, only to break off in a sobbing groan.

As she paused, Tío grabbed my arm and whispered, "That's Pastora Pavón, *la Niña de los Peines*—the girl of the combs. She is singing a *saeta*, a type of *cante jondo*—deep song."

As Pastora's song moved upward, through the verses of the mode, her voice pierced the air almost cruelly; then, returning to the tonic, her voice suddenly seemed to come from a different singer, metallic and veiled with softness. She broke again into sobs as she resolved the phrase, at which the whole crowd shouted, "*¡Olé!*"

Pastora resumed with a slightly different melody, strident now, and I felt the overtones vibrating in my head, chest, and pelvis. I looked over at Gerda, and she was weeping. Then Pastora reverted to the softer voice and ended her saeta, again breaking off at the tonic, and retreated without fanfare through the open door of the balcony. I had an urge to rush into the building, find her, and embrace her in a sort of spiritual sisterhood.

The costaleros hoisted their load once more and continued, pushed along by the blaring trumpets, and we all sighed and waited for the next paso.

At about three in the morning, the plaza became even more packed with townspeople anticipating the entry of the true queen of Seville, whose full name is María Santísima de la Esperanza Macarena. Her followers had accompanied her from her working-class neighborhood for her triumphal passage through the arch that bears her name. The public rose to applaud as the Macarena's canopy came into view, undulating rhythmically to a brisker march. Past the countless dripping candles and snowy carnations, I could make out her golden crown, encrusted with precious gems, and, with just the right light, her face. Along with the usual tears and furrowed brows, the Macarena's anonymous seventeenth-century sculptor had imbued her with a strength and a resolve that I imagine mothers of murdered children must summon in order to survive and carry on. Her parted lips revealed her effort to control her breathing, another survival technique.

It was nearing four o'clock by this point, and we all felt stiff and cold, so we willingly headed toward the cathedral. Our guidepost was the Giralda, the tower built by the fierce fundamentalist Almohades that was originally part of the mosque, partly destroyed to accommodate the enormous cathedral. I imagined the tower functioning as the minaret for which it was designed, the call to prayer launched from deep within the muezzin's body and echoing through the narrow streets. Perhaps it was the hour or the cold, but the sight of the cathedral in its entirety occasioned in me a slight wave of nausea and a chill. The size itself was intimidating and dizzying, and I imagined the process of construction across centuries and styles, and the domination of the building mass itself over the people living in its shadow and beyond.

As we approached an entrance, I saw the horseshoe arch of the doorway, now called the Puerta del Perdón (Gate of Forgiveness). That doorway was part of the original mosque, Tía Lola pointed out, and I was able to mentally block out the toga-clad saints affixed to the walls on either side of the entrance and receive the comfort offered by the graceful shape of the doorway and its delicate carvings, an unexpected contrast to the famously warlike nature of the Almohades.

We passed through the doorway and into what is today called the Patio de los Naranjos, the courtyard of the orange trees. This area was also part of the original mosque, the area in which the faithful made their required ablutions before entering for services. The rains of the night before had lingered on the azahar, which was now releasing its fragrance as the approaching daylight warmed it, causing me to feel grateful that this area had been spared the zeal of the conquering Christian armies.

Once inside the cathedral, I again felt overwhelmed, overwhelmingly separate and different, but I made myself concentrate on the tombs of some of the notables buried there—Christopher Columbus, among others, and the same Pedro I, dubbed both "the Cruel" and "the Just," whose boastful inscription Clarita and I had seen in the Reales Alcázares.

Finally, I took Liese's arm, Spanish style, and we all agreed that we were tired and hungry. Tío Julio knew just what we needed, and by six o'clock, we were seated at a lovely, marble-topped counter in the bar El Comercio and dipping freshly fried *churros* into cups of thick and steaming hot chocolate.

It was a short walk back home, and after we arrived, I asked my uncle to explain the words of the saeta we had just witnessed. His response was a nod and a squeeze of my arm, whereupon I repaired to my room for a refreshing nap. I awoke a few hours later to find a piece of paper laid on my bureau, in his handwriting, which I can now translate:

> *Lo clavaron con fiereza,*
> *Lo coronaron de espinas;*
> *Sangre mana su cabeza,*
> *Sangran sus ojos y cejas,*
> *Sangran sus sienes divinas.*

They nailed him up, savagely.

They crowned him with thorns.

Blood flows from his head,

Blood from eyes and eyebrows,

Blood from his holy temples.

SEVILLE, Easter Sunday, 12 April 1925

Today marks the event that defines the Christian religion: the resurrection of
Jesus Christ. To believe in this event is to be a Christian, and to be a Christian
is to believe in this event. Tío announced to us yesterday that today's plan
included a bullfight, as well as attending Mass in the morning. We will probably be spending the day packing for tomorrow's trip back to Berlin, as none
of us has the least desire to see a bullfight. Too terrible to contemplate, and I
fail to see any connection with the Christian holiday unless it is that of pain,
sacrifice, torture, and spilled blood.

I was wondering the whole time we were here, even during our improvised Seder, if Tío would try to convince us to become Catholic. I plan to talk
about this to Mama and my sisters. He seemed to me to be quite objective
and matter-of-fact as he explained the traditions and beliefs of Holy Week.
I'll admit that I was made sharply aware of my Jewishness, from the moment
when Tío imposed his rule of silence and especially when I witnessed and
felt in my insides the judgment of the Spanish Catholics toward the Jews as
responsible for Jesus's death. Yes, a slight feeling of guilt, or perhaps only
of sorrow, but mostly a desire to refute the false legend. I had an entirely
different sensation when seeing tangible evidence of the coexistence between
Jews, Muslims, and Christians during Spain's Middle Ages and feeling the
entwined roots of generations coursing up into my body from the solar of
what was once the Great Synagogue of Seville. It was as if I could have lived
during those times without feeling the stigma of difference I feel here—and

in Germany even more. I can change my beliefs, but not my ancestry. I try to imagine what it would feel like to be a part of a nation that would allow me to feel so at home.

To crown our visit to Seville, we all gathered at Restaurant El Cabildo, located near the cathedral. The spot was spectacular—and typical, with its lovely arches and columns and comfortably appointed interior with warm lighting and spacious rooms. Most meaningful to me was an actual section of an Almohade wall forming one side of the dining room in which all fifteen of us (including Baby Carmencita) were seated. I rubbed my hand across its rough, earth-colored surface and tried to inhale and draw into my body some remnant of its builders and of others who had come in contact with the wall. Though I know walls like this were constructed to keep people out, I felt that I was enclosed within it with ancestors I never had but who were accepting me and keeping me safe.

We ordered the oven-roasted leg of baby lamb, called *lechal*; its pungent, sweet aroma mingled with that of the wall, and its taste suggested a return to the space-time visit I had experienced at the Reales Alcázares and to the sanctity of the Santa Cruz solar that had filled my body.

SEVILLE, Monday, 13 April 1925

We spent most of the morning making final preparations for our return trip. Today was considered a holiday, *Lunes de Pascua* (Easter Monday), and the pace of life had slowed. Schools and many businesses were closed. I decided to ask Tío Julio's permission to accompany him on his daily walk, as I wanted to speak to him about something I have been thinking about very strongly, and even dreamt about last night.

I posed the question as we strolled arm in arm toward the Alameda de Hércules:

"Onkel, I know I have not spent a long time in Spain, and I have many things yet to learn, but do you think I would do well in Spain—I mean, to live and work? Are there opportunities for a female scientist who is a Jew, even if a lukewarm Jew, and a Communist?"

"*Ach*, I think we need a quiet place to sit and talk," he said and steered me to the nearest bar. (Yes, bars were open today.) We took a seat at a small, tiled corner table and ordered a couple of finos and a dish of olives, the specialty of the house. I purchased a small jar of them to take home, as I don't think I can bear to return to life in Berlin without these heavenly morsels, and I also want to introduce Papa to this taste of Seville.

"Well, Klara," resumed Tío, lowering his voice, "science has taken some big steps so far this century. The nation began to examine its conscience and its place in the modern world after the humiliating defeat of 1898, and to look outside the country for models. People even began to study abroad—in Italy, mostly, but also in Switzerland. I used to hear the expression, probably coined by the philosopher Unamuno, '*Que inventen ellos. . . .*' How to explain: 'Let the others invent'—and in fact, since the dictator has taken over, progress in science has indeed slowed a bit, as university posts are handed out to Primo de Rivera's allies. But I can say that advances are being made in Spain in all fields of science. Professors and scientists are even coming here from America."

This last sentence was pronounced with pride, and I realized how thoroughly my uncle has adapted to life in Spain, a sort of conversion that is perhaps stronger than his religious beliefs. We proposed a toast—to science—over our first sips of fino.

"Our family's chemical company and other foreign companies have dominated the industry here for many decades. But this may change as our educational system changes, especially propelled by the *Junta para la Ampliación de los Estudios*, even though the dictatorship makes efforts to hold on to the status quo."

"What is this *Junta*, Tío?" I asked, leaning in toward him to bring myself closer to his knowledge.

"This is a government institution created by royal decree and presided over by the wonderful Dr. Ramón y Cajal since the beginning of the century, to compensate for the lack of progress in the sciences here. And," he went on, "did you know that before the 'Royal Goose' took over in February of 1923, Albert Einstein was awarded a doctorate of science, *honoris causa,* from the University of Madrid, and that he came here in person to receive it and met with the king and with local scientists?"

I sat back in my seat. "My goodness, I did not know that!" I exclaimed. "But who is this 'Royal Goose,' Primo de Rivera?"

"Ha, ha," he laughed. "Right! That is one of Unamuno's chosen names for him—which is one of the reasons behind Unamuno's 'involuntary leave of absence' from the University of Salamanca. He seems to have more freedom to think and to write from his exile in France, and the dictator is not spared in his prose or his poetry, nor is the king himself." He lowered his voice even more. *"Halevai"*—I love this Yiddish expression, which means something like, "May it be so"—"when the dictator falls, and may it happen soon, Einstein's ideas, not only about relativity but about pacifism, shall prevail in our country." He took my hand, and tears welled up in his eyes as he added, "And may you have the courage to help bring us progress and peace."

I also began to weep, feeling so moved at his recognition of my beliefs and of his acceptance of my life's mission.

We walked home in silence, and I again clasped my uncle's arm, feeling love and admiration for him, and a renewed sense of dedication to the possibility of Spain as a location for my life.

Just as I was about to come up to my room, Tío handed me this photograph of him. I shall always treasure it.

BERLIN, Saturday, 25 April 1925

Home again and anticipating the results of the election. Our train trip back from Spain included an animated conversation. Rain fell heavily on the new crops and made rivers swell, a comforting backdrop that encouraged confidence and privacy.

I put the first question to Mama: "When Onkel was explaining the Holy Week traditions to you, do you think he was trying to get you to convert?"

"Not at all." Mama placed the magazine she was reading in her lap. "He was as impartial as a paid guide. But later I did ask him what had led him to become a Catholic. He told me that he realized before leaving Kassel for Spain that he was going to be working and living in a Catholic country. He never actually went through conversion but rather began his new life by simply going through the motions."

"Did you ask him if he misses being a Jew?" asked Liese. "I was not sure if he wanted to participate more in our little Seder in the plaza."

"Yes, I did, and though he did admit that he missed some aspects of Yiddishkeit, he confessed that he feels safer in Spain as a Christian, even a nominal Christian, than as an admitted Jew."

"What about you, Mama?" asked Gerda, lowering her voice. "Do you still feel safe as a Jew returning to Germany, now that you have been in Spain? Those horrible pogroms of 1391, incited by an insane demagogue? Couldn't this happen in Germany?"

"Now Gerda, we have talked about this before," Mama said adamantly, tipping her head to one side. "We have lived in Germany for centuries. We are Germans first. We speak German—in fact, we speak better German than most Germans. Your father's work makes him an accepted part of German society. After all, his business makes the uniforms that our troops put on every day, in many lands, even in Africa. Your brother served as a medic in the German Army in that horrible war, and he and Gina have patients among all types of Germans. We make positive contributions to the welfare of the German people."

"But what about the notices plastered on all the public buildings, especially in the south, and that wild beast, Hitler, and some of the messages around the election that the country would be better without Jews?" Gerda protested.

"People have always said bad things about Jews," Mama said dismissively, waving a hand in the air and picking up her magazine. "That is never going to change. We go on about our lives in an honest way and we do not let a few crazy people intimidate us."

"I hope you are right, Mama," I said. "But this election runoff could point in a dangerous direction."

"Well, you will do what you need to do, Klärele. We are going to be just fine."

BERLIN, Tuesday, 28 April 1925

So now I am trying to come to terms with the results of the second election. I am not surprised, but I am disturbed and also hopeful that we can address some of the conflicts within our Party. What is not surprising is the fact that Hindenburg has emerged triumphant, if unwilling, with a bare plurality of votes. Thälmann and the German Communist Party received a mere 6.4 percent, even less than in the first round. I'm sure that many Party members chose to vote socialist this time because of their distaste for Thälmann. This leads me again to speculate that if the KPD had been able to overcome our differences with Marx's Social Democratic Party and the German Democratic Party, forming a left coalition, we might have been able to put people in power who can truly eliminate class conflict and the cult of personality and instead address the common needs of the working classes. I can only imagine an increase in militarism, and even in imperialism now for Germany, with Hindenburg's advocacy of *Lebensraum*.

BERLIN, Saturday, 2 May 1925

I so miss Tío Julio, and I miss being in Spain, especially speaking Spanish and the way people touch each other. Since our return, I have noticed how far apart Germans stand while conversing, compared to Spaniards. I also realize that in Spain, even though my language skills are limited, I found myself saying things that I would hesitate to say in German. I spoke about myself in more personal terms, and addressed others—Clarita or Asun, for example, or even people I didn't know—in more personal ways than I would in German. That chemical shift I felt in Seville is still with me, and my feeling of difference here in Germany is stronger on return than it was before.

BERLIN, *Friday, 30 October 1925*

Gerda has thrown herself into her work with the immigrant children at Siegfried Lehmann's Jüdisches Volksheim. She has returned to her mission of carrying donations through the streets and, since she has let her hair grow out naturally, presents quite a wild spectacle. She has also been devoting herself to teaching her beloved kindergarten group, which five-year-old Putzi has now joined. She sometimes appears to be in a sort of trance, not responding when spoken to and staring into the distance. She even lets Putzi bring our dachshund Lumpi to school and reports that the other children adore him and are learning to bestow tender care on animals. Here is a picture of them in our garden.

BERLIN, *Friday, 15 January 1926*

My niece Ellen's fourth birthday is coming up next month, and I have been asking Artur and Gina to let me have her for the day. I would love to take her to work with me. She is very interested in people and is already beginning to read. A serious child, she knows exactly what she wants and asks a lot of questions. I love to hear her formulate them, though I am not always able to answer her in a satisfactory way.

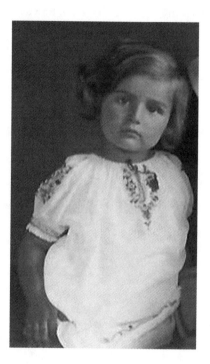

BERLIN, *Wednesday, 15 December 1926*

True, I have not opened my diary for quite some time and have been attending too many meetings to recall or comment upon. The Party purchased a huge building last month just off the "Alex" (Alexanderplatz) to serve as headquarters and has named the building "Karl-Liebknecht-Haus." The *Rote Fahne* newspaper will be published here, and offices are still being installed in the building. While it is wonderful to see such a major landmark named for a stellar founder of our Party, one whose voice was raised against war and its capitalist origins, I only wonder why the building was not named for Rosa. When will landmarks be named for women, for Communist women?

Artur and Gina are expecting their third child in May. Gina continues to go to her office and see patients. She is such a strong woman; I have come to admire her. Since returning from Spain, I have been going out to Nowawes and spending time with the little girls: Ellen, who will be five in February, and little Renate Eva, who just turned three this past summer. Ellen explains all of Renate's needs to me with great authority, and Renate is so adorable that people in the street stop to comment on her beauty. I love hugging and kissing them, another trait that Spain has engendered in me, and they now run to me with open arms when I arrive, shouting, "Tante Klara, Tante Klara!"

NOWAWES, Saturday, 14 May 1927

It's girl number three! Born two days ago, healthy but very tiny and must spend some days in hospital. They have named her Nora Teja Susanne. Gina had been thinking about giving her baby a Hindi name, and Teja means both "light" and "strength."

I am staying at their home while Gina and the baby recuperate. They have a nursemaid, but the girls had been asking for me, and I am more than happy to care for them and take them to the park in this lovely spring weather. Artur continues to see patients during his consulting hours, and his home and office addresses are listed in the Nowawes section of the Potsdam directory.

Papa's business has not been doing very well. For extra income, he and Mama are planning to rent out Liese's former bedroom to a student, and they have posted notices at the University.

BERLIN, Saturday, 1 October 1927

Our new boarder has moved in. Leo Szilard is a physicist from Budapest, and actually an instructor at the university. He is quite handsome and youthful, with a friendly, jovial nature. He dined with us this evening and mentioned that he is well acquainted with Einstein and is actually collaborating with him on some inventions. Pressed by Papa, he explained that his family changed their surname from Spitz when Mr. Szilard was an infant. He explained the "Name-Magyarization" campaign promoted by the Austro-Hungarian monarchy, in the name of national unity. It seems like a loss to me, especially as it forces people to conform to an official policy. And does it not also stamp Jews as lesser beings—people not qualified to participate in the society at large? How can one be expected to hold allegiance to a society that does not allow one to retain one's traditional name?

Mama did not join us at table. She has had a head cold for about four days and is reading in her room.

BERLIN, Tuesday, 4 October 1927

Mama is now complaining of sudden chills and chest pain and seems to have influenza. We don't want to take her out as the weather is unseasonably cold, windy, and rainy. We will have Artur recommend someone to come to the house to look at her.

Tonight at supper, I noticed that Mr. Szilard was looking intently at Gerda across the table. She blushed and looked downward. He stated that he was interested in the arts, but I think it is actually Gerda who is the object of his interest. Gerda appears rather neutral about the attention, and she is certainly not talking to me about it.

BERLIN, *Saturday, 8 October 1927*

Mama has developed a high fever and stays in bed, taking only tea and thin soup. She is very irritable and wants me to sit by her bed; then she tells me I'm not doing something correctly, or rather that I'm not doing *anything* correctly. Doctor L. says she should be kept covered and encouraged to sweat and has issued a preliminary diagnosis of pneumonia. So I pull the woolen blanket over Mama, and she throws it off and orders me either to freshen the cool cloth for her forehead or to leave the room. This afternoon I tiptoed in, and she bolted upright and—staring into space and waving her arms—shouted hoarsely, "Get Lumpi off my bed! Get him out!"

I took her hand. "Lumpi is not here, Mama. It's me, Klara."

She sank back down and appeared to sleep.

BERLIN, *Monday, 17 October 1927*

Mama awoke this morning drenched in sweat and demanding coffee, lox, and rye bread. Birgit and I gave her a sponge bath and helped her to put on fresh clothes, and she devoured the food and added generous portions of cream and sugar to the coffee, which she sipped with gusto. Her temperature has dropped, but she still feels too weak to get up. She must have heard us talking about putting her in the hospital, for she keeps repeating, "No one is taking me to any hospital. I'm staying right here."

Dr. L. believes she has passed the crisis but that she will take quite a while to convalesce.

BERLIN, *Monday, 24 October 1927*

Today was Artur's birthday and we all celebrated it together here on Prinzregentenstrasse. Artur brought a bottle of plum *schnapps*, making Papa very happy. Heinz and Putzi are handsome and well-mannered and very respectful toward Mama, who was up and dressed and beaming at the children, though quite a bit thinner. Artur and Gina's three girls are wonderful, and Gina is happy to have returned to work. Ellen, the eldest, is very proud of her reading skills and asked permission of Mama to read to her little sisters from our well-worn edition of *Der Struwwelpeter* (Shaggy Peter). Even baby Nora, only five months old, opened her eyes wide as Ellen declaimed very dramatically and with much expression, and Renate shrieked both with delight and horror at the antics of the bad-mannered children, her blue eyes sparkling. Gerda took a turn reading and even improvised melodies to the verses, and Liese rushed to the piano to accompany her, skillfully creating dissonant harmonies *à la Viennoise*. This bizarre "opera" set Mama to laughing uproariously, which turned into spasmodic coughing that forced her to return to bed.

Mr. Szilard did not join us, and Gerda did not seem to miss him. After everyone had left, she and I sat in the kitchen, sipping the delicious, aromatic schnapps.

"Klara," she said after a few moments of silence, "I am thinking about assisting Siegfried Lehmann in his Ben Shemen project, perhaps even moving to Palestine."

"Oh, really, Gerda?" I was surprised. "So does this mean that you believe that Palestine should be a Jewish homeland?"

"Well, from my work among the *Ostjuden*, I see the threats to Jewish children in Germany. There is really no future for them here as things stand."

"That may be true, but I would feel more sympathetic toward Palestine if a Jewish working class could settle there, work the land. Besides, I don't think that a religion should be turned into a nationality."

Gerda set her glass down, frowning. "What do you mean?"

"Well, if Palestine becomes a 'Jewish' homeland, would that mean that people who are not Jews could not make their home there?"

"Oh, I never thought of that," Gerda admitted.

We finished our drinks and kissed good night.

It is now very late. I am back in my room. I must have slept for about an hour and then got up to use the bathroom. Just as I reached my door, I noticed Gerda slipping silently down the hallway in a peach-colored silk negligee and, instead of turning right toward her bedroom, turning left toward Szilard's room. A deep stirring arose in my body at the sight of my little sister evidently going to meet her lover. Back in bed, alone, I imagined myself with a lover and attempted to satisfy my longings.

BERLIN, *Monday, 30 October 1927*

Mama's fever has returned, and she stays in bed, coughing with much pain and congested with thick mucus. I have been staying home from work with her and observing her breathing, which is becoming more labored. Gerda continues to volunteer with the children at the Jüdisches Volksheim and to operate her little kindergarten class, while she often dines out with "Leo" and has begun to meet him and Herr Einstein at the Café Wien in the afternoons. I would also like to meet Einstein and have let Gerda know this, but I think that Mama really needs me now and that this is where I need to be.

BERLIN, *Friday, 4 November 1927*

I can't stop weeping! Mama died during the night. She had been having episodes of apnea for the past twenty-four hours. She was so patient through these periods, not panicking (as some of us did) and assuring us, by patting our hands after each paroxysm of coughing, that she was going peacefully. Toward sundown I sensed it would be her last night, and I wanted to crawl in bed with her, but I reluctantly left her room at around midnight. This morning Papa stumbled into my room, weeping, and told me, "Mama is gone." When he woke she was still and not breathing. We telephoned Tío Julio in Seville,

and it was somehow easier for me to speak to him in Spanish. Tío offered to
contribute to the announcement we posted in the *Berliner Tageblatt.*

Gerda is reacting to Mama's death most intensely, as she had not been
spending much time with her during her final days. She has emerged from
some sort of stupor, and she is suddenly activated and has covered all the
mirrors in the apartment in preparation for sitting *shiva.* She has taken the
streetcar alone to Weissensee to make the burial arrangements, for tomorrow
at two o'clock.

As the middle female child, between Liese marrying at twenty-four and
having children and Gerda with her singing career, I had taken on the responsibility of caring for Mama and protecting her in a way that Papa did not seem
able to do, as he is so engaged in his business. I cannot believe she is gone
and that I won't be able to clasp her hand to steady her (and also to reassure
myself). Here is a picture of the two of us on a hike in the Bavarian Alps,
about ten years ago. Dear, sweet Mama, adieu!

BERLIN, *Tuesday, 22 May 1928*

Good news about the Elections: The KPD won 10.6 percent of the votes, giving us nine more seats in the Reichstag—the lower house. And Helen Overlach won a seat—a hollow victory, in my opinion, as the women in this body are only expected to act on traditional "women's issues" like education, childcare, and reproductive rights, and to stay within the limits of their parties. I know that in previous years, women have met across party lines to discuss political matters, but most recently have been discouraged from doing so by the men leading the various parties. And I fear that women of the other parties do not feel sufficiently competent to pierce through the smoke and noise in order to speak about politics. This is probably why we lag behind Great Britain and Denmark in electing women to positions of power. The Bolshevik idea of the "new family" sounded wonderful, but Soviet women are expected to continue their full-time roles in their homes as they join the workforce outside.

BERLIN, *Tuesday, 9 October 1928*

An exciting day: Leo invited Gerda and me to join him and Albert Einstein for tea at the Café Wien on Ku'damm 26! And what a magnificent place! Beautiful, polished wood, round tables with artists discussing their creations, and various floor levels, including a Gypsy cellar—all of it modeled on the Viennese coffeehouse, brainchild of Karl Kutschera. Quite a few degrees above the Romanisches Café in elegance, with less emphasis on *rachmunis*, to use the play on words in Yiddish ascribed to the very noisy, Bohemian location (*Rachmunisches—pitiful—Café*).

The men were already seated in the café when we arrived. Einstein had lit his pipe, and smoke curled through his shaggy hair and drifted above his head. He had tipped his chair and was leaning back. His legs stuck out, and I noticed that he was not wearing stockings, despite the cool weather. During the introductions, he impressed me as quite charming, a bit shy and self-effacing, unlike Leo. He seemed to avoid eye contact and to be talking to himself rather than to us, but he did tell Gerda that he had heard her sing in Munich and that her voice was lovely. He asked her if she had ever performed Mozart, to which she blushingly answered in the negative, though she, of course, has studied many Mozart arias.

Gerda's interest in what Einstein could tell us was very different from mine. She explained to him: "Herr Einstein, Leo—Herr Szilard—may have told you that I am very interested in Siegfried Lehmann's Ben Shemen project in Palestine. Besides rescuing poor Jewish children from life in the city and from the . . . problem we are now facing in Germany, and teaching them to work the land, Herr Lehmann has joined the movement to carve out a new and safe homeland for the Jewish people. Might I have your opinion on the subject of Zionism?"

Einstein grunted and scratched his chest, looking into the distance. "Well . . . I am planning on attending the Sixteenth Zionist Congress next year in Zurich, in July . . . but I should tell you that I have signed up as . . . a non-Zionist."

"Ah," sighed Gerda, her eyes wide.

His gaze returned to Gerda and to me, as he began, slowly choosing his words: "The Ben Shemen project is very promising. I would like to help these children. But please remember . . . that there are people already living in Palestine, namely, Palestinian Arabs." He paused and took a puff on his pipe. "They had established . . . flourishing civilizations . . . even before Abraham arrived." We nodded as he added, "The best condition under which Jews could live there would be in a binational state. The worst thing that Jews could do in Palestine would be to perpetuate nationalism *à la Prussienne*." He tapped on the tabletop to emphasize his next words: "This is precisely our greatest threat in Europe."

Gerda looked down in thought and then solemnly replied, "If I were to travel to Palestine, I would try to remember your words."

I told him sincerely that I agreed with his point of view and continued: "Herr Einstein, I am very interested in your stay in Spain."

"Ah, yes, 1923. I was awarded an honorary doctorate from the University of Madrid."

"Ah," I responded eagerly. "I visited Seville in the spring of 1925 with Gerda, my mother, and our older sister, and I am fascinated with Spain. I am actually thinking about going there to live and work." Gerda turned her head abruptly to look at me. "Do you know of something I might do there, and are you in contact with anyone in the field of chemistry in Spain?" I immediately regretted what must have sounded like a breathless and inappropriate outburst.

He chuckled a bit before replying, "Well, I did meet with the king. I hope you are not intending to move into the Royal Palace." We all laughed at that possibility. "But there are laboratories associated with the wonderful *Institución Libre de Enseñanza*—the Free Institute of Learning—that might have a place for you. When the German Embassy hosted me at a dinner in Madrid, I met a very interesting woman, María de Maeztu, an educator who advocates for the study of the sciences for women. I had almost forgotten her, as the dinner itself was rather dreadful. There was talk about her connections with the dictator, so I was not too eager to form an alliance with her."

These words and the little joke about the Royal Palace gave me courage to go on: "I am already able to speak some Spanish and have done some reading in my field—bacteriology—in that language."

"You are doing better than I am in that respect," replied Einstein. "I speak absolutely no Spanish, but fortunately I am still in touch with a wonderful Catalan scientist, Rafael Campalans, who was able to communicate with me in German while I was there."

"In what language did you lecture in Spain?" I asked.

"I did my best in French, which is not so good, but when I was offered a good translator, like the splendid philosopher Ortega y Gasset, I was able to lecture in German."

Then Szilard intervened, and I thought I detected a twinkle in his eye: "Herr Einstein, if you know of a position that Klara could fill in Spain, I will be happy to let her know. And I think she might be interested in some of your stories about your influence in Spain."

"Ah, of course," responded Einstein wryly. "Everyone in Spain is suddenly an expert on relativity, light, and curved lines." To illustrate his point, he pulled out of his jacket pocket a wrinkled clipping from the Spanish newspaper *El Sol* showing a cartoon by Lluís Bagaría of a working-class man in the street, commenting aloud about an attractive female passerby, with the caption: "*¡Ay, qué curvas! ¡Viva Einstein!*" ("Oh, what curves! Long live Einstein"!)

BERLIN, Tuesday, 6 November 1928

Today we had Mama's unveiling ceremony, amid heavy rainfall. Onkel Julius traveled from Spain, and Szilard also attended, which moved me a great deal. Papa and Tío Julio stood together, and both were weeping. The rain did my weeping for me, as I concentrated on helping Gina keep baby Nora out of the rain. As the oilcloth was removed from the stone, Gerda stepped away from Szilard's side, closed her eyes, and began to intone the chant for the soul of the departed, "El Malei Rachamim." The rain's strumming on the earth provided a constant drone for Gerda's unwavering voice and offered her strength to sustain the beautiful ornaments, which she prolonged in tribute to our dear mother, who had given so much of herself to us and made such efforts to brighten our lives. I have never heard my sister sing in such a way that connected us to our ancestors and at the same time was reminiscent of the cante jondo that had affected us so strongly in Seville. After the final amen, all was silent, even the children, save the hissing of the rain as it rushed through the trees to its final drumming on the ground.

Birgit had prepared a warming meal at home. After we had eaten, Tío called me into the kitchen, and we perched on stools at Birgit's work table. He watched my face as he ceremoniously unwrapped the bottle of fino he had brought me from Seville. This made me very happy, but not as happy as what he then told me:

"Clarita, I have been in touch with some people from the University of Madrid, specifically the International Institute for Girls and the School of Medicine. Our new generations of scientists are struggling against the restrictions of the dictatorship as they attempt to pull Spain into the modern world. The number of women students is gradually increasing, as are new courses in the sciences. There will be a need for laboratory assistants for these courses."

I gasped. "I have been doing more research in bacteriology in this past year since Mama's death, reading articles by some Spanish scientists in the *Biochemische Zeitschrift*. Would you have any connections in this area?"

I searched for Mama's cordial glasses as Tío considered his response.

"I could probably help you make some contacts. I think the *Junta para la Ampliación de Estudios*, the Council for Further Scientific Study, emerging as it does from the *Institución Libre de Enseñanza*, would be the place to start. This organization represents the heart of progressive scientific thinking in Spain, in fact of humanistic culture in general. You would of course need some good references."

I poured us each a generous glass of fino and responded with a chuckle, "Well, Tío, I think I might be able to produce quite a good reference. You have heard, I suppose, of Doctor Albert Einstein?"

"Ha, ha, ha! Are you serious?" laughed Tío.

"Quite serious. He has been collaborating with Szilard, our boarder and Gerda's . . . friend . . . on some inventions, and we actually met a few weeks ago at the Café Wien. I feel confident that he may be able to write me a brief letter of recommendation, with a little . . . *nudzh* . . . a push . . . from Szilard. "

"Well, let us toast that nudzh, Clarita," declared Tío (echoing the Yiddish word I had hesitated to use with him), and we clicked our glasses and sipped some delicious fino to cement the possibility that I may really be going to Spain.

BERLIN, *Sunday, 18 August 1929*

After many attempts, I have finally established a correspondence with the director of the International Institute for Girls in Madrid, Dr. Mary Louise Foster, an American chemist and professor. I had written to María de Maeztu, mentioning Einstein, and I think that his name was the magic formula. She had evidently mentioned me to Dr. Foster, who in the fall of 1930 will be returning to Madrid from Smith College in Massachusetts, to supervise the modern laboratory at the *Residencia de Señoritas* that was dedicated last year. Called the *Laboratorio* Foster, this is the first chemistry lab devoted to female Spanish students of the sciences. Now to get my documents in order.

BERLIN, *Sunday, 3 November 1929*

The financial world has fallen to pieces, and I am so worried! Following a crash in the US Stock Market, businesses here have had to shut down or let most of their employees go. Papa's factory will remain open, though he has had to dismiss some workers, since his business was supported by our government, rather than by American banks. But who knows if the government will be able to repay America for the loans made to upgrade our highways and rebuild our factories and bridges after the war? People are rushing to the banks to withdraw their savings, and the funds are not being replenished.

Against this backdrop, Gerda has left for England, which is also feeling the shock with its losses in world trade, though their businesses had not been propped up by America as extensively as ours had. The chemical industry, in which the Monds have prospered, may not be affected as strongly, so Gerda is hopeful that she can convince some family members to offer financial support to the Ben Shemen project.

In the Marxist papers, people are saying that the crash was simply a climax to what had already been building up: a steady decline in the capitalist economy. The delights of Berlin during this past decade have been enjoyed at the expense of the poor, and now perhaps the classes will become more equal, but not in the way we would have hoped.

I am still waiting to hear from Spain about the possibility of a position in the Foster Laboratory at the Residencia de Estudiantes. I understand that things like official matters and even daily negotiations take a little longer to materialize there, so I am concentrating more on my Spanish lessons and have hired Comrade D. as a private tutor. We meet twice a week, and I find I am able to answer and ask questions in Spanish and actually understand D.'s responses.

BERLIN, Monday, 10 February 1930

The letter came today: I have been accepted to a position in the laboratory of the University of Madrid, beginning in September! From the sections on Spain in the German newspapers, I have also learned that the Spanish dictator, Miguel Primo de Rivera, has resigned. There has been much pressure on him from the liberal sector as well as the military to step down, and he had put down several coup attempts, besides the fact that the man was probably simply worn out and in very poor health, diabetic. The king has already replaced him with a military man, Dámaso Berenguer. Spanish hopes, at least among the bourgeois and the intelligentsia, are that Berenguer will restore normalcy. I'm not sure how much justice can be expected under a king who backed the coup that put Primo de Rivera in place. This new government is being called a *dictablanda*, coining a very clever (and untranslatable) Spanish play on the word *blanda*, meaning *soft* (in contrast with *dictadura*, as *dura* means *hard*). Despite relaxation of government control in many areas, the Communist Party is still completely outlawed, being the closest ally of the working classes and enemy of the monarchy. But I will soon be able to learn more and perhaps even participate in the downfall of the dictatorship: such an exciting prospect!

Artur and Gina are planning a trip to an island in Denmark in July, as a holiday and also to explore the possibility of moving there. They made me very happy when they asked me if I could stay with the girls, which I would love to do. I will end my job at the lab at the end of summer, and I will leave for Spain soon thereafter.

NOWAWES, *Wednesday, 9 July 1930*

I have been with the girls for five days now. The housekeeper, Ilse, helps with laundry and cleaning, but I have been cooking meals with the girls and spending much time with them out of doors. Last night we all camped out near the Havel River. I let them run a bit wild and also feel somewhat wild myself, without the pressures of work and Gina's restrictions, and also realizing that I will soon be in Spain. The girls take their shirts off, and we drive through the woods with the top down and let the wind tangle their hair and the sun bronze their little bodies. Here's a photo Ilse took of us, with Ellen at the wheel of the Opel.

BERLIN, *Friday, 18 July 1930*

More people than ever are now begging for coins in the streets. Hindenburg has dissolved parliament and called for new elections, set for September 14. Not only will I be unable to vote, as I will be in Madrid, but it will be difficult for me to participate in the campaign, as my support for the KPD and Thälmann is frankly no longer my greatest concern, though I wish I could be here to vote against Hitler. His "Nazis" (abbreviation for the National Socialist German Workers' Party) are modifying some of their tactics in order to look good to industrialists and the upper classes. Hitler is taking advantage of the economic crisis by presenting himself as the savior of the German people. His speechmaking tactics are theatrical and calculated: he seems to be present in every district of the country at once, and he delays his appearance to build up tension and then blasts through the crowds with military music, protected by brown-shirted SA (Storm Detachment) troops. I have actually stopped listening to the radio, as the formula is always the same: he begins speaking quietly and hesitatingly, then gradually creates a crescendo of volume and pitch, in his characteristic accent with its prolonged rolled guttural R's. The speeches all end in screams, first from Hitler himself and finally in the echoed "Heils" exploding from the audience. He addresses the spellbound throngs and offers them everything they long for: jobs for the jobless, prosperity to the bankrupt, classlessness to the young idealists, and a return to the glory of the Fatherland to the disillusioned. He vows that he will end the payment of war reparations, dissolve the treaty of Versailles, end political corruption, stamp out Marxism, and of course, put the Jews in their place. Do the people believe all this? Amid such desperation, logic has been replaced by wishful thinking.

II

MADRID, *Tuesday, 9 September 1930*

I arrived early this morning. The Spanish train system has improved somewhat and is a bit more efficient and punctual under the dictatorship. Perhaps this is a case of what we call in Germany "enlightened despotism." I'm looking forward to seeing how far the enlightenment extends into daily life and for what people. Once at the Atocha-Mediodía station, I called for a porter to help me with my very heavy valise and asked the driver of the late-model Renault to drive me to what will be my home in Spain: a room with a family in a third-floor walkup in a newish building at number eight, Calle Donoso Cortés, in the Chamberí district. We pulled up in front of a rather large structure, on the corner of Magallanes Street. The exterior is fairly ordinary looking, but much to my surprise, I was greeted by a beautiful, modern, wrought-iron gate and a marble-lined, well-lighted vestibule or lobby in neoclassical style. The driver helped me up with my valise. In addition to my books, I had to bring many more clothes than I normally do for travel. I had been warned about the extreme climate of Madrid. The Spanish expression, I was told, is rhymed as "*nueve meses de invierno y tres meses de infierno*" (nine months of winter and three months of Hell), so I brought light clothing for the warmer weather and heavy woolens, boots, and trousers—though I was not sure about what was acceptable in Madrid—for the expected winter.

The woman of the family was the only one at home, and she received me with a hug and the usual double Spanish kiss. Her name is Hortensia Alonso Villaseñor (Spanish women retain their maiden surnames)—she is small and round, with reddish-brown bobbed hair and greenish eyes. Her husband, Severino Jurado, works in construction and was expected home for the midday meal. Hortensia's mother had died earlier in the year, and they needed some extra income, given the worsening financial situation in Spain, so they decided to rent out her room. I left my valise, followed Hortensia to the kitchen, and asked her if she needed help. Suddenly, at the smell of frying ham, I realized that there was a decision I had not yet made: I had not told anyone that I do not eat pork, and I also had not told anyone, no one at the university, that I am Jewish. And now, how to approach this dilemma? The studies on trichinosis that I have been reading would probably not have been an appropriate topic at that moment, so I took a breath and plunged ahead with a lie:

"Oh, I'm so sorry that I forgot to tell anyone that I'm a—sort of vegetarian—though I do eat fish. My doctors have told me that too much meat is not good for me . . . for my heart. I'm sorry that you have gone to so much trouble to prepare a special meal. If you like, I can go down to eat at the corner restaurant."

"Don't even think of it," insisted Hortensia. "I'm also making cabbage and potatoes, and we have a nice salad of lettuce, tomatoes, onions, and carrots. You will not go hungry."

At that moment her husband, Severino, stomped up the stairs and entered the kitchen. I offered my hand when Hortensia introduced us and he took it very gingerly, which surprised me, considering that he is a construction worker. He told me he was working on a residential building project on nearby Calle Alonso Cano. A wiry build, dark blond hair, and blue eyes.

The meal was pleasant, and the time was mostly spent with Hortensia asking me questions about my plans. I surprised myself by the degree to which I understood what she was asking me and at the ease in which I was able to reply to her questions. I'm feeling grateful to Comrade D. for her patient coaching.

Afterwards Severino lit a cigarette, a *Ducados*. Its odor rushed to penetrate everything and lingered as he retired to another room to rest before returning to his construction site. This was the famous black *tabaco negro* that I had been warned about. I tried not to cough and at the same time to avoid inhaling the tarry smoke. After my pronouncement about my dietary peculiarities, I didn't want to make more trouble.

I helped Hortensia wash the dishes, which we placed to drain in very convenient metal cupboards with slits in the bottom that allow for the water to drip out into the sink, and then she showed me my room. Besides a small bed and a nightstand with a lamp, a chiffonier with a basin, pitcher, and mirror, there is an armoire in which I will hang my clothes. I will have to unpack only the clothing for the rest of the fall season and keep my winter clothes packed away. No place to store my books. The window overlooks the street, and I can see beautiful trees, still clinging to their red-tinged leaves, and more red-roofed buildings. I took photographs of the children out of the valise and kissed each one before placing them on the nightstand, which inspired Hortensia to ask me about them. I miss them already!

Hortensia asked me if I cared to have a siesta, to which I eagerly agreed, as I will be meeting Dr. Foster tomorrow and would like to explore the city later today. So I should now lay my diary aside and try to sleep on a pillow that feels like a sack of concrete. Still thinking about my decision about the pork. Have I decided to hide my Jewishness while I am in Spain? It feels strange to even think about it, but it might be easier than I thought. I look more like the people here than I look like the Germans. I remember the tone and the gestures accompanying the word *judío* as I heard it uttered during Holy Week in Seville, too reminiscent of what we have been hearing in Germany. I want to start my new life at an advantage. So I shall keep my ancestral religion—such as it is—to myself. Enough to say that I know who I am.

MADRID, *Wednesday, 10 September 1930*

After a breakfast of *café con leche*, toast, and *mermelada*, an auto came by to take me to meet Dr. Foster at her pleasant office in the Residencia de Estudiantes. The pavilions making up the Residencia are mostly long and low, all brick, on a tree-lined avenue. They invite one to enter, concentrate on studies, and share new ideas. The Residencia is also encircled with gardens, and happy birdsongs greeted our arrival.

Having read Dr. Foster's stellar biography and some of her articles, I was rather dazzled and a bit intimidated at first in her presence. She rose, holding her tall body erect, extended her hand to me, and surprised me by addressing me first in German. Then we tried switching to Spanish, and we finally settled into English, which I was happy to do. I started to pull a straight-backed wooden chair toward her desk, but she gestured to a more comfortable chair, where I gratefully seated myself. She had a stately and restrained manner reminiscent of some of Mama's British cousins and seemed to have no color at all in her skin or hair, her attire matching these neutral tones. Her blue eyes were framed in round, dark-rimmed spectacles. Once I allowed myself to look into her eyes, I noticed a warmth that had not seemed apparent before. She addressed me as though we were colleagues and not in a haughty or superior way, as she explained how I had been chosen for this position.

"Spain is changing," she began. "You are probably aware of this from the simple lack of scientific writing coming out of Spain during times when the rest of the world was advancing. I am sure you know about the Junta para la Ampliación de Estudios and about don Francisco Giner de los Ríos, who inspired Spanish intellectuals to make greater and deeper reforms in the sciences and in education. Modernizing the sciences in Spain began as a rather Quixotic goal, but let us hope that it is fast becoming a reality, despite the current political restrictions. Spain needs to open itself to new ideas and methods that are in practice today in Britain, France, and Germany. The fact that you are German and that you speak Spanish is highly in your favor. The referral from Dr. Einstein was very well-received."

I lowered my head, smiling and thinking, *Ah, that explains much.*

"Now, equal education for women is another task we are undertaking," she went on, smoothing her softly waved hair, which I now observed to be a lovely silvery gray. "Women in Spain were historically secluded and impeded from public life, under the Moorish influence that persists to modern times."

I began to cough and clear my throat on hearing that statement, and Dr. Foster offered me a glass of water. Having sympathized with Seville's Islamic past, I had done some research on contributions of Muslim women to the sciences, like Zubaida of Baghdad and Walladah bint Mustakfi of Córdoba.

I also thought of Mama's cousin, Mathilde Mond Mathias, whose daughter Marie-Thérèse married the son of a Muslim princess, called Salama bint Saïd, who not only learned to ride and shoot but taught herself to read and write and published her memoir. As I sipped the water, I gathered my thoughts. How to respond?

"Perhaps we should look at other, local tribal influences as well," I managed.

"Ah, yes," she responded vaguely, looking away, "but that is a job for anthropology, I think." She folded her hands and nodded, now looking steadily at me: "We are very happy to have you here in the chemistry department, and especially to work with the few female Spanish medical students. Do you know that the great majority of women who traditionally studied here studied only pharmacy, and that those who studied chemistry suffered under horribly antiquated teaching methods? Students have told me that a question on their final examinations might consist of recalling how many cubic centimeters of hydrogen chloride, specific gravity one point zero one, were required for experiment fifteen on page seventy-three! And the laboratories themselves were nothing but pitiful."

"That is scandalous!" I exclaimed.

"You are also very fortunate to be associated with the College of San Carlos, which has been a part of the Central University since the last century. But come! Let us visit our new laboratories."

Dr. Foster then escorted me to two splendidly furnished labs. There were desks for all students, and installations of water and gas. When I exclaimed to Dr. Foster that I had not seen such completely laid-out labs even in Germany, she proudly stated that she had reproduced her own laboratories at Smith College here in Madrid. Unlike the strictly research laboratories with which I am familiar, the teaching laboratory in which I will be assisting is designed to allow women to become respected and valued experts in their field.

I write this seated in an outdoor café on the Paseo de la Castellana, on my way to the German Embassy, to present my documents. The avenue bustles with strolling Spaniards of all ages, most of them well-dressed, despite the obvious economic hardships. On park benches along the way, I saw the occasional servant girls, dressed in neat striped uniforms, wheeling perfumed, lace-clad babies in prams and chatting flirtatiously with young soldiers. A sharply sweet, sexual tang in the air. I picked up a used photo album in a kiosk, and one page of the album held a photograph of the German Embassy, a lovely two-storied neoclassical building, fiercely guarded by two *Reichsadler*, imperial eagles, between which I will probably have to pass shortly.

MADRID, *Tuesday, 16 September 1930*

The German election results came out yesterday afternoon and are even covered in today's *ABC*, a Madrid daily newspaper. I am able to read the Spanish paper well enough to see nothing but contradictions: The party getting the most votes was the Social Democrats, but they lost ten seats in the Reichstag. Getting fewer total votes was Hitler's National Socialist Party, but they gained an astounding number of seats (ninety-seven, with a total of 107). Thälmann and the Communist Party gained twenty-three seats but achieved a total of only seventy-seven. Hitler will not even be seated in the Reichstag, but the *ABC* calls the results for his party "a great triumph for the extreme right." And there is nothing contradictory about the fact that Hitler and his party appealed to the people desperately looking for a way out of the financial crisis and needing something (and someone) to blame it on.

ABC reports street battles yesterday afternoon in Berlin between communists and "*racistas*"—a new word for me but one that I am afraid that I will need to learn and use. More than five hundred people arrested, two dead, many injured. I almost wish I were there in the streets of Berlin.

This morning, as I descended the tram about a block from San Carlos, a shabbily dressed man approached me indirectly and opened his shoulder bag, revealing a newspaper with the banner *Mundo Obrero* (Workers' World) and a tiny hammer and sickle in the corner. I snatched the paper, hastily tucked it into my handbag, and dropped a few coins in his pocket, whereupon he quickly rounded the corner of Calle de Atocha and disappeared. How brave these comrades are to risk their lives to compile and publish a clandestine Party newspaper, not to mention to sell it in the streets!

When I returned home, Hortensia asked me if I had plans for Sunday, and I wondered if this was an implied question about my religion. I mumbled something about not being sure what I would do. Then she suggested that we walk to the Mercado de San Miguel and visit *el Rastro*.

"What is *el Rastro*?"

"Ah . . . *el mercado de pulgas*."

I still looked puzzled, and then she made a gesture as if crushing a flea on my arm between her thumbnails.

"Ah, the flea market! Like the Berlin Seventeenth of June Street!"

"Yes, I suppose so! We should get there around nine thirty for bargains."

"Maybe I can find a bookcase there, for my room."

"You can find anything there! I would love to have a day of Rastro exploration with you and maybe a taste of vermouth at the Mercado de San Miguel. Oh, and a piece of advice: at el Rastro, don't accept the first price quoted."

MADRID, *Sunday, 21 September 1930*

Hortensia and I left the house at about eight o'clock this morning, which was overcast and chilly. We both took woolen scarves that we wrapped around our necks. Severino remained in the kitchen, smoking and reading the paper. It took us about half an hour to reach the Mercado de San Miguel, as there were many turns and street changes, befitting an ancient European city built on a circular grid. The Mercado itself looked quite spectacular and elegant from the adjoining streets, completely roofed and covering about one city block, girded with delicate cast iron and charming touches of ceramic. Large glass panes revealed the colorful array of produce and exotic sea creatures displayed within.

Once inside, Hortensia guided me around the building, an experience that was almost like visiting a museum, and we finally perched on stools before a marble-topped counter and ordered two enormous steaming *tazones* of café con leche.

"Have you tried *mil hojas*?" Hortensia wanted to know, gesturing toward some innocent-looking golden-layered rectangles clustered in a glass case.

"No—what are they? A thousand leaves of what?

"Ah, *hojaldre*," she responded with a chuckle. "I think you should order one."

I agreed, and soon the dish was placed before me, and Hortensia turned to watch me. As my fork dove downward, a *shushing* sound, accompanied by a sweet, warm, fragrance, rose up. The pastry met my teeth, the crisp, puffy layers offered little resistance, and then my tongue discovered the more solid filling of almond paste and honey. I wanted to retain the pleasure in my mouth as long as possible and discovered that my lips were holding some tiny pieces that my tongue could entice to return to the inside of my mouth, and finally to be swallowed. I didn't realize that I had closed my eyes and felt utterly transported, if not to the Arabic-tinged delights of Seville, then to the Muslim and Jewish ancestors who were not mine but with whom I knew that I must have coexisted at some remote time.

One more turn around the Mercado, a kaleidoscope of edible colors and textures, and then we continued southward toward el Rastro, together with families and groups of students who all seemed bent on the same objective: hunting for bargains. The sudden sight of canvas-shaded stalls occupying block after block along the Ribera de Curtidores and spilling over into the side streets was something I had not expected, coupled with the rather anarchistic way business was conducted, compared to Berlin's *Trödelmarkt*. Vendors shouted out the names and prices of their wares, musicians strolled among the crowds, children picked up and played with toys scattered on blankets, and people seemed to be bargaining for the least essential items, from wooden fish crates to empty glass jars. I soon spotted some wooden furniture, including a small bookcase with two shelves, and began my quest:

"*Joven*—young man—how much is this bookcase?"

"Only eleven pesetas, Señorita. All solid wood," replied the young man, who did not seem terribly enthused about closing a deal or about me as a potential customer.

Hortensia subtly nudged my side with an elbow, as a reminder against accepting the asking price. I ran my hand over the smooth wood and shook the case gently. It seemed quite solid, but I replied, "That's quite a lot for this. I'm going to continue down the street."

"You won't find anything this nice, Señorita. I can let you have it for ten," offered the young man, now more interested in my offer.

"Ten pesetas represents two days' pay for most *madrileños*," Hortensia murmured.

"I'm not prepared to go over seven," I said, shaking my head and beginning to turn away. The case would fit perfectly in my room, but I wanted a better deal.

"Wait, I'll let you have it for nine."

"Well, how about eight?" I offered.

"Fine. I can hold it for you if you'd like to bring an auto later, at about four o'clock."

"I think I can do that. Can you give me a receipt?"

The young man did not seem prepared to offer a receipt, so I opened my handbag to look for some paper, and he caught a glimpse of the *Mundo Obrero* that I had kept in my bag. I tore off a corner and quickly shoved the newspaper back into my bag and he looked more closely at me as he wrote, "*Recibí cantidad 8 ptas por estantería. Agustín G.*" (Received amount eight pesetas for bookcase [signed] Agustín G.). Then I asked Hortensia, "Is it getting close to the vermouth hour?"

"Yes, I think so."

We retraced our steps to the Mercado de San Miguel, where we enjoyed samples of vermouth and some delicious fried *calamares* (my first time eating squid: no fins or scales!). As four o'clock approached, we hailed a taxi, returned to the Ribera de Curtidores, and picked up my newly purchased bookcase. Agustín loaded it in the back of the taxi and thanked me, looking steadily into my eyes. The driver kindly helped me carry it up to my room, where it now resides with its first supply of books.

I had bought some lovely-looking mushrooms at the mercado, and Hortensia said that they would make a wonderful addition to this evening's omelet, which she called *revoltillo*, less firm than a tortilla and deliciously sautéed in olive oil. After the last dish was put up to dry, I returned to my room to read the copy of *Mundo Obrero* and pulled out the receipt for the bookcase. Then I noticed something the young man had written on the scrap of paper: "*28-IX las ventas.*" Back I went to the kitchen, where Hortensia was folding some napkins and Severino was sitting at the kitchen table, enjoying a Ducados and reading the paper.

"Hortensia, what does this mean? Is it a special sale?" I held the scrap in front of her.

She simply clutched my arm and looked at it more closely: "*Veintiocho de septiembre* (Twenty-eighth of September)," she said aloud, "*Las Ventas.*"

Severino looked up sharply: "Are you interested in liberty?"

"Very much so. But what are *las ventas*?"

"Las Ventas is the name of the bullring here in Madrid."

"Oh," I responded quickly, thinking I must have misunderstood his question. "I don't think I would like to see any bullfights. I was invited in Seville but just could not bear to go."

The couple both laughed.

"Next Sunday there is a public meeting in Las Ventas for those who would like to see the Republic return to Spain," explained Severino. "We are planning to go, and you are welcome to join us."

I thanked them and agreed to accompany them to the event. I felt so relieved: Another Sunday in which I don't have to make an excuse to stay away from a church!

MADRID, *Tuesday, 30 September 1930*

I have been waiting for the papers to come out, hoping that there would not be very severe censorship of Sunday's huge republican solidarity meeting in the bullring, Las Ventas. This picture from *ABC* of course could not be censored.

MADRID. EN LA PLAZA DE TOROS
ASPECTO DE LA PLAZA DURANTE EL MITIN DE SOLIDARIDAD REPUBLICANA CELEBRADO EL DOMINGO. (FOTO ALFONSO)

I have also been waiting to read the accounts. Despite the amplification of the speeches through loudspeakers, I need to see in print what I had difficulty understanding. The press even admits that twenty thousand people attended the meeting. *ABC*'s editorial staff quoted directly the words of Manuel Azaña, who promised that the Republic would be "bourgeois, parliamentary, and radical." Before uttering that conciliatory phrase, however, Azaña declared that "the Jury shall be the People, the Courtroom shall be the Street, and the Sentence shall be the Republic." These are wonderful, promising words, but how would such a policy be implemented in a bourgeois government?

MADRID, *Wednesday, 15 October 1930*

Outside the German Embassy this afternoon, I noticed a wizened old man selling foreign newspapers from a wooden crate on the sidewalk. I had never seen him there before. I spied a single copy of yesterday's *Rote Fahne*, paid the overpriced one peseta without bargaining (the paper costs three *pfennig* in Germany), and stepped into a café to read it undisturbed. But when I opened to the third page and read that Hitler's SA troops had been let loose in Berlin to smash the window panes of Jewish-owned stores, I quickly closed the paper, stuffed it in my bag, and took a tram to the Telefónica to call Papa (Hortensia and Severino do not have a telephone).

I waited nearly an hour for a booth in the local cold and damp Telefónica, an elegantly tall building on the Gran Vía. I was so happy to hear Papa sounding strong over the weak telephone connection. He reported that he is in good health, at age seventy-eight. All the children are fine, and he sees them as often as possible when he is not working. After these pleasantries, he laughed nervously and suddenly lowered his voice, making it even more difficult to hear.

"The first session of the Reichstag occurred yesterday. I'm sure you know that the Nazi party won a total of one hundred seven seats in last month's election. Well, the talk is that they put on quite a show of power, starting with their entry into the building. All the Nazi representatives, dressed in their brown shirts—yes!—marched noisily into the hall and took their seats. As their names were called, each one of them shouted out, 'Present! *Heil Hitler!*' Ha!" scoffed Papa. "A real circus! And the SA joined them later in the day to top off the performance by breaking store windows around Potsdamer Platz. They did quite a spectacular job on the Wertheim department store on Leipziger Strasse."

The situation as Papa described it did not seem laughable, and my throat tightened with worry.

"Oh, Papa," I exclaimed, "I saw that in the paper! And they are calling it a 'German pogrom!' Do you feel safe there? Can Gerda help you get to England?"

"England? What should I do in England? Moritz and I are in the business of making uniforms for Germany. That is not about to change. They need us for that. Artur and Gina may go to Denmark, as they can work anywhere, but my work is important here, no matter who is in power. And remember that the Social Democrats still control the Reichstag, and even your Communist Party has gained some seats."

We had to hang up at that point, as my time in the booth was limited, and others were waiting to make their calls. I am feeling very concerned, and next week I am going to try to contact Gerda in London and ask about the situation there. I'll also ask her to find out how the Mond family would feel about helping some of the Philipsborns gain immigration into England. Germany may no longer be safe for us, but I felt safe emerging onto the Gran Vía and not onto Potsdamer Platz. I began to breathe more easily as the light autumn sunshine stroked my cheeks.

This afternoon as I was leaving the laboratory, some women who identified themselves as medical students approached me and asked me to have tea with them in the cafeteria. It was raining heavily, so it was a pleasure to take refuge in the glassed-in area, and the insistent rushing of the water against the panes accompanied the equally insistent conversation of the women. They all seemed to want to talk at once, so I asked them to simply introduce themselves, one at a time, and let me know what it was that each one was concerned about. I had to ask them to repeat and to speak more slowly, which they tried hard to do, as I took notes. Here are some of their concerns, to the best of my understanding:

"You are the only female lab assistant, and you actually listen to us," began Julia, a young woman with soft-looking cheeks.

"Did you know that the four of us are the only women medical students this academic year, out of a total of over two thousand medical students?" demanded her sister Pilar, looking around and nodding indignantly. She kindly wrote out the number "2,000" and showed it to me.

"There are some female students who are considered 'unofficial' and only come here to take their exams or the classes that prepare for the exams," she added.

"They haven't received their parents' permission to live here, and their parents probably were reluctant to give permission for them to study," commented Julia.

"Yes," added Pilar, "they come here in special buses and return home immediately after their exams. We try to talk to them as much as possible."

I felt a tremendous admiration for those women as well as those who were seated around me and attempted to praise them.

"We do as well in our exams as the men do. But you would never know it, because the professors—all of them male—never address us in class," insisted Herminia, a young woman with an impish smile.

"It has only been legal for women to study at university for the last twenty years," affirmed Julia, tapping on the table for emphasis, then displaying her fingers for the number "twenty" in case I did not understand.

I was definitely not aware of that fact.

"Some of the male students have written satirical poems about the absurdity of females wanting to become doctors when we should be at home having babies and cooking for our husbands." Pilar laughed scornfully and gestured the rocking of a baby and the stirring of a pot.

"Do you know how we are placed in our microbiology class?" continued Herminia, setting down her teacup and lowering her voice a bit. She drew a diagram on a sheet of paper as she explained: "Professor Matilla has assigned us seats in the front row. Then he makes all the male students leave three rows empty and all of them pile in behind the empty rows. Does he think our *feminidad* is contagious? And he doesn't so much as glance our way. The few times that he looks up from droning through his utterly boring lectures, he looks right over our heads, into the masculine throngs."

As the women nodded and chortled bitterly, I suddenly realized that, at that moment, whatever I said or did would affect their lives. I laid down my pen and took a sip of my tea, and for a moment simply looked each of them in the eye. Then I tried to echo their statements in a way that would let them know that I had heard them and that I cared about them:

"You feel . . . invisible." I paused and looked at them again. They all nodded, and many said, "Invisible, yes!"

"You would like your work in the lab, and in your classes, to be . . . acknowledged . . . as equal to that of the male students."

The response was again, "Yes!"

"And you would like to be acknowledged as human beings equal to the male humans here at the university."

An overwhelming chorus of "Yes!"

"We should probably call ourselves *Las Invisibles de la Resi*," remarked Herminia, tossing her head. "That is how I felt during the time of my secondary *bachillerato* studies in Ceuta. I was the only girl, and I may as well have been invisible."

I laughed bitterly and then responded, "Of course you know that I am a foreigner. I have only been in Spain once before this year. I am not really . . . accustomed to the way Spanish women are viewed or treated here. But I think the first thing is to become more visible. Please know that I admire you all so much for just being here, not to mention for your academic accomplishments. Do you think it would be a good idea for Doña María [de Maeztu] to know that you are not treated equally in your classes?"

"Señorita Philipsborn, that sounds wonderful. But we would not like you to get into trouble for trying to push things forward more quickly than the administration—and especially the faculty—is willing to move right now," stated Julia.

"Oh, I see." I lowered my head and stared into my teacup as I thought for a moment, hoping that the tea leaves would guide me, as Mama had often shown me. I felt even more responsible and was touched that they were so considerate of me, as busy as they are with their studies. But I am a foreigner and to an extent on probation here in Spain and at the university. "Perhaps I could mention it in a subtle way if it comes up in conversation. But meanwhile, I would like to know in what ways I can help you. . . . Would you like to meet here maybe next week at this time?"

They welcomed this plan, and we will take a table at the Residencia next Wednesday after classes. I thanked them for their trust, and the women hugged me as we stood up to leave the cafeteria. Meanwhile, the next time I speak with Dr. Foster, I will see if there is a diplomatic way to make a case for her to convince her colleagues to really accept the female students, not simply as bodies that have been placed in their classrooms through royal decree, but as equal participants in the university curriculum. This may be a more difficult task than the chemistry exams I have been compiling.

MADRID, *Wednesday, 12 November 1930*

It is nearly midnight, and the day has ended in tragedy and death. I had told Hortensia not to wait for me for the midday meal, as I would be meeting with the medical students at the Residencia. It was about three o'clock as I approached the house, and I was surprised to see Antón, the *sereno* (night watchman), on our street in broad daylight. He grabbed my arm and began speaking rapidly, his voice breaking, in a frantic mixture of Spanish and what must be his native dialect. I tried very hard to understand and to confirm what he was trying to tell me:

"*Señorita, nun ta la señora!*"

"Mrs. Hortensia is not home? What has happened?

"*Ye una catástrofe, ho!*"

"A catastrophe? What happened?"

"*La casa na que trabayaba el señor—fundióse.*"

"The house collapsed? The one on Alonso Cano, where he works? Is Severino all right?"

Antón made me know that Severino was fine but that some workers were wounded and even some dead. I understood that Hortensia had left to be with him.

"Oh, I must go and help," I said, anxiously. Can you show me which way to go?"

"*Sí, cai Alonso Cano, treinta y seis,*" he replied, pointing eastward, then held up four fingers: "*Solo unes cuatro manzanes p'allá.*"

I covered the four blocks in a desperate rush. As I approached the site, breathless, hundreds of people had gathered around the collapsed building. Everyone seemed to be shouting at once—it was completely chaotic. The building looked horrendous: the lower three stories had collapsed over the ground floor, but the upper stories at the rear still hung precariously over the lower portion, and the fire department was attempting to pull them down. They had allowed some of the workers to assist in the rescue efforts. The dead—four in number—had already been removed to the *depósito judicial* (the morgue, as I was able to understand).

I heard my name called and felt so relieved to see Hortensia and Severino standing with some workers. I made my way toward them, and we embraced tearfully.

"We're all headed for the Casa del Pueblo," Severino told me, "to plan our next action. The CNT (*Confederación Nacional de Trabajadores*) and UGT (*Unión General de Trabajadores*)—my union—will be represented there, and workers from the building next door to this one will also come."

That was the first mention of workers' unions I had heard from Severino or Hortensia, and I quickly said, "I'd like to come to that meeting with you."

Accompanied by other workers and families, we all boarded the tram, and as I looked around, I saw that many men were covered with gray dust—they had barely survived the disaster. My heart went out to them. We arrived at the Casa del Pueblo, a beautifully elegant building on Calle del Piamonte, at around four o'clock. Many of the people had probably not eaten anything that day, and the kitchen workers dished out bowls from a gigantic pot of soup and quickly made large omelets.

Once we entered the meeting room, two men took seats at the front table, each with a pad of paper. They took turns addressing the group, and then invited testimonials. I will try to note here what I understood of the meeting.

"Comrades, at this terrible time, it is urgent for all of us to be united. Here are the names of our fallen brothers." (As they read out the names of the four dead, I heard sobbing and "*ays*" from the group.)

"Our brave brothers risked their lives to rescue their comrades. Some of you are present here."

"As you may know, Quiñones, the contractor of the project, is also the owner of the property. Once he got the foreman to go through the list of workers and saw who was missing, he left immediately. We declare him and the architect, Fernández Urosa, responsible for the lives of four humans and perhaps more." (Applause and murmurs from the crowd.)

"We want to make an account of what you witnessed. We especially need to know the condition of the building materials. Comrades, please raise a hand to be recognized, and we will make a note of what you tell us."

Many men then raised their hands and were recognized, one by one, by the men at the table. They were all dressed in overalls or *monos,* and many were wearing simple *alpargatas* or rope-soled canvas espadrilles, not solid work boots, and many had scratches on their hands and faces. As each man stood to speak, illustrating with gestures the terrible conditions—the flimsy building materials and the lack of concern of the bosses, and expressing their solidarity with their dead and injured comrades, I experienced their outrage.

The men at the table announced the wake—*el velorio*—for the fallen workers, for Friday morning. They then stood up and raised their fists, followed by everyone in the room, as all began to sing the "Internationale." I do not know the words in Spanish, so I mouthed the German words, "*Wacht auf, verdammte dieser erde. . . .*" buoyed by the strength of the voices of the workers in the hall and their families. All my years of labor theory and Communist rhetoric were made real and tangible in that space, and Rosa's memory and ideals stood by my side.

MADRID, *Friday, 14 November 1930*

Stories about the collapsed building spurred all of Madrid to take part in today's procession, which resulted in three more funerals and the largest public spectacle I have ever witnessed. Four horse-drawn funeral carriages, decorated with wreaths, flowers, and insignia of the builders' union, headed the procession, which was interrupted when some of the participants attempted to alter the route toward the Puerta del Sol to allow more people to witness the event. When their request was denied, mounted police rushed in to halt the hail of rocks and bricks hurled by protesters. I was horrified to see police viciously slashing at people's heads with their sabers in the Plaza de Cánovas. I backed away from the charging horses, but when gunfire broke out, I realized that I was truly risking my safety and fled. I was able to run through the crowd to the nearest metro entrance and am now grateful to be alive and at home.

Severino arrived late this evening from a union meeting. Seated at the kitchen table, he read the names, ages, and addresses of the many injured and three dead workers. Hortensia and I both wept. At least twelve of the injuries and all three of the deaths were from gunshots. All of these casualties were workers, none of them police. Four policemen had head injuries from thrown rocks. Many workers had suffered severe scalp injuries from being slashed by the sabers of the guardsmen. Then Severino informed us that the Executive Commission of the Central Committee had declared a *huelga general* of building workers, to begin tomorrow morning, November 15, ending Monday at five in the afternoon, as a statement of protest against the police action. The union is also calling for the removal of the chief of police and is demanding that the State subsidize the families of the dead and compensate the injured workers so that they can receive proper medical treatment. There is also a demand to free all arrested workers and to head for the streets tonight. He laid the paper before him on the table. "Calling for a work stoppage at such a late hour is in reality a *huelga relámpago*."

"Oh, please let me get my dictionary," I pleaded—"that is a new word for me." I rushed to my room to retrieve my Langenscheidt and found that the word *relámpago* means "lightning." I thought that was a brilliant way to express the phenomenon. "Isn't that a revolutionary move? It will really stir people up."

"That is exactly what we intend to do," replied Severino, punctuating his words by rapping on the table with his closed fist. "Dictadura, dictablanda—both are enemies of the people."

Severino had never acted so openly in front of me and had never revealed his convictions so strongly. I let his words sink in for several seconds, then agreed, "*De acuerdo,*" and looked over at Hortensia, who nodded, wiping her eyes. I finally stood and hugged them both, wished them a good night, and made my way to my room. Though I am exhausted, I am also exhilarated to think that I have landed in a revolutionary household.

MADRID, *Saturday, 15 November 1930*

The first full day of general strike ended yesterday at midnight, and I am writing by my predawn candlelight. Different editions of the papers gave wildly varying estimates as to the number of those who participated in Thursday's funeral procession. The right-wing press (*ABC*) announced the lowest figures (about seventeen thousand), while denouncing demonstrations in public places, while more liberal papers (*El Imparcial*) showed more sympathy for the workers and estimate the crowd at one hundred thousand.

Yesterday morning's classes were held without disturbance. Then at around ten thirty, the lab door opened, and a man, who the students informed me was the university rector, took a couple of steps in and announced, "Classes are suspended for the rest of the day, to honor the construction workers' strike." He then continued down the hallway, presumably doing the same for all classes on our wing.

"Señorita Philipsborn!" The woman student I was assisting turned to face me and grabbed my arm. "We are all going to the *centro* (downtown). Will you come with us?"

"With pleasure," I replied and started taking off my lab coat, animated by a new sense of belonging.

"Leave the *bata* on," interjected Herminia. "We are all wearing ours in solidarity with the workers and to show that we are doctors against dictatorship."

After visiting the bathrooms, we all stopped by the cafeteria, which was still open and offering little bags of almonds, hazelnuts, raisins, and other dried fruit and nuts, which the students called "*músicos*" ("musicians," for some unknown reason). I dropped a couple of bags in my rucksack and headed for the exit doors, and we were quickly surrounded by what appeared to be a hundred medical students, all wearing white coats.

"Let's take La Castellana," someone shouted, and we all began moving southward. It was early enough in the strike schedule that some bread dispensaries were still operating, and lines of people, mostly women carrying shopping bags and some with small children, stretched for blocks. Mounted police rode closely alongside the people waiting for bread. I noticed firearms, sabers, and nightsticks attached in various locations to the police or their horses. I wondered what or whom they were protecting: private property, the State, police violence? And what kind of society calls in police against citizens buying bread?

The students decided to head toward the centro, and I was with them, feeling that their cause was mine, as workers tried to persuade others to close shops or stop transporting people. I heard the word *esquiroles* hurled at those who refused to strike: *streikbrecher,* I assumed. If transit drivers did not join the strike, some workers banded together to turn the ungainly vehicles over. Security guards and the Civil Guard used their weapons freely, and at one point—I think it was in the Gran Vía—they separated people into two groups, one of which was shouting "*¡Viva la República!*" and the other "*¡Viva la Dictadura!*" and then went after each other with fists and anything they could pick up. Some worker groups tried to enter the Telefónica but were pushed back by the *Guardia Civil,* and I heard some shots nearby and again felt threatened. I moved away from the crowd and headed for home. I assume that the whole school will be shut down by the strike.

Everyone in this city seems to know the roles they are supposed to play in such a situation. I am not yet certain about mine, but I do feel part of the obvious alliance demonstrated between the students and the workers I joined in the streets today.

MADRID, Saturday, December 13 1930

It looks like we may have moved one step closer to the Republic unless we have moved one or even two steps back. Everyone is talking about what happened yesterday in Jaca, an ancient, fortified city near the French border, in Aragón. Two brave captains from the Jaca garrison, Fermín Galán and Ángel García Hernández, declared that we were a republic, gathered their troops, and were joined by other citizens on a march toward Zaragoza. Unfortunately, the anticipated assistance did not materialize, and the two captains were quickly surrounded by government troops and have surrendered.

The front page of today's *ABC* is blatantly fascist. The uprising is called a "criminal intent," and an "*inexorable*" punishment is demanded for those responsible. Today *El Sol* printed an announcement the government has sent out to all the papers that until further notice the press is to be censored concerning any news from Jaca, public demonstrations related to the uprising, and also any ongoing union strikes. The only "authorized" reports will be those coming directly from the government.

As I have come to know the Spanish people in this brief period of time, I doubt very much that censorship of the press will be able to stem the people's ability to communicate the deeds and the plans of those who are striving to undo the cruel alliance of monarchy and dictatorship. I sympathize so deeply with the two captains and am aghast at the censorship and the rigid policies of the government.

MADRID, *Thursday, 1 January 1931*

My first semester in Spain has ended with crushed uprisings, ongoing strikes, and twelve swallowed grapes. The two young captains who led the Jaca rebellion were summarily executed just two days after their valiant attempt to proclaim a republic, and they have already acquired martyrs' status among workers and students—the people with whom I am now in daily contact. Stories single out Fermín Galán, who expressed his dedication during the impromptu trial and with his last breath. When approached by a priest for last rites, Galán reportedly replied, "Don't bother. Just give me a hug—as a friend. That's what I really need now. As a priest, you're wasting your time with me."

Before the firing squad, both men refused blindfolds, and Galán himself gave the order to fire, shouting out, "¡Viva la República!" just ahead of the bullets that forever silenced his voice.

The official line of the Party is that the revolution is not going to come about through the agency of small groups but will be accomplished only by great masses of the people. If Communists and Socialists cannot collaborate to overthrow this repressive government, I'd like to know how the Republic will ever get off the ground. Will the fate of all the Spanish people be at the mercy of ideological differences? This situation feels so similar to what is happening in Germany. Perhaps one reason why I am beginning to think of myself as a Spaniard.

The first snow has fallen on Madrid, and yesterday a group of students gathered on the steps of the Residencia to commemorate the New Year. Then they shrieked in laughter as they accumulated enough snow, not in its purest white state, to construct a gigantic snowball. I am saving space to post the photo once it is developed.

New Year's Eve (last night) conveyed a mood of anticipation and hope that the year will bring a change of government. I celebrated with students at the Residencia de Estudiantes, to which the women students were invited (males are not allowed in the Residencia de Señoritas). Despite the clumsy attempts we have witnessed at instituting the Republic, students expressed hope for a democratic transition to a republic that would allow a free press, women's rights, including the right to vote, separation of church and state, divorce, and even socialization of private property.

The most unusual event for me occurred at the stroke (or rather, strokes) of midnight. Just before then, three students circulated around the room, passing out exactly twelve lovely white grapes on little glass plates. I stretched my fingers out to eat one, and Herminia, who was at my side, grabbed my arm, laughing, and warned me to wait. All the windows were then opened, and at exactly twelve, the nearby church clock began to chime. With each stroke we had to pick up one grape, pop it into our mouths, and eat it. Some students (those who had consumed a bit more sparkling wine) were feeding the grapes to each other, as they proclaimed twelve wishes for the coming year. Wishes like "*salud, prosperidad, y amor*" were soon overpowered by those of "*libertad, democracia, y república.*"

May it be so!

MADRID, *Thursday, 26 March 1931*

The first three days of this week at the Medical School have witnessed what has been called the "Siege of San Carlos." Another experience with actual conflict in Spain, along with November's funeral procession for the Alonso Cano workers. I shall attempt to describe the events of each day.

Monday: As I walked down the halls toward my office, low-pitched conversations were issuing from each classroom before the professors arrived. Once in the lab, my students seemed restless and unable to concentrate on their projects. One of them asked me if I knew where he could find a piece of *cartón*.

Cartón, I thought, *must mean "cardboard," just as it does in German.* "What for?" I asked. "Your project doesn't involve cardboard."

"No," he replied, lowering his voice, "but the Spanish people's project does."

"Ah," I replied, and pulled the copy of the *Heraldo* out of my rucksack, showing the word *Amnistía*. He nodded vigorously, blond curls falling onto his forehead. "Wait a moment," I offered. "I think I know where I can find some cardboard."

I excused myself to the students, stepped out of the lab and headed for the stairs that lead down to the supply room. On the stairs were gathered about twenty students, speaking excitedly in hushed tones. "We need to make some *pancartas*," one student was saying, his open hands on either side of his body.

This word was so similar to German *plakat* that I assumed he was talking about signs. "Do you need cartón?" I interrupted, repeating the Spanish word for cardboard I had just learned.

"Ah, yes, please, right away," came the enthusiastic response.

I continued down to the supply room, opened it with my key, my heart pounding, but at the same time I felt encouraged by the resolve of the students. After a bit of a search, I found some large pieces of cardboard on which had been printed charts showing types of shoulder injuries, the anatomy of the brain, causes of syncope, leading causes of death, etc. They looked to be a bit out of date, so I assumed they would not be missed, gathered up a large armful and took them up to the students on the stairs, reserving a choice sample of anatomy of the teeth for my curly-haired lab student.

Classes continued in a more or less orderly manner, but when students attempted to exit the building, now holding signs saying "*PEDIMOS AMNISTÍA*" (We demand amnesty), they were met by security guards, and once they had pushed onto Calle de Atocha, by Civil Guardsmen and mounted police. Some students were chased through the streets, and a few improvised signs were snatched and torn up by police and by supporters of the monarchy. The red flag of the FUE (the University Students' Federation) was unfurled from the top floor. Some workers in the street demonstrated their solidarity with the students by hurling bricks at the police. In the building, others formed a group and met with General Mola, the security director at the School of Medicine, requesting permission to hold a legal demonstration tomorrow. Mola dismissively denied their request, and they left. His denial was worth nothing, as they planned to meet and continue to strategize.

Tuesday: Morning classes took place as usual, but promptly at noon, all the students put away their materials, stood up, and headed for the assembly hall, and I joined them. A number later estimated at three thousand filled the hall, with designated speakers declaring that classes were suspended for the rest of the day and that any students who wished should adjourn to the street in a public demonstration to demand amnesty for the political prisoners. General Mola's resignation was demanded by students who claimed that he had confused the streets of Madrid with the Rif Mountains (where he had served in the war against Morocco). Herminia and Pilar were sitting on either side of me, and we decided to go to my office, to observe from my window, which overlooks Calle de Atocha. Crowds of students had poured out to the street, many carrying signs. Soon some of them returned, this time with armfuls of bricks snatched from nearby construction sites. As soon as they were inside, the building was surrounded by Civil Guardsmen, who prevented anyone inside from going out. By that time, the students had reached the top floor and started pelting the police with bricks and chunks of pavement. The police retreated, serenaded from the rooftop by a youthfully roared version of the "Marseillaise." We could also see neighbors come out to their balconies and from one balcony a banner was unfurled proclaiming "Viva la República." Another female student, Carmen, burst into my office, breathless, her voice breaking:

"The boys are pulling out the chairs from the dental school and using them as projectiles!" And at that moment, we were shaken by two tremendous crashes on the street and looked out to view the shattered remains of two dentist chairs on the sidewalk below.

By one o'clock the battle had not dissipated. More armed police arrived, and just before two we began to hear shots. When we saw some people on the street fall, I closed the shutters on my window, fearing that we would become targets. I tried to calm the three women, but I was terrified myself. We later heard that students who had been throwing objects from the balconies had been shot and pulled inside to the clinic for treatment by their fellow students and by professors.

At two-thirty the shooting stopped, the students ran out of bricks, and once most of the police had retreated, we all left in groups and headed for the Puerta del Sol where we were joined by other citizens. Some people began to shout pro-dictatorship slogans, and fights broke out, and it appeared that the police were not interested in maintaining order, so I ducked into the metro and returned home.

Wednesday (yesterday): The information I am entering here I have gathered from newspaper accounts. I am frankly exhausted from Tuesday's tension. And yesterday, though a twenty-four-hour student strike was called, students managed to break in and occupy their school, opening the doors to more students and to professors, and then heading quickly to the roof where they hurled roofing tiles at the police, who continued to shoot into the building, even damaging operating rooms and injuring and terrifying patients. The *Heraldo* interviewed the Dean of the Medical School, Doctor Sebastián Recaséns, who severely criticized the actions of the police and mentioned that he had to crouch on the hospital floor to telephone the Ministry, since the police were aiming at students through the bars on the windows.

Thursday (today): Not surprisingly, *ABC* has expressed its opinion on the clashes, calling the students' revolutionary attitude "frankly intolerable and excessively tolerated," denying that students have civil rights, and defending the actions of the police as "fulfilling their arduous task of impeding disorder" by responding with fire *to shooting initiated by the students* (yes!). The editorial complains that the government is too lenient with students, whose only right is to study, not to prevent from studying those who do not agree with their politics.

Meanwhile, one death has been reported, that of a Civil Guardsman, of a bullet wound, some students are in critical condition with gunshot wounds, and many people (police, students, and passersby) have suffered injuries from thrown projectiles. There is quite a bit of damage to San Carlos, but classes are scheduled to resume on Monday.

MADRID, Friday, 10 April 1931

So it is happening. Municipal elections are scheduled for this Sunday, the twelfth, and election issues and politics in general have consumed the mentality of all Spain. By scheduling elections, the king hopes to show that the Spanish people are at heart monarchists, but the office for which people will be voting is only that of *concejal* or city councilman, and I do mean literally council*man*. I was aware that, as a German, I would not be voting in the Spanish election, but it was only on Wednesday that my "Invisibles" informed me that Spanish women are not permitted to vote.

I have never thought of Spain as a woman's paradise, and I am aware of the problems that female students are having in mixed classes with the satirical poems and the segregation by gender, but I hope to see Spanish women obtaining equal rights within their lifetimes.

MADRID, *Monday, 13 April 1931*

HERALDO DE MADRID

Año XLI.—Núm. 14.102   No se devuelven los originales   Lunes 13 de abril de 1931   Red. y Ad., Marqués de Cubas, 7.   EDICIÓN DE LA NOCHE

OCHO AÑOS DESPUES
EN EL GRAN PLEBISCITO DE AYER
ESPAÑA VOTÓ POR LA REPÚBLICA

They are calling it a plebiscite (though monarchists received majority votes in many areas), and they are calling Spain a republic (though the election was for city councilmen only). This headline was borne out by the mood of people today in Madrid, and "¡Viva la República!" was the cry I heard echoing along the streets from balconies and shouted in a chorus of thousands in the Puerta del Sol. The municipal elections have actually had national results. The colors red, gold, and purple, which had been banned if appearing together, are now worn proudly on lapels. On the way to the laboratory this morning, I saw images of the Jaca martyrs Galán and García Hernández plastered on shop windows and even on the windows of taxicabs.

I am witnessing a historic moment in Spain: the first time that a government has been unseated through the electoral process. I feel as if I have participated in the process and that the victory is partially mine. The story going around (already!) is that Aznar, the interim president picked by the king just two months ago, walked into the palace this morning, and was confronted by the press, who asked him, "Do you think there will be a crisis?" His answer: "A crisis? What more crisis do you want from a country that goes to bed as a monarchy and wakes up as a republic?" Results tallied as percentages are:

Republicans, 43.05 percent, Monarchists, 23.84 percent, Socialists, 5.97 percent, Communists 0.08 percent, and others, 27.06 percent.

I arrived a bit early at the Medical School this morning, not knowing what to expect. A few Civil Guardsmen stood near the entrance, looking rather sheepish, as if they did not know who was in charge and what they were supposed to do in any case. The tricolored flag of the Republic and a red flag were draped from balconies on the façade of the building. Glass and other debris from the demonstrations and the police attacks had been removed, but some windows are still boarded up. I expected the students to be jubilant today, and indeed I was greeted with many smiling faces in the lab. Santi, the student who had fashioned a pro-amnesty sign out of the tooth anatomy display, caught up with me in the hall as we recessed for a break.

"I'm glad to see that you are all right, Señorita Philipsborn," he began.

"Thank you! And how are you feeling, Santi?"

He lowered his voice a bit and moved closer as we walked. "Frankly, I'd like you to know that I come from a province where the pro-republican vote was in the minority. Many of my own family voted for monarchical candidates. In my town, and even here in Madrid, I have witnessed violent opposition to the new system that will be implementing a parliamentary form of government and conceding rights to groups long considered enemies of the State."

"What groups are those?"

"I'm talking about workers, particularly if they are organized in unions, and about intellectuals, and students."

"And—how about women?" I asked, hesitatingly, not really knowing Santi's views on women's rights and female suffrage.

He stopped walking and turned to look at me, as if he were just noticing that I was a woman. "Well, yes, even women," he conceded.

"Maybe—*especially* women?" I asked, playfully.

"Ah, *cuidado:* watch out!" he rejoined, equally playfully, tapping my arm. His touch stirred up my blood a bit, and I turned to look at him as he strode down the hallway. Spanish people touch each other a lot, but this felt different.

MADRID, *Wednesday, 13 May 1931*

I never thought I would experience a day like today, but I will begin with this event: eight religious structures in Madrid have been deliberately burned in the past two days. When I was in Seville, I should have realized the importance of the power of the Catholic Church over the people and people's resistance to its sway, but it has now been brought home to me. One of the principal conditions of the new Constitution protects religious freedom and expresses the goal of making Spain a secular state, cutting the ties to the Church that were a hallmark of the monarchy.

By yesterday, seven more churches had been burned, and some of their contents—valuable cultural and artistic treasures—with them. Marx has called religion "the opiate of the masses." Perhaps the exhilarating sense of power conveyed to people after dethroning a king and a dictatorship and replacing them with a republic has simply replaced one opiate with another.

And something that I definitely did not expect to happen: I went back to my office in the evening, after meeting with "Las Invisibles" in the cafeteria and was seated at my long table, drafting some notes for an experiment we were to do tomorrow. I had opened my window, and the fragrance of new flowers drifted inside, along with the demanding calls of the first night birds, when I heard a gentle tapping on my door. I opened, and there stood Santi, looking rather lost.

"I saw your light," he began, and I stepped aside, offering, "Come sit."

He came in, and we both moved to the table. He sat beside me, and we began to look at the papers I had spread out in preparation for tomorrow's session. Suddenly, he turned toward me and asked if I would like him to assist me in the lab with some of the student projects. I looked closely at him. With his tousled blond hair and earnest eyes—much like one of the Raphael *putti*—I couldn't resist his offer. "Oh yes, thank you, Santi!"

Then he abruptly changed the subject: "Señorita Philipsborn, are you familiar with the works of Rabindranath Tagore?"

A question I had certainly not expected to hear from a medical student in Madrid.

"Ah, yes, the Indian poet. My sister and I have some of his poetry, and he visited my university. Just before I left Germany to come here, I read that Tagore met with Einstein. They were seeking meanings in common of Beauty and Truth, and I think they actually ended up agreeing on many issues. Why do you ask?"

"Haven't you seen the posters up in the hallways? Tomorrow evening Professor María de Maeztu will be conducting readings and presenting her commentary on Tagore's poems, right here at the Residencia. They were translated into Spanish by Doña Zenobia de Camprubí, the wife of the poet Juan Ramón Jiménez. I plan to be there. I think you would really enjoy this event."

"Oh, yes, I probably would," I agreed. "So you enjoy poetry?" I asked, leaning back in my chair to get a better look at Santi. With the warmer weather I had hung up my white lab coat and was wearing a flowered print dress and had thrown a light shawl over my shoulders.

Santi lowered his head for a moment, looked up again, and murmured, "Señorita Philipsborn, I do enjoy poetry." He paused, leaning toward me. "Though I am neither Tagore nor Einstein, the Truth for me . . . right now . . . more than anything . . . is the Beauty of you in that dress. You are a garden in springtime." As he said those words, he stretched his arm along the back of my chair. My breathing accelerated. What to say or do? I turned my head toward him, and began, "Oh, Santi. . . ." At that moment, he slipped his hand under my shawl, and I felt the warm pressure on my bare shoulder.

"What I mean to say is"—he now broke into the intimate *tú*—"that you *are* Springtime and Beauty and Truth—and Poetry," he whispered hoarsely, and with a gentle pressure, with each word, drew me closer to him. I leaned in and brushed his lips with mine . . . my thigh pressed against his . . . I asked myself what on earth had gotten into me, but my body knew exactly what I was doing. I placed my hand on his cheek and pulled back a bit.

"Santi, it's late—I need to go home now—I am expected."

He also pulled back: "I have my *moto* here. I can take you home."

"Oh, I have never ridden on a motorcycle," I protested . . . but part of me yearned to ride on a motorcycle!

"There's room for you. I'll drive carefully."

We stood up to leave and he reached for me again. We embraced and kissed once more and, feeling his body against mine, I suddenly wished I had a sofa in my office, but I made myself pull away, grabbed my bag and dashed out the door. Santi followed.

The echoing roar of the motorcycle made any conversation impossible, and the speed through the darkened streets and the vibration of the Gimson's motor between my thighs increased my excitement, as I pressed into Santi's young back. I wished I could bring him up to my room, but of course that was also impossible. As we pulled up in front of Donoso Cortés, I slid off the vehicle, saying, "Tomorrow," to which Santi also replied, "Tomorrow," before speeding off down the street.

None of the fires set by anarchists, republicans, or communists can duplicate the heat that is keeping me from sleeping tonight and promising, "Tomorrow."

MADRID, *Thursday, 14 May 1931*

This morning on awakening, I felt more like an adolescent schoolgirl than a practically middle-aged lab assistant. I tried to tell myself to just enjoy the feeling and let it play out. I rarely pay much attention to what I wear to work, but while I was soaking in the tiny bathtub, I remembered that I had brought to Madrid the dress I wore to the *Zaubernacht* ballet in Berlin nearly ten years ago, so I pulled it out of my valise, smoothed it out a bit, and stepped into it. The dress still fit, though it is probably *démodé*. I also found a tiny vial of jasmine oil (*esencia de jazmín*) that I had bought at the Rastro and dabbed some of it on my neck, my wrists, and, yes, behind my knees and between my breasts. I found a pair of high-heeled shoes, impulsively pushed them into my bag, and drew on a pair of silk stockings, over which I laced up my white lab shoes. I had absolutely no appetite so just took half a cup of café con leche and let Hortensia know that I was going to an event at the Resi and would be late returning. I pulled a light raincoat over my dress, lest I be ogled in the street, and hurried down the stairs.

Riding in the tram on the way to the lab, I pondered why this was happening to me now, since I had had virtually no thoughts about sex and certainly had not been attracted to any man for years, maybe since university. But just a touch and a few sweet words from a young student have stirred all the cells in my body into action and my mind into questioning: Is the Spanish springtime awakening me? What are his motives? Am I really so attractive? Because I am older, does he think that I'm more available than the young women of the Resi, who are officially here to be protected? He didn't actually invite me to tonight's event. Did I imagine it?

The hours of work in the lab seemed to drag by. In the session that Santi attended, I tried to avoid eye contact with him, and it appeared that he was doing the same. He did not repeat his offer to assist in student projects and seemed to be in a hurry to leave at the end of the hour. *Oh God*, I thought, *does he regret what happened last night? Klara, you are a mature woman. You must be in control here. This position is too important for you to lose your head over what is basically a boy.*

I did some work in my office until the event was to begin, at eight o'clock. Then I drew the little shoes out of my bag and slipped into them, trying a few steps around my office. Such a change from the practical flat things I wear to work each day, but by the time I reached the door, I remembered how to adjust my spine, arching backwards a bit, thrusting my chest forward, and stepping first with my toes rather than my heels. It took me longer than usual to reach the library, and when I got there the room was filled and I moved to the back row. I spotted Santi immediately, sitting with a small group of students around the speaker's empty chair. This time we made eye contact, and my legs began to tremble and weaken, and I grasped the chair in front of me and took a seat.

At that moment, Doña María entered and took her seat, holding a book and a sheaf of papers. She looked radiant, her Spanish features chiseled sharply by her British heritage. She introduced the life and works of Tagore briefly, mentioning his connections with Spain and the fact that most of his poems had been translated to Spanish from English versions, rather than the original Bengali. Then she stated that a selection of poems from his book *Crescent Moon* (translated as *Luna Nueva*) would be read aloud by students and that she would comment on each one. So that's what Santi was doing at the front of the room! One poem, about right livelihood (*"Vocación"*), delighted my Marxist heart with its images of ideal work, and I found myself becoming more able to concentrate on the musicality of the verses and of Doña María's commentaries. But just at that moment Santi stood, threw a glance briefly in my direction, and began to read his poem, in a deep, determined voice I had never heard from him:

"*Ah, estos jazmines, estos blancos jazmines. . . .*"

These white jasmines! The jasmine fragrance on my own body and the words issuing from the mouth of this beautiful young man aroused a memory I had never had, and with the lines "like a bride who lifts her veil to receive her lover" I became the Shulamite of the *Song of Songs*. I scarcely heard or understood Doña María's commentary, after which it was announced that it was time for intermission. I stood and looked again at Santi, who looked at me and turned his head and pursed his lips in the direction of a rear door in the library, toward which he began walking. I immediately understood and went back through the door through which I had entered and proceeded toward the hallway.

I wasn't certain which way to turn, so I simply stood for a bit, and then spotted Santi coming around the corner. He stopped as soon as he noticed me, and his mouth dropped. He was not seeing the white-robed, flat-footed, stooped lab assistant at that moment! Then he turned, with the same head movement he had made in the library and proceeded to the staircase. I began to climb, leaving space between us for anyone else who was going that way (no one was). I was careful to step on the balls of my feet, which slowed me down a bit, and I noticed Santi turning to make sure I was following. At the top of the stairs, he turned to the left and around the middle of the hall, placed his hand on a doorknob and opened the door. There was still no one in the hallway when I reached the door and stepped into the small student room, furnished with bookshelves, a small desk and chair, a colorful little rug, and a small bed.

Santi stood in the middle of the room and seemed not to know what to say or do.

"So this is your room?" I blurted, stupidly.

"*Our*_room," he responded, and took me in his arms. "Oh, that fragrance," he exclaimed at once, inhaling deeply. "What is it?"

"Jazmines," I responded, "of course. For Tagore and for you."

This time he pressed his lips to mine, then pulled away. "Would you like to sit down?"

"Oh yes," I responded gratefully—"my feet"—and took a seat in his desk chair, stretching out my legs—"*Ay, mis pies!*"

"No wonder," he murmured, "they are in prison, *los pobrecillos* (the poor little things). Let us free the prisoners." With that he knelt down before me and carefully removed my shoes and began to gently rub my feet, through my silk stockings. I sighed and moaned in relief and pleasure, at the pressure from his hands and the smooth texture of the silk on my skin. With that he began to move his hands up my legs, while looking into my eyes to see my response. We soon found ourselves atop his little student bed, which proved ample enough for frantic and eager lovemaking.

"I knew you would be wonderful," he soon whispered. "Did you know I always wanted you?"

"No idea," I responded, truthfully.

But reality soon returned.

"I have to go down to the reception," he said. "I'll tell them I wasn't feeling well and came to my room to rest. What will you do?"

"I will just go to my office and hope no one sees me leaving here. I didn't recognize anyone at the recital, except for Doña María, and I don't think she noticed me."

"Just go out the back door and around to the front of the building on Miguel Ángel."

I did just that and don't think I was spotted. I barely remember returning home, so I'm thinking that I must have flown. The scent of jasmine still lingers on my skin, and the manly juice is beginning to seep from my body. I hope the odors stay with me all night.

MADRID, Friday, 15 May 1931

I woke this morning earlier than usual, feeling like a different person, connected now to Spain through my sex and shared breathing and whispered language. As I took off my nightgown, I let the harsh cotton fabric slide along my skin and it excited me. I chose my clothes carefully, not sure of what the day would bring, but as the air felt warmer, I picked a flowered print dress and some silk underclothing, but I left the high-heeled shoes in my armoire. I smoothed on some moisturizer and a few drops of jasmine oil, and finally applied a bit of lip rouge.

From the tram I gazed out at the budding trees and the people rushing to work or to market. I felt a circulation shared with all of them—trembling tram, budding trees, rushing people.

The familiarity of my white lab coat and shoes against my body steadied me somewhat, and I was able to direct students and suggest some new projects for them. Then finally in the last session, the one that Santi attends, toward the end of the hour he asked, loudly enough to be heard by the others, "Señorita Philipsborn, would you still like me to assist with some student projects?"

"Oh, yes, thank you, Santi. I could use some help . . . choosing equipment for experiments in biochemistry. When can you start?"

"I'm available right after class."

"Wonderful. I'll wait for you in my office."

As soon as I reached my office, I pulled off lab coat and shoes and slipped on a pair of espadrilles that I keep in a drawer when I work late. I opened a window, spread some papers out on the table, took a seat, and finally—oh evil temptress!—I unbuttoned the top button of my dress. I started making a list of equipment our lab did not have, principally for distillation, when the shy knock on the door came. I opened to him, and we sat at my table, side by side, just looking at each other but not saying anything. I pointed to the list and began, "Here are. . . ." when Santi took my hand and turned completely to face me.

"I have been looking at your mouth all hour," he murmured, almost groaning. I also turned in my chair, until our legs were interlaced. He took my face gently into his hands and began kissing me, making small, tender sounds, and then our tongues found each other. I granted to him what my mouth had promised, and he then satisfied me—on my table top. Santi sat back in my chair, pulling up his trousers as I slid to the floor and reached for my underwear.

"That was a first for me," I admitted, breathless.

"Me too," he replied. "Do you really need help with that equipment?"

"I really do. I don't know what is available here, and I assume that you do."

He recommended some equipment that he thought was available in the supply room, and then said that he had to leave. I walked him to the door. No mention was made of the upcoming weekend. What was I expecting? As he stepped into the hall, his friend Javier walked by.

"*Oye*, Santi, we were supposed to be studying for the physiology exam! Do you still have time?"

"Oh, sure, Javi, let's go," replied Santi, and he walked away with Javier without looking back.

I sat back down at my table and considered that last little scene, reminding myself: This is a young medical student with a full schedule, and I am a professional foreign woman in Spain on a work visa, maybe twenty years his senior. I have just indulged in the hottest sex of my life, and I think I have given him the same. But I cannot expect an equal relationship, with dinners out, moonlight walks, and babies. It probably doesn't mean the same to him that it means to me. He may just be seeking experience for future relationships as he matures, while I have actually been rejuvenated and awakened to new aspects of myself. A new me in a new land. We are moving in different directions, and I mustn't make this the first priority of my life. But oh, if he came back right now, I'd gladly take my clothes off for him again.

Now I am seeing notices of a Party meeting over the weekend to discuss some recent writings of Trotsky about Spain and called "The Ten Commandments of the Spanish Communist." I will take my new self to Party meetings and try not to lose my heart at San Carlos.

MADRID, *Monday, 18 May 1931*

Today's lab sessions went according to routine. I felt very nervous before the last session and could not help noticing that Santi busied himself completely in the work of helping other students, without a glance in my direction. Toward the end of the hour, I asked him pointedly, "Santi, are you willing to assist me in another project today?"

"I'm sorry, Señorita Philipsborn, I'm in a study group for final exams, so I won't be able to continue that activity."

At that moment I realized how close we were to the end of the term and that after exams, many students would be leaving the city while some would be staying to take summer courses.

As classes let out, I caught up with him in the hallway and took his arm and simply asked him, "So what are your summer plans, Santi?"

"I will be going back to my town." He looked away, then finally into my eyes. "There's a girl," he continued, quietly.

My heart could not decide whether to explode out of my chest or stop completely. Somehow out of my throat squeaked the question, "Your girlfriend?"

"Yes—we are planning to get married as soon as I finish medical school."

The primitive female *Clarita* was urging me to scream and cry and throw my arms around his neck. Instead, the stoic, white-clad lab technician *Señorita*

Philipsborn swallowed, took a step back, managed a smile, and proclaimed, "Ah, congratulations. What a lucky girl!"

"Thank you," he replied, relieved (I think he feared what might have happened if *Clarita* the *vilde chaye*—the raging beast—had been unleashed—God knows he had experienced her firsthand!). He turned and continued down the hall.

I rushed to my office—returning to the "scene of the crime," so to speak—slammed the door behind me, began to sob, and searched for any remnant of *"that activity."* Unfortunately (or otherwise), the custodians had done an excellent job of cleaning my office, depriving me of any trace of Friday's torrid moments, so I locked my office door and left the building, then headed directly for the tram stop. It was somehow comforting to help prepare supper tonight and to sit at the table in the company of Hortensia and Severino, like returning to home and family after wandering lost through unknown streets.

Yesterday's Party meeting was held at the Salón de Variedades, a small theater near the hospital, on Calle de Atocha, 68. Identification was checked at the door—I wondered under whose authority. The underlying plan was to draft statutes for an upcoming assembly, so Trotsky's "Commandments" were suggested as a sort of yardstick. Thinking about the meeting and reading my copy of the "Commandments," it just seems more humane and less bureaucratic to fashion a political system that considers the local traditions and customs, rather than attempting to force people into a system based on that of a country with whose history they have nothing in common.

MADRID, Monday, 29 June 1931

Today I am grateful for two birthday gifts, the renewal of my contract for the coming academic year, and the results of yesterday's general elections: left-leaning parties have gained a majority of seats in the *Cortes* (the Congress). With no classes or other activities at the Residencias over the summer, I plan to attend concerts and public lectures here in the City. Most students have left Madrid, including Santi, of course. I wouldn't say that I am heartbroken—it happened so unexpectedly and was over so quickly that I don't think it has left a deep impression in my life—in fact I sometimes wonder if it even happened. He will return to finish his studies, and then he will marry the girl from his little northern monarchist town. And he never called me by my first name.

III

MADRID, *Wednesday, 15 July 1931*

I have filled my tagebuch and am now using this handsome new volume, purchased at Nicolás Moya's medical bookstore, just off Sol. The Republic's new *Cortes Constituyentes* have assembled, ready to work on drafting the new Constitution, and seated in the Parliament are now three women members, ironically elected without having been able to cast votes themselves.

One of the women elected to the Cortes is Victoria Kent, the first female lawyer in Spain. Another irony: Victoria actually opposes female suffrage, believing that Spanish women, so heavily influenced by the Church, lack political sophistication and would vote for conservative candidates. She thinks that women don't really "feel" the Republic. I certainly cannot comment on that opinion. Margarita Nelken, now representing Badajoz, Extremadura, in the Cortes, also opposes the vote for women.

The third female parliamentarian is Clara Campoamor, who does support women's right to vote and equality of the sexes in general. One voice among so many opposing voices. I hope that hers prevails and that she is able to convince her male colleagues that women are indeed capable of making decisions for the good of the Republic.

Artur and Gina have sent me this sweet photo of the girls, taken on their holiday in Denmark. I shall frame it and put it in my room. They all look so adorable, and I hope they are as happy as they look. I miss them so much and wish they could visit me here.

MADRID, *Wednesday, 7 October 1931*

Classes began last week for the new term and with it a new role for the women of Spain: The Cortes have voted in favor of woman suffrage. Three of the "Invisibles" contacted me to continue meeting on Wednesdays, and this afternoon I got together with Carmen, Herminia, and Pilar to discuss some of the many issues that have arisen around this momentous decision.

The three young women were eager to talk about the vote and the debates.

Carmen had brought last Thursday's *Heraldo*, showing the opinions of the women seated earlier in the Cortes, and began, "Señorita Philipsborn, look at this first page: Clara Campoamor is given one hundred percent responsibility for the Cortes vote."

"Oh, was it so easy? How did she do it?"

"She simply used logic and her persuasive skills learned as a student of law," replied Carmen.

"Wait a second, Carmina," intervened Pilar. "Victoria Kent is also a lawyer, as are many of the other members of the Cortes. Her argument *against* woman suffrage is that women have been so conditioned by the Church that they are incapable of making reasoned decisions. And I know a lot of women—some of them in my family—who might be described that way."

"But is that because women are innately prone to being conditioned," I asked, "or because institutions like the Church have undertaken the conditioning of women, almost from the day of their birth?"

"Victoria is also thinking of the number of women in Spain who are illiterate," added Herminia. "How can women inform themselves if they cannot read?"

"And why can't they read?" I asked. "Isn't that also a type of conditioning? Who is responsible for that?"

There followed a trio of ragged polyphony:

"Men!"

"The government"

"The men who run the government!"

"The king!"

"The dictator!"

"The priests!"

"*We* are responsible," proclaimed Carmen, rising to her feet, "unless we stand up!"

"And that is why we are here," added Pilar, taking Carmen's hand and calmly pulling her to her seat. "We persuaded our parents that we were responsible for our safety and capable of studying in an atmosphere dominated by men and studying material that men deemed us incapable of learning."

"Yes," agreed Carmen, "but our parents still had to be convinced that their weak, vulnerable, virgin daughters would be housed in an atmosphere protected from the penetration of the probably no less virginal but decidedly more powerful sons of other parents."

"Power," I mused, and paused. I tried to explain the German concept of the three "K's": *kinder, küche, kirche,* and asked them if there was an equivalent expression in Spanish.

"It's even worse," laughed Pilar, and they all recited, almost in unison, "*La mujer honrada, la pierna quebrada y en casa*" (The honorable woman: her leg is broken, and she stays at home).

"Either way, she has no power," I suggested. "Maintaining her in that state is what gives all power to the men. It is the reason that they are in opposition to declaring women as equal to men, and to allowing them to vote. Victoria Kent claims that women will vote for their oppressors and that the recently elected members of the Cortes will then lose their seats—their power. We must thank Clara Campoamor for convincing one hundred sixty-five of them that if we are living in a true democracy, they must accept the rights of women."

"And the one hundred twenty-two of them who voted against it will also need to be convinced," added Carmen, and we all laughed.

After that conversation, my thoughts turned to Santi, who has completed his chemistry lab requirements and whom I have barely glimpsed. He was certainly not virginal and was definitely powerful, but I did not feel as if we were competing for power. His girlfriend will certainly benefit from our brief affair, and I am happy to give myself credit for that. He looks embarrassed if he sees me, and I must confess that my heart skips a beat. Does that mean that he took some of my power? While it was happening, I admit that my wiser self did surrender to some sort of fool, the weak female that we are accused of being. Perhaps I was "voting for my oppressor," as Victoria Kent suspects. The image of Carmen rising from her seat to express her own power inspires me and reminds me of what I can learn from these young students.

MADRID, Friday, 25 March 1932

My elder sister Liese's forty-sixth birthday! I telephoned her this evening, and everyone seems to be well, aside from the growing apprehension around the looming presence of Hitler and National Socialism. The family is planning a gathering for Papa's eightieth birthday in August, and they expect me to be there. I am definitely looking forward to it.

BERLIN, Sunday, 7 August 1932

I have been here for about two weeks, for various reasons: to renew my visa for Spain, to vote in the July 31 election, to say good-bye to Gerda before she leaves for Palestine, to celebrate Papa's eightieth birthday (and Putzi's upcoming twelfth), to visit the rest of the family, and, ideally, to get Santi completely out of my mind, though my body still retains his pulsing imprint. The train ride northward through Spain was characterized by some moments that made me uneasy. Scarcely had we pulled out of Madrid when a police official, along with a pair of Civil Guardsmen, strode through the aisles and demanded documents of me and a few other people. This act was repeated as the train entered various provinces. And as we approached Catalunya, I noticed an agent standing in front of my compartment and occasionally glancing in. There was much less surveillance after crossing the Spanish border into France, but once in Germany, the frequent document checking began again, accompanied by that piercing look at what I can only describe as my physiognomy. I had fortunately had my hair bobbed and waved and my eyebrows tweezed, so at least I don't think I looked as exotic as I might have. Even so, and despite the German passport in my hand, I actually felt a twinge of nausea crossing the border into my homeland. I must look even less German. Who am I now? It was as if I had left the familiar behind and had entered an alien realm.

As for local politics, the Reichstag has been dissolved since June. The ironies are rather staggering: I've come from a country that just unseated an absolutist government through democratic elections to form a republic, to my homeland that unseated a democratic republic and is now in chaos, with the SA and SS reinstated. And the anti-republican bloc is made up of both the Nazi and the Communist parties, not at all friendly bedfellows!

Papa tells me that brown-shirted thugs continue to roam the streets freely, clubbing people who look Jewish and chanting this horrendous song:

Blut muss fliessen,	Blood must flow,
Blut muss fliessen,	Blood must flow,
Blut muss fliessen knuppelhageldick!	Blood must flow, like hail so thick!
Haut'se doch zusammen,	Let's smash it up,
haut'se doch zusammen,	Let's smash it up,
Diese gottverdammte Juden Republik!	This God-damned Jew Republic!

Today was Papa's party, and we had the whole family here in his new apartment on Motzstrasse. Birgit is still working for Papa and obviously keeping him in the best of health for his age. She had prepared chopped liver and noodle pudding and had set out pickled herring in sour cream. She has also evidently learned how to render chicken fat, preserved in the refrigerator as the golden *schmaltz*. I had forgotten how much I missed this food while in Spain and hovered over Papa in the kitchen as he sampled a bit of everything, as did I, with equal gusto.

"Take a *schtick* rye," he offered, spreading some schmaltz on a couple of slices he cut from the fragrant loaf and handing me a piece. The first bite afforded me a sort of cultural communion, and I felt the presence of dear Mama in the kitchen with us and a renewed connection to the soil on which I was born.

Papa still runs his factories and makes deliveries and does other errands on foot through the streets. I am very worried about him, given his age and the increase in anti-Semitic activities, which seem to be almost officially tolerated, at least not punished, since the recent elections. I have tried to encourage him to emigrate, perhaps to Denmark or to England, to join the Mond family, though he speaks no English. I broached the subject again this afternoon before the family arrived. We had poured a couple of glasses of schnapps in the small sitting room and toasted his age up to one hundred twenty years, Yiddish style. His argument is still that he and Moritz manufacture uniforms and that their business will always be in demand in Germany, and besides, he doesn't look Jewish.

I was tempted to comment, "Really? An old man schlepping schmatas around the streets of Schöneberg doesn't look Jewish?" but I could not bring myself to puncture his self-image and his pride.

Liese and Moritz were the first to arrive, with the boys, whom I hugged and kissed eagerly. Heinz, now twenty-one, brought a young lady named Ellen, to whom he is about to become engaged. Putzi will turn twelve on the seventeenth and is becoming quite the handsome young man. He's preparing to become a bar mitzvah and now insisting that we call him Günther, which I am trying to do.

Artur and Gina and the girls arrived soon afterwards. Artur is approaching fifty and already seems to have slipped into the role of old man, in contrast to Papa, who circulated busily from person to person, asking everyone if they had enough to eat and drink. Artur piled a plate with sweets—*rugelach* and chocolate *babka*—and moved his chair back, as if to observe everyone from a certain distance. I heard Gina comment, to whom I'm not sure, "That's what he's eating? I can't keep sweets in the house."

Szilard took a seat next to Artur and greeted him perfunctorily, watching the door or getting up several times to go to the window, no doubt waiting for Gerda.

I was so impressed with Ellen, who turned ten in February. She has inherited Gina's musty brown hair which, along with her serious expression, lends her the air of a wise woman. I felt drawn to speak to her and brought her a little plate of cake, for which she thanked me quite graciously.

"Ellen, are you enjoying school?"

"I suppose so, Tante Klara, though as one of the few Jewish students in my classes, the teacher is not giving me full credit for my work."

"Oh, Ellen, how do you know that it is because you are Jewish?" I asked, shocked.

She placed her fork carefully onto the plate and wiped her mouth with a napkin. "Teacher often tells the whole class that Jewish students will not be able to succeed in the professions. She also marks my papers more harshly than the papers of other students. My friend Helga shows me her papers, which I don't think are as well written as mine, and her scores are higher than mine," she replied, in a very matter-of-fact way.

I simply did not know what to say, so fell silent, stroking her hair, then asked about Artur: "Is your papa all right? He seems very quiet."

"Oh, ha, ha, Papa!" Ellen chuckled. "He certainly talks enough at home. He has something to say to all of us. And now that Nora is five, he lectures her almost as much as he does us."

"And what is the topic of his lectures?" I asked, rather sarcastically, thinking of Artur's tendency toward the pedantic, and then regretted it, given Ellen's young age.

"He mostly wants to make sure we keep up with our studies, especially languages. Renate and I are doing very well in English, which he makes us practice with him. I think our pronunciation is actually better than his. Nora doesn't understand and starts to cry. I don't think Papa understands Nora," Ellen confessed.

I was so impressed with her maturity and her compassion and was about to tell her so, when the door swung open, and Gerda made her grand entrance.

She had swept her hair up and was wearing a long dress, which added to her prima donna aura. Szilard stood up abruptly but couldn't approach her without asking Artur to move, so he sat down again. Gerda helped herself to a bit of food without even glancing at Szilard and sat down next to Gina, who started asking Gerda about the *Jüdisches Volksheim*, from which Gerda had just come. Gerda then made a special point to relate her plans for her upcoming trip to the Ben Shemen Youth Village in Palestine.

"You are very brave to travel to such a rough country," commented Gina.

"Ah, it is not a question of being brave," responded Gerda, "but doing what is the right thing to save our children."

Gina evidently felt that she was outdone with that phrase, and then turned to face me, and in a louder voice, queried, "So, Klara, tell us about Spain. Has this adventure been worth your while?" I felt the room go silent and all eyes, not to mention ears, were on me.

"Well, I suppose you know," I began, "we now have a republic in Spain, voted in last year by the electorate, an all-male electorate, I should add. The men in power have finally conceded the right to vote to women, though they won't be able to actually exercise this right until next year. But in many ways, it feels as if Spain is going in the reverse direction of Germany."

I took a small bite of the sweet babka and felt like I had to go on: "It seems like in Germany you"—and I did say *you*, conscious of the fact that I was separating myself from my country and my family—"are moving away from a democratic republic and throwing yourselves into the arms of a dictator who may do away with us all."

Loud protests greeted that remark.

"Klara, we didn't vote for Hitler," protested Moritz. "Of course, we didn't vote for your Thälmann either—at least Liese and I didn't—but I can assure you that none of us voted for Hitler!"

"Hitler is being raised to power by people and forces in this country who don't care about your positions or how you change your name or if you go to *shul*," interrupted Szilard. "We can call ourselves German and speak German and bring money into the German economy," he insisted, glancing at Papa, "but at the end of the day, to the brown-shirted mobs, a Jew is barely human, better off dead."

"So what can we do?" asked Liese, almost as if challenging him.

"We can leave," responded Gina.

"Yes," added Gerda, dramatically. "Palestine is now being settled by people who want to make a homeland for Jews. These poor orphan children from Lithuania, instead of being destined to die in the streets as beggars, are learning to work the land, a land that they can claim as their own."

"Gerda," I began, as patiently as I could, "do you remember Herr Einstein's words that day at the Café Wien? He reminded us that there have been people who are not Jews, living in Palestine and working the land for generations. Besides, it is a mistake to make a nationality out of a religion, if indeed we still have a religion."

"So what then?" asked Liese again, gathering her two younger nieces in her arms, as if suddenly needing to protect them from some approaching foe.

"Well, maybe leave," I conceded. "America might be the best idea. I for one will be returning soon to Spain. It is definitely not perfect, but at least the people there look more like me—like us—than do the Germans—and I am respected for my work. And how about England? Did you know that Mama's cousin Robert Mond was knighted just a month ago? Let us keep studying English," I concluded, hoping to lighten the conversation a bit. "Perhaps the British will not sing evil verses about us."

At that moment Birgit entered, as if on cue, with a tray loaded with glasses of champagne, offering a welcome relief from the strain of the conversation. We all raised glasses to toast Papa, who eagerly and gratefully joined us.

MADRID, *Tuesday, 8 November 1932*

The results of the November German elections have been announced in today's papers and, even though Hitler's National Socialist Party earned the number one position, it lost thirty-five seats in the Reichstag. The president is still Hindenburg, and he seems to be viewed as a kindly but ineffectual figurehead, sort of an easily manipulated grandfather. And Chancellor Franz von Papen seems to believe he can manipulate both Hindenburg and Hitler.

I have decided to give Hortensia and Severino a radio for Christmas. They have been so kind to me, and the quality of the programming seems to have improved in the time that I have been here. Hortensia spends many hours at home, and I know she would enjoy listening. The radio is also utilized for important government announcements and for news items that would make events immediately available to all of us.

While searching through today's *Socialista* for adverts of radios, I came across this one, the first one I have noticed, for *preservativos*. Contraceptives and birth control were strictly forbidden in Spain during the dictatorships (both "hard" and "bland"), owing to the teachings of the Church, which are basically against pleasure (as I understand it). The Republic has relaxed that prohibition, accepting the usefulness of condoms in preventing pregnancy and venereal disease.

This little notice made me exclaim almost aloud, "Gottenyu, Klara!" as it suddenly struck me that I had considered neither the real possibility of pregnancy nor of venereal disease last spring during the brief affair with Santi, and he certainly did not mention it or take any precautions either. I'm not sure if it is men or women who are expected to take responsibility, and I certainly had not. Was I temporarily insane, driven by my awakened libido and by the flattery of my feminine ego? It was certainly a way to join me to the Spanish earth. I am thinking that if I ever chance to be in the neighborhood of *"La Discreta"* I will have a look at their free catalog and perhaps purchase some samples, in case the opportunity ever arises again. I have certainly seen—and treated—the effects of venereal disease and of unwanted pregnancy.

MADRID, *Monday, January* 30 1933

The snarled words came hurtling through the radio and crashed like fists into my stomach as I entered the kitchen this morning:

"Die grosse zeit ist jetzt angebrochen! Deutschland ist nun erwacht! Die macht haben wir uns in Deutschland gewonnen; nun gilt es das Deutsche volk zu gewinnen!"

Hitler's bellowing voice was mercifully interrupted by the Spanish announcer, who translated: "The time of greatness has now erupted! Germany has now awakened! We have won the power in Germany; now we have to win over the German people!"

Adolf Hitler has manipulated his way into the Chancellorship of Germany, appointed by the senile Hindenburg, whom von Papen convinced in order to gain a vice-Chancellorship for himself, thinking that he could in this way control Hitler through a coalition which could then outnumber the Communists.

Since no major papers come out on Mondays in Madrid (except for the *ABC*), I called Artur and Gina immediately after work. They are more convinced than ever that the best plan for the family is to emigrate, and they are already planning to enroll the girls in schools in Denmark.

"And has Gerda written you from India?" Gina asked, moving to a new topic.

"India? No. When did she leave Palestine?"

"Last month. A man from the university met her in Bombay and escorted her to Delhi."

"Well, at least she is out of Germany," I commented, and Gina agreed.

Next, I called Liese, who sounded dreadful and was sobbing. "I had such a hard time getting Günther to calm down and go to sleep. He wanted to go out and stop the victory parade single-handed. Heinz is out with Ellen, and I'm so worried about them! The vibrations from the drumbeats and the marching boots shook the windows, which we had closed tightly. Worst of all, the awful 'Horst Wessel-Lied' came roaring out—I can't say it was sung—at the top of everyone's lungs—men, women, and children. There were SA and SS troops carrying torches and passing out armbands with swastikas."

"Horrible! What does Moritz think?"

"He's with Papa now, still at the factory. It's unbelievable, but they are not as worried as I am. I hope you can talk to them."

I remained at the Telefónica and called Papa at around ten o'clock. "Papa, are you all right? Have you been affected by the actions in the streets?"

"We are fine, Klara! Moritz is here with me, and we're working late to get out a new batch of uniforms."

"You are making uniforms for the SS and the SA?"

"We just do the cutting and sewing. We are not taking part in politics."

I was stunned into silence. My own father says this! Finally, I managed to suggest, "By being who you are and where you are, you are taking part in politics, Papa."

"I am a manufacturer of military uniforms and children's clothing. That is who I am. My work is needed by whatever government is in power."

"Will Hitler want his uniform to be sewn by (I lowered my voice, an instinctive habit) a Jew?"

"Hitler, *Schmitler!*" scoffed Papa, "Uniforms are needed, children need clothing, and we are here to make them."

I felt a pang in my stomach as I realized that there was nothing more I could say. I told Papa I loved him and wished that he and Moritz be safe. My stomach is still in a knot as I write these lines.

MADRID, Wednesday, 1 March 1933

I would not have been surprised if the Reichstag had *only* been dissolved, which Hitler convinced Hindenburg to do on his first day as Chancellor, but the building itself has actually *burned*, and with it, any pretense at a parliamentary government in Germany. I have just received the latest issue of the *Rote Fahne*, which shows clearly the murderous Nazi plan well before the burning of the Reichstag. Hitler arrived on the scene and declared to reporters that the fire was "the beginning of a great epoch in German history." I am completely enraged. Such a transparent destruction of democracy sets a flaming inside me. And Hitler then demanded of Hindenburg a decree "for the protection of the people and the State," which of course Hindenburg signed, and which effectively deprives all Germans of their civil rights. I feel so helpless and far from home at this moment.

The only Spanish paper not seduced by Hitler's rhetoric is today's issue of *El Socialista*, which attributes the burning of the Reichstag to "fascist provocation." I met with my "Invisibles" this afternoon, who concurred completely with that opinion, saying "What else could it be?"

"*Más claro, ni el agua*," added Carmen. (Not even water is clearer than that!)

MADRID, Sunday, 2 April 1933

Germany has taken its first step with its "Enabling Law." Yesterday, at 10:00 a.m., brown-shirted SA men stationed themselves before major Jewish-owned businesses in Berlin, plastering on shop windows posters that proclaimed, "Germans, defend yourselves! Don't buy from Jews!"

I plan to call family tomorrow to see what the effects were and if the boycott will continue. I fear most for Papa, who does not seem to have a clear idea of the reality of the situation. For me, so far away, it is also difficult to imagine what this must be like.

MADRID, Tuesday, 4 April 1933

This evening I was able to make two telephone calls, one to Papa and one to Artur and Gina. Papa reported that the SA officers felt rather embarrassed at having to stand in front of his door.

"This boycott thing is not serious and will not continue," Papa insisted. "In fact, one of the SA men told me, 'Herr Philipsborn, we have been commanded to stand guard here. But we are not allowed to prohibit anyone from entering.'

A few of our regular customers, gentiles, came to shop for Easter outfits for their children. One woman even faced up to the officers and told them that she had a right to shop wherever she wanted."

I was simply unable to respond to Papa's words. Is doing business so important to him that he will accept being humiliated? And does he even feel humiliated? I myself was mortified but could not ask him that.

"So how are things at the apartment?" I asked, hoping to change the subject.

"Ach, well, Szilard has left, for Budapest. He does not see a future for himself here." I thought I detected a somewhat scornful tone in Papa's statement.

"Oh, I hope he finds success—and safety—in his home city, and I hope you will be safe, Papa."

I next spoke briefly to Artur, who said he did not want to talk, and passed the telephone to Gina. Her tone and words were far different from Papa's.

"We don't feel like Germans anymore! Ellen and Renate are taunted daily by their classmates, and a girl asked Ellen if she was getting ready to celebrate *Karfreitag* (Good Friday), since she had killed Christ!"

I gasped, "Oh, poor Ellen! How did she respond?"

"She reminded the girl that the Romans killed Jesus, and added, 'I didn't kill anyone, and I don't plan to kill anyone.' I will not raise my daughters in this atmosphere."

"So what do you plan to do?" I asked, feeling so proud of my dear niece, her wisdom and her ability to speak up, but devastated at the treatment she is receiving in Germany.

"Artur is looking into South America and Australia. But I think it would be easier simply to move north to Scandinavia. We have read that the king of Denmark, Christian the Tenth, is favorable to the Jews, despite pressure from Hitler. So I am investigating schools where we can send the girls while we make permanent arrangements."

I might have suggested to Artur and Gina that they think about Spain as a possible future home. That is, before I read an article in today's *ABC* titled, "*ABC en Berlín*," ostensibly about the boycott. Actually, the fact that the boycott took place seems to serve as an excuse for the writer, César González-Ruano, to express his visceral hatred of Jews. Though he offers no ideological basis of Marxism, he feigns surprise that no one realizes that it was the "Marxist Jews" who took over the Power (yes, capitalized!) in the German government after the end of the Empire, as if that were sufficient justification to boycott Jewish businesses. Though he alleges to have sent his story in from Berlin, this writer has no access to the reality of life. His statement that Germany has Jewish merchants and bureaucrats but not a single Jewish worker must have been penned in a castle or perhaps even on another planet.

After seeing what is accepted as objective reporting in a country whose Constitution proclaims freedom of religion, I am glad that I have decided to conceal my Jewish identity in this country, which feels more like my own, at least for now.

MADRID, Monday, 1 May 1933: MAY DAY!

Oh, irony of ironies! As my adopted country emerges from the frying pan, my native land plunges into the fire! The irony intensifies with the praises by some Spanish intellectuals (!) for German National Socialism. I am now holding a copy of the daily, *La Libertad,* with an article filed in Berlin by yet another terrifying Spaniard, Felipe Fernández Armesto. For this writer, the fact that Hitler has proclaimed May Day as a "National Workers' Day" is the most natural act and in fact a work of art. He claims that "logic is Hitler's forte" and that the festival has become an arm of national politics. He even quotes Göbbels: "All Germany must deck itself out in green garlands and national flags!" And the most painful phrase of all: "All Germany will live this day under the motto: Honor labor and appreciate workers!"

I find myself gasping for breath and my eyes tearing up at such a profanation of Workers' Day. With writers like Fernández Armesto and González-Ruano working in Socialist Spain, I realize now that the tricolored flag can wave over multicolored ideologies. Perhaps the red flag—or maybe even the black flag—is the only one I can trust.

MADRID, *Wed., 10 May 1933*

I stopped by the Telefónica today to call Papa. He was of course at work, at the shop on Dirksenstrasse, which indicated to me that he was in good health. I was more concerned about Papa's response to the May Day outrage, and as usual, his replies were utterly nonchalant.

"It was a *big* circus," he proclaimed, dramatically deepening his voice.

"Did you go out and see it?" I asked, trying to keep my tone casual.

"Ha, no, I've seen plenty of circuses in my lifetime. My workers told me I did not miss much."

"Your workers?" I asked, anxiously. Papa has always employed gentile workers, and now I feared that they may have been taken in by the theatrics of the new, pseudo-legal, regime.

"Their working conditions could not be better, so I think it is just fine that they went to the show," he replied, obviously realizing my concern. It was evident that Papa did not want to worry me, and I changed the subject.

"*Nu*, anything new in the family?"

"Ah, yes, Regina and the girls have received exit visas and are moving to Denmark. They leave in July, and the girls will start school there in the fall. Artur will remain until he receives his papers."

I realized with that statement that tremendous pressures must have been placed on them, as Artur and Gina have enjoyed successful careers as psychologists in Nowawes. It was obvious to me that it is more important to Gina to keep her girls safe than to attempt to prolong a career in Germany with dubious outcomes. I told Papa I loved him, and we hung up, after which I placed an immediate call to Artur and Gina. She answered the telephone, and her tone sounded guarded. Again, I tried to remain calm as I began: "So, Papa says you and the girls are leaving soon for Denmark. I am planning on coming home and would love to help you pack."

"Klara, you are not helping us pack and you are not coming home. Once I have told you everything that has happened in the past month you will understand." Her voice was firm as she fired off facts as if from a machine gun:

"April first: boycott of Jewish businesses. April seven: 'Law to Reestablish the

Civil Service.' All civil servants of Jewish descent must retire. April twenty-two: Jews may not serve as patent lawyers or as doctors in State-run insurance institutions. April twenty-five: the number of Jewish children permitted to enroll in public schools is limited. April twenty-six: Göring creates the *Geheime Staats Polizei* (Secret State Police), now popularly known as *"Gestapo."* Brown shirts are now legally members of the *Hilfspolizei,* and they stop and search anyone on the streets, especially those of us who 'look Jewish.' And all of this crowned on May first, by the Grand Nazi Circus. I will send you a page from—of all things—the Sunday *Berliner Tageblatt* that illustrates my point. Should we stay and simply wait for more restrictions? And even if you are permitted to enter, will you be permitted to leave? We have had to bribe horrible people and buy connections in Denmark and even in America to get these permits."

I remained silent for many seconds, trying to digest all the bitter events she had mentioned. With each new restriction, I felt as if I were being removed one more step from Germany. Finally, I managed to offer her any help I could and asked her to kiss the girls for me. The girls! I may never see them again! I hung up, sobbing, and once again received some stares along the Gran Vía as I exited the Telefónica. I will again save a space here for the clipping that Gina is sending me. I feel more alone than ever before. Do I belong anywhere? A terrifying feeling.

SEVILLE, *Friday, 18 August 1933*
(or early Saturday morning)

I have just arrived in sweltering Seville, after an eight-hour train ride from Madrid. What brings me here was this piece of sad news: Tía Lola died earlier this month, and I didn't learn about it until this past Tuesday, when the notice appeared in the *ABC* of Seville. I immediately telephoned Tío Julio, who sounded weak and, for the first time, old. He even spoke to me in German and begged me to come spend some time with him. I packed two lightweight black dresses and boarded the train right after work. Again, my passport was scrutinized several times during the trip, as was my person (this from a modest distance).

The taxi stand beside the Moorish palace which is the Seville train station was heavily guarded by Civil Guardsmen when I arrived after midnight. The city is under a strike, but I must not have looked suspicious, as a woman traveling alone and dressed in black, so I was able to get a taxi without difficulty.

The moment we passed through the Arco de la Macarena, I again felt a sort of transformation as we entered the historical center—really the kernel—of the city. Calle San Luis was quiet, and I noticed some renovations and improved lighting. We soon pulled up in front of number 42, the Mond family home. I expected that everyone would be asleep at that hour, but once the sereno had let me in, to my surprise Asun was waiting up in the vestibule, fully dressed (in black) but without her apron. We embraced fondly and kissed noisily, and I began to weep when she said to me, almost immediately, "I am so sorry about your mother's death." She then showed me to my room, which was the one formerly occupied by Cousin Clarita, now married to Gerardo and with two children. I had brought some *manzanilla* (chamomile tea) and honey, along with those wonderful mushrooms from the Mercado de San Miguel, and I suggested that we go to the kitchen and make the tea. I noticed modern touches in the kitchen: a new refrigerator and new blinds for the windows, though the charming tiles still remained.

Asun has obviously aged in the more than eight years since we have seen each other. There are now deep lines in her face, and she donned a pair of eyeglasses to measure the fragrant flowers into the teapot. Her black hair, which she still wore pulled back into a severe bun, showed streaks of gray. She seemed to have the same steady, calm presence and the intelligence that allowed her to preside over the household, albeit from a subordinate position. I was happy that she addressed me with the familiar "*tú*," a tiny confirmation of my hopes for a classless society. Then I asked her about my uncle.

"Don Julio is taking Doña Lola's death very hard," she began, as she took a seat with me at the table. "His appetite has diminished, and he is less active. He has even stopped taking his walks. I am worried for his health. He was also very sad when he came back from your mother's funeral but was happy that you might be coming to Spain."

That statement made me feel much love for my uncle. "He was also very helpful toward my finding employment in Madrid."

"Well, in fact, now you talk like a real madrileña," she interjected, patting my arm.

I was so flattered by that statement. I know I still have an accent but every day it is a bit easier to pass for a local, that is if I don't say too much. I took a sip of tea and plunged into the next subject: "Have you been affected by the strike?"

"The strike? *¡Bah! ¡Mucho ruido y pocas nueces!*" she exclaimed, throwing her hands in the air.

I understood this to mean something equivalent to "Much ado about nothing," with the literal meaning of "a lot of noise but not many nuts."

"This is the so-called *Sevilla la roja* (Red Seville)," she continued. "Even now that we have the Republic, the groups can't agree, someone is always on strike, and we workers have seen no benefits."

I shook my head in disappointment, thinking, *The bourgeois Republic: what else could I expect?*

"Maybe the revolution will come from the jails," she added. "My friend Petra has a son who is in jail, and he told her that the prisoners are being punished by being given stale bread after singing the "Internationale" in the exercise yard. So what do you think they have decided to do? A hunger strike!"

"Oh, *ojalá* (God willing) that will be effective," I exclaimed, suddenly realizing that I was letting Asun know my political ideas, perhaps encouraged by her use of the word "revolution."

"Ojalá," she responded.

I was relieved to hear what seemed like a statement of solidarity and suddenly felt tired. I helped Asun wash the teacups and teapot and retired to my room.

And just now that I am completing this entry in my diary, it occurs to me that Tía Lola was the last person—or perhaps the *only* person—in Tío Julio's family to be aware of the Mond family's Jewish ancestry. The thought stirs up a strange sensation of being cut adrift, but at the same time is rather exhilarating. A way to begin anew, to create one's identity. Am I on this path?

SEVILLE, Saturday, 19 August 1933

This morning I awoke and raised my blinds to look down at the patio, and then opened the window to take in the fragrance that the geraniums and carnations shared with me from their many pots below. Asun had told me about a huge Saturday *mercadillo* which was held on Calle Feria, just west of Calle San Luis. I knew I could not miss this opportunity, returned to my room and closed the blinds tightly against the sun, and prepared to go down to the kitchen and greet Tío. I found him seated at the kitchen table before a plate of *churros* and a generous tazón of café con leche. As he stood to embrace me, pressing on the table for balance, I noticed that his body was quite bent, and he appeared thin. His color was sallow, and his eyes were teary. I gave him the strongest hug I thought he could bear, as he uttered, "Klärele, Klärele, Gottenyu!" He was dressed in shirtsleeves but wore a black armband and black trousers.

We both took a seat and Asun poured hot coffee out of one silver pot and hot milk out of the other for me, just the right proportions, as if she remembered how I like it (which she probably did).

As I had already expressed my condolences to my uncle when we spoke on the telephone, I suddenly felt that it was my duty, almost as medical protocol, to try to lift his mood. "So what are your plans for the day, Tío?"

"My goodness, you are actually speaking Spanish. Better than I, even." He added a sugar cube to my coffee and was about to add a second, when I stayed his hand.

"*Ach*, Tío, you are flattering me as you sweeten my coffee. Will the girls be coming here?"

"Yes, I have invited them all to come tomorrow. Lolita's children are away studying, so they may not be able to come, but she is planning on coming, and Carmela and Clarita are very eager to see you."

"I'm very eager to see them too," I offered enthusiastically, "especially Clarita's little one, also called Clarita, right?"

"That's right. I hope you have gotten used to this custom."

"I have, in fact I scarcely notice it now. I would also love to go to the mercadillo on Calle Feria before it gets too hot. Will you accompany me—to keep me from spending too much money?"

Tío smiled briefly and put his hand on my arm as he said, "I think I will have to trust you to control yourself, Klärele. Do protect your handbag and remember that you are in the capital of the *cacos*."

"Oh, yes, the *carteristas* (pickpockets)." I laughed. "I have kept myself safe from them so far."

"*Ptu, ptu, ptu!*" To my surprise, Tío enacted the family ritual of warding off the evil eye, feigning to spit over his left shoulder. He quickly looked around to see if Asun had noticed. I certainly had and repeated the gesture myself. I wondered if he had passed it along to any of his children but did not ask.

"What I want to do is to go and hear Mass at eight thirty this evening. I know that the Church is not a part of your life, but I would be so pleased if you would accompany me."

"I will be happy to do that, Tío—but oh, I did not bring anything to cover my head." I have accompanied students to Mass on occasion and know that women cover their heads in church, but I had not thought to bring anything to Seville.

"We can find you a mantilla—of Lola's," he suggested, his voice almost breaking. "Asun," he called, turning in his chair to face Asun, who was scrubbing the tiles along the sink, "would you please go and find a mantilla for Clara to wear to church? Black, of course."

"Of course," Asun echoed, "right away, Don Julio."

Asun dried her hands and disappeared, returning soon with a beautiful black lace mantilla, which I took to my room.

I left the house, walked up toward the Plaza Pumarejo and took the long Calle Relator all the way to Calle Feria. What a sight! Colors upon colors, bright polka-dotted flamenco dresses for little girls, full-length pastel-colored gowns for women. Men and women, assisted by some children, sang as they laid out multihued trinkets on colorful blankets, potted flowers were grouped in graceful patterns, books were being arranged on tables, and caged birds trilled bravely from canvas-draped frames.

I began to stroll about comfortably among the crowds, aware of glances toward my pocketbook, which I held tightly against my body. I noticed many of the vendors looking at me. I simply greeted them as normally as I could. I soon realized that I had begun to drop the sound "S" from various parts of my speech, and I actually got fewer of those quizzical looks when uttering *"Bueno' día."* I stopped first in front of a blanket displaying used metal items. There was a brass box that I thought would make a lovely cigarette case, and I used my now almost natural bargaining skills to get the price down to three pesetas and purchased it as a gift for Severino. Across the way was a table with baskets of bracelets. I finally settled on a simple polished wood bracelet for Hortensia and continued down the street to the bookstall. I picked up a copy of *ABC* for ten céntimos, bought a *granizado de limón* from a little booth, found a bench shaded by a palm tree under which to sip the frozen lemonade, and opened the paper. I had only to reach page eight when the enemy rose up and hit me in the stomach: a photo of Hitler, looking almost normal, superimposed over a peaceful scene from his Austrian birth town, Braunau am Inn. The article, more a love poem than an example of reportage, had been written by César González-Ruano, the same fascist hack who authored the encomium to the boycott of Jewish businesses. The title, *"El día de Hitler,"* attempts to show a typical day of "the peasant, by the grace of God" as he travels by airplane between his difficult job in Berlin dressed in that uncomfortable uniform and the *gemütlich* (yes, Ruano uses the German word!)—sweetly homey hours he whiles away in the Bavarian country-side, discoursing on Teutonic music and art with his fellow peasants, clad in his charming native garb, surrounded by the snow-capped blue mountains, the white flowers, and the little blonde maidens.

Impelled to launch a Wagnerian finale, Ruano produces this phrase: "Many secret forces are still waging a silent battle against the dawning state led by the swastika-sporting *caudillo*." By that time, not only was I burning with anger, but the sun had pushed past the protective arms of the palm tree and was scorching my unprotected skin. I returned to the house, tempted to burn the paper, but I had decided to save one clipping for my diary, so it came back with me and will soon be hidden in my valise.

For the midday meal, Asun had prepared a refreshing *gazpacho*, followed by a revoltillo using the mushrooms I had brought. Tío and I ate together alone, seated at the long mahogany table in the dining room. I had bathed and changed into another black dress. The blinds were still drawn, and the room was serenely cool. I considered bringing up the topic of the article that had offended me so deeply but then remembered my plan to try to do something to lift Tío out of the depression over his wife's death while still allowing him to grieve for her and miss her.

"Asun, the gazpacho was delicious—thank you," he remarked, looking up at Asun, as she removed the soup plates from atop the dinner plates.

"Thank you, Don Julio. Now you are going to taste some wonderful mushrooms that Doña Clarita brought from Madrid, mixed into a revoltillo, your favorite."

"Ah, that will be stupendous. Klärele, would you like some wine? Asun, how about that *rosado* from down in the cellar? It must be cool and will go perfectly with the egg dish."

"Yes, good idea, Don Julio. Let me bring that up first."

Tío began to explain, as Asun left the room, smiling and walking briskly: "This is a wine from one hundred percent *garnacha* grapes."

"From Sevilla?"

"Ach, no! These grapes are from Aragón, and the wine was a gift from a vintner with whom my cork factory does business."

I noticed that he was sitting up straighter as he enthusiastically described the wine we were about to taste.

"The grapes are grown at a fairly high altitude: over six hundred meters. The altitude here in Sevilla is only about ten meters above sea level. We could never grow such grapes here. And we will need the correct glasses to enjoy this rosado. Take some bread. To neutralize your palate after the gazpacho."

He rose from his chair and walked without his cane to the rosewood cabinet with a *vitrina* that held many wine and water glasses of varying shapes. He opened a glass door and drew out two that seemed to be shorter versions of the glasses used for red wine and placed them on the table.

"This is fine Bohemian crystal, the best vessel for wine," he declared. "Oh, one moment." He turned back and pulled out one more glass. "For the cook— she well deserves it," he announced, just as Asun entered the room with a bottle of a pale pink liquid with a slight salmon tinge. She set the bottle down and turned to go to the kitchen, but Tío stopped her. "Wait for me to open this and please pour yourself a glass."

"With pleasure." Asun opened a drawer in the cabinet to pull out a strange-looking metal device with wings or arms, handing it to Tío.

"This is the latest gadget," announced Tío proudly, "just invented and patented by Domenico Rosati. It requires a minimum of effort to open bottles now." He inserted the point into the cork, remarking, "This is one of our corks," rotated his hand to turn the device, pressed down on the "wings," and the cork obediently rose and emerged from the neck of the bottle. "It feels cool," he noted, after closely inspecting the cork and gently palping the bottle. "It will be fine to leave it on the table so the flavor can develop." He then poured a small amount for himself, hoisted the glass by the stem, and held it up to the filtered light. "Beautiful color, eh?" He took a slight sniff, commenting "Tropical fruit—rose petals" and next took a sip: "Fresh, substantial . . . we can drink this!" He then poured a glass for Asun, one for me, and filled his own glass. "Hold the glass by the stem, not by the bowl. That way you don't change the temperature with your fingers. Now let us toast to our health."

I stood and lifted my glass to touch it to Asun's and to Tío's as we all chorused, "¡Salud!" Everything Tío had said about the wine was confirmed. The temperature was cool but not icy, and I did fancy that I could taste and smell fruit and roses. Asun took her glass to the kitchen, and Tío and I returned to our seats. He still seemed to be sitting straighter in his chair.

"How do they get this pink color, Onkel?"

"Ah, there are some secrets. The region is very dry, the grapes are harvested at night, and the skins of the grapes are removed when the pink color is achieved."

"I'm learning so much from you. I can use this information in my chemistry labs," I said, laughing.

"Yes, of course, much about wine is chemistry. The rest . . . is magic," he declared, taking another sip of wine.

Asun returned with a platter of the egg-mushroom mixture, along with a smaller platter of red peppers and olives.

"What a banquet, and just for me!" I exclaimed, as I served myself and Tío and took a bite of the revoltillo. The mushrooms lent an exotic, earthy dimension and a rich color to the dish.

"You deserve it, Klärele. You are my last connection with family." Tío's voice broke as he uttered this last statement.

I was about to say, "Come back to Germany" when I realized, with a shudder, that not only would he not be returning to Germany, I probably would not either, and Germany was no longer my home. But I had embarked on a sort of mission to pull my uncle out of depression. I raised my glass, calling out, "To family! To grandchildren and great-grandchildren!" Saying this brought me back to where I was at that moment, and it seemed to do the same for Tío.

"Yes, to family!" he repeated, touched his glass to mine, and took a final sip of the rosado. "They will be here tomorrow. The house will be once again filled with children."

We rose, hugged, and retired to our respective rooms for a welcome siesta.

I woke and bathed again and donned the other black dress, which Asun had washed and pressed. Clothing dries so rapidly in this African air. It had cooled considerably by eight o'clock when I met Tío in the front room, and we prepared to leave the house. His color seemed to have improved since the meal and the siesta. He had put on a black jacket which the people here call *americana*. I had put the black lace mantilla over my head and simply let the ends drape over my shoulders.

Tío took a step back and remarked, "Now you are really dressed de Hebrea."

"Oh!" I exclaimed, remembering that phrase as describing the way the Virgin was dressed for Holy Week, head and shoulders draped in a shawl—as a Jew. "Well, I imagine I have a right to do that." I laughed.

The still light sky was promising a display of purple when we stepped outside. I took Tío's right arm, and with his left hand, he clutched his cane, supporting each step he took with the right foot. It reminded me of how Mama used her cane, on exactly that side. (Papa has always refused a cane and exaggerates a brisk walk to display his agility—and his stubbornness.)

Just a few steps south of our front door, I gasped to behold what looked like a reduced version of the Giralda looming up at the end of the street. "That is the tower of our San Marcos," Tío commented with what sounded like pride.

"Was it a minaret?"

"No, but since it was built on the remains of a mosque, I think the four-teenth-century architects and builders probably had the Giralda in mind."

I remembered a word from my first visit to Seville, and suggested, "So could we call it Mudéjar?"

"That's right," confirmed Tío. "They call it 'gótico-mudéjar.'"

Ah, yes, the hybrid: proof that we can all reconcile. And I was quite comfortable with both those labels. The arch was flanked by two figures of saints (Gabriel and Mary, as Tío explained). I was about to ask about the figure at the center, above the apex of the arch, when I realized it was meant to be God, holding the orb of the earth in his hands. I was shocked to actually see this depiction, forbidden in all of Jewish law as I understand it, and wanted to cover my face—but I simply looked away. Fortunately, it was time for Mass to begin, so we entered the church, where Tío dipped his hand in the holy water and made the sign of the cross as I again averted my face.

During the actual Mass I looked about at the sculptures as they lay or sat in repose. What a contrast to the way they had been during Holy Week, emerging alive to display themselves to the townspeople, sharing their suffering, their triumph over death, and their promise of salvation! Do they sleep all year, like forgotten dolls, only to be brought out to be dressed up and played with at their owners' whims?

MADRID, *Friday, 6 October 1933*

We have a new resident at the Resi, and I may have acquired an ally. She is Dr. Käthe Pariser, a geneticist from Berlin, and she will be working at Professor Antonio de Zulueta's Natural Science Museum on the Paseo de la Castellana. Doña María proudly introduced her at a tea in her honor on Wednesday, and I was able to speak with her briefly and invite her for tea (*merienda*) at the Café Gijón this afternoon at six o'clock. I thought it would be nice to distance ourselves from the Resi, at least geographically, since some of its luminaries do frequent that café. She was waiting inside when I arrived and stood rather formally and stiffly when I approached her table. I had to remind myself that she had arrived only recently from Germany and probably did not expect to be hugged and kissed immediately, which has become my first impulse. I took her hand, removed my raincoat, and dropped it onto the chair where she had placed hers. Though no one in the Resi had mentioned whether she was Jewish, I assumed from her name that she was, and I somehow needed to find out. So as we took our seats at the marble-topped table, in an attempt to break the ice, I smiled, looked into her eyes, and began, "Fortunately, this place does not at all resemble the Romanisches Café."

Her smile and her chuckle were immediate: "And it especially does not seem like the *Rachmunisches* Café either, *Gott sei dank* (thank God)!"

We both enjoyed a subdued laugh, and my question was answered. She is tall and solid-looking, with pale skin, blue eyes, and prominent cheekbones. She wore no makeup, and her light brown hair was tightly pulled back, probably in an attempt to control curls (like mine). Her hairline came to a point in the middle of her forehead, a shape the English call a "widow's peak," adding a distinctive dimension to her face. Her lips were fleshy, also pale, without lip rouge. About my age, perhaps a bit older.

"Are you coming directly from Berlin?"

"No—I left in April and have been living in Zurich. Life in Berlin"—she lowered her voice—"Germany, I should say—has become impossible."

"Yes." I nodded. "Some of my family have already left, for Denmark and for Palestine. Some are still in Germany, and I wish they would leave already.

My father and my brother-in-law are still able to work, making clothes, and my two nephews are still studying."

"My father is also in the textile business. My brother Robert has been living in New York but travels a lot because he is an importer."

A waiter arrived to take our orders. Both of us ordered café con leche, and I chose a mil hojas puff pastry from a tempting tray he displayed to us. Käthe chose something with apples and cinnamon, which I believe I will try the next time I am there. Her Spanish was halting and heavily accented. The fact that I noticed made me think that perhaps I am finally losing my German accent.

"How do you know Professor Zulueta?" I asked.

"I met him at a genetics conference in Berlin, in 1927. I had studied with Richard Goldschmidt, and he introduced us. Our research interests had much in common, as it turns out, though his work is primarily with the beetle (*Phytodecta variabilis*). He is truly a pioneer in Spanish genetics. And what is your mission here, Fräulein Philipsborn?"

"Please call me 'Klara,'" I insisted. She was using the formal *Sie* address in German, and I realized how much Spain has changed me. People here, especially people on the left, have begun to use the informal *tú* form much more readily, and to greet each other with an earnest "Salud." "I came here in 1930 to work in the chemistry laboratory in the Medical School. I had a recommendation from Dr. Einstein, which seemed to help."

"Ah, wonderful. Did you know"—she leaned forward and lowered her voice again, though I doubt that anyone within earshot understood German—"that he has renounced his German citizenship? His Berlin bank account has been seized, and he may move to England or to America."

"Oh. He had been offered a chair here in Madrid ten years ago. Perhaps he would have been safe here."

"Do *you* feel safe here, Fräu— . . . Klara?"

I hesitated for a moment since she doesn't know anything about my politics. "I do," I answered, "though not very many people know that I am Jewish." This time it was I who lowered my voice.

The coffee and pastry arrived at that moment, and it saved me from admitting that I have been hiding my Jewishness. I added a sugar cube to the cup, marked with the initials of the café, "CG," stirred it and we took the first sip together, acknowledging the rich gift of the hot, dark beverage. "So you will be working with *tritones*—with newts," I began. "What type of research will that be?"

She took a sip of coffee and explained. "I have been crossbreeding them, and I will use types of newts found in two areas of Spain. I am looking at intersexuality and what I have found so far is that if species are crossbred, they are more likely to produce female offspring, and if they produce males, the males are far weaker than the females and often die young." She became more animated while talking about her research, and some color appeared on her cheeks.

I pictured this prim woman extracting sperm from slimy little male newts and inserting it into the slimy vaginas of unsuspecting female newts and then waiting to harvest their slimy offspring. As I could not imagine how her research could produce a classless society, I failed to see the benefits, but wished her well in her endeavors and promised to assist her in acclimating to life in Madrid. I returned to the Resi with her, she thanked me, we hugged tentatively, and she retired to her room. After this encounter I am feeling more Spanish than ever and wonder if I too should be renouncing my German citizenship.

MADRID, Tuesday, 31 October 1933

I telephoned Artur on the occasion of his fiftieth birthday, last week, on the 24th. The telephone line to the island of Bornholm in Denmark was every bit as clear as the lines to Germany. My brother was his usual pedantic self, but actually congratulated me on living away from Germany. When I asked him what he liked about Denmark, he complained that the Danes did not pronounce half the letters in their language, but that he did like a Danish version of *pfannkuchen* or pancakes. I am not surprised that Artur would focus on a sweet treat. He soon handed the telephone to Gina, who felt compelled to inform me about yet another shocking series of policies issued by the Nazi government. I was thankfully sitting down as she enumerated these unbelievable rulings. It became clear to me why Käthe Pariser had left Germany:

"As of last month, all non-Aryans and their spouses are prohibited from government employment." Gina had lowered her voice, as if she were still in Germany and fearful that someone was listening.

"'Non-Aryans'? What does that mean?"

"Hitler says the Aryans are the pure race, which he equates with Germans."

"Germans? *We* are Germans, aren't we? And is that a race? I thought Aryans were from India." I somehow could not let her go on without interrupting with questions that probably had no answers and certainly no logic. She attempted to explain further:

"The Nazis are saying that an Aryan is a person of the 'superior race' (*Herrenrasse*), is tall, and has blond hair and blue eyes. A Jew is by definition a non-Aryan."

Though the weather has been very cold and rainy this month, I found myself getting overheated in the little phone booth. It was difficult for me to control my anger and my disbelief.

"What?" I exclaimed. "And tall, blond, blue-eyed Jews?"

Gina could not respond to that question, and went on: "Since around the same time, Jews are banned from all cultural and entertainment activities including literature, art, film, and theater."

"Do you mean Jews cannot create art? How is that possible to prohibit?"

"It means that Jews cannot even attend cultural events."

"But how do the Nazis know that people attending events are Jews?"

Another question that Gina could not answer, except to say that people are regularly stopped in the streets outside events and forced to produce their papers. People with Jewish-sounding names are turned away. Cultural events in Berlin with no Jews on stage, in the audience, or behind the scenes?

"One more thing," she continued, "Jews are prohibited from being journalists, and all Jewish newspapers have either been shut down or placed under

Nazi control. I'm not sure if you know that Theodor Wolff was dismissed as editor of the *Berliner Tageblatt* just after the Reichstag fire. You probably know that the fire was blamed on Communists but probably set by the Nazis. It created an opportunity to get rid of Wolff and require the paper to print Nazi propaganda. The Nazis are holding the *BT* up now as an example of 'free press.'"

"Free press, indeed!" I thought I would explode if I heard any more news of this nature, so I forced myself to slow down my breathing and ask about the girls.

"They are getting along very well in their new school," Gina replied, her voice sounding more normal. "They are learning Danish and making new friends. I think they are happy. Nora has now started school, and her teacher is very pleased with her."

"I am so glad. Dear Baby Nora! Please tell them I miss them and send big hugs and kisses." I began to sob even before I hung up and made yet another tearful exit. I am probably becoming known as the Weeping Woman of the Telefónica.

And just this week, in an elegant Madrid theater, *La Comedia*, a meeting of extreme right-wing elements was held. The principal speaker was José Antonio Primo de Rivera, son of the dictator. And some of the phrases from his speech, culled from among vague and inflated expressions of patriotism, bear no resemblance to comedy, and in fact burn me with rage:

"Dialectics is fine as the first tool of communication. But the only acceptable dialectics is the dialectics of fists and pistols when justice and the Fatherland are offended."

General elections are scheduled in Spain for November 19. The right is uniting as the left divides. Miners, construction workers, and many others are on strike. Severino spends most of his days at the Casa del Pueblo. Bombs explode daily on city streets, and the son of the dictator, viewed as a clown by the liberal and socialist press, wishes to return Spain to its supposed historical glory and is received in a comedy theater packed with thousands of people saluting with arms upraised.

MADRID, *Friday, 17 November 1933*

Madrid is covered with political posters, some of them in several layers. Most of the newspapers are sensitive to the fact that women not only will be voting but can be reached by advertising. As expected, the *ABC* has posted slogans on every page, urging their readers to "Vote Rightist." And here is a graphic from yesterday's *El Socialista*. The message seems to be that Socialism supports birth control, although my impression is that the topic is still taboo and not yet discussed openly in the Cortes. And while the words are rather vague: "Woman, rebel against your life, made miserable by poverty: Vote for the Socialists!" the image shows the sad reality of the exhausted, gaunt mother and five (or is it six?) barefoot children, suggesting a way out of poverty through socialism and birth control.

The Communist Party has created a new group for Spanish women, *Agrupación de Mujeres Antifascistas* (Anti-Fascist Women's Group), *AMA*, as a section of the international organization, Women against War and Fascism. The group became active in Spain just following Hitler's ascent to power and is headed by the wonderful woman from the Basque Country, Dolores Ibárruri, called "*Pasionaria*." And they advocate for issues that are not strictly within Party parameters, such as equal rights in work and in education for women and health concerns of women and children. Pasionaria contributes articles to *Mundo Obrero* and is a powerful and eloquent orator, as well as a candidate in Sunday's election.

MADRID, Wednesday, 6 December 1933

Despite the faint promise of a Socialist victory in the first round of the elections, the results of the second round award the victory to Gil-Robles' *Confederación Española de Derechas Autónomas* (Spanish Confederation of Autonomous Right-Wing Groups). The Madrid press is divided as usual, showing delusionary denial and self-browbeating (if such a term exists) among the more liberal press, along with the expected right-wing triumphalism.

The *ABC* is, of course, overjoyed, displaying a frothy, hyperbolic column from Nazi zealot César González-Ruano. His choice of words for the title, "*Reconquista de España*," evokes the Christian campaign that required seven centuries to wrest Spain from the Muslim rule implanted in the eighth century. In pulsating purple poetic prose (I cannot resist the alliteration), Ruano salivates over a map of Spain, dripping extra foam over each area that voted right-wing. In fact, in thirty-one regions the majority of votes went to the CEDA, with eleven regions voting Republican.

The two women previously seated in the Cortes, Clara Campoamor and Victoria Kent, were defeated in this election, while Margarita Nelken gained a seat, as did Ángeles Cid, representing the right-wing CEDA. The dictator's son, José Antonio Primo de Rivera, won a seat representing another new right-wing party, known as the *Falange Española*.

MADRID, Monday, 15 October 1934

How could so many changes take place in such a short time? The Spanish government has been dissolved and reassembled, Catalan autonomy proclaimed and withdrawn, a mineworkers' revolution in Asturias has arisen and been brutally struck down, and the struggle continues. Perhaps now I can proclaim, "The revolution is dead: long live the revolution!" Some progressive (or relatively progressive) newspapers are now back in circulation after being shut down or after closing down in solidarity with the strike, called on Friday the fifth, under the leadership of Francisco Largo Caballero. Meetings of the Communist Party were prohibited as were meetings of the CNT, which did not openly support the strike in most of Spain. Discussions took place in private homes, in student dormitories, and in cafés. The Assault Guard searched citizens in the streets, reminding me of accounts from Germany. It feels very eerie and confusing.

Now what? Although these events are extremely discouraging, I know that the left must reunite, if not through the next parliamentary elections (fostering bourgeois ideology?), then with further revolutionary tactics.

MADRID, Wednesday, 24 October 1934

"Las Invisibles" met today in my office. We are all missing the presence of Pilar and of Herminia, who has moved to Zaragoza with her family for her last year of medical school. Her colleagues here gave her a farewell party in the spring.

I ordered tea for all of us from the cafeteria and sat back a bit in order to encourage the students to direct the group activities. We were joined by a new student, Aurora, who has just been released from the Las Ventas prison.

"Aurora, I'm so glad your case was dismissed. What was your 'crime'?" asked Tere, younger sister of Pilar and Julia. Julia left the Residencia and her studies to get married, but Tere is now a student of chemistry, like Carmen.

Her resemblance to her sisters is striking, with the same round face and intense expression, often relieved by a sweet smile.

"I was posting fliers with my friends Víctor and Antonio announcing a meeting of the Communist Party Plenum. I was accused of 'spreading Communist propaganda.' My lawyer, José Ballester Gozalvo, visited me every day and explained to me that I had the right to do that, as stated in our Constitution."

"Oh," commented Tere, and there was a pause in the conversation, which I decided to fill.

"I think I know that right rather well," I offered, and cited Article 34 directly: "Every person has the right to express freely his/her ideas and opinions, using any means of dissemination, without submitting to previous censorship."

"Yes, freedom of expression!" exclaimed Aurora. "And fortunately, the judge supports the concept of free speech and agreed with the arguments of my attorney and the attorney of my comrades."

"Not to mention the suspension of the free press during the uprisings," added Carmen bitterly. "Was the government adhering to Article 34 when they shut down *El Socialista* and *El Heraldo*?"

"What do you think?" I asked and continued citing the Constitution: "No newspaper can be ordered shut down except through due process."

"*ABC* is certainly enjoying protection now," commented Aurora, tossing her head. "Has anyone noticed how *ABC*, and even *El Sol*, have been referring to those brave revolutionaries as monsters, animals, garbage, filth? It is so obvious that we are moving toward fascism if we are not there already. Members of the Cortes are equating the army with the State."

I ended the session by recommending the Friday evening lecture-recital on Beethoven by Sofía Novoa, Residencia alumna responsible for the integration of music into academic life. I am so looking forward to Beethoven's mind-centering sonorities.

MADRID, *Friday, 15 February 1935*

This year has begun with wishes from what seems like the entire Spanish population that the New Year should be better than the last, as it couldn't possibly be any worse. The CEDA government, however, does not appear to be trying to make this happen. Every newspaper must now undergo government censorship, which I imagine must pose enormous challenges, except possibly for papers like *ABC*. *El Socialista* has been completely shut down.

President Azaña was released last month from prison and has begun to speak publicly about allying his *Izquierda Republicana* (Republican Left) with other leftist groups, no doubt in view of the national elections to be held one year from now. Communist Party members are doubtful and claim that Azaña has never been a friend of the masses. It would be pleasant to think that his three months in prison with members of the proletariat have influenced his views.

MADRID, *Thursday, 19 September 1935*

I called Gina this evening on her birthday (forty-fourth!). She let me know that life is fine in Denmark and that the girls are doing well. They have constructed a home in the little town of Svaneke on the island of Bornholm. Artur, together with Liese's son Heinz, has set up a youth camp in the woods near the shore that serves both boys and girls from ages six to twenty.

Gina then went on to relay news from Germany that approaches the inconceivable. At a Nazi Party rally in Nuremberg on Sunday, new laws were introduced by the Nazi Reich's Ministry of the Interior, whose aim is to further isolate Jews from the rest of humanity by defining them genetically, mathematically, and, I dare say, hematologically. This new classification has as its end the denial to Jews of full German citizenship.

I next spoke with Liese, and her voice shook with worry: "Heinz had to leave medical school. His Jewish professors have been ousted and replaced by

barely qualified Nazis, some showing up to teach, or whatever they do, in full
Nazi regalia. He has been working with Moritz and Papa and helping Artur
organize the summer camp in Denmark. He and Ellen are awaiting the birth
of their first child any day."

"Oy! And Putzi?"

"Günther has kept studying, despite being spat at and having stones
thrown at him and his friends. When the Citizenship Law is implemented
in a couple of months, he will probably no longer be able to attend the State
school since Jews will no longer be German citizens."

"No longer citizens?" I was incredulous. "Of what country will we all be
citizens then?"

"The word being used is 'statenloos'—'stateless.'"

I have been keeping up my legal status and my Spanish work visa with the
German government, and in the light of the political news from Germany, I
was also considering renouncing my German citizenship in favor of Spanish
citizenship. But if I will automatically become *statenloos,* I can skip this phase
of the process—that is, if any country will grant citizenship to a stateless
person. And I will probably never again pass between those fierce Reichsadler
that guard Madrid's German embassy.

After Liese and I said good-bye, I asked myself if I still felt homesickness.
Yes, I am homesick for the Germany—the home—that is no more. So what
does that make me now? Our family, my generation at least, has always considered itself German. I am adapting to life in Spain but still feel occasionally
separate, but then I also *always* felt separate in Germany as a Jew. Perhaps I
would feel more certain if I could free myself of having to ally myself with a
group, be it national or "confessional." From my gymnasium class in Latin,
I recall the phrase from Terenz (*Terentius*), "*Homo sum; humani nihil a me
alienum puto.*" (I am human, and I think that nothing human is alien to
me.) If I could actually internalize that phrase and live by it, I would need no
homeland. My reactions tell me that I am—at least now—too torn to live by
Terenz's lofty creed.

MADRID, *Monday, 25 November 1935*

Hitler has issued the final wording on the so-called Nuremberg Laws, which in effect decide who in Germany is Jewish and to what rights they are no longer entitled. The laws became final on November 14 and were published in the November 20 issue of the *Jüdische Allgemeine Zeitung.* Liese sent me a copy. The paper covers almost nothing else. The explanations state that Jews may not vote in elections or be elected to office. Jews who already hold elective posts must vacate them by December 31. Another concept driven clearly home is that there must be a complete divorce between "Germanness" (*Deutschtum*) and "Jewishness" (*Judentum*).

As I was completely baffled by the concepts of "protected German blood" and "Jewish blood," I thought I might benefit from the knowledge of a geneticist, so I contacted Käthe Pariser, and we made another date to meet at Café Gijón yesterday. This time I arrived first and took the same table at which we had sat before. Perhaps we will become regulars at this spot. Käthe gave me a generous hug and two kisses as I stood to greet her. She is quickly becoming acclimated to Spanish ways. Before we ordered anything, Käthe reached into her bag and pulled out the paper that was supposed to solve the "Jewish question."

"This chart explains who is permitted to marry whom, according to how much 'Jewish blood' a person has," she began.

I examined the paper for a bit, then looked up and asked, "But how does one measure the amount of Jewishness in a person's blood? What is the science?"

"Ah, that's exactly the problem!" Käthe retorted. "This configuration might work when applied to fruit flies or even to yeast, but we are talking about humans! It is all cloaked in a mantle of science, but I say it is non-science, anti-science."

"And supposing I converted to Christianity: would I get a black circle or a white circle?"

"In that case the Nazis would refer to ancestral records. If your parents were registered as Jews with the Jewish community, you would be labeled a Jew, even if you had become a Roman Catholic and more papist than the pope!"

I laughed to hear one of my favorite expressions coming from a renowned scientist but felt a bitter revulsion at the deeper meaning.

"They do consider religion in some cases, however," she went on. "Look at the bottom of the page: If a *mischling* marries another *mischling*—"

"Mischling? What does that mean?"

"It is a word used for a person of mixed Jewish and gentile ancestry. If they both practice the Jewish religion, which is still permitted, their children are legally Jews. And now they are applying measurements to people's facial features. Supposedly a Jew is recognizable simply from appearance."

"But supposing a blond, 'Aryan' Christian from Sweden living in Germany converts to Judaism? Where is he on this chart?"

"He is not there at all. And if he converted because he wanted to marry a Jew, that would not be permitted anyway."

"You can't win."

"Well they lose. They have lost us."

"And we have gained freedom. Let's order a little glass of schnapps and toast our freedom," I suggested.

"Schnapps! Do they have that here?"

"Well, something similar: *aguardiente de trigo* (wheat brandy)," I replied, proud to produce this obscure detail. A waiter was standing by our table and seemed to be peering at the chart. I patted his arm and ordered two shots of aguardiente and a couple of pastries, which sent him away, and motioned to Käthe to put the paper back in her bag.

The drinks arrived at the same time as the apple-cinnamon pastries, and as we clicked our glasses, we proposed a toast to freedom. I did feel a slight touch of the promise of the *Homo sum* phrase of Terenz. The liquor produced a mild burn in the throat as it mated delightfully with the pastries, as happily as a first-degree mischling would mate—freely—with a second-degree mischling.

MADRID, *Thursday, 16 January 1936*

This year, which began with the usual twelve grapes and more than usual noise in the Puerta del Sol, has also begun with much promise. The newspaper, *El Socialista*, reappeared on December 18, giving hope to a free press with the sentence, "External injuries mean little when the spirit has not been broken."

After the bitter lesson imparted by the victory of the monarchist, pro-fascist CEDA over the fragmented, fractious left and the drastic erosion of the democratic rights laid out in the Constitution, previously rival parties and groups have joined in a pact, signed just yesterday and proudly heralded on page one of today's issue of *El Socialista*. The language looks forward to February's elections on the sixteenth and lists the organizations participating in the pact. The designation *Frente Popular* is being bandied about as an umbrella term, covering the eight organizations whose names it is so pleasant to see together.

Some of the major tenets of the Communist Party (the distribution of lands to peasants, the nationalization of banks, government compensation for unemployment, and a worker-controlled government) appear to have been abandoned in favor of the coalition. What is proposed is again a bourgeois form of government, not one rooted in economics or class. Still, the goal of the Republic expressed in the pact is that of elevating workers' spiritual and material conditions to the maximum.

Despite the current disarmament movements and the powerfully organized antiwar women's groups, I have not seen any promises to demilitarize the State or to weaken the power of the Church. Even if the groups supporting this pact are elected one month from now, won't the people of Spain still be at the mercy of the generals, the priests, and the Guardia Civil?

MADRID, *Wednesday, 19 February 1936*

All the evidence necessary to judge the nature of the three principal Spanish political elements can be found in the editorial reactions to this week's election results. *El Socialista* opens its headline with "The Republic rescued (or redeemed)," followed by "Frente Popular victorious in all of Spain," followed by two editorial columns, one stressing the need to assume power and the other calling attention to the losers who have headed for the borders. The liberal *Heraldo*, gratefully patriotic, proclaims "Long live Spain! Here the only leader is the people! All power to the leader. . . . The left-wing Frente Popular has scored a big win in Madrid and the provinces."

The most interesting phenomenon for me is the response of *ABC*. If I had picked up that paper exclusively of any other, beginning the day after the elections, I would have missed the fact entirely that elections have been held and won by the left. And finally, it is only today, on page seventeen, that a tiny piece states that Sunday's election results have been confirmed and that Don Manuel Azaña will form a government that is exclusively republican.

MADRID, *Tuesday, 14 July 1936*

Two political assassinations occurred over the past weekend, and all of Spain is now on alert. They did not occur in a vacuum—violence has been escalating since February's election, created both by those dissatisfied with the results and by those determined to avenge the wrongs of the so-called *bienio negro* (the "black biennium," i.e. 1934–1936). Armed mobs roam the streets, large areas of agricultural land have been seized by those who believe that they are entitled and that the Republic's proposed agrarian reform does not apply to them, churches have been burned and clergy members attacked, and the central government seems totally alienated from what goes on in the streets, despite the lofty ideals maintained by the *Frente*. Powerful generals like Franco and Mola, after having declared their allegiance to the Republic, hover ominously in the background. Primo de Rivera has been in prison since March.

The first assassination was that of *Teniente* (Lieutenant) José del Castillo Sáenz de Tejada of the Assault Guard. His sympathy for left ideals and perhaps his membership in the *Unión Militar Republicana Antifascista* earned him the enmity of the right. Assigned to put down the October 1934 revolution in Asturias, he is reported to have rebelled against an order to shoot to kill, declaring, "*Yo no tiro sobre el pueblo.*" (I don't shoot the people.) Blaming Del Castillo for the murder of a right-wing Carlist student, four men ambushed him and gunned him down on Sunday night on the street as he was on his way to report for night duty.

His comrades quickly swore revenge and hoped to take it out on CEDA boss Gil-Robles, but when they failed to find Gil-Robles at home they proceeded to the home of José Calvo Sotelo, leader of the right-wing, monarchist *Renovación Española*, drew him out with a false arrest warrant, placed him in an automobile, shot him, and left his body at the East Cemetery.

The government is also trying to play a role, closing union halls and political meeting halls, arresting many, suspending congressional sessions, and calling for "respect for human life." Appeals for public disarmament over the past months have gone largely unheeded. Hortensia has been stocking up on tinned food, and Severino says he may be buying a pistol.

IV

MADRID, *Saturday -Sunday, 18-19 July 1936*

I am not certain what day today is, officially. And the word "official" is ringing hollow at this point. Yesterday (Saturday) morning, Hortensia entered my room at what felt like the middle of the night. It was the first time she had ever done so, so I knew that something was wrong.

"Clara, you had better wake up and come and listen to the radio. The government is making some very confusing announcements."

I ran to the bathroom, threw on my robe, and rushed to the kitchen. Hortensia and Severino were both seated, leaning forward with their elbows on the table, their chins resting on their hands. The first (eight o'clock.) broadcast from Unión Radio had been superseded by the government, and from the speaker were issuing the words, "*nadie, absolutamente nadie*" (no one, absolutely no one). The message: "*No one* in Spain has joined in the effort of Spanish officers in Morocco to overthrow the Republic. The Republic has overcome the uprising and the situation is now totally normal. The government is in complete control, and all is quiet."

"This is serious! I'm going to the Union Hall," announced Severino.

The government says that all is quiet and Severino is headed for the Union Hall? What do I know about Spain?

"How? Azaña has shut it down," Hortensia reminded him. "But let me make some coffee first," she added. "Workers will be gathering on Calle Fuencarral at any rate for more news and for instructions." She dropped a few spoonfuls of coffee into the *cafetera* and poured some milk into the enamel pan to heat. "You'd better take some food with you too," she suggested, and cut a hunk of cheese, another of sausage, and another of bread and put them all in a metal hucha with a folded cloth napkin for Severino.

As Severino left, I assisted Hortensia. Where will I go? I pondered. Party offices are probably closed. Classes are not in session.

The radio broadcast continued with the usual daily programming: stock market reports, the weather, the saints of the day—no more word about the Morocco uprising. I had to find out more. I decided to go to the streets, where the people know what is really happening.

I walked the few blocks past the Metro Quevedo stop toward the local Party office. People had gathered near the entrance, talking in low tones and gesturing agitatedly. Posters calling for "*armas para el pueblo*" (arms for the people) had been plastered on the walls. Looking around, I spotted Aurora, entering from Calle San Bernardo with two young men. We hugged, and she introduced me to Antonio and Víctor, who had been arrested with her for posting Party fliers.

"Any news, Comrades?" I asked anxiously.

"Just rumors for the moment, Camarada Philipsborn. But we have been given this paper, in case war is declared," replied Víctor, whose curly blond hair, dense eyebrows, and intense green eyes reminded me a bit of Santi (Santi!). He slipped a small piece of paper into my hand.

("In case war is declared!") My heart knocked against my chest as I took the paper. The cryptic message read simply "*Cole sales Estrecho.*" I had no idea what it meant.

"We are going back to FUE headquarters now," said Aurora.

I was tempted to go with them but thought it better to return home, have something to eat, and stay close to the radio. Hortensia had put some garbanzos on to soak the night before and was now cooking something similar to a *cocido madrileño* (Madrid-style stew), with a beef bone and chicken instead of pork. A year or so ago I broke down and told them that I now could eat meat, as long as it wasn't pork. I haven't yet explained why. As we sat down to eat (Severino had not returned), I showed the paper to Hortensia and asked if she could explain the brief message.

"Hmmm, '*Cole sales*'—ah, it must be the *Colegio Salesiano*," she replied, wiping her hands on her apron as she sat down beside me. "It's a religious order, in the Cuatro Caminos district. Up Calle Bravo Murillo, near Metro Estrecho. That explains the '*Estrecho*.'"

"Is it called 'Estrecho' because it is located on a narrow street?"

"Ha-ha—no—I think it is named for the *Estrecho de Gibraltar* (the Strait of Gibraltar), but I'm not sure why."

As we finished eating, a little after two o'clock, the music coming through the radio was interrupted by another announcement. The government reported that it had received a notice from Radio Ceuta which purported to be transmitted from Seville, saying that the Ministries of War and of the government had rebelled in the Andalusian capital.

"Seville!" I gasped, "I must call my uncle! Do you think the Telefónica is open?"

"I imagine that it is."

I hurriedly helped her wash the dishes and headed out for the Telefónica. It was indeed open, and there were long lines of people waiting, a fairly usual occurrence for Saturday, but people were conversing with an urgency similar to what I had noticed in front of Party offices. After nearly an hour, I was finally assigned a booth after being told that I had a three-minute time limit, and I placed my call. Asun answered the telephone and delivered devastating news:

"Don Julio is very ill and cannot speak to you, Clarita. We are having nurses come in to care for him."

"Oh, Asun" —my voice broke as tears stung my eyes—"I am so sorry, and I wish I could be there. But we are receiving disturbing news about Seville. Asun, are you all right? And what is happening there?"

"I am fine, Clarita, but the nurse who came on the afternoon shift told me that a garrison has declared that it is joining forces with officers who have led a rebellion in North Africa against the Republic. The rebels have arrested the general in charge and replaced him with General Gonzalo Queipo de Llano. This thing is being directed from the north by General Mola, who is very powerful."

"The Madrid government is not saying anything about that," I said. "They are trying to keep the people calm, I suppose, but how can we organize and defend the Republic if we do not have the facts?"

"We were getting news from Unión Radio Sevilla, but I think it has been taken over by the rebels. They are saying that they will take Sevilla and 'rescue' all of Spain. We are hearing gunfire in the streets."

"Horrible! Now I must hang up, Asun. Please send all my love to Tío. May I call you again?"

"Yes, of course, dear."

I don't know which made me feel worse, the fascist takeover of Seville or the illness of my dear uncle Julius. By the time I returned home, Severino was back and seated at the kitchen table, hungrily spooning up the cocido. He let us know that UGT-head Largo Caballero had just arrived from abroad and had stated that the union would declare a general strike if a state of war were declared.

"Largo is saying that the main objective is arming the entire citizenry," he announced, brandishing a piece of bread in the air.

Hortensia told us that there had been another radio announcement, at around three o'clock, stating that the "aggression" against the Republic was limited to Morocco, that the insurgent generals and officers have been arrested there, and that all was normal on the Peninsula.

"Well, now we know that is not true," I argued. "The 'aggression' has already begun in Seville, and it is moving forward. The radio and parts of the army have already been seized and a new general is in command, eh . . . Queipo de Llano."

"Now that's just great!" Severino leaned back in his chair and threw his hands up into the air, surrendering to an invisible enemy. "Which side is he on now? You never know! ¡Traidor, canalla, hijo de puta!" he shouted, his face reddening. I had never heard him swear before and somehow it felt satisfying to hear this man called traitor, scoundrel, and son of a bitch. I would have liked to swear as well but have not really become accustomed to doing so.

At that moment, at around 5:20 p.m., the music on the radio was once again interrupted by Unión Radio, with the government announcement that the rumors that rebel ships were headed for the Peninsula and that war had been declared were false.

"I suppose we can assume that everything we hear on the radio is the opposite of what is really happening," suggested Hortensia.

"Well, I'm going back to the Union Hall," announced Severino. "We should probably prepare for a general strike, whether or not the office is closed."

I suddenly felt exhausted and came to my room for a bit of a nap. It is still quite warm outdoors, and my room is cool and dark with the blinds drawn.

At eight in the evening, I awoke and bathed, went into the kitchen, and turned on the radio. Hortensia and Severino were not at home. I took some bread and cheese and a glass of wine and had just sat down when the broadcast was interrupted just after nine. This time it was an announcement by Socialist and Communist parties that completely contradicted the previous announcements. It stated that Gil-Robles and General Francisco Franco had led the insurrection now centered in Seville. Then there came a plea from the Frente Popular, calling on workers to be prepared for street battle. I noted down two messages word for word and translated them here into my diary: ("The Popular Front must back up with arms the victory it gained at the polls. . . . When the order to battle is given, we must roar down like an avalanche.") Once I fully understood the meaning, I knew I was ready to serve the Frente and the Republic, with arms if necessary and certainly with my nursing skills. I left Germany too soon to fight fascism and anti-Semitism there, but I can do it here in Spain. I am feeling very Spanish at this moment, ready to defend my homeland.

At that moment Hortensia and Severino returned, and I showed them my notes.

"Inspiring words," remarked Severino, "but now it is time for deeds. We need arms to fulfill that pledge. We have just come from the streets, along with half of Madrid, calling out, '¡Armas! ¡Armas!' The government is deaf to our cries and to our real needs."

About an hour later, a government broadcast came over the radio announcing the dismissal of several generals, including Franco and Queipo de Llano, who had been relieved of his post at *Carabineros*—a bit late, I should say—and the dissolution of military units that are in rebellion. Again I felt the urgent need to know what was happening in Seville. Back to the Telefónica, where fewer people were using the telephones and I was able to call Asun right away. My uncle, she said, was resting comfortably, but the streets were in turmoil.

"What is even worse is that Queipo de Llano used the radio tonight to intimidate the population," continued Asun. "He squealed into the microphone that the rebels will show everyone, especially the women, who is in charge. Since women are communists and anarchists, and practice free love, they will find out who are the real men, not the militias and the 'fairies,' no matter how much they kick and scream."

"¡Hijo de puta!" I exclaimed and felt immediately satisfied by uttering that phrase at that moment. I sent hugs to Asun and to Tío and returned home, just in time to hear that Dolores Ibárruri was about to broadcast a statement directly from the government ministry. Pasionaria's clear, inspiring voice came on at about ten minutes after midnight, declaring that she was speaking on behalf of the Central Committee of the Communist Party of Spain. She appealed to the regions campaigning for autonomy (Catalunya, Galicia, the Basque country) to defend the Republic, calling them "Spaniards, all of you," and ended with a phrase I shall also copy here: "*El fascismo no pasará; no pasarán los verdugos de octubre!*" (Fascism will not pass; the October executioners will not pass!)

We all stayed in the kitchen, supplied with generous tazones of café con leche, and waited for the next broadcast, which came at two in the morning, a government announcement that President Casares Quiroga had resigned and Azaña had replaced him with Diego Martínez Barrio. Two hours later, a new government had been formed. Another announcement came on at five stating that forty airplanes had left the Cuatro Vientos airbase to fly over various Andalusian and North African cities (not Seville) with pamphlets and with bombs to be dropped if necessary.

It is beginning to get light outside, and I am now going to try to sleep a bit. I shall keep repeating to myself Pasionaria's declaration, "*¡No pasarán!*"

MADRID, *Sunday -Monday, 19-20 July 1936*

Days and nights are still blending. Yesterday (Sunday) I was again awakened at eight to hear that the newly appointed president, Martínez Barrio, had refused to include Socialists in his government. What a disappointment!

"We have just chosen the Frente Popular," exclaimed Hortensia, standing at the foot of my bed and tapping my foot for emphasis, "and now the government thinks we should be ruled by monarchist moderates who would probably like to throw in their lot with the insurgents, just to be safe!"

I was soon dressed and in the kitchen, and we continued listening to the radio over breakfast. Another president, José Giral, had been named. Severino and Hortensia remarked that not much could be expected from this change. Then, a little before noon, it was announced over Unión Radio that, in response to the heavy demand, the government had finally decided to hand out rifles. Members of the CNT and the UGT could gather at their respective union halls and receive munitions. We all looked at each other and stood up.

"Let's go get those rifles!" declared Severino.

Hortensia echoed him immediately.

"I'm coming with you," I offered, "but armed with medical supplies." I went to my room, put on a white lab coat over my dress, hastily stuffed another one in my medical bag, along with a few personal toiletries and my tagebuch, and returned to the kitchen, feeling elated. It was the first time I was about to participate in a battle for my ideals, and I would be using my skills to save lives!

We soon arrived at UGT offices on Calle Fuencarral, along with a wave of civilians lined up to receive arms. A man standing in a doorway announced himself as the person in command. His voice roared out hoarse and gravelly as he tried to address the crowd above the din of excited voices:

"Camaradas, camaradas, we have just five thousand rifles to give out. I am sorry to announce that the bolts to over fifty thousand additional rifles are being held by the insurgents at the Cuartel de la Montaña. We will not be able to hand over the rifles with missing bolts."

Roars of surprise and rage erupted from the crowd. Hortensia explained (shouting into my ear) that the Cuartel was a large barracks near the Plaza de España.

Men and women were slowly entering the building, and some were emerging from another door, clutching the rifles from among the limited supply of those with bolts. After about half an hour, the raspy voice delivered another announcement:

"The Ministry of War has issued an order to the colonel presiding at the Cuartel, Moisés Serra, to turn the rifle bolts over to the government. Colonel Serra has refused the order. The Cuartel is now our objective."

Loud cries of, "To the Cuartel!" burst from the crowd. We finally reached the entrance of the Union Hall, and I went in with Severino and Hortensia. We could see several tables staffed by union officials and behind them, large wooden crates containing the coveted rifles. Severino produced his union card and stated that his wife would be joining him. The union officer noted down their names and handed a rifle to each of them and informed them that instructions for use would be given in the Plaza de España. Hortensia seemed to grow taller as she grasped her rifle.

We all headed toward the Plaza. Crowds that had gathered in doorways and on the sidewalk were applauding and cheering us on with "¡Viva la República!" and "¡No pasarán!" Many people joined us, some armed, some not. At one point, Severino grabbed my arm saying, "Look at that!" Passing us on the left was a beer truck atop which sat an unwieldy-looking cannon, also bound for the Plaza de España. The sight of that formidable weapon heightened my dedication to the Cause and quickened my steps.

The Plaza had been transformed into a battle post. Sandbags were piled to create a barrier that people had gathered behind. The cannon we had seen carried by the beer truck was now installed right next to the statue of Cervantes. I was hoping that Don Quixote would join in, shouting out, "Do not flee, cowards!" Members of the Civil Guard and of the Assault Guards were demonstrating the use of rifles to small groups. For a moment I considered requesting instruction, but then I realized that where I belonged was in the San Carlos Hospital-Clinic. Though much of the staff is on vacation, I thought that it would be the place where medical personnel would be called to volunteer.

Upon arrival at San Carlos, I was greeted by Professor Gustavo Pittaluga, director of the National School of Health. He directed me to a room that was to be used as an intake station. He informed me that, owing to my seniority, I should act as triage nurse. He then introduced me to three young men who explained that they had formed a sort of ad hoc Committee of the Hospital-Clinic, representing the Frente Popular. One of them, Santiago Tabares, told me that the hospital would now be functioning as a frontline hospital.

More nurses called in by Dr. Pittaluga began to arrive. Some of them are members of the Communist Party, and we recognized each other from meetings. We all scrubbed and began taking a quick inventory of the boxes and cabinets that were labeled with names of instruments, drugs, bandages, and plaster, as well as refrigerated supplies of blood and other liquids. I was very glad that Dr. Pittaluga was there, given his specialization in transfusion.

"Let me introduce you to the triage doctor," added Santiago, and we moved into another room to meet a young man who appeared to be in his late twenties, with a sweet smile, generous cheekbones, and a hairline featuring a "widow's peak." He looked familiar and introduced himself as José Ramos Mimoso. His accent piqued my curiosity.

"Where are you from, camarada?" I asked. This question is asked all the time in Spain, where in Germany it might be considered impertinent.

"I'm from Bayamón, Puerto Rico. I just graduated from the Medical School here in Madrid, and my wife and I came here to help." He reached out his arm to gesture to a petite young woman who was rolling bandages with another woman, both of them having hastily thrown lab coats over their civilian clothes. His wife approached and shook my hand.

"Violeta Toral," she introduced herself.

"I am Clara Philipsborn. I have been working at the Medical School chemistry lab since 1930. I'm so glad you have come."

At that moment two stretcher-bearers rushed through the door carrying a man bleeding profusely from the face and neck. He was dressed in workers' clothing and wearing a single alpargata.

"Machine-gun fire," they announced. "He is aspirating blood!" and they placed the stretcher on a gurney. The stretcher-bearers sat down, and two other volunteers took a new stretcher and rushed back to the scene of battle.

"We must suction the lower airway," called Dr. Ramos. "Tracheotomy!"

With two other nurses, I gathered morphine, cleansing supplies, surgical knives, and tubes. A nurse injected the man with morphine for pain, and another washed the wound on his neck. Dr. Ramos opened the wounded man's windpipe below the larynx, and a student inserted a tube as instructed, removing the blood so that the air could reach his lungs. Once that was done, the hemorrhage was stopped, and I checked his pulse and the damage to his face, which had two embedded machine-gun bullets.

"Radial pulse weak," I called.

"He will need a transfusion for shock and blood loss and will have to have surgery to remove the bullets," ordered Dr. Ramos.

It was about seven in the evening when the stretcher-bearers returned and sat down to rest, sending the first team back to the battle. We all were anxious for the latest news from the "front," and the two men explained as well as they could.

"The new man in the Cuartel is a General Joaquín Fanjul," said one. "He slipped into the barracks dressed in civilian clothes, put on a uniform, and declared himself in command."

"Since about five o'clock the Cuartel has been completely surrounded," continued the second. "The Civil Guard, Assault Guard, and the Carabineros are backed up by armed militias of people loyal to the Republic."

"How many Loyalists are there?" asked one of the nurses.

"We are hearing the number eight thousand!"

All of us in the room cheered, and I felt such love for my fellow workers.

"The militias have been joined by five thousand miners from Asturias, bringing hand bombs!"

More cheering.

Just then a new team of stretcher-bearers came in carrying a woman on the stretcher. They noted that she had a fractured clavicle, probably from a rifle shot.

"This wound must be kept clean at all costs," Ramos emphasized. "It will have to be debrided and the fracture realigned, but first, morphine and a small transfusion. So please cleanse and open the wound and divide the fascia. Once that is done, you must immobilize the limb, and she can rest and receive the realignment."

Violeta explained as she worked: "The debridement Dr. Ramos has ordered is a procedure developed late in the past century, of excising all contaminated flesh from open wounds before attempting to close them. Infection is avoided, and many lives have been saved by this procedure."

The stretcher-bearers sat and had a drink of water and a bite of food donated by one of the unions, while they responded to another barrage of questions from the medical volunteers:

"We now have mortars, tanks, and machine guns to stop this fascist uprising."

"A captain of the Assault Guards commanded over a loudspeaker that the rebels should stop shooting and exit the fort, but the only response was more machine-gun fire."

"Airplanes from Getafe have flown over the barracks and dropped leaflets demanding surrender."

By about eleven it had grown quieter outside. Some of us went to the door and looked out. Passersby told us that the lights had been turned off in the Plaza and evidently in the Cuartel as well. The wounded woman was resting. People dispersed in small groups to find bathrooms and then rooms for sleeping, in case this quiet represented a respite from more injuries. Santiago suggested that we sleep in the rooms that had been vacated by the nuns. Representatives from CNT and UGT were taking small trucks to all the emergency stations and hospitals with meals prepared and donated by Loyalist supporters. We took our welcome supper in the cafeteria, and I was quite sure that I tasted ham or some type of pork among the lentils and vegetables. If I am to be strong enough to defend the Republic, I must be able to nourish myself. I'm certain that I have full forgiveness from my ancestors and probably from God, and I must admit that the flavor was delicious. I slept below a cross, fully dressed, my dreams punctuated by gunfire.

At first light this morning (Monday), firing began again, this time sounding like heavier artillery. This went on for what seemed like an hour, and then the building rocked with enormous explosions. Some bottles fell from shelves and broke. Through the windows we saw two airplanes overhead, which had obviously just dropped at least one bomb on the Cuartel. Soon two teams of stretcher-bearers arrived, bringing one Civil Guardsman and one civilian, both injured by machine-gun fire. They deposited the patients and immediately left for more. We were at capacity and could not take any more wounded.

At that moment, another team of stretcher-bearers rushed in with astounding news:

"Camaradas, did you hear what just happened? The insurgents draped a white sheet out a window and when our troops moved toward the door they were fired on from inside."

We all gasped, and I heard the now-familiar "¡hijos de puta!"

"So they retreated and fired cannons on the barracks until they heard no firing from within. They were able to rush the Cuartel and take Fanjul prisoner. Colonel Serra has been killed. The government has declared it safe to go into the streets."

"So the streets are ours!"

"Victory is ours!"

"¡Viva la República!"

We hurriedly began returning all the supplies to their containers. With mixed emotions we volunteers hugged each other amid hopes that today had seen the last manifestation of this bitter hatred.

On stepping outside of San Carlos I was shocked at the change in mood and struck by the wave of jubilation in the streets. People were hugging, laughing, weeping, shouting vivas to the Republic. I was also weeping, and I received hugs and thanks from many people. We began a victory march toward the Puerta del Sol. José, Violeta, and I boarded a truck that had been refurbished as an ambulance and marked with a red cross. The driver honked the horn rhythmically as we rolled slowly along the Gran Vía, which was packed with exhausted but elated men and women, still clutching rifles and pistols and raising their fists. Someone began singing the lively *"Himno de Riego"* (the unofficial anthem of the Republic), which was taken up by the crowd, keeping time with their marching feet. I have only learned the words of the refrain and was able to join in: *"Soldados, la patria nos llama a la lid / Juremos por ella vencer o morir"* (Soldiers, the Fatherland calls us to battle. Let us swear to conquer or die for her.) (Yes, it is odd to refer to the Fatherland as *her*, but I did not create this language.)

As we neared Sol, the triumphant chords of a band reached us. The crowd in the square was enormous and jubilant. People who had obviously just come from battle were mixed in with "civilians" who looked clean and rested in contrast to the sooty and disheveled militiamen and women. Many fighters were hoisted onto the shoulders of the crowd. Soon a truck made its entry into the square, loaded with militias waving their rifles and their fists and singing the "Internationale," which inspired the band to join in, albeit in a different key. Another truck marked with the letters UGT rumbled into the square, and I was thrilled to recognize Hortensia and Severino among those perched in the truck bed. I hopped out of the ambulance and began waving, and I tried singing more loudly and finally shouting. They then spotted me and slid down from the truck, rifles in hand. Their skin was blackened and their clothing filthy, but I hugged them both tightly. They reeked of smoke and gunpowder.

A few people began shooting into the air, which I thought could be potentially dangerous, so I gestured, as conversation was impossible, that we should leave the square. We walked toward the metro entrance, Hortensia clasping Severino's arm. I kept trying to ask them about their experience, but both of them were having a hard time hearing me and I realized that they must have suffered some inner-ear damage from the bomb blasts.

Back home at Donoso Cortés, Severino was adamant, voice still raised: "It's hard to believe how treacherous those military fascists are. Every time there was a pause in the gunfire, some men would run out of the building into the yard, and the rebels would shoot them. I suppose you could use the word 'heroic' for the officers who shot themselves rather than surrendering."

"Maybe," added Hortensia, "but to shoot their own men, whether they were attempting to return to the Republic or they were *falangistas* or monarchists or just cadets is just cowardly. And how about you, Clara? Were you able to save anyone?"

"I certainly hope so. I was working with a wonderful team of professionals and volunteers at San Carlos."

"And now," Severino said, "I am in dire need of a bath." He walked into the bathroom, followed by Hortensia.

I also obviously needed to bathe and rest but decided to return to the Telefónica to speak to Seville again. The tall building was extremely busy, with people entering and taking elevators to the upper floors. The woman who assigned me my booth told me they were journalists, including foreign correspondents, filing reports on the recent events. Asun's news was quite alarming. Bands of supporters of the Republic have burned several churches, among them San Marcos, my uncle's spiritual home.

"His heart is broken," she admitted, her voice quivering. "I wish no one had told him what happened, but we can smell smoke from the fires from here."

"Unbelievable! And how are my cousins?"

"They are trying to stay at home because women are not safe on the streets. The nurses who come to care for Don Julio are terrified."

"*¡Ay, Dios mío!* I hope you are safe, Asun," I said, and I sent my love to Tío before we hung up. My beloved Sevilla la roja—and my dearest Tío Julio—smothered in the fumes of hatred and intolerance!

The battle is over, but the fighting continues in the mountains to the north. Tomorrow I will be going to the Salesian headquarters to volunteer as a nurse with the *Milicias antifascistas obreras y campesinas* (Antifascist Worker and Peasant Militias). Another phase of my life has begun.

MADRID, *Tuesday, 21 July 1936*

Here in Madrid I am noticing a palpable mood of victory, as uprisings in other garrisons have been suppressed and insurgent leaders killed or imprisoned. The Azaña government holds sway, at least in some areas. Barcelona as well has triumphed over its own insurrection.

Reports are coming in that Republican troops are in control of the mountain passes, having defeated the falangistas, Carlists, monarchists and other would-be insurgents who took to the mountains (Sierra de Madrid) at the beginning of the coup. General Mola's troops are approaching from the north to attempt to capture the Sierra and heavy fighting is expected.

The Party had circulated thousands of half-page fliers around the city calling for volunteer militias of all anti-fascist persuasions and all professions to resist the insurgency. People were instructed to prepare for a medical screening and to bring some type of certification proving their anti-fascist allegiances. Instructions were to report today at two o'clock to the former Colegio Salesiano, now taken over as a center of resistance by parties on the left. Since the nursing profession is still dominated by nuns, who are being ousted or are fleeing on their own, licensed nurses are especially in demand.

In the morning I had decided to make an early visit to the Natural Sciences Museum on La Castellana, as I was concerned about Käthe. I am struck by the way in which I am somehow comforted in the company of another Jew. Even if Yiddishkeit is not the topic of conversation, which it usually is not, and even if I am not particularly close to the person, it occasionally feels as though I am in need of a nutrient that has been lacking in my diet. I passed just before noon through the well-kept gardens and was a bit surprised to be confronted by a pair of Civil Guardsmen blocking the entrance to the Museum. To one side, uniformed men were loading large crates into a truck.

"Good morning, camaradas," I began. "I would like to speak with *Doctora* Käthe Pariser."

"What is your business with *Señorita* Pariser?" the guardsman asked me sternly.

"We are friends and colleagues. I wanted to make sure she is all right."

"Documentación, por favor."

"Certainly, camarada." I replied, feeling somewhat queasy as I drew out my German visa along with my university card identifying me as an employee of the Medical School. The other guardsman approached and with his companion looked from my documents to me and back again. I know I do not look German, and my Spanish is becoming more natural. They mumbled something to each other, then handed back my papers.

"Wait here," the first guard said. He entered the building briefly and returned to stand guard with his companion.

I took a seat on a shady stone bench to wait, feeling puzzled and confused, as I reflected on the fact that the guardsmen had not referred to Käthe as "Doctor," a perfectly well-earned title. I sat up straight on the bench as a pale young man, possibly a museum employee, emerged from the building and gestured for me to approach.

"Come with me, Señorita Philipsborn," the young man ordered.

Why is he calling me Señorita? I wondered as he led me through the cool museum lobby to an elevator. We entered, the door clanged shut, and the elevator began to descend, amid desperate creaking. I glanced at the man's face to try to determine his plan, too intimidated to ask questions. He simply stared at the fleeting images as they rose through the glass of the elevator door, hands at his side, as the light flickered weakly. We seemed to be moving endlessly downward, and my stomach was in my throat. Finally, the elevator stopped with a resigned shudder and the man gestured for me to step out.

"Ten minutes," he stated tersely.

At the end of a long, dank corridor, through an open laboratory door, stood Käthe. She looked haggard, her hair disheveled and her body slightly stooped, her lab coat showing dark stains. I was so glad and relieved to see her and embraced her tightly. Behind us, the elevator was already making its way upward, squealing in protest. Käthe and I stepped into the lab, and she closed the door. It was obvious that she was in the process of packing up equipment.

"I have been ordered to have these articles sent to the Banco de España, for safekeeping," she explained. "And then I must leave—leave Madrid, leave

Spain. Zulueta will remain, but I fear that my funding will be cut off, and besides," she added, lowering her voice and looking toward the closed door, "I do not feel safe."

"Where will you go, Käthe?"

"I will need to stop in Germany to obtain some documents."

"Will they let you in? Will they let you out?" I asked, anxiously. "We have been deprived of our German citizenship!"

"Oh, they want me out!" Käthe exclaimed. "I have reserved an exit visa for Palestine, but I want to continue on to Australia."

"Ah, that sounds like the right decision." Then I noticed the aquariums stacked against one wall. They were empty. "But what is to be done with your little subjects, the newts?"

"I—I have—had to—sacrifice them." Her eyes filled with tears. Then— almost in a whisper and looking over her shoulder toward the door—"I released them into the river. I hope they will survive. Some of them are unnamed species, crossbreeds. I feel so bad at having created these poor little monsters."

I really did not know how to respond and took a step back. "They will probably be happy to be free," was all that it occurred to me to say. I suppose a newt, even an unclassified newt, is capable of feelings, but it seemed so remote from my consciousness and from the real and immediate needs of these days. "But *your* freedom is important now, Käthe," I continued. "I wish you a safe journey, and please keep in touch if you can."

Käthe accompanied me to call the elevator and waited with me until it finally arrived. We hugged once more before I stepped into the cage, and I felt sorry and at the same time relieved to leave the forlorn woman standing alone in the dimly lit hallway as I moved toward the surface and emerged into sunlight, where I bade farewell to the pair of Civil Guardsmen with a brisk "Salud, camaradas" and didn't wait to see if they decided to address me.

I next took the metro, two trains, in fact, all the way up to the Estrecho stop where I easily found the Colegio Salesiano, a very large complex of out-buildings spreading out from a Byzantine-looking domed church and fronted by a huge courtyard. There I joined a line of people, about three deep, extending from the entrance gate to an archway or arcade leading to the church. People holding hand-lettered signs walked along the line. Some of the signs had names or abbreviations of political entities (CNT, PCE, JSU, MAOC, SRI), and people who responded to the signs were directed to walk directly to the arcade.

I was soon approached by a woman carrying a sign marked "*Batallón Femenino*" and nodded to her, whereupon she pointed to one of the arcades. As I grew nearer, I saw a table with two women seated behind it, and other women forming a new line in front of the table. There were men in Civil Guard uniforms and Republican Army uniforms going from table to table and monitoring the recruitment process. It was pleasant to be in the shade and also to be in the company of what I assumed were like-minded women. Rather than having people fill out applications, the women seated at the table were filling out the forms by questioning the prospective volunteers. I thought it was a rather inefficient way to organize, but then I realized that it was probably because of the persistently high illiteracy rate in Spain, especially among women, despite all the best efforts of the Republic.

Most of the women there appeared younger than I. The woman who took my information was tall and slender, with a sweet face. I had to spell my name, which I am now accustomed to doing. When she asked for my birth information, I made an immediate decision. I had seen a sign, limiting the age of volunteers to 28 to 45 years, so I gave my birth year as 1902. She next asked me to produce proof of my anti-fascist affiliation, and I showed her my faded card from the Communist Party of Germany.

Another problematic issue was that of my nationality. If I am no longer German, what am I? I had sincere doubts that this woman was familiar with the Nuremberg Laws, and I didn't think she had any idea that I am Jewish. So I told her that I was German, which is true, isn't it? When I told her I had been working at the School of Medicine, she told me she had lived at the Residencia de Señoritas until her marriage, in 1930, the year that I arrived here. She said that if all went well with my application, I would be assigned to volunteer work at the *Hospital Obrero* (Workers' Hospital) on Calle Maudes, before being given a more fixed assignment. She had taken a moment off from signing up other women, and it was a pleasure to speak with her, as she seemed very well-educated as well as friendly and kind. I had told her that I had worked at San Carlos during the assault on the Cuartel de la Montaña.

"Much work will be needed on Calle Maudes, camarada," she said. "This hospital has been used as a tuberculosis sanitarium and has been in the hands of the Church. The SRI—*Socorro Rojo Internacional* (International Red Aid) has taken it over, and it will be our task to transform it into a frontline hospital. The nuns who are working there now will be phased out as volunteers are put in place. I would like to work with you there to organize the transition."

"I would be very happy to do that, camarada. What is your name?"

"Matilde Landa. Now, are you willing to undergo weapons training? All medical personnel will be required to be able to use firearms. Madrid can be attacked any day."

"Yes, of course."

"Good. If your physical condition is approved at your medical examination, please report here on Thursday. Then, if your application is accepted, you will be photographed and your training and volunteer schedules issued."

I thanked her and shook her hand and made my way past a sign labeled "*RECONOCIMIENTO: MUJERES*" (EXAMINATION: WOMEN) into a part of the original monastery that had evidently been a classroom, signed my name on a sheet of paper, and looked around the room. I was overjoyed to see the medical student, Aurora Lafuente there, dressed in overalls, and I took a seat at a desk next to hers. I asked what she had done during the siege of the Cuartel de la Montaña.

"I was behind the barricades, shooting out the windows of the Cuartel," she explained proudly. I noticed that her voice was louder than usual and concluded that she also must have suffered some hearing damage from the cannon blasts.

"How about you, camarada? What did you do?"

I had just begun describing my experience at San Carlos when Aurora's name was called, and she walked through a door to be examined. I thought that it must have been a fairly perfunctory examination, since in less than ten minutes she was back, flushed and happy. She told me she had been approved on the spot and would also return on Thursday for additional military training.

"Are you also going to participate in the medical training?" I asked.

"I think I would rather join the Batallón Femenino," she asserted.

"You are so brave, Aurora."

"But you are also brave, camarada. Medical workers also risk their lives."

"If I can save one person to fight fascism. . . ." I began, and at that moment my name was called. I stepped through the door expecting to be asked to remove some article of clothing, but the female volunteer simply checked my weight and blood pressure, listened to my heart and lungs, and looked into my mouth and at the inside of my eyelids. She asked my age and I again said I was thirty-four.

"You are approved, camarada. Come back here on Thursday, first thing in the morning, and look for your group assignment."

I returned to the classroom and smiled at the waiting women as I walked past them, then out and past the lines of people who had gathered to volunteer to save the Republic, peering into their faces and wanting to hug them all, as my sisters and brothers, perhaps even more closely related than the terrified zoologist I had left this morning.

MADRID, *Thursday, 23 July 1936*

Today I have come away from the former Colegio Salesiano (now referred to as the Cuartel Francos Rodríguez de Cuatro Caminos, named for the street and the urban district where the headquarters are located) more certain than ever of my place and of the path ahead of me. Yesterday I got my hair done (straightened, bobbed, and waved) and my eyebrows tweezed, so I felt that I had been doubly renovated, physically and professionally, my nursing skills enhanced by the variety of emergencies I had dealt with at San Carlos during the taking of the Cuartel de la Montaña, and my anti-fascist fervor reinforced by the spirit of the people of Madrid.

Severino has joined forces with the UGT militias and left yesterday for Toledo, where rebel forces have joined with the Guardia Civil and have occupied the huge fortress called the *Alcázar* as well as hospitals and the munitions factory. Hortensia will stay in Madrid, and I appreciate her presence, though I am aware that I may mobilize to other areas. I realize that I had begun to think of Hortensia and Severino as family. Families all over Spain must now be feeling this pain of separation.

As I crossed the vast patio of the new Headquarters there were no more lines for interviews but instead clusters of people gathered around the columns of the arcade, on which had been posted long sheets of paper. I finally found my name (albeit wildly misspelled) on the paper headed *Servicios*, with sub-headings *Intendencia* (administration), *Armamento, Transportes* and finally, *Sanidad* (health care), supervised by Dr. Juan Planelles Ripoll, whose name I recognized as the Chief Health Officer of Madrid and also a member of the Communist Party. The sign directed me to *Sala* 46, which turned out to be another one of the classrooms of the former monastery.

In the room a group of people, including Matilde Landa, the woman who had signed me in on Tuesday, stood by the chalkboard talking in low tones. After a few minutes the classroom had filled, with people having to stand against the walls.

One man from the group, dressed in an undistinguished khaki uniform that looked as if he had slept in it, came to the front of the room and began to speak. His face was soft, and his eyes were drawn downwards at the outer corners, his fingers pudgy. His talk impressed me deeply, not only for the words but for the way in which the man seemed to place an arm around all those assembled, eliminating any differences. He introduced himself simply as Juan Planelles. He expressed gratitude to all of us for being there, saying that the commitment that we were making was as important as the commitment of those who would be taking up arms to defeat fascism. His essential humanity was obvious as he reminded us, "Everyone in this room is dedicated to saving the lives of our fellow human beings, irrespective of social origins. Beneath our healing hands, all are equal. Now, though it is true that all of you as Communists are working toward a classless society, after you take the oath administered to you by our camarada Dolores, you will be associated with an elite army of the people. Yes, it sounds like a contradiction in terms. But this association, to be known as the Fifth Regiment (*Quinto Regimiento*) of the People's Militias, will be distinguished for its discipline and its culture but also for its support of our Republic and its Constitution."

He next introduced Matilde Landa, who also welcomed us all and then read off a list of those who would be assigned to the transformation of the hospital on Calle Maudes to a workers' hospital and a frontline hospital. I was thrilled and relieved to hear my name included. She instructed us to report tomorrow to a small nearby hotel, to begin the organization of health workers. Our uniforms would be issued and our photographs taken today. She then yielded the floor to Dr. Julio González Recatero, whose task was simple: to introduce Pasionaria.

I can only describe my sensation as being sent into a spin as this woman strode into the crowded classroom. I had heard her speeches in enormous public forums and on the radio, but to be contained in a small space with this compelling energy was almost too much to bear. I had the feeling that her black eyes (were they really black?) were penetrating mine, calling forth my devotion. Then her voice, uttering the simple words, "Please rise, Comrades, to take the oath of the Fifth Regiment," lifted my body and raised my clenched fist, as it did for every other person in that room, and then we repeated after Camarada Dolores, phrase by phrase, the entire oath.

People then shouted out, "*Prometo!*" (I promise!) and someone in the room was inspired to begin singing the "Internationale" as we all stood facing Pasionaria, and I must confess that it was difficult to articulate the words with my tightened throat and tears coursing down my cheeks. She immediately pivoted and swept out of the room just as she had entered, no doubt ready to inspire yet another group of dedicated volunteers. Dr. Recatero then instructed us to go to the next classroom to receive our uniforms and to put them on and report to the assembly hall, where we would be photographed. May I be worthy of the pure whiteness of my uniform and of the dedication inspired by the words of Dr. Planelles and of the oath administered by our Pasionaria!

MADRID, Friday, 31 July 1936

I certainly did not think that I could use the word "fascinating" to refer to an assignment to transform a Church-owned hospital into a frontline hospital for victims of a fascist revolt. If the task did not include driving seventy kilometers each way to the front lines in the Sierra to collect the wounded, sometimes under fire, and returning to continue the frantic race to save their lives, I would almost consider my duties at the Hospital Obrero de Maudes to have been awarded to me as a gift.

The transition team has been put in place, expertly motivated by Dr. Juan Planelles Ripoll. The same bond I felt he had created with the members of the introductory health care group at the Francos Rodríguez Headquarters is at work now in this collective, mostly made up of high-powered women. We all feel that we have been conceded autonomy, not so much in any words Dr. Planelles has spoken but simply in the fact that he steps back and remains in the background as we make the major logistical, medical, dietary, even military decisions.

Another thing that unites us, something I would never have considered possible, is that all of us possess firearms. Most of us were trained at the Headquarters, and my particular weapon is a nine-mm. Astra 400 38 "la Puro" pistol. Regulations state that we are not to carry firearms in medical settings, but under certain circumstances, soon to be explained, it is a must. We were told that around twenty-five thousand of these models have been handed out to Loyalist forces. Given the atmosphere of enmity now hovering over the streets of Madrid, I do feel somewhat more protected while walking between metro stations by the fact that "la Puro" lies armed and at the ready in my medical bag next to my stethoscope.

The Headquarters have been quickly converted to a real home base. A newspaper, *Milicia Popular*, is now being published, movies (mostly political, some Russian) are shown in a theater on site, a center to care for children of militia personnel has been set up, and there are poetry readings and political lectures nearly every day.

The daily—as well as nightly—tasks at the hospital are made more bearable by the company of the other volunteers. I will start with Matilde, the woman who signed me up initially. We rode the metro together on the day we first entered the hospital on Calle Maudes, and I now feel an even deeper kinship from the words we have shared. She was born in Badajoz, Extremadura, into a family that was closely associated with the Institución Libre de Enseñanza, and she had studied sciences, unusual for a woman in this country. I remembered that she had lived at the Residencia de Señoritas, and I gained some new insights.

"So how did you like living at the Resi?"

"It was convenient, and definitely promoted studying. But I may as well have been confined to a convent!" she added, tossing her head.

"How do you mean?"

"The girls were required to attend mass every day. Practically commanded to do so by Doña María."

Of course she was referring to María de Maeztu, so famously progressive and professedly feminist. I know that parents put much pressure on her to keep their daughters "safe," which no doubt in their minds included regular church attendance.

"What place do communion and the body of Christ have in science?" she went on. "Not in my science! Don't you agree, Clara?"

"Of course I agree. I am a Communist. But you, Matilde?"

"I was not baptized," she admitted. "My parents were progressive—were even married in a civil ceremony and did not wish to sacrifice their children to the empty, retrogressive ritual that binds people to a repressive system.

But the fact that one is a Communist today does not mean that one was not brainwashed in one's youth."

"Well, I am a different kind of Communist," I began. I wondered, *Am I going all the way with this?* She was confiding in me. I would reciprocate. "I also—was not baptized—in fact, I am not a Christian." I paused to see how she would respond. She simply smiled, as her eyes widened under her heavy brows, which lay in a straight line across her forehead, awaiting the rest of my "confession." I lowered my voice: "I am a Jew."

"Ah," she nodded. "Well, so were Marx and Rosa Luxemburg, and so is Trotsky, and so is Margarita Nelken, and so are Irene and Kety Lewy."

We had just arrived at the Cuatro Caminos stop, and I put my arm around her shoulders as we climbed the stairs.

The sight of the hospital as we approached was something I had not expected, to say the least. I thought, *This is a hospital? Are we in Spain? Am I going to be so fortunate as to work here?* The first glance conjures up an English castle. Getting nearer, we noticed that the building, which seemed to reach out in various directions at once, was not made of the usual brick one sees in Madrid but of granite and limestone. It occupies an entire city block.

We were directed to an administrative office near the main entrance, where some other women were seated and chatting with Dr. Planelles. He welcomed us all and asked each of us to state why we were there. I reported that I had been invited by Matilde. When her turn came, Matilde mentioned a "*Comandante* Carlos," and her face seemed to redden as she mentioned that name. Another woman, called simply "María," quite attractive, around forty years old, also referred to Comandante Carlos, and I thought I detected an

Italian accent. Each time Dr. Planelles referred to María, it sounded as if her name were a pseudonym. And another beautiful woman, in her mid-twenties, introduced herself as María Luisa, speaking in an accent similar to that of the Puerto Rican doctor I'd met during the battle of the Cuartel. María Luisa said she had actually fought in that battle, using a pistol she had been issued, and that she had been solicited for work at the Hospital Obrero through the Socorro Rojo Internacional and also via Comandante Carlos. My curiosity to meet this comandante is certainly piqued.

Dr. Planelles then delivered a summary of what we would be doing there. He first explained the layout of the hospital, a sort of X-like cross or star extending from a central octagon, with administrative offices at one end and a church at the other. He illustrated the architecture using a chalkboard, which was helpful. Patients would be housed along the arms of each cross, characterized by natural lighting and ventilation that prevents contagion by too much enclosure (as I understood it). He explained that we were inheriting a building with progressive beginnings, conceived in 1916 as a hospital for workers who were treated free of charge.

We next moved toward the patient wings, while Dr. Planelles explained that the nuns who had been working there had refused to treat victims of war. I wondered if that was due to some type of vow of pacifism, or if perhaps they feared that they would have to put their hands on Communists. We reached the first door, and it appeared to be locked. We then moved on to the next door, which was obviously also locked.

"The nuns are still trying to keep us out!" exclaimed "María."

"¡Ay, mi madre!" exclaimed María Luisa. (I don't think I had never heard that expression.) "I know what we can do about that!" she declared, drawing a handgun out of her pocketbook.

"Wait!" exclaimed Dr. Planelles. "This is not a gangster movie!"

"What? Do we have time to call a locksmith?" I asked, pulling my pistol out of my bag. "We need these doors open now!"

Matilde did the same and we all formed an ad hoc firing squad.

Dr. Planelles backed away, shaking his head, as we four women moved to the first four doors, stood at a safe distance across the hallway and fired at the locks. With the successful freeing of each door, our aim improved as we moved methodically along the corridors, which echoed with the blasts from our government-issued pistols. Fortunately, this small gun battle for a safe space to care for our wounded soldiers was won privately and without bloodshed.

MADRID, Wednesday, 12 August 1936

Wounded men and women continue to pour in to our hospital, largely from the Guadarrama Mountains, with Mola's column inflicting heavy casualties as it advances toward Madrid. There are of course many well-trained nurses, doctors, and assistants at the Hospital Obrero, but caring for the wounded is a learning experience for many others. María Luisa and the Italian woman called "María" began by simply observing and assisting when instructed, but now María Luisa is able to distinguish a single bullet wound from a shrapnel wound caused by bombing or by hand grenade, while "María" has taken over the kitchen, much to the delight of wounded and staff alike. Her chef's coat consists simply of a large man's shirt, tossed over her regular clothing. She displays a knack for combining cured meats with beans and vegetables (grown by the few neighbors in this almost rural zone of Madrid) and has somehow been able to acquire barley to add to these creations, all simmered in a huge pot and which can be puréed to be fed to convalescing soldiers.

"*Ma che*, don't you have corn meal here?" she demanded. "In *Messico* I was able to use it to make polenta." Some of us tried to explain to her that corn (maize) in Spain is considered food for pigs, and she simply snorted and replied that Spain must be a very backward (*arretrato*) country if they feed their pigs better than their people.

As for María Luisa, she has already proved an expert shot, having learned from her father, an Olympic marksman, and we can thank her bold actions for the fact that we were able to open all the hospital doors. She was born in Madrid but raised in Cuba (which is why I thought I had detected a Puerto

Rican accent—it must be something about the Caribbean). A member of the Communist Party, she became involved in progressive education there. And last Saturday she even demonstrated her skill at the wheel of an ambulance, as our usual driver was ill, when we had to journey through the mountains on dizzying roads and under fire, to the front line at Buitrago de Lozoya to pick up two wounded men and one woman. Men working along the road waved and raised their fists in glee at the sight of a female driver.

María Luisa seemed to be close to "María," and yesterday as we were checking the dressing of an anesthetized patient, I asked her what "María's" connection was with Mexico, as she seemed to be Italian.

"*Chica* (Girl)," she began (as she often begins sentences addressed to other women), "don't you know? She came here—with—*him*." Her face reddened, as it had when I first met her.

"Him? Do you mean Comandante Carlos?"

She simply nodded. "He will probably be here on Sunday for Ti—'María's' birthday. Will you be here?"

I hadn't known about the birthday or the visit but promised that I would be there, and I wondered what she meant by saying "Ti—".

Tonight I brought home the fifth issue of *Milicia Popular*. Below the story of the *Brigada de Acero* (the Iron Brigade) is a caricature of none other than Comandante Carlos. I am trying to puzzle out from this drawing the magnetic effect the spiritual father of the Fifth Regiment obviously has on the women with whom I am now working. I will have to wait to see what effect he has on me in person.

EL COMANDANTE CARLOS, DEL QUINTO REGIMIENTO

MADRID, *Sunday, 16 August 1936*

I arrived home very late tonight. Fortunately, the metro is still running. Hortensia had left a back issue of *El Socialista* on the kitchen table, so I've been sitting up reading and am now back in my room recording my thoughts here.

I knew I would not be able to sleep after reading the front-page article from *El Socialista*, titled "Arms and Letters: An English journalist wisely defeats General Franco in an interview by displaying his terrible emptiness." The article was cited from the *London News-Chronicle*, and the writer conducting the interview was Jay Allen, who is American and not English, but the nationalities are sometimes conflated here in Spain. I remember that the "arms and letters" theme is based on the classic dichotomy of the military lifestyle vs. the lifestyle of wisdom and learning. The perfect, Renaissance-type individual was one who was able to balance the two. According to *El Socialista,* that of arms comes out the clear loser.

Selections from the interview:

"How did you manage to cooperate with the government for so long and apparently so loyally?" (Franco was Chief of Staff in 1935.)

"I cooperated loyally as long as I thought that the Republic represented the will of the people."

"And the February election (February 16, in which the Frente Popular was victorious), did it not represent the will of the people?"

"Elections never represent (the will of the people)."

"What would your government do if you were victorious?"

"I would implement a military dictatorship and later I would call a national plebiscite to see what the nation wants."

So elections do not represent the will of the people, but you will call a plebiscite to see what they want? Are you really such a fool?

The next question reveals the more terrifying plans of the little general:

"How long do you continue to keep up this slaughter?"

"There will be no compromise, no truce. I will keep advancing toward Madrid. I will save Spain from Marxism, no matter the cost!"

"Even if you have to kill half of Spain?"

"I repeat: No matter the cost."

"Hijo de puta," I thought—in fact I am saying it now as I write, gritting my teeth.

Today was "María's" fortieth birthday (I hear that her real name is "Tina," but I have been cautioned not to use it, perhaps a wartime measure), and she decided to celebrate in the hospital itself. The patients love her so much, for her cooking as well as her movie-star beauty, which I am convinced is an aid to healing, giving the wounded and the ailing something to live for. She had baked a heavenly dessert, in large enough quantity for us to be able to distribute generous slices to all the patients who were well enough to enjoy them.

I was in the kitchen as she was preparing the dish that she called *strucolo de pomi*, which, after sampling it, I can only call *apfel strudel*, though "María" used pears rather than apples, which have not quite reached their full ripeness in Madrid. The pears were perfect. She told me this dish is typical of her town, Udine, in the Friuli-Venice region. She explained the Austrian influence, which in turn explained the origin of the pastry. I asked her about Mexico, and she was beginning to tell me about her work there with the photographer Edward Weston when a man entered the kitchen and grabbed "María" around the waist, growling, "*Cosa stai dicendo?*" (What are you saying?). She gasped and stopped talking and turned to kiss him. He wore a leather jacket despite the heat, was rather portly, and his skin shone. He then turned to face me and "María" introduced us: "Carlos, this is Clara. She's a nurse practitioner."

I said a few words in Spanish—I don't remember exactly what—and he exclaimed, "*Ah, Tedesca* (Oh, a German)!" He clasped my hand—his was pudgy and damp. I could feel the heat coming from his body. His lips parted in a fleshy smile. He had the underbite of the caricature, and he seemed to have too many teeth, all of them vying for primacy inside his mouth. His hairline receded above a broad forehead, and his nose was in the shape of a shark's head. He kept my hand in his.

"So, what brings you to Spain, camarada?"

"I am a chemist and have been working—at the School of Medicine." As I pronounced those words, the school, the students, and even my position there retreated to some remote place and time, and the only thing that was real was the heat invading my body and the imperious presence of Vittorio Vidali, alias Comandante Carlos. His eyes penetrated mine, and at the same time, I sensed that he was sizing up everything else in the room, as if he were preparing to dash away.

"Ah, *brava*, and 'María' was telling you about *Messico*?" He glanced toward her as he asked this and released my hand.

"Yes, I was interested in her photography and also in some of her cooking ideas from there and from Italy. She has introduced some delicious dishes to the hospital."

"Ah, *certo*." He turned away as Matilde entered the room, was immediately at her side, and greeted her by pinching her waist. She looked surprised and flushed red again.

"Clara," called "María" from in front of the oven, "can you please take these trays of strucolo to the patients?"

I was relieved to have been given a specific assignment—anything to pull me out of the gravitational field of Comandante Carlos, who seemed to have completely forgotten about me as well as "María" and was now conversing with Matilde and with her husband, Francisco López Ganivet, who had entered from the patio. Moving among the patients and being able to share the delicious strudel-like pastry with them and chat about their recovery and their efforts to defeat fascism reminded me of my purpose for being there and helped to return me to reality.

Now I must try to sleep. I still feel the heat in my body—whether it is from the rage at the interview with Franco or from the presence of the commander of the Fifth Regiment, which has had a strangely visceral effect on me that I am at a loss to describe.

MADRID, *Friday, 28 August 1936*

Bombs have fallen on Madrid, dropped over the course of last night by a German Junkers Ju 52. I was in the main building of the hospital at around eleven, getting ready to leave, when the first explosion shook the building, followed by two more. I turned around, my hands shaking, and put my uniform back on and scrubbed again, along with other volunteers. About one minute later we heard and felt two more blasts, which seemed to be coming from another area but with the same volume and intensity as the first blasts. We all looked at each other and held our breaths, but there were no repetitions of the bombings. We were expecting ambulances to be delivering wounded victims, but the only ambulance coming in was from the Sierra. Comandante Carlos soon rushed in to report:

"The bombs have been dropped on the Ministerio de la Guerra (the War Ministry) and on the Estación del Norte (not far from the Cuartel de la Montaña). One death has been reported. Most of the wounded have been taken to San Carlos."

We were relieved at this last piece of news, but I was concerned about the symbolic nature of the bombings. The Ministerio de la Guerra is right next to the iconic Plaza of the Cibeles, a statue of the Phrygian goddess Cybele, mounted imperiously on a chariot drawn by two lions, her spirit-animals. To me she represents both fertile motherhood and orgiastic ritual, and I associate her with the Spanish Republic (also sometimes depicted as a woman in Phrygian garb).

"Are the fascists attacking our goddesses?" I cried, probably in somewhat desperate tones.

"Ah, Tedesca, you are worried about our goddesses! I am sure they will thank you. The government has ordered that they all be covered with sandbags. No more worrying, *cara* Tedesca!"

Comandante Carlos moved toward the kitchen, probably to check on "María." As he passed by me, he pinched my waist, just as I saw him do to Matilde last week. I turned to look at him, but he had disappeared into the kitchen.

I joined several other nurses to receive the incoming patients and for the next two hours we labored to remove the horrible pieces of shrapnel that had done so much damage to the bodies of our valiant *milicianos* and *milicianas*. Some of the wounds contained stones and fragments of metal and even wood and clothing, blasted into bodies by the exploding grenades, and the doctors instructed us to remove the damaged and contaminated tissue to allow for healing, that is if infection had not set in first. One young woman had lost much blood, both legs had been nearly severed, and her respirations were shallow and infrequent.

By around three in the morning, the patients were resting, and a few of us, including "María" and María Luisa, had repaired to the kitchen to sit and put our feet up. Suddenly "María" offered an unusual suggestion:

"Chicas"—under María Luisa's Cuban influence?—"let's sing! The bombing is over."

"Oh, I know some Italian songs," responded María Luisa. "Both my parents sang. I learned more than shooting and riding from them. How about 'La Donna è Mobile'?"

We all sang as much as we remembered of the aria, "María" more than the rest of us, and then moved on to "O Sole Mio," which we dramatized with gestures toward the sleeping sun-god, amid much laughter. "María" has a quite lovely voice. Then I recalled hearing Gerda practice "Mi chiamano Mimi" and the lyrics reminded me of the fact that "María" was of course what "Tina" wished to be called, so I stood and faced her and started singing it, for the first time in my life, though in a lower key than the original. I summoned up Gerda's talent and even made it through the upward *glissando*. Somehow my sister's voice seemed to emerge through my body as Puccini's aria transported me to another era, another space. I took my seat as the group applauded and María Luisa asked, "Chica, where did that voice come from?"

"My sister—was an opera singer."

"Oh, is she deceased?"

"Oh, God no—she's in India, teaching." I suddenly missed Gerda ferociously and felt comforted by evoking her through music and singing with other women.

Just then another volunteer entered to inform us that the injured woman had died. Her body was being taken down to the morgue, and of course we were all saddened as we returned to the reality of war amid the joyous respite that singing had brought.

I now felt that it was time to make my way home. Just as I was about to exit (for the second time), Comandante Carlos suddenly appeared in front of me.

"Camarada Tedesca, would you like to sample some good Russian vodka tomorrow?"

Without waiting for an answer, he continued, "I will bring it tomorrow night. Come to Room Eighteen at eleven."

Barely looking at me, he turned and strode away, leaving me to look for the stairs, wondering where I was and how I would find the metro station.

MADRID, *Sunday, 30 August 1936*

Although those around me are behaving as if everything were normal, I am having to remind myself how to perform each task and how to interact with fellow workers and patients. It helps to gaze at my *carnet* or identification card from the Fifth Regiment, which I was just issued.

And behind all this is what happened yesterday. It was another very hot day, and two other ambulance loads of wounded had been brought in from Somosierra. "María," Matilde, and María Luisa have Saturdays off (so ironic—I, the Jew, must work on my Sabbath). Those who worked with me yesterday were actually trained nurses, a rarity, almost making it unnecessary to have the supervision of a doctor. Mola's troops have evidently been rearmed and have inflicted deep and vicious wounds, this alongside the bombings that are so frequent in the Sierra. We are still experimenting with new techniques of treating compound fractures.

I welcomed the advice of these experienced nurses, as my thoughts kept moving to the eleven o'clock time proposed by Comandante Carlos. My mind spun with questions: Why would he invite me to drink with him? Has he invited others? How do I feel about him? I am definitely feeling something, and it is clear that he and my female colleagues are linked in some sort of hypnotic coterie. Perhaps it is that magnetic pull that I am feeling. The easiest solution was simply to follow routine automatically and hope that my patients would benefit.

By ten thirty the bulk of the work had been done, and I wrote reports for the three patients in my care. Then I allowed myself some time to wash my face and apply a bit of lip rouge and a touch of jasmine oil. I tossed my uniform into the laundry bin and moved slowly toward the "elite" wing.

The door of Room 18 was closed. I knocked softly and there was no response, so I entered, switched on the light, and closed the door. The room was empty and clean, with a little table with two chairs by a window, a small bed, and a small W.C. I took a seat at the table. An enormous and almost-full moon threatened to thrust through the window, and I closed the blind. By fifteen minutes after the hour no one had come, so I stood and began to walk toward the door. Had I imagined that late-night invitation? At that moment the door opened abruptly, startling me, and in strode Vittorio Vidali:

"Ah, Camarada Tedesca, you are already abandoning me?" He was still wearing a leather jacket, which he removed and placed on the back of one of the chairs by the window after setting down a leather pouch on top of the table. He signaled me to sit.

"This is a special vodka," he announced as he took a seat, pulling a roundish bottle out of the pouch. A picture of Stalin was prominently displayed on the label. "I have been keeping it refrigerated, hidden among the blood supplies. I am sure that you have not tasted it."

"I hope no one has used it for transfusion," I remarked playfully. "And in fact I have never drunk vodka in my life."

"Ah, *mai* (never)? Well, I am happy to introduce you to this 'little water,'" he declared as he pulled two small glasses out of the pouch, set them down, and filled them with the clear liquid. "This is a transfusion that will definitely bring you back to life. It is from a special distilling, in honor of the new Soviet Constitution and the new prosperity," he explained, raising his glass to mine.

"So you think I am not alive?" I hoisted my glass as I found myself succumbing to the flirtatious banter.

"That is what I would like to find out!" he replied, lowering his voice.

I tried not to guess what he meant by that. I had still not tasted the liquor, and now I raised the glass to my nostrils. "Oh—it smells like ether—mixed with earth."

"Well, you will see that it tastes better than it smells. What shall we toast?"

"How about la Cibeles?" I suggested, recalling our conversation about the need to protect Madrid's emblematic goddess from bombardment.

"Por la Cibeles," he agreed, clinking his glass against mine and then downing the contents.

I took a tentative sip. The cool liquid stung the roof of my mouth, and then I noted a sweetness I hadn't expected. I trustingly swallowed. Then, on impulse, I drank the contents of the glass, which he refilled immediately before refilling his own.

"And now, a Russian toast: *Na zdorovya!*"

"Na zdorovya!"

We clicked our glasses again and I emptied mine in two swallows. He set his empty glass down.

"*Allora*, what brings the pretty German nurse to Spain?" he asked, looking into my eyes. At that moment I realized that his eyebrows, which had been rendered with four light strokes of the pen by the artist of the caricature published in *Milicia Popular*, were actually thick and dark, and each one came to a point in the middle, almost like inverted V's. His initials, upended and emblazoned upon his forehead—two warning signs.

"I have been living and working in Madrid since 1930." I tried not to sound defensive. Was he just making conversation? I was beginning to feel a bit dizzy. "I've loved Spain since I first visited my uncle in Seville in. . . ." I was about to cite the year but then realized that he probably did not realize that I am close to ten years his senior, so I ended the sentence there.

"Ah, you have family here. Are there others?"

Others? What did he mean? "No, just me and my uncle."

"Do you return to Germany for visits?"

"Whenever I can, but I really feel like this is my country."

"Ah, brava," he said.

My eyes dropped to his chest, bulging beneath a blue-striped shirt unbuttoned at the collar. Must keep talking, I told myself as I imagined the heat of his bare chest.

"So, do you think that—Comrade Stalin"—I gestured toward the bottle—"really wants the bourgeois Spanish Republic to prevail, or does he simply want . . . to extend his power? Execute people as he did with the Politburo?" I heard myself ask, thinking, Is that my voice?

"Oh, Jews. . . ." he muttered dismissively.

Did he really say that?

He filled our glasses again, and I took a sip, without benefit of a toast. I now felt a burning in my throat and, putting one hand to my neck, set the glass down. It became more difficult to talk.

"I think the vodka—is irritating my throat," I managed to say.

Carlos put down his glass and moved his chair next to mine. He put his hand on my throat and slid it down to my breasts, inside my dress. His hand was hot and heavy, and I think I moaned at the sensation.

"*Poverina la tedeschina* (Poor little German girl)," he murmured. His other hand turned my face and his full lips pressed mine as his hot, thick tongue pushed into my mouth.

What happened after that I simply cannot remember. I awoke on the bed, alone—the room was in total darkness. A sheet lay draped over my legs, and I was not wearing underwear. A wave of nausea suddenly overpowered me, and

I nearly fell off the bed as I staggered to the bathroom and vomited violently. I washed as well as I could. I felt that I had been penetrated but could find no evidence. He must have used a *preservativo*. Well, I am grateful for that. But had I willingly had sex with Comandante Carlos? Why couldn't I remember?

I looked at my watch: it was 3:20 a.m. I found my underwear on the floor beside the bed and headed for the door.

The night guard wished me a good night as I exited the hospital for Metro Cuatro Caminos, which bore me quickly and safely to Metro Quevedo. Antón, the sereno, let me into my building, with a "Working late again, eh, Camarada Clara?"

V

LA CABRERA, *Wednesday, 2 September 1936*

I am writing these words in a cool room with solid granite walls, seated at a small table beneath an arched window that reveals the thickness of the walls and opens onto a courtyard graced by what the people here call *chopos*, which I think are poplar trees (*pappel*). Their yellowing leaves are brushed by the last rays of today's sun. Over the bed hangs the unsurprising crucifix. I am now housed in a monastic cell, part of the former *Convento de San Antonio*, taken over by the Fifth Regiment and converted to a field hospital, about two kilometers uphill from the center of the mountain town of La Cabrera. Not all remnants of religious life have been completely obliterated, hence this crucifix that faces me. My room is just a few steps away from the *puesto de socorro*, or aid post, located within one of the five apses of the church portion of the con-vento. Here I will be the only licensed nurse practitioner, together with vol-unteers, rotating physicians, and stretcher-bearers. We will be receiving the first streams of wounded, classifying their injuries, and sending them to one of the other sections of the hospital or all the way to a base hospital in Madrid. I was informed about these arrangements on the drive here from Madrid on National Route One (N-I) by Felipe, a medical student-turned-miliciano assigned to deliver me to my new assignment. Our method of transportation was a passenger automobile equipped with two empty stretchers, one above the other. As Felipe explained, "If we paint a cross on the roof, the Germans will bomb us."

"So Geneva Convention be damned, I suppose."

"Alas, yes! In the minds of the Nazis and the fascists, no targets are off-limits. You can expect patients to be shot in their beds and bombed in ambulances."

Felipe skillfully maneuvered the sharp mountain turns while describing situations that I might expect. As we continued our ascent into the Sierra, I rolled down the window to appreciate the air, which had become more rari-fied and smelled sweeter than that of the city.

Once we arrived at the convento, Felipe helped me to the admitting office with my valise, and we said good-bye as he went to pick up two wounded to transport to a rehabilitation hospital in Madrid.

The office is staffed by an older woman adept at using the typewriter and at dealing with the public. She delivered my instructions in such an efficient way that it seemed as though the war had been going on for years:

"Your room will be in the eastern apse, number eleven, one of the larger rooms. Two volunteer nurses will share the room next to yours, and the doc-tors, whose shifts will also rotate, will take number eight. The bathroom is at the end of the hall." She nodded her head toward a telephone on a side table. "This telephone is available to staff, but there is a waiting list you must sign. You may give out this number"—she handed me a piece of paper—"but personal calls are limited to five minutes."

"Will I be assigned exclusively to the puesto de socorro?"

"No, in fact, given your experience and your title, you may be needed to work in any one of the areas of the hospital at any time."

The city already seems far away. Perhaps it is the pure air I am breath-ing here and the cool quiet inside the walls of the convento. Bidding fare-well to Hortensia (Severino is still fighting in Toledo, and the siege of the Alcázar continues as Franco and his troops approach) was sad, as we had become very close, but we'd both known since the July 17 fascist rebellion that circumstances would be changing for all of us. "María," María Luisa, and Matilde all wept with me as we hugged and wished each other health and safety. I made a special point of letting "María" know where I would be. Of course, she does not know what happened between Comandante Carlos and me, nor am I myself certain about it. I haven't seen or heard from him since that strange night in Room 18, but I somehow would like him to know where I am. I also miss my students and especially "Las Invisibles" and hope that they will be able to continue their studies. Classes have not resumed at the university. With no formal dissolution of a contract, I consider myself de facto discharged from duties there and free to continue my commitment to the Fifth Regiment and the Republic.

I am going to try to sleep now, as my shift is due to begin tomorrow, but my new coworkers may arrive at any moment, and the war does not wait.

LA CABRERA, *Tuesday, 15 September 1936*

I had been advised that I might be needed in the main hospital area, and what we accomplished today justified every one of my reasons for being here. I was awakened by the usual cannon blasts and was soon inside the puesto de socorro. Just before noon, young volunteers Catalina and Verónica and Dr. M.R. and I had just completed a first repair on a young miliciano's fractured thigh and sent him along for surgery, when we heard screeching brakes, and a pair of stretcher-bearers burst through the door, bearing a young woman whose right arm was wrapped in layers of blood-soaked gauze that radiated an odor of antiseptic.

"She didn't scream or cry when it happened," explained a miliciano who accompanied them. "The dynamite blew up in her hand!"

"They said she was making a bomb in a milk tin," added the first stretcher-bearer. "They took her first to Buitrago and they treated her for tetanus and for gangrene."

"This camarada," added the second stretcher-bearer, referring to the miliciano, "has probably saved her life. He used the straps from his alpargata to fashion a tourniquet for her arm. We are lucky that we even got here, driving in the daytime. By some miracle we were not fired on."

We carefully removed the gauze to reveal that her right hand had been mostly severed and was attached solely at the radius. The ulna appeared shattered. Her fingers hung uselessly and looked shredded. No X-ray equipment was needed to assess the severity of this woman's injury. Verónica leaned in to look and abruptly fainted onto the floor. Juan Pedro, one of the stretcher-bearers, carried Verónica into the next room. I moved to the woman's left side to ascertain her pulse, which was very rapid and weak. Catalina was eager to assist, almost shrieking, "She needs an operation! Take her to surgery!" but Dr. M.R. and I looked at each other and pronounced, almost at the same time, "Shock!"

"We must treat her for shock first," I explained to Catalina. "How far from here is Buitrago?"

"About sixteen kilometers," responded the miliciano, called Toquero.

"That is a long way to travel in a state of shock," I said.

"Yes," responded Dr. M.R. "Shock must be treated first. We must try to replace the lost fluid and treat for pain."

We have few or no blood supplies at the puesto de socorro, and there was no time to group her blood.

"What do we have to give her, Doctor?"

"Given her weak pulse, we'll begin with an injection of glucose thirty per cent with insulin, one unit per three grams of the glucose."

"Catalina, please get that," I ordered. "Shall we also use morphine?" I asked Dr. M.R.

"Yes, of course. Catalina?"

She hurriedly brought the needed supplies, and I applied a fresh tourniquet. Then I moved to the woman's head to monitor her responses as the medications were slowly administered. I gasped as I found myself looking into the face of a beautiful child. Her black ringlets fell damply across her pale forehead and her eyelids flickered. Prominent cheekbones adorned the small, round face. Her lips were moving, but there were no intelligible sounds. I began stroking her forehead, murmuring, "*Mi niña, mi niña, estás bien, estás bien* (My child, my child, you're all right, you're all right)." Then I asked Catalina to bring a blanket, as the girl was now shivering. I covered her tightly and within about ten minutes, her pulse began to beat more firmly.

"She will recover from the shock," pronounced Dr. M.R., "and then she must be taken to the convento for surgery, for a complete amputation. We will have to identify her and make out a report."

Verónica had recovered from her faint and was returning to the room as she heard these words. I walked over to her and put my arm around her shoulders.

"Could you find her papers and read off her information?" I asked her. I thought this would be a task that she could handle.

The girl was wearing a typical blue mono, and on her left arm was the armband of the workers' militias of our Fifth Regiment. She wore alpargatas, which we loosened and removed, and Catalina began to massage her feet, which I thought was a lovely touch. Around her waist she wore a canvas belt with pockets for dynamite cartridges (fortunately empty), and attached to the belt, next to her tin plate, her canteen, her fork, her spoon, and her knife, was a pouch with her papers: "Rosario Sánchez Mora, Nationality: Spanish, born 21 April 1919, Villarejo de Salvanés. Profession: Seamstress. Affiliation: Communist Party. Fifth Regiment, Galán Column."

As Verónica read aloud, Catalina noted these details in the medical report, along with the procedures that had been followed, the immediate prognosis of the patient, and Dr. M.R.'s instructions for amputation.

Rosario now appeared to be sleeping and Dr. M.R. instructed the stretcher-bearers, "All right, camaradas, now you can take her across to San Antonio. The tourniquet should stay in place while she is being transported but must be checked immediately on arrival at surgery. I am turning her over to chief surgeon Captain José Escobar."

The two young stretcher-bearers picked up the stretcher and began to carry Rosario tenderly out the door toward one of the surgical areas.

"Oh, wait, camaradas," I said, "I want to go with you. Dr. M., are you all right to carry on without me for a while?"

"Yes, go ahead, Camarada Philipsborn. We'll send for you if we need you."

I hurried to catch up with the stretcher-bearers. Somehow, I could not let this girl go alone into surgery. I think she needed me to be with her. We reached the physician in charge and the stretcher-bearers handed him the paper with the report and introduced me as the head nurse. The doctor picked up what looked like a telephone mouthpiece and broadcast a message:

"Prepare for amputation, Room Thirty-Four." Then he addressed me and the stretcher-bearers: "Place her on that gurney. The volunteers will wheel her into surgery. Camarada Philipsborn, you may accompany the patient. Dr. Escobar will join you shortly."

We approached Room 34, which appeared very aseptic. I scrubbed as Rosario was wheeled in and covered in sterile wrap. I was given covers for my shoes and a clean uniform and a mask and gloves and was directed to proceed to her left side and monitor her pulse. I simply held her hand and stroked her arm between moments of monitoring. Dr. Escobar entered, in full surgical attire, and began to administer a light concentration of sulfuric ether "Abelló" with a Bégouin mask, and the amputation proceeded.

After one hour, concentration of the ether began to be gradually reduced.

"We will take four minutes to withdraw the ether altogether. And then we will see how this *bella durmiente* (sleeping beauty) awakens," announced Dr. Escobar.

It was almost exactly four minutes from that time that Rosario began to moan and to shiver. We hastened to cover her with a blanket. She coughed for a while and finally half-opened her eyes.

"*¡Ay, mi mano* (Oh, my hand)!" she groaned, and I wasn't sure if she was remembering the explosion or feeling pain. I have read about phantom pain and wondered if that was occurring.

Dr. Escobar moved back in then and in a kindly voice that inspired confidence—definitely a medical skill—he explained, "Rosario, you are in the hospital. We have operated on your hand and you are going to be just fine. You will be staying here for a few days." Then he turned to the rest of us, smiled, said, "Gracias, camaradas," and strode out of the room, peeling off his mask, gloves, gown, and shoe covers as he went. He tossed all of it into a bin and was gone.

The *practicante* (assistant) informed me that Rosario would soon be moved to a ward, as the operating room would need to be cleaned and prepared for more wounded.

"I will stay with her as long as I can," I offered. Someone would have to explain to Rosario that her hand had been amputated. Someone would have to be there as she inevitably experienced pain, confusion, sadness, who knows what else. I followed closely, as an orderly entered to wheel her into what had obviously been an apse of the church: oddly frescoed ceilings, stone arches, an altar consecrated solely with medical supplies, and the smell of incense overpowered by that of ether and alcohol, blood and vomit. Moans rose from some of the beds and quiet conversation from others. I found another nurse to help me remove Rosario's soiled mono and give her a sponge bath. We left her armband on the bedside table. She seemed to be still half-unconscious and had not yet seen her bandaged arm, now ended at the wrist. Just as we got her dressed in a gown, she roused and asked for water. I helped her sit up and gave her tiny sips. I told her again that she was in the hospital, suggested that she sleep a bit and said that I would be back soon.

My next stop was at the admitting office, to implore the woman in charge, Florencia, to allow me to telephone the puesto de socorro in Buitrago, to report on the condition of Rosario Sánchez Mora. She kindly consented and fortunately no one had signed up for that hour. I let them know that the steps they had taken there had been crucial in saving Rosario's life.

"This is very important, camarada. We will let Madrid know about this brave miliciana. Salud."

I returned to the ward just as Rosario was waking. I pulled a stool to her bed, on her left, and introduced myself. "Do you remember what happened to you, Rosario?"

"Yes. I was testing a fuse. It was damp from the rain. I didn't feel the heat and it blew up in my hand. . . ."

I interrupted her before she could turn to the right:

"It actually blew your hand off," I explained, as gently as I could. "Here in the hospital the doctors took away the destroyed parts and stitched you up. Have you looked at your arm?"

She turned her head to the right and gasped, "*¡Ay!*"

I took her left hand and squeezed it tightly. What she said next amazed me:

"It's too bad I couldn't throw that bomb at a *fascista*! I will have to learn to make bombs with this hand," she declared, now looking at her left hand and clenching her fist.

"Do your parents know you are here?"

"My mother died when I was little. My father married someone else and has other children. He doesn't even know that I enlisted. He thinks I just became a seamstress." She smiled for the first time and her cheekbones popped out happily.

"Rosario, are you hungry?"

"Oh, yes. I don't even remember the last time I ate."

I brought a bowl of lentil soup from the kitchen as she continued to stare at her bandaged arm. "You are also going to have to learn to *eat* with this hand," I remarked, placing a piece of bread in her hand. I took a tray from the bedside table and placed it on her lap with the soup, which I began to spoon slowly into her mouth. I was concerned about the amount of blood she had lost and was happy to see that she had a healthy appetite.

Then I called for someone to assist Rosario in using the bathroom and I kissed her and told her I would try to be there tomorrow. I walked out of the building, crossed through the arches and followed the path upward, toward the mountains. There was no moon and I don't think I have ever known such total darkness. The cannon fire that awakened me that morning had ceased. Stillness reigned everywhere. I sat down on a smooth rock, glad to have brought a woolen shawl, which I draped around my shoulders. I drew the fragrant air into my lungs, recalling the Bavarian Alps and memories of dear Mama, in the cool silence and the dark protection of that moment.

Back in my "cell," I am so struck by the bravery of this girl who would fashion a bomb from a milk tin to save the Republic against fascism. I hope to be able to visit her tomorrow, as I think this seventeen-year-old girl is the most inspiring person I have met in Spain.

LA CABRERA, *Tuesday, 22 September 1936*

Rosario continues to recover, as all around her people bleed to death, brought in too late to be saved, even as we labor all night to stop the hemorrhaging. Despite her immense loss and her young age, Rosario shows compassion for the condition of her comrades and also for those of us who are caring for them. She is eating well and recovering color in her face, with its lovely olive skin, and will probably soon be strong enough to be moved to Madrid for additional rehabilitation. She is already giving herself little exercises to perform with her left hand, completely on her own, and each time I visit her she demonstrates progress. The scar on her right arm is healing well and cleanly.

I am rather surprised at the depth of feelings I am having toward this valiant young woman, perhaps because I am missing my dear nieces and nephews so much. Even though I cared for them as much as possible, the degree of intimacy I have felt caring for Rosario from the moment she was brought, bleeding and unconscious, into the puesto de socorro, is something I do not recall experiencing. And I must also admit to a feeling of pride. Thanks in part to me, she survived a trauma that could have killed her. What I feel at each step of her rehabilitation is what a mother must feel as her child develops. As if I had given birth to her and raised her and now must encourage her to move on to her next phase, without me.

LA CABRERA, *Thursday, 1 October 1936*

Too much loss at one time! To begin with the deepest and most personal: Yesterday someone brought me a note from the Admission office that I should telephone my uncle's home in Seville. A weeping Cousin Clarita took the call. My beloved Tío Julio died yesterday. Asun had mentioned to me that his heart was broken in response both to the violent military takeover of Seville (from the right) and the burning of churches, including that of San Marcos (from the left). I am sure that it is possible to die of grief over such devastating events, and then of course there was the passing of Tía Lola three years ago, which no doubt laid a burden on his heart. Clarita told me that the funeral would be held at the church of San Luis on Saturday, the tenth of the month, and that one death announcement was being placed in the Seville *ABC* and another in the Madrid *ABC* (which has recently turned "red" while the Seville paper is completely in fascist hands).

The family would like me to be at Tío's funeral. Train connections between Madrid and Seville remain, but I cannot say the same for ideological connections. Besides the difficulty of obtaining permission to take time away from the hospital, I believe I would be risking my life to enter what has now become for me enemy territory. Another loss: my dear "Sevilla la roja," the witness, or perhaps the impetus, to my first awareness of myself as a border-crosser—the borders being those of time, space, religion, culture, to the possibility that "home"—my home—is not a fixed, static, even a geographic entity. What sustains me is my belief that Seville remains, eternal as Rome or Jerusalem. But until women can stroll freely along her azahar-scented streets and sing and dance and make love and sip fino, I must remain here among my comrades, safe as long as a fascist bullet does not pierce my heart. The funeral of Don Julio Mond Kaiser will have to proceed without his Communist Jew niece who is working daily to defend her Republic and to bring about a workers' revolution, and who gave her body over one night, albeit stunned by an overdose of vodka, to Comandante Carlos.

The next terrible loss is that of the besieged Alcázar of Toledo, after more than two months of persistent attacks. The so-called *nacionales* holed up inside were outmanned and outgunned by our valiant militias, but our soldiers were no match against the impermeable foundations laid by the Romans on the solid rock of Toledo's heights. And then the long-awaited arrival of Generals Varela and Franco assured the victory of the rebels and permitted the fascists to claim a symbolic superiority in the progress of the war. We are now left with hundreds of wounded in a city now in enemy captivity. I worry about the safety of Severino, among the other brave Alcázar soldiers.

Rosario has been discharged today, to continue her program of rehabilitation. Regiment officials (Carlos not among them) gathered in the Assembly Hall (once one of the five apses of the convento) to honor her. Members of her medical team, I'm happy to say, were included in the ceremony. She insisted on donning the blue mono of the milicias, but has exchanged her summer alpargatas for a new pair of boots, as the weather is turning quite cold. On being invited to speak, she declared, "I thank all the camaradas who have taken such good care of me. I hope to return soon to the front lines as soon as the next medical team gives me the go-ahead." She then raised her left fist—her only fist—to exclaim, "¡Viva la República! ¡No pasarán! ¡Salud!"

I could not help weeping as I echoed her call, together with the others, and found myself hoping that she would *not* return to battle, but this is what a mother must feel at her child's decision to face the uncertain future, one in which the mother can no longer play a role.

LA CABRERA, Saturday, 17 October 1936

The cross and the notice conspired to stab me in the heart, delivering the devastating notice of the passing of my dear Tío Julio, the last of his siblings to die. The announcement was published in the *ABC* on the very day of his funeral.

I am wondering how and why my uncle obtained a blessing from *Su Santidad*, "His Holiness" (the pope), but I do not intend to ask. I had been waiting for the notice to appear in the papers, and this afternoon I telephoned Liese to deliver the sad news and promised that I would ask *ABC* Madrid for extra issues to send to her and to Gerda in India. I asked about Moritz and the boys.

"They are all now working in Papa's business. The boys' studies have been . . . discontinued."

Liese lowered her voice as she said this. It was obvious that there were topics that she could not discuss over the telephone, and I know that Jews are no longer permitted to study for the professions. I wondered how the business was doing but hesitated to ask. But I especially wanted to insist that they all emigrate from Germany. So without mentioning the Monds by name or even using the word "cousin" or "England," I asked, "Will you be visiting Robert?"

"Oh, we'll see," replied Liese, vaguely. "How about you?"

Just then a third voice came on the line, saying, in crisp German, "Your three minutes have expired," and the connection was severed. I felt a sudden chill as I realized the danger that my sister and her family are in. And Papa? I am afraid to even try to call him, though from Liese's report, gathered that he is still hard at work, at age eighty-five.

Since last month, Britain has influenced Léon Blum and France to sign a Non-Intervention Agreement. Germany and Italy are completely flouting the agreement; otherwise this war might have not reached this point. And now Stalin has announced that, since Germany and Italy are in total violation of the agreement, the Soviets will now send armaments to the Republic, to stem the rise of fascism in Europe.

Snow has come early to the Sierra, and our militias are now traversing the countryside on skis. The advantage is the speed they are now afforded, but staying warm is an enormous challenge. We are already seeing cases of frost-bite and have had to amputate the feet of two brave men, both of whom cried out, "*¡Madre!*" (Mother!) above the horrendous sound and sensation of the sawing away of bone, despite high levels of sedation and anesthesia. I could only hold their hands tightly as we administered more ether.

MADRID, *Friday, 6 November 1936*

Here I am once more, at the Hospital Obrero on Calle Maudes, lodged in one of the patients' rooms, here for about a week now. The enemy is literally at Madrid's door, and our help is needed if we are to save the city. I have filled yet another volume of my tagebuch, and fortunately Nicolás Moya's medical bookstore is still open.

Today at around noon, the entire Spanish government left Madrid for Valencia and declared it Spain's interim capital. CNT members have been added to the government roster, and Largo Caballero has appointed General José Miaja to remain here as head of the newly formed *Junta de Defensa de Madrid*. Medical personnel have been drawn in from outlying areas, and I had to leave La Cabrera, which was becoming like a home to me. I probably should not develop attachments in wartime—should that be a general rule for me at any time? I miss the sweet, herb-scented air and the piercing clear nights of the Sierra and the solidarity I experienced among the workers and the patients at the convento, but I have pledged to support the Republic, and of course my first responsibility is to save lives.

We are starting to see food shortages, especially of meat, milk, and "luxury" items like coffee. Food is rationed, and people are going hungry. "María" remains at the hospital and is still doing wonders in the kitchen, creating warming broths that the convalescing wounded need so badly. And speaking of attachments, I did not see Matilde Landa, and asked "María" about her. "María" used the hem of her apron to wipe her brow and leaned against the sink. Her mouth sagged and her voice trembled as she muttered, "She left for Paris . . . with *il comandante*."

"Oh," I exhaled, and suddenly felt as if my legs would not hold me up. Fortunately, I was standing next to a table and put out a hand to steady myself, hoping that she hadn't noticed, and the other hand on my face, as I feared that my lips were also trembling. I tried to think of something positive to say: "I—I hope they are convincing Blum to withdraw from the Non-Intervention Agreement," somehow stumbled out of my mouth. I surprised myself at the feelings I must still harbor for Carlos.

"Yes, I'm sure they will be able to do that, as we know that the French people support our cause and are already sending needed items," she said as she turned to face the sink again and continued filling a huge pot with water.

"Would you like some help, camarada?"

"Ah, no, thank you, I have everything I need and just need to add water."

If she noticed my reaction, she certainly did not seem to care or did not want to even think about it, and I definitely did not wish to hear any more details. It is obvious that "María" has also been captivated—if I can say that—by this man. Who knows how many other women can number themselves among his conquests. It lightens my mood somewhat to recall Leporello's aria cataloguing Don Giovanni's "beauties" and in particular the line, "*Ma in Ispagna son già mille e tre* (But in Spain it already adds up to one thousand three)."

After a restless night interrupted by two calls to assist at surgery, yesterday I requested permission to leave the hospital. I felt a need to walk through Madrid's icy streets. I took Metro Cuatro Caminos to Metro Quevedo to visit Hortensia and witnessed a city transformed. Sidewalks become trenches, barricades sprouting from gardens, and the metro itself now a military transport line. Its tiled walls displayed rifles, grenades, picks, shovels, sandbags, even mattresses. Uniformed militias occupied large areas of the cars. Posters calling for the defense of Madrid were plastered everywhere.

It felt like I had been away from Calle Donoso Cortés for an eternity, and I certainly did not expect to be greeted at the door of my former home by a black-clad Hortensia. She was not expecting me, since she still has no telephone, and we both burst into tears the instant I realized what had happened.

"Toledo!" she sobbed. "Severino was killed in Toledo trying to dislodge the fascist bastards from the Alcázar. They never found his body—just declared him missing."

"*Ay, mujer*," I murmured, hugging her tightly, also sobbing. "How did you find out?"

"Someone from the UGT came by. The moment I opened the door, I knew what had happened. But come in and sit."

I had brought her some goat cheese from La Cabrera, and we took seats at the familiar kitchen table. Her face was red and her eyes swollen, but she wiped her eyes, managed a smile, and thanked me for the gift.

"Are you getting any assistance?" I asked.

"The union promises me a pension. But with the war and all the efforts to defend Madrid, who knows when that will happen? The women from UGT have brought me food and moral support."

"Is . . . my room occupied?"

"No. Two men answered the advert I placed, but they smelled like fascists and I told them the room had already been taken. That's all I needed!" she snorted sarcastically.

"Yes, no room for fascists in Chamberí!"

I knew she would refuse an offer of money, so I asked to use the bathroom and left a ten-peseta note in the medicine cabinet there before returning to the kitchen.

"I must get back to the hospital. Please come by if I can help you with anything. I'm not sure how long I will be here but am pledged to resist along with the brave madrileños and madrileñas."

I gave her another big hug before making my way down the darkened staircase and back to the streets. A freezing rain had begun to fall, and I pulled my coat around me and wrapped my scarf over my head and about my neck before ducking back into the metro, this time accompanied by a troop of mono-clad women sporting rifles and singing the "Himno de Riego" to some kind of anticlerical lyrics. Their beauty and their positive spirit buoyed me up after hearing about Severino's cruel death and sharing Hortensia's sorrow, and I was able to return to the hospital feeling confident that Madrid would indeed resist the imminent fascist onslaught.

MADRID, *Tuesday, 10 November 1936*

The enemy has entered the Casa de Campo and is approaching the campus of the university, while the Loyalists are bravely resisting. Wounded men and women are brought in a constant stream into our hospital and into many others, as well as to hotels that have been converted to hospitals. Most of the wounds we are seeing are from shrapnel, requiring complicated surgery, and surgeons are operating almost round the clock. Fewer women are fighting as *milicianas* now than in the first couple of months of the war, since Largo has been discouraging women's participation in battle, in favor of more domestic roles. And the progress in women's rights realized by the Republic and our 1931 Constitution? Yes, someone needs to prepare the meals and mend the clothes, but can't men share these tasks? I felt the resentment expressed by some of the "Invisibles" and wished we could express our anger together at this new, official blow to women.

It is no longer possible for me to occupy a private room in the hospital, so I have taken my old room with Hortensia for a few hours of sleep and the occasional meal. The metro continues to run and to provide both supply space and shelter, and it is now run by women—probably not the domestic roles that Largo would have assigned them. Here are two clippings from today's *ABC*:

I hope Largo sees the illustrations and realizes that women's place is also on the front lines and that they can pilot a vehicle as well as any man!

A beautiful and encouraging spectacle occurred Sunday on the Gran Vía, as men from the newly arrived International Brigades marched through the streets of Madrid, wildly cheered on by crowds shouting, "*¡Vivan los rusos!*" (Long live the Russians!) though they have come from all over the world. I am amazed at the hope that the people are placing in the Soviet Union despite the Pact of Non-Intervention, which has probably been completely abandoned at any rate. The Brigades are mustered out of a town called Albacete, in Castilla-La Mancha, the land of Don Quixote, where they have been gathering since October. *Kominterns* of various countries are sending volunteers and helping them get here through France.

MADRID, Friday, 20 November 1936

If there is such a thing as Hell, it has come to Madrid now, and it is a Hell created by human beings. Perhaps I should retract that phrase, since the devastation inflicted from the air on the civilian population by German, Italian, and, yes, Spanish bombers cannot possibly be a product of a divinely created human spirit. The Junkers airplanes swarm overhead in groups of three, which people are calling "*las tres viudas*" (the three widows), unleashing their deadly cargo at all hours of day and night, despite the fact that city lights now remain dark. Their targets? Madrileños, in their beds, on the streets, and with them Madrid's most beloved institutions and landmarks. Poorer areas of the city are targeted over the more affluent. The Cuatro Caminos site of the hospital is constantly attacked, while the Barrio de Salamanca is largely spared.

The attacks come in three stages: the first is the launching of enormous two-thousand-pound bombs, which plunge through buildings, producing craters in what were once basements. In the second stage, smaller bombs turn what remains into further rubble. Incendiary bombs then light anything combustible. Fires rage everywhere, lighting the night sky and of course also producing devastating burn injuries which we have a horrible time treating. The Museum of the Prado was even bombed two nights ago, and people are taking steps to remove the priceless art and send it to Valencia, where it is hoped it will remain safe. Carloads of children are also being sent to Valencia, the new seat of the government, leaving their parents to defend the city, parents whom they may never see again.

As if the thousands of wounded from the hand-to-hand fighting around the university were not difficult enough to tend to, with the air raids we are seeing a greater variety of horrific wounds. Even wounds that seem superficial often involve deep destruction of tissue that requires immediate surgery. And bombs often fall while we are in the midst of surgery, cutting off the electricity or spewing glass shards and masonry into the operating room. I join my comrades as we shake our fists and curse the enemy, and their dedication reminds me that this is where I belong. People have taken to the metro tunnels to sleep, and some have even learned to sleep through air raid sirens. Trams are used to transport troops to the front line, which is now a part of the city.

Yet somehow the mood of resistance is high. Huge banners proclaiming, "¡No pasarán!" are draped on buildings, spanning city streets—also banners urging "*Evacuad* (Evacuate) Madrid." People still go to the cinema and to the bars, while hunger is widespread. I am occasionally able to bring some surplus lentils or garbanzos to Hortensia but am of course reluctant to take food from patients and comrades.

Franco has reportedly ordered these air raids in order to demoralize the population and as a sort of last resort, since the rebels have not been able to win the streets. General Mola had declared on the radio that he would be having coffee on the Gran Vía on October 12, with members of the *quinta columna*, the "fifth column," the term coined to refer to the local supporters of the four columns of fascists advancing by land on Madrid. The message I am getting is that the streets still belong to the people, and that Franco, Mola, Varela, and Queipo have had to have their coffee somewhere else, because here in Madrid, ¡No pasarán!

MADRID, Thursday-Friday, 31 December– 1 January 1936–1937

After spending a "red Christmas" here in Madrid, I am preparing to turn another page in my life, as I tear yet another leaf from my calendar. On December 24, representatives of the SRI, together with the *Intendencia* (the Administration) and the Frente Popular, came by the hospital and distributed what are called the *aguinaldos del miliciano* (the soldiers' Christmas boxes) to the workers and the patients. They told us that one hundred thousand of these aguinaldos were being given out to hospitals and primarily to soldiers in the trenches around the university campus, which is now occupied by the rebels (*my university! my hospital!*) in the Parque del Oeste and the Casa de Campo, and to people housed in evacuation centers who have been bombed out of their homes.

I brought my aguinaldo home to Hortensia, who had already received one from the UGT. Our inventory: *turrones* (almond candy that we call *nougat* in German—my favorite kind is what is called *jijona* and it reminds me of halvah, which of course is made from sesame seeds), a fresh orange, some kind of preserved meat, and a cigar. Included was a message, written in Spanish, French, and German, stating that the aguinaldo "is not a Christmas dinner—we have no reason to celebrate a Catholic holiday—but rather a token of our desire for the union of all who struggle against fascism." Hortensia suggested that we take the cigars downstairs to Antón, who accepted them gratefully, and we then invited him up for a glass of wine.

"All right, but I am on duty and the *tres viudas* may want to pay a visit while I am enjoying your wine," he retorted, but I was happy that he did come sit with us for a while to share a glass of *clarete* and to take a few puffs of the aguinaldo cigar. He hugged us both and kissed Hortensia before returning to patrol the street, ready to duck into doorways if the sirens begin to sound. Another brave soul defending Madrid. I feel so grateful.

Yesterday a meeting was called by Dr. Rudolf Neumann, who is chief of Health Services with the International Brigades, headquartered in Albacete.

Fortunately, our hospital was chosen for the meeting, and even more fortunately, there was a pause in the bombing. Dr. Neumann is from Germany but speaks excellent Spanish. Thin, with reddish-blond hair and blue eyes, he gestured nervously while speaking. The purpose of the meeting was to channel medical workers into what will be called the *Servicio Sanitario Internacional*—SSI (International Health Service). He enumerated several reasons for this shift from a civilian hospital staff to one centrally managed (by the Party) and laid out his plan for the new system. He had drafted a list of new hospitals to be created or rehabilitated from existing structures. After the presentation I approached him and introduced myself (in German), explained what I was doing, and offered to serve in one of these new field hospitals. The closest one I saw that has a need for speakers of German, English, and French is located, or will be located, in the town of Ocaña. Dr. Neumann told me he would like me to work in the Evacuation Department, so that I could begin repatriation procedures for the wounded according to their countries of origin. That is an interesting possibility, but I would not like to stop rendering medical assistance altogether. And I wonder what would be done to repatriate the hundreds of German Jewish volunteers, now officially stateless.

Ocaña is about sixty-five kilometers to the south of Madrid, in the province of Toledo. There is no adequate hospital there now, so its prison, called *El Penal*, will be converted to a hospital, ideally in time to receive and treat wounded and to accommodate those who need to convalesce. So I signed up to be transferred to Ocaña and will no doubt vacate my room on Donoso Cortés and say good-bye to Hortensia yet again. I spoke to "María" about the move, and she said she may be moving on to Andalucía—perhaps to Málaga. I did not ask her about Carlos. Midnight arrived, and she had somehow managed to produce grapes for all of us to gobble down, as Saturnino, one of the practicantes, emulated the chiming town clock, intoning, "*Tan . . . tan . . . tan. . . .*" The kitchen has no windows, so we could not hear any actual clocks chiming, and we would not easily have been able to hear at any rate, as it was raining heavily. Once we had swallowed all twelve grapes, we all offered vivas: to the Republic, to Spain, to freedom, and to peace in the midst of war.

MADRID, *Sunday, 31 January 1937*

My father is dead! Papa, *mein Tate!*

Jacob (Koppel) Philipsborn, eldest son of Jeremias Philipsborn and Ernestine Bernhard Philipsborn. Clothier to Germany, her children, and her armed forces at home and abroad, husband (widower), father, grandfather, bon vivant, "feinschmecker." Born in Bentschen, Posen, Prussia, on 7 August, 1852, died on the streets of Berlin, 30 January 1937. Predeceased by his wife, Ida Mond Philipsborn and siblings Abraham (Albert), Simon, Friedericke, and Marcus (Georg). Burial at Weissensee.

This may be his only obituary, and who will read it? Who will mourn him? Who will sit shiva for him? Will Birgit remember to cover the mirrors? I shall send a copy of the announcement to Cousin Robert Mond, who is now in Paris, I think, and one to Cousin Robert Moritz Mathias in London, only hoping that the post will get through.

Liese telephoned me late last night at the hospital, sobbing hysterically. I gasped and cried out and began to weep. Papa was struck down by an automobile as he was carrying packages of children's garments from his shop to God knows where. The vehicle did not stop. God, how awful! Was it an accident? An ambulance took him to the hospital on Achenbachstrasse, where he died of his injuries. Liese will be accompanying his body today to Weissensee, where he will be laid beside Mama. Liese said she was about to telephone Artur. I will write to Gerda in India, who I know will be heartbroken. I hate to be the one to deliver this bitter news. Oh, how I wish I could be there at Weissensee with my sisters and brother! And how I wish I could have cared for Papa after he was injured! Perhaps I could have saved him! I added a black armband to my uniform today at the hospital and received sincere condolences from my comrades and even from some of the patients. We Philipsborn siblings are all orphans now. At the same time, now that one more tie with my homeland is loosened, severed, I feel one more degree of freedom. Freedom both from a homeland that does not recognize me as its citizen—as its child—and freedom to choose a home that resonates for me. Am I freed from the idea itself of "home"? Right now, I feel connected to Spain by blood—the blood that is being shed to free this nation, the blood that each day soaks my hands and my white gown.

OCAÑA, *Tuesday, 2 February 1937*

We arrived late tonight, amid this relentless rainstorm that began last month and does not seem able to stop. Even though on a map the road to Ocaña from Madrid looks quite straightforward, offering not much more than a two-hour drive, our driver, Hermeto, had to take a long alternate route around the town of Getafe, which has fallen to the enemy. He must have inherited the vision of a bat, as we passengers could not see anything from the interior of the vehicle, a large sedan converted to an ambulance, without exterior markings, of course. We had to keep wiping the windows with whatever rags we had at hand and even with gauze bandages, as they kept fogging up. About three hours after departing we finally arrived at the town of Aranjuez, which has not been taken. We were able to stop for a few moments, refill the gasoline tank, and buy coffee for Hermeto, who had performed such an admirable service, before we continued on the last few kilometers to Ocaña.

I cannot yet say what the town of Ocaña is like, as the rain continues to pelt down. I did get a glimpse of the façade of the prison/hospital, however. It was dimly illuminated by a single feeble lamp, showing a solid, light-colored archway that led to a rather squat-looking brick building, no more than two stories high. A few volunteers welcomed us, brought in our equipment, and showed us some wards on the main floor that had been converted to living quarters for the director and for the doctors in residence. They next directed us down a staircase to our sleeping quarters on the lowest level, unmistakably prison cells. We were promised a more thorough tour tomorrow. There is no window in my cell and not much air to speak of, especially with the blanket hung over the bars of my door for some semblance of privacy. Happily, the electricity is functioning, and we cell-dwellers are probably fairly safe from air raids at this location. Water in the bathroom is cold only, but there is running water and even a shower. I am glad I brought my own soap, a bar of Heno de Pravia, which I shall guard jealously, in a very un-socialistic manner. I hope my cot is comfortable, with its mattress consisting of a folded quilt. I am exhausted, but I am not sure I will be able to sleep, feeling so far from any known center and having just lost my dear Papa. May I be able to create my own center and my own comfort, and to find freedom, here in this former prison. Tears come to my eyes as I realize that my new family are the valiant Spaniards and internationals who come to me for help to heal the fierce wounds of their battle against fascism.

OCAÑA, *Saturday, 6 February 1937*

I am already observing a fellowship here that I did not notice at the Hospital Obrero in Madrid. It is largely generated by the women, volunteers who had worked previously at the Madrid Casino, also converted to a hospital, and which has been abandoned to the attacks of the Junkers and the sabotage of the "fifth column." The generous spirit here makes me aware for the first time of the constant feeling of competition I had experienced with the women with whom I was supposed to be collaborating: Matilde Landa, María Luisa Lafita, and the one called simply "María." Though we accomplished together the work of the hospital as well as we could, given the limited supplies on hand and the intrusions of fragments of glass, concrete, and other biproducts of bombings into the operating room, I always felt the underlying need to perform my duties more efficiently, to garner more attention from the doctors, and even to look more attractive than the other women on my "team." I am not at all proud of myself for this trait, especially since I am pledged to participate in a war effort in order to liberate all peoples from the petty competition engendered by capitalism. And I suspect that Comandante Carlos somehow played a role in that dynamic. I am not experiencing any of those feelings among the women here at the Penal (as everyone still calls it). They show such pride in their transformation of a filthy, lice-infested dungeon into a welcoming, whitewashed facility with gleaming red tiled floors, and windows (on the main and upper floors) from which the bars have been removed and replaced with pots of geraniums. A huge central patio connects with all the sickrooms and allows us to let the wounded get some fresh air and even occasional sunshine. And today is the first day of full sun after almost a month of constant rainstorms, which provides a definite lift to the spirits. Also off the patio is what is called the *rincón de cultura,* the culture corner. In that room, moving pictures are shown, there is a table for newspapers and political pamphlets, sofas, and even a piano. The volunteers are all helpful and happy to explain the workings of the system, which still houses a few prisoners. The lower story houses the operating room, created ad hoc, the pharmacy, still pitifully undersupplied, a room to store uniforms and civilian clothes, a laundry room, food storage, a barber shop, and the dining hall. The Admission and Evacuation offices are also located there, and I have been spending much time in Evacuation, as patients are processed to leave for rehabilitation hospitals. Each of the offices has a telephone and a telegraph machine. The kitchen is off the dining hall, toward the rear of the building, and includes a bakery.

One woman in particular who has impressed me is a scholar from Asturias called María Josefa. She is a specialist in languages and dialects of Spain and seems to be the organizing force among the volunteers. I am looking forward to conversations with her.

Though I am kept somewhat busy in the Evacuation office, I do assist at surgery regularly and am sometimes called to translate for German or French patients. And we are expecting an influx of wounded, as a new offensive has been launched today by the so-called nationalists, in the Jarama Valley, about sixty kilometers north of here. We are all accustomed to responding to the bell that rings each time a new patient is brought in or an ambulance is sighted. I feel my stomach tighten at the sound, and I need to tell myself each time that the bell is my reminder of my commitment to do away with fascism and to save Spain. Franco's plan is to cut off the route between Madrid and Valencia, the city that houses the government and is also now serving as a refuge for children and for the art of Madrid's museums. If that highway is captured, the war will effectively be over, and fascism will reign.

OCAÑA, Monday, 8 February 1937

This morning Néstor, a worker in the Evacuation office, offered to fill in for me so that I could take some time off, and I gratefully accepted. God knows I was due for a break. Wounded from Jarama have already begun to arrive, and I am often called to two places at once and at times am barely aware of which place I am in. The hospital is a self-contained world, and it is easy to forget that there is life consisting of more than bombs, blood, and ambulances. A newly arrived Spanish doctor, Dr. Martínez, gallantly offered to accompany me on my outing, but I explained to him my method of tourism: taking my time and perhaps wandering without rhyme or reason. I promised him that I would not get lost and that I would return by afternoon for a scheduled surgery session. I was intrigued by his promise to show me what he called the "Spanish method" of treating compound fractures. I would also like to know more about him, as he carries an air of elegance that is unexpected and intriguing.

Once I reached the bottom step of the hospital, I inhaled deeply, in what seemed like the first time in several days, and was rewarded by the bittersweet aroma offered by two almond trees that had just begun to blossom, welcoming me to the streets of Ocaña and promising springtime. The cobblestones had been rain-washed, and the sun had timidly emerged, leaving a few wandering gray clouds to vary the palette of the flat Castilian sky.

I ended up in the Plaza Mayor (the main square), containing the Town Hall—its architecture a modest version of Madrid's. It was the day of the mercadillo, and I found two pairs of alpargatas at such a low price that I did not even dare to bargain. Men were seated at low tables exchanging coins and stamps as if there were no war, and for a brief moment I tried to pretend that I was in a country at peace. I took a table and ordered an *infusión* of chamomile, which I sweetened with a little honey; then I wandered the streets (yes, without rhyme or reason) and returned to the Penal. As I ascended the steps, I felt hungry and eager to share a meal with the comrades, ready to return to today's world, war and bombing and head lice notwithstanding. I was so glad to sit with them and stepped into the kitchen afterwards to thank the cooks for the delicious white beans, in which I did not detect the usual indigestible Russian meat; in fact, I don't think it contained any meat at all.

"Come and scrub for surgery, Señorita Philipsborn," called Dr. Martínez from the kitchen doorway.

Señorita? I hadn't heard that term for quite a while, but there was no time to speculate. I followed him into the large room that had been prepared for surgery. Accompanying him was another fairly new arrival, a rather stocky man with a wide forehead whom he called simply "Carrasco."

The patient was a young man of seventeen named Roberto Ruiz Hernández, of the 19th Mixed Brigade from Villena, in the province of Alicante. He had been shot in the battle of Jarama and had sustained a compound fracture of the left femur. Carrasco was assisted by Lucy, a sweet young woman from the Basque country who had also been volunteering in Madrid. Braulio, one of the practicantes, stood at the sink mixing plaster of paris for the necessary casts.

As we scrubbed, Dr. Martínez explained, "This boy arrived early this morning from Jarama. Fortunately. the puesto de socorro on the battlefield administered the first treatments. They gave him morphine and a small transfusion. You can see that his wound has been fairly well cleansed and opened, and these splints have been put in place to immobilize his legs."

Both legs had indeed been hastily splinted, in order to assist in his sedation.

"So far this procedure is similar to one I witnessed when I was assisting at the taking of the Cuartel de la Montaña," I said.

"Uh," he grunted. "I think that what we do next may be new to you." (I wondered if he was trying to demean me.) "He is pretty well sedated," he continued, "but we will need to administer ether so that he can endure the surgery. Let us remove the splints, and then we will cleanse the wound more thoroughly and cut away all damaged tissue."

I placed the mask over the boy's head and began the ether drip but felt it necessary to respond, "I have also assisted in this type of procedure."

"At the Cuartel de la Montaña?"

"Well, yes, and also at La Cabrera, when we performed an amputation."

"Ah, well, we plan to save this leg."

I helped him cleanse the wound, as he proceeded with the debridement of the damaged tissue. Much of the soft tissue had been ripped by machine gun bullets, and we actually extracted a couple of them. The boy groaned, "Madre," and Lucy stroked his forehead, intoning musically, "Lo-lo, lo-lo," in Basque.

Once the debridement was complete, Dr. Martínez stepped back a bit and asked Lucy and me to pack the wound with sterile gauze. Fortunately, there was no infection and no excessive bleeding. A credit to the puesto de socorro team and the cool weather. We placed a small rubber drainage tube in the wound.

Dr. Martínez donned a fresh pair of rubber gloves and instructed me to do the same. "All right, Señorita, let us realign this fracture."

That phase was difficult and delicate, but we managed to mesh the broken ends of the bone.

"Braulio, is that plaster ready? Do we have some bars or slabs to reinforce it?"

Braulio brought the tray with the wet plaster, as well as some light boards to be used to further immobilize the limb. Carrasco raised Roberto's leg gently while I wrapped it first in gauze, from the top of the leg to the ankle, and then wrapped more gauze around to hold a board in place on the side opposite the wound. Carrasco continued to hold the leg while Braulio spread the plaster thickly.

"This will be firm and dry by tomorrow morning. Please stay with him all night until he regains consciousness. You can give him Sedol for pain." Dr. Martínez removed his gown, mask, gloves and shoe covers and exited the operating room, humming to himself. It was as if he had just shaved or tied his shoes, so casual and lighthearted was his attitude. "Oh," he added, turning in the doorway, "this cast will need to stay on for weeks, no matter how bad it smells."

This statement came as news to me, but I assumed that this was part of the "Spanish method" he had mentioned earlier.

It was close to midnight. I shooed Lucy away to sleep and gave Roberto another injection of Sedol. Then I sat and opened this diary to record today's events. Roberto's peaceful breathing comforts me.

OCAÑA, Tuesday, 9 February 1937

The heavy rains have returned, fortunately slowing the murderous process of the war and the influx of wounded warriors. The weather is also causing us all to stay indoors and to engage in conversations, along with the monitoring of our patients. Roberto awoke from his procedure and has begun to eat. We are encouraging him to wriggle his toes in order to bring circulation to his wounds and promote healing.

Yesterday afternoon, on the way to the dining hall, the volunteer from Asturias, María Josefa, greeted me and asked if I would consider giving a little German class to some of the workers at the Penal.

We agreed to start the next morning (in other words, today), and while we were eating (garbanzos again—with that unidentifiable Russian meat), I racked my brain to decide how I would do the teaching. We certainly did not have textbooks. I thought that it would help to use pictures and rhyme, useful tools for me, at least. Then I remembered that at the bottom of my valise I had packed the old family edition of *Der Struwwelpeter* that had provided us with so much entertainment on Artur's birthday, now almost ten years past.

So this morning, right after breakfast, I brought my *Struwwelpeter* to the unused room with a table and overhead lamp in the lower level that we had chosen for our lessons, walked in, and greeted the group already seated there: "*Guten morgen.*"

The four of them—María Josefa, Dr. Talamantes, Braulio the practicante, and Néstor from Evacuation—all responded appropriately, and I knew I could proceed in this way. Next I introduced myself—"*Ich bin die Klara.*" I said this a few times as I patted my chest and then reached my hand out to María Josefa, knowing that she was a linguist, and continued, "*Und du?*"

"*Ich bin die María Xosefa,*" she responded.

I smiled, relieved, exhaling, and said, "*Ach, ja, die María Xosefa!*"

Once I felt that everyone had a grasp of what was going on, it was time to show Heinrich Hoffmann's famous cover of *Der Struwwelpeter*. I pointed to the picture as I slowly enunciated the verses.

I then had them repeat each line, pointing to Peter's hands, nails, and hair, and gesturing for the verbs "to look," "to stand," "to cut," and "to comb" and shaking my head and waving my index finger for the word "*nicht*" so they would get the meaning without reverting to Spanish.

One more round of introductions and, exhausted, I dismissed the class until tomorrow (*bis morgen*).

María Josefa stayed behind with me for a while, sitting next to me at the table. "I took a German class in Madrid, and I think I have spoken more German in this hour than I did in that whole class," she said.

"Oh, thank you! Were there other women in your class?"

"No, in fact I think I was the only one."

I laughed bitterly and told her about "Las Invisibles," whom I suddenly missed terribly. I wondered where they were and how the war was affecting them. I took her arm and said, "Perhaps if we win this war, women will no longer be invisible. We will be learning alongside men and also teaching them."

"If we 'win the war,' what will we have won?" she asked wistfully, shaking her head slowly. "And who are 'we,' anyway? Of course, you are not Spanish, but in this war, we are all 'we,' children of God, brothers and sisters." She opened her arms as if to embrace the world. "No one is winning, and everyone is losing." She dropped her hands into her lap and lowered her head.

"Then—" I hesitated, not knowing exactly how to ask but wanting to understand her commitment to the Cause. "What brings you to Ocaña to volunteer for the Republic?"

She hesitated, and her dark eyes filled with tears. "What brings me? My humanity. Life."

I felt in my heart a kinship with her and gratitude that she shared with me her grief for the human loss she witnesses each day. But suddenly I began to question my own commitment to Spain, to the Party, to the war. It is becoming clear that consolidating the revolution, with all the accomplishments entailed, is far more important than winning the war.

"So you don't agree with what la Pasionaria says: 'Better the widow of a hero than the wife of a coward'?"

"I am not saying that it is good to be a coward, but what is the virtue of a heroism that creates widows—and orphans?"

"Oh! I think I can learn from you, camarada," I admitted to her, and as I said it, I felt a deep admiration for this young woman. We stood up to leave, and I hugged her and reminded her "*bis morgen*" before we started off in opposite directions—I to see how Roberto was recuperating, and she to spread her love for humanity to those in need of it.

OCAÑA, Thursday, 11 February 1937

This morning as the sun valiantly emerged above huddled, slate-colored clouds, the Evacuation office received an urgent cable from Dr. Oskar Telge, one of the Bulgarian doctors who has replaced Rudolf Neumann as head of the SSI. The message was grim: Fascist forces, headed by Moroccan troops, have crossed the Jarama River and have taken the bridge at Pindoque. There are heavy casualties and more expected. The International Brigades are assisted by Soviet machine guns, tanks, and aircraft. Dr. Telge informed us that they know that the English-speaking Spanish surgeon, Dr. Eduardo Martínez Alonso, is here and that he should be informed and prepared. I went looking for Dr. Martínez and found him sitting on a bench in the sun in front of the hospital, enjoying a smoke. He patted the bench beside him, and I took a seat. He looked very dapper, with his legs crossed, swinging a foot elegantly shod in wingtips, and offered me a cigarette from his packet of Gold Flakes, which I declined. His moustache was trim, and his light brown hair combed straight back from the "widow's peak" in the middle of his forehead. A smallish, wiry man who exudes an air of importance. I relayed the Bulgarian doctor's message.

"We are pitifully understaffed here," Dr. Martínez commented, shaking his head. "But I have a plan." He flicked an ash over the side of the bench. "I am going to visit the Convent of San José of the Discalced Carmelite nuns, just down the street from the Penal, to see if I can get some of them to volunteer to be trained. It couldn't be any worse for them than being imprisoned or killed."

I winced at the fact that he was referring to the anticlerical actions that some on the left have carried out, but decided to overlook it and change the subject: "They say in the office that you speak English. That is very rare here."

"So true, and it has opened many doors for me. I was born in Vigo but have lived just about everywhere. I did my medical studies in Scotland and England and have lived in Uruguay and have just come from Madrid and Extremadura. But my English is a gift and has been a life-saver for me."

"I understand. Speaking more than one language allows one to live in more than one world."

He chuckled knowingly. I wondered if I should offer to go by the convent with him, but thought that I would not be the right person to do that.

"Are you thinking of asking one of the female workers to accompany you to the convent?"

"Now that is an interesting thought. I was thinking of just taking Carrasco, the assistant who came with me from Extremadura. Do you have anyone in mind?" He turned to face me and moved a little closer, looking into my eyes with eyes the color of honey. "Yourself, perhaps?"

I moved back a bit. "I don't think so, but I wonder if María Josefa would be a good person to go with you. She is so compassionate, and I think she could persuade the nuns to come and help."

"Ah yes, I know who you mean." He sat up straighter and stubbed out his cigarette. "The girl from the Madrid Casino—the scholar from Asturias. Large black eyes. I will go and ask her now. We have no time to lose. Thank you for that idea."

I followed Dr. Martínez as he strode briskly up the stairs and into the building. The moment I reached the door of the office, Néstor grabbed my arm, his face white.

"Oye, camarada! They are bringing in fifty wounded from Jarama now. They are the survivors of the André Marty Battalion from the Twelfth Brigade"—he choked on saliva and continued—"the ones whose throats were not cut in the night by the Ifni Marksmen. Please stay here to receive the wounded and I will go and make sure that Dr. Martínez is on hand."

"Dr. Martínez is on his way with Camarada María Josefa to recruit more volunteers," I told him. "We will have to cover until they have returned."

"All right, camarada." He rushed back into the office. "I hope the loudspeaker system is working. I will make the announcement." He picked up the telephone receiver that served as a transmitter for the loudspeaker system and tapped the mouthpiece. "Attention, all hospital personnel. Doctors, nurses, practicantes, volunteers, please report to stations. Suit up and scrub to receive incoming patients. Stretcher-bearers, please report to the ambulance entrance." His voice echoed metallically through the hallways and, we hoped, into the dining, recreation, operating, and other rooms used for triage and emergency treatment.

No sooner had he hung up the receiver when we heard the first ambulance pull up. Our stretcher-bearers rushed to bring in the first wounded as the ambulance personnel returned to their vehicle to bring in two more. Blood loss was our first concern, so I followed the patients to the large room where the practicantes and nurses were attempting to staunch bleeding and treat for shock and pain. I recorded the identities of the wounded as they were being treated. The Spanish-Canadian Institute of Blood Transfusion had fortunately sent some refrigerated blood supplies from Madrid. Thanks to the Institute's founder, Canadian surgeon Norman Bethune, and to the Socorro Rojo Internacional, our loyal citizens, mostly the women of Madrid, have been donating blood and it is safely stored, as long as we have electricity to run our refrigeration system. The doctors here at Ocaña know how to perform a transfusion, and I didn't want to think of having to train nuns in this art.

After about an hour and the arrival of two more ambulances, Dr. Martínez arrived with María Josefa and three frightened-looking women in tow, of varying ages, wearing ill-fitting street clothing. Who knows how he had convinced them to "volunteer" in a field hospital for the Republic. Dr. Martínez asked me to train them at least in hygiene and in following instructions and handling instruments, and then he rushed with María Josefa to the operating room to scrub and to continue with the patients who had been sedated and somewhat stabilized.

I was not sure how to address the nuns, so I called them "*camaradas hermanas*" (Comrade Sisters) and asked them to come with me to the dining hall. As they took seats uneasily at a table, I went into the kitchen and asked the cook to prepare a pot of *tila* (linden-blossoms) with honey, which soon made its appearance and soothed the nerves somewhat. I thanked them for being willing to help save the lives of their fellow human beings, and then, as well as I was able, I instructed them in the essentials of hygiene. I told them that the white uniform that we were asking them to don not only identified them as health care givers but also added to the hygienic nature of medical care. They seemed relieved at this additional way to camouflage themselves. Since the outbreak of the war, nuns, monks, and priests have been discouraged from wearing religious garb. I asked for their names and told them that we would address them as they wished, which also reassured them. Once we had finished the tea, I suggested that the best way to learn would be to go from room to room and observe what was being done.

Ambulances had stopped coming, and it was nightfall as I supervised my charges while they scrubbed and drew on white gowns. In the first room, Carrasco, Dr. Martínez's assistant, had selected a bottle of blood from the correct group (Group II, also my blood group—my donated blood is stored here) for a Czech Brigader, and first injected Novocain into the median cubital vein (in the bend in the boy's elbow). Then he sliced into the vein and was about to insert a cannula for the transfusion, when Beatriz, the youngest nun of the three, sighed, "¡Ay, Señor! (Oh, Lord!)" and collapsed onto the floor. Carrasco threw me a disgusted look and indicated with a toss of his head that I should clear out of his room with my pious entourage. We gathered up the semi-conscious Beatriz and helped her to a chair in the hallway where she could put her head down and recover. I wondered about Dr. Martínez's idea to make wartime medical workers of women dedicated to the spiritual life , but the other two nuns encouraged Beatriz to buck up and suggested that they could do work that did not involve blood.

That gave me an idea, and I took a few steps back and addressed all three of them. "The place where you all could do the most good is with patients who have come out of surgery and need to rest and recover. You could monitor them for vomiting and anxiety and soothe them with calming words. If they seem to be in pain, you can ask a practicante to inject them with analgesia,"

I added, glancing at Beatriz to see if that idea would trigger another fainting spell. She simply nodded her head, and I was satisfied.

At that moment Dr. Martínez appeared in the hall, still in his surgical gown, though he had removed his mask and gloves. He approached Beatriz and bent over her. "Have you recovered from the fright, *hermanita*? It looks like your color has returned," he added, touching her cheek. She drew back a bit and flushed red. I have not spent much time among the religious, but I think that I have never heard a nun addressed as "*hermanita*" ("little sister" or "sister dear").

Dr. Martínez returned to surgery, and I signaled the three women to follow me and led them into a large room with about eight beds, all of which were occupied by our beautiful and valiant soldiers garbed in various uniforms, some cut away for surgery or torn away by gunfire. Each nun settled in a chair close to the beds as I approached a very young British soldier whose uniform still smelled of the thyme in which he must have been lying on a hill at Jarama when the stretcher-bearers picked him up. His head was bandaged, eyes covered, but he seemed to be awake. I touched his hand to let him know I was there, bent over, and greeted him, "Hello, Comrade."

He turned his head toward me and asked, desperately, in English, "Did we kill the fascists? Are they gone? I can't see."

"We did not kill them all. They are still there. You are in the hospital." His arm was bandaged where he had evidently received a transfusion. "We have given you new blood. That will help you get well. I will stay with you until you go to sleep. My name is Claire."

"I am Nigel. I don't want to sleep. Please help me get up." He grasped my hand and tried to pull himself up and cried out in pain.

"Nigel, if you want to kill the fascists, you must rest. We will give you something to help you sleep." I went to the cabinet and pulled out a vial of Sedol and gave him an injection. I held his hand until he calmed down and finally surrendered to sleep. Then I gathered the nuns and took them downstairs to show them their sleeping quarters and the bathroom. I apologized for the humble cells in which we all sleep, but Sisters Teresa and Úrsula reminded me that they had all taken vows of poverty and had slept in more uncomfortable circumstances. I have something to learn from these women.

OCAÑA, Saturday, 13 February 1937

Breakfast this morning was peaceful. No casualties had come in since last night. Two men had died of their wounds and the rest were recovering. So when Dr. Talamantes greeted me with *"Guten morgen!"* I knew what to do next. I took the few steps to the next table, where María Josefa, Néstor, and Braulio were seated, and uttered a cheerful *"Guten morgen,"* followed by *"Guten appetit."*

"Hay clase hoy?" asked María Josefa.

"Ja, heute!" I replied, nodding, grateful that the words for "today" in the two languages sounded so similar. I pointed to my watch and then held up all ten fingers as I added, *"Um zehn uhr."*

By ten o'clock I had retrieved my copy of *Der Struwwelpeter* and was walking into the basement room that was serving as our classroom. I began again with the introductions and then proceeded to have my four students introduce themselves to each other and then to the next person. But then, while about to view Shaggy Peter's habits, we heard the crackle of the loudspeaker and then an announcement, broadcast by Juan José, who was filling in for Néstor in the office. The urgency of his voice reached us through the distorted sound system:

"Attention, many British casualties arriving from Jarama. Everyone please report to stations."

That announcement was the prelude to the heaviest day we have had yet at Ocaña. We worked constantly without eating or even using the bathroom. Men who were conscious and could speak told us that this battle was for a hill called Pingarrón and that many of their officers had died on the battlefield. They had witnessed so many losses that they were calling the area "Suicide Hill." Wounds were ferocious, and I was not surprised to hear British soldiers calling out, "*Mama!*" as we performed phlebotomies or debridement, often with little or no anesthesia. Supplies began to run out at about eight o'clock, including blood, and some of us had to resort to direct transfusions, arm to arm. In desperation, I found myself asking the nuns if they would volunteer to donate, and I felt so relieved when they all consented, even young Beatriz. I encouraged her to look at me, away from the practicante, and I squeezed her hand while her blood was being drawn.

OCAÑA, *Sunday, 14 February 1937*

I must have fallen asleep over my diary last night or early this morning—difficult to distinguish, as ambulances continued braving the mountain roads and the bombs to bring us patients that we can barely handle but somehow find space for, in hallways, in cells . . . I had neglected to wind my watch, so it could have been any time when I tiptoed past the nuns' rooms, from which no sounds issued, and all seemed well. I continued down the corridor, toward the south wing of the basement, where a few prisoners are housed. As I neared the end, the unmistakable voice of Dr. Martínez, sharp and furious, drew me further along the hallway. I made out the words "Send another cable . . . surgical units . . . casualties. . . ." and finally arrived to observe an armed guard unlocking a cell door, permitting Dr. Martínez to emerge.

"Clara—Señorita Philipsborn! What are you doing here?" He took a step backwards, his mouth agape.

"I—I couldn't sleep . . . checked on the nuns. . . ."

"Well, you may as well stay for a while." He addressed the young miliciano who had accompanied the guard: "Young man, please bring us some tea." The miliciano scurried off to do his bidding, and the guard followed him. Dr. Martínez regained his composure, smoothing his moustache.

With a regal sweep of his arm, he invited me to step into his cell. Now it was my turn to drop my jaw as I took a seat at a small table on which lay a few books, a green, half-finished bottle of gin, and an ashtray. He took a seat on his cot, which was padded with woolen blankets and a soft-looking quilt—he even had a pillow. One wall was recessed to form a little cubby, in which hung neatly pressed shirts and trousers. Well-polished boots and shoes sat on a shelf in the cubby. He switched on an electric lamp that stood on a night table and began:

"Yes, you see before you a prisoner at the Penal de Ocaña. The only thing that allows me to continue breathing and smoking is the fact that I followed the profession of Galen, in keeping with my father's wishes."

"But—why are you—imprisoned?" I had to ask.

"I was too close to the king and queen—a sort of favorite of theirs, I might say. When Alfonso and 'Ena'"—(*Ena!* I thought. *On such familiar terms with Queen Victoria Eugenia?*)—"had to abdicate and leave Spain, I was working at the Red Cross Hospital, where I was needed for my ability to speak English . . . the Queen's English, as it were. Once the war started, I cared for wounded Reds," (*Reds!* So that was why he never called me "camarada"!),"but I also rescued some priests and some nuns, in Madrid and then again in Extremadura," (Ah, *rescued*—hence his idea to recruit the discalced sisters), "so they finally caught up with me, and here you have me. I persuaded them that as a surgeon I would be of more service to the Republic alive than dead, and they obviously believed me. Even so—who knows?—any day these sumptuous quarters of mine may be invaded and I invited to be the recipient of the dreaded *paseo*—the one-way stroll to the cemetery wall. Ah, the tea."

The miliciano shuffled in and set down a small wooden tray holding a teapot, two porcelain cups, two teaspoons, and a few sugar cubes (rationed sugar!) and was about to leave when Dr. Martínez put up a hand.

"Don't forget to send that cable—marked urgent—to the Chief Medical Officer, González Recatero. And he had better get this one. We simply cannot continue to operate without supplies and without more surgeons." He communicated the order as if he were seated behind a desk in a neatly appointed military office, complete with maps, typewriters, and filing cabinets, a framed photograph of Largo Caballero and perhaps one of Stalin, on the wall. He was issuing the message in order to save lives in a death-struggle against fascism—and yes, also against monarchy, papacy, and capital. *Which side is he on?* I wondered as I poured tea for both of us, dropped a sugar cube into my cup, and stirred it, but I struggled to formulate the question:

"So—your political loyalties are. . . ."

He spared me from completing my thought: "No political loyalties. As a Spaniard and a surgeon, I am on the side of those who need my help."

"And the British? The Belgians? The Irish? All those whose lives you probably saved last night?"

He added two sugar cubes to his tea and then reached out to pull a small tin of condensed milk off another shelf and added a splash to his cup. The milk tin reminded me momentarily of Rosario Sánchez Mora and her self-destructing dynamite bomb, but I brought my attention back to his reply.

"Listen, camarada"—this said rather sarcastically—"a casualty to me is simply another human being who needs my attention."

Another person here, at this hospital, who thinks this way, who lives this way! María Josefa, probably the nuns, and now Doctor Martínez! Is that what it means to be human, to be a doctor, or to be a Spaniard? But that does not explain the atrocities, the hatred that spills so much blood each day. These few people constitute an antidote to the poison administered by *la bête humaine* who dwells within us all. I am now remembering what the rabbis used to teach us about the rival human conditions of *yetzer ha-ra* and *yetzer ha-tov*: We are born with both evil and good inclinations, and we can either succumb to the evil (yetzer ha-ra) or choose the good (yetzer ha-tov). But what is it that determines which one we choose? The pious speak of God and of Satan—the adversary—neither of whom fit in my system of understanding.

I moved upstairs to begin the day's work. I will certainly not tell anyone of my strange discovery, as I am sure that Dr. Martínez would not like the general hospital population to know that he is a prisoner here. I imagine that many people must know, however, since he is kept under scrutiny as a possible "enemy" and as a flight risk, not to mention a possible candidate for the paseo and the firing squad.

Fewer casualties arrived today, enabling us to better attend to those who had poured in yesterday. Ambulance drivers have reported that Russian T-26 tanks are holding off the nationalists. Roberto is eating well and feeling sensation in his injured leg. We continue to urge him to wriggle his toes and to exercise his "good" leg. We are not allowed to remove the casts, in accordance with the "Spanish" method. Nigel is facing surgery for shrapnel in both eyes and may lose them.

The nuns had told María Josefa that they needed to return to the convent to retrieve changes of clothing, and María Josefa asked me to accompany them. We decided to wait until nightfall to lessen the danger of bombardment. We all wrapped ourselves in woolen shawls against the cold and I thought we all looked like nuns as we slipped beneath the hospital's arch into the receiving night. There was no moon that I could see, but the sky was spattered with stars. María Josefa asked me for the German word for "star" and I replied, "*Der stern,*" and then gestured toward the heavens and exclaimed, "*Wie viele sterne* (How many stars)!*" She repeated the phrase, followed by Beatriz, who enunciated the German with a high-pitched sigh. We all laughed softly as we ascended the steps of the convent, united in a surreal sisterhood.

OCAÑA, Saturday, 6 March 1937

Dr. Martínez has disappeared from the Penal! He completed a surgery late last night—on poor Nigel, whose eyes had to be removed—and this morning in the dining hall people were wondering why neither he nor Carrasco had appeared at breakfast or been seen at all. When I entered the Evacuation office, the guard I had seen letting Dr. Martínez out of his cell was talking excitedly and in low tones to a man I had not seen before. They stopped talking the moment they spotted me. I tried to appear casual and unaffected and walked out of the office. After a few visits to patients, I took the stairs to the basement and repeated the walk down the south wing. When I arrived at his cell, the door stood open, and I took a hasty look inside. My breath caught in my throat: the doctor's clothing, his boots, his books had vanished. I continued down the corridor, toward the nuns' rooms. Sitting on Beatriz's empty cot were Teresa and Úrsula, quietly weeping.

"She is gone!" Teresa cried. "Gone! What happened?"

I sat down with them as I began to make the connection in my mind. As gently as possible, I said, "I think the sister has left the hospital—with—Dr. Martínez."

They both gasped, and Úrsula made the sign of the cross as they continued to weep.

"She is very young and perhaps not as committed to her vows as others," I continued. "Perhaps the doctor accepted a position at another hospital—and—realized how helpful she had been to him." Then my brain began sending me more disturbing messages: Why am I making excuses for *him*? A monarchist, possibly one of the loathsome parasitic *señoritos*, maybe even an outright fascist! Was he sincere in professing his devotion to Hippocratic principles? But—worst of all—was I a bit taken by his urbane charm?

They calmed down somewhat, and I continued, "I know that you are here because of him. I am sure that you will be welcome to stay, as you have become quite useful, and you may also be safer here." I hugged them both and stood to leave. "Our patients need us, and I hope to see you upstairs."

A lesson for me, perhaps: discovering my more than professional attachment to this man showed me that I may not be as obsessed with Carlos as I had thought—just as well. And I hope that I can apply a phrase from Sophocles we learned at school: "If you try to cure evil with evil, you will end up in more pain." It definitely will not bring the revolution any closer.

OCAÑA, Tuesday, 9 March 1937

The Jarama Valley battle has ended with our forces holding open the highway between Madrid and Valencia, but at great cost of lives, those of loyal Spanish under Líster, Miaja, and "Modesto," as well as those of the valiant internationals who defied the policies of their own countries to fight against fascism in a strange land. This significant but costly victory has widened the battlefront, and the fascists are trying to come up with other ways to conquer Madrid, which continues to resist.

At yesterday's mealtime I wished a happy Day of the Woman to my female comrades. The remaining two nuns from the convent smiled, apparently pleased to be regarded as women rather than disembodied spirits. Perhaps they will be more forgiving of the errant Beatriz as they recognize our common status.

OCAÑA, *Wednesday, 28 April 1937*

Can there be a more cowardly act than that of bombing innocent civilians from the air? I am recalling the interview that the American journalist Jay Allen conducted with Franco last summer. Franco had sworn to "save Spain from Marxism, no matter what the cost," up to destroying half of Spain. Not deterred by Madrid's brave resistance to the aerial bombings of this past November, Franco and Hitler tried it again on the civilian population of Albacete in February. Then, last month, on the thirty-first, the fascists bombed the Basque city of Durango on a market day.

But even more enormous was the raid conducted just two days ago on another Basque city, Guernica. Again, it is the civilian population that is the victim. The German-made weapons were designed to pulverize buildings and to annihilate civilians: women, men, babies. As in Madrid, incendiary devices ignited fires in the structures that had already been bombed, and as in Albacete, people fleeing toward the fields and the hills or toward shelters were machine-gunned by low-flying airplanes. Again, it was a market day and people had flocked there from outlying areas where food supplies had become scarce. One target of the "nationalists" was the tree of Guernica sacred to the Basque people, the *Gernikako árbola*. So bombing a tree is now military strategy?

This evening at nine o'clock, for the daily war report someone had tuned the radio in the Culture Corner to Radio Nacional, the "official" Falangist/ fascist frequency, and a few of us gathered around. The world has rightfully accused our enemy of mass murder, and while Franco and company recognize the horror of the destruction of Guernica, rather than admitting to having created it, they cast the blame on—who else? The Jews! I will translate as well as I can the passage that was broadcast:

"The Jewish and Masonic world press and the hypocritical mourners in Valencia rent their garments and slandered the Caudillo, whose name, clear as our skies, they tried to besmirch with their drooling false accusations . . . Such immense destruction could only have been caused by arsonists and dynamiters."

Everyone in the room groaned, a few swore, and one of the patients hobbled to the piano and struck up a ragtime strain. The piano is so out of tune that I could not bear to hear it through, and the harsh sounds fueled my rage at the murderous fascists, so I retired to my somewhat comfortable cell with some back issues of *Frente Rojo*.

OCAÑA, Thursday, 29 April 1937

I am noticing many Party publications that equate Trotskyism, as well as adherence to the POUM, *Partido Obrero de Unificación Marxista* (United Marxist Workers' Party) with fascism and even with Nazism. Stalin's "masterful" speech on the subject is paraphrased across a few issues of the *Frente Rojo*. No matter the effort I make to understand how adherents to Trotsky's ideas are considered "enemies of the people," and exactly what are the principles of Trotskyism to which Stalin objects, the arguments I see in Stalin's reasoning are simply hollow accusations. Trotskyism is regarded not as a political current born of the working class but rather as "a band without principles and without ideas, made up of saboteurs, of terrorist agents, of spies, of assassins, a band of sworn enemies of the working class paid by the information services of foreign states."

Trotskyites are also accused of serving fascist Italy and Japan and Nazi Germany and of killing workers and members of the Bolshevik Party in Russia. None of these accusations offer examples or names. There is no explanation for the liquidation (the purge) of people like Grigory Zinoviev (real name Hirsch Apfelbaum) or Lev Kamenev (real name Lev Borisovich Rosenfeld, who also happened to be Trotsky's brother-in-law), for simply opposing Stalin's rule.

Is Stalin collaborating with Hitler in eliminating the Jews? And if the Party accuses other members of the Party of being "enemies of the people," who are the people?

OCAÑA, Saturday, 1 May 1937

This year's May Day was observed valiantly at the Penal/Hospital, with a special meal: mule meat, I think, instead of the horrific, undisguisable Russian excuse for meat, and with potatoes—harvested where?—interrupting the interminable stream of garbanzos. Franco has outlawed the holiday itself in all the areas of Spain now controlled by his murderous henchmen. Outlawing May Day: Isn't that equivalent to nullifying workers? Or at least rendering us invisible?

Tonight in the Culture Corner we viewed the Soviet motion picture *Chapaev.* A volunteer, Marika, translated the Russian dialogue as the movie played. The story is that of a leader of the Bolshevik Red Army during the Russian Civil War, Vasily Ivanovich Chapaev, a "man of the people" and war hero.

"Part of our Thirteenth International Brigade bears his name: the Chapaev Battalion," she explained. "There is even a marching song, with music by Samuel Pokrass."

I was struck by hearing many characters begin sentences with "*Nu?*" which I've always associated with Yiddish and have not heard in such a long time. It made me feel comfortable with the Russian language. The music, mostly folk tunes sung by the characters themselves, was absolutely beautiful. One particular song about a black raven lodged in my heart. After the film ended—sadly, with Chapaev, wounded in one arm, drowning in the Ural river—I asked Marika about the song, and to my great surprise and to the delight of everyone present, she sang it! She had been standing to one side of the screen, and now she stood in front of it and looked heavenward, stretched her arms upward and began, "*Chorny voron. . . .*" in a rich, low contralto voice. Even for those of us who did not understand the words, Marika's voice and gestures conveyed a feeling of conflict, longing, and ultimate surrender. With the final strains of the song, the room was hushed. A few seconds passed, and then Dr. Talamantes volunteered the fact that in medieval Spanish literature a raven flying overhead represents an evil omen. He asked Marika to explain the message of the song.

"Indeed, I think the raven in the song represents death itself. The singer at first rejects the raven but he finally tells the raven to bid farewell to his mother and to his sweetheart. His last words are, 'Black raven, I am yours.' He surrenders to the raven and to death."

At that point, María Josefa stood and hugged Marika. "We are all familiar with that surrender," she said, "though it is so difficult for us. Thank you for giving us a song about it."

We all sat in silence for a moment, and then Braulio spoke up: "Marika, what about that marching song you were telling us about?"

"Oh, yes . . . I think I can sing the chorus." Her body straightened, and she brushed aside a wisp of blond hair and began to sing, rhythmically, in a strong, clear voice that sounded as if it were coming from an entirely different person from the one who had drawn sobs from us minutes before, "*Tak pust ye krásnaya. . . .*" (I am approximating the sounds as I think I heard them.)

People began to clap, and at the end of the chorus, Eddie, an American patient with a red, curly beard who is recuperating from a fractured thigh sustained at Guadalajara, hauled himself to his feet, still wearing a heavy cast, and announced, "We of the Abraham Lincoln Battalion also sing this song." He made his way to the piano, holding on to the backs of chairs for support, sat down, swinging aside the awkward cast, and began to pound out the military chords as he blared out his version:

> Against the Hitlers, the Mussolinis
> Against the fascist enemy,
> For peace and progress,
> For truth and freedom,
> For people's true democracy!

We all cheered as Eddie continued to play the marching chords. Then Nigel, the now eyeless British boy with head still bandaged, rose and offered, "Here are the words of the British Battalion." Eddie continued to accompany as Nigel sang in his shrill tenor:

> And we will Franco—his ranks demolish;
> The great Mïaja leads us on
> And on our rifles
> Depends our freedom:
> No pasarán, no pasarán!

The whole room roared the last line as Eddie's piano repeated the phrase. Some staff and patients, including some who are forming romantic couples, remained in the room, seated on sofas, as we assisted the more severely injured patients to their beds.

Now back in my room, I admit that my pulse was somewhat stirred by the patriotic music and the May Day celebration. But now my mind returns to the raven song. I am thinking that the most difficult task for someone in the healing profession is the surrender to death. Perhaps if I think of the beautiful black raven as soaring away with the life of the patient I could not save, I will be able to surrender.

OCAÑA, *Tuesday, 1 June 1937*

Nazi Germany and Fascist Italy chose the last two days of May to demonstrate, with the murderous power of their weaponry, their refusal to adhere to the Non-Intervention Agreement. Claiming retaliation, a German battleship and four German destroyers fired on the Andalusian civilian port city of Almería in a dawn attack, and the following afternoon an Italian submarine slithered into Spanish waters and torpedoed the motorship *Ciudad de Barcelona*, sinking the ship and causing the deaths of over one hundred people.

Hitler's early-morning raid on Almería continued for over an hour and killed over fifty and injured an equal number of people. Unlike the attack on Guernica, this time the Nazis did not attempt to disguise themselves or deny their responsibility.

Mussolini's comeuppance was directed toward the *Ciudad de Barcelona*, ironically an Italian-built ocean liner, as it sailed just four hundred meters from the shore of the Catalan fishing village of Malgrat. The Italian submarine launched two torpedoes. The first one flew wide but the second one hit the engine room directly and the ship capsized within five minutes. The *Vanguardia* article states that the ship was carrying food, and the *ABC* adds other items, including trucks and sidecars, all supervised by the Non-Intervention Committee. Malgrat villagers, including fisherfolk in their small boats, rushed to the rescue but only one hundred twenty-five people, including the captain, Francisco Nadal, survived. My rage at the murder of civilians only increases.

OCAÑA, *Saturday, 5 June 1937*

The life of another bloodthirsty fascist scoundrel has reached a well-deserved end: a small airplane transporting General Mola to inflict more pain on the Basque people in Vitoria crashed into a foggy mountainside two days ago, killing him and his crew. His body was so completely destroyed that he was identified solely by the insignia on his uniform. Mola's entire career can be summarized in his Machiavellian military *credo:* to give the *impression* of domination, "while eliminating unscrupulously all those who do not think as we do." Dedicated though I am to the saving of lives, I cannot help but feel triumphant over Mola's fate, though sorry for the deaths of his innocent crew members.

OCAÑA, Saturday, 19 June 1937

Against a dismal background, the fall of Bilbao to Franco's troops, I am about to be assigned to a new hospital, a new town, and a new area: Benissa, in the province of Alicante, on the Mediterranean Sea, is opening a military hospital for the International Brigades, on the site of a Franciscan convento. It will not be a surgical hospital but a basic rehabilitation site of up to 350 beds. It has been used as a rest center for military personnel on leave and will form a part of the network of rearguard hospitals set up by the SSI.

I am scheduled to take the train on Monday, spending one night in Albacete, so today I walked to the Plaza Mayor to get my wildly overgrown hair cut. When I returned to the Penal, some of the men looked at me as if they had never seen me. Yes, the moon is nearly full, but now it is transporting me from the bars of a prison to the open climate of the Mediterranean Sea and to whatever it has in store for me.

VI

ALBACETE, Monday, 21 June 1937

The sky was fortunately overcast at about four in the morning when I descended the steps of the Penal for the last time and climbed into the unmarked ambulance, where Hermeto waited at the wheel. I looked up the steps for a last glimpse at the building, a place of punishment transformed into one of healing. I became more human in Ocaña, maybe more Spanish as well, even as I shared my blood with our soldiers. Something about this place raised morale. Even the wounded healed more quickly. The red-headed American, Eddie, played the first movement of the "Moonlight Sonata" for me late last night, miraculously drawing Beethoven's contemplative arpeggios from the battered piano. Not everyone was aware that I was leaving, and I was especially sorry not to say good-bye personally to María Josefa.

At the entrance to the train station in Madrid, heavily armed guards scrutinized our papers. They required patients to show their surgical scars, to prove their stories of returning to battle after being wounded, even though their discharge papers were in perfect order. We were finally permitted to board, and as the day awakened, so did the landscape, with the sun gradually revealing and illuminating reddish earth, silvery olive trees, and greening vines. I soon noticed a few women working in the fields and realized that they were probably replacing the men who were off to battle. I had brought along what must be the last copy of the POUM publication, *La Batalla*. Since the organization is now outlawed, at least in Catalunya, I had tucked my copy between the covers of my medical report log. One never knows who is looking over one's shoulder, and the fifth column is definitely capable of boarding a train out of Madrid.

It was night by the time I disembarked at the Albacete train station, and I noticed that all the street lights glowed bluish, making enshrouded ghosts of the elegant buildings. I stepped into an auto-ambulance provided by General

Headquarters, along with a few soldiers. Much of the road had been rerouted around gaping craters. The driver was eager to tell us about the February bombing by the Condor Legion, his voice laden with emotion.

"This was the worst part," he concluded. "As people tried to flee the city, the moon illuminated them, and the scoundrels flew low and sprayed them with machine-gun fire."

"Just like Guernica!" I cried. "But what is the purpose of the blue lighting?"

"It makes it more difficult to see the buildings."

At that point we arrived at our destination: the beautiful Gran Hotel, International Brigades headquarters, also partially equipped with a forty-bed infirmary. I was fortunately expected and did not have to wait too long to get my documents inspected and approved. The French officer explained, barely glancing up from my papers, "Tomorrow morning at eight, camarada Ernesto will come from the Auto-Park and drive you and two soldiers on to Benissa in order that they may enjoy their leave time and continue their convalescence process. You will be issued the medical leave papers for the soldiers. You may have breakfast here in the dining room. *Bonne nuit*, camarada."

I am now sitting on my small hard bed with a tiny light timidly illuminating my diary. Through the window the full moon promises more light, duplicitous though she may be. Will she choose to light the way for the enemy to come bombing yet once more?

BENISSA, *Tuesday, 22 June 1937*

I have been set down in a pine-scented, moon-splashed paradise. The journey could have lasted forever, and I would have still been content. It began at a little after eight this morning when I was sitting in the hotel dining room enjoying the last few sips of coffee—which actually tasted like coffee.

"*Kamerrada Klarra?*" a quiet deep voice inquired. At my side stood a tall man in his thirties, dressed in khaki fatigues and boots, goggles pushed up into slicked-back black hair that curled around the straps.

It was unmistakable: the "R's" were forced through the throat in a way that only a German can produce them. I smiled as I rose to my feet and put out my hand. "Clara Philipsborn. Camarada Ernesto?"

"*Sí. Errnesto* Liefmann." He smiled and briefly took my hand. His face was lean and angular, clean-shaven, gray—or green—eyes. "Let me help you with your bags."

"Don't trouble yourself," I answered in German. "I am accustomed to it."

"Ah, so you *are* German." He picked up my heavy valise and waited for me to gather the rest of my things. "I was wondering about the name."

"Yes, it is not very common. Do I detect a Hamburg accent?" The way he said *Deutsche* sounded very northern.

"Indeed, I am from Hamburg. And you? Ah, the auto is outside, just in front, in the plaza."

"Born in Kiel, but I lived in Berlin for many years."

"Ah. More northern than I, then. Oh, I will wait for you to stop by the control office to pick up the medical records for the soldiers we will be taking to Benissa."

I received the documents, and we descended the steps of the hotel. I paused to look across over the Plaza del Altozano and imagined the terror that people must still be experiencing since the deadly air raids, recalling the horrendous scene last night's driver had described. Workers—older men, mostly—were engaged in repairing the damage from the bombing and working to complete the huge underground shelter. The morning air was cool, but the sun heralded a warm day as it spilled cheerily into the plaza.

In the rear seat of the ambulance, a donation from the Scottish Ambulance Unit, sat two young men. Ernesto introduced them as David and Bernard, from England and from Palestine, respectively. I introduced myself in English as "Claire" and settled into the comfortable front seat with my large handbag in my lap. Ernesto skillfully and slowly maneuvered the vehicle past the construction workers and their equipment, and around the bomb craters. Then he turned onto the *Carretera* (Highway) *de Valencia*, which would take us to the town of Almansa, our first stop. The soldiers in the back seat were communicating in a mixture of French and English, assisted by gestures. I turned to Ernesto.

"Is 'Ernesto' a pseudonym?" I know that many Brigaders and Brigade leaders have assumed names, sort of *noms de guerre.*

"No, it's simply my name since I am here. I suppose that 'Ernesto' is the closest equivalent in Spanish of 'Ernst.'"

"Ah. I'll call you 'Ernst' then." I began using the familiar *du* form. "When did you get to Spain?"

"Only last October. I came with the Tank-Brigade, but now I am just working for the Auto-Park at Albacete. And—you?" he asked, also using the familiar form of address, somewhat hesitatingly, as he is evidently not yet accustomed to the Spanish usage taking hold since the establishment of the Republic.

"I am here since 1930. I was working in the chemistry department at the School of Medicine in Madrid when the military coup occurred. I enrolled right away in the Fifth Regiment as a nurse and translator."

"Ah, admirable! Have you already signed up at Albacete?"

"No, not really, since I'm not officially a member of a Brigade. But I'm wondering why this small town is so important to the Cause that it was chosen as the location for the headquarters. And do you know the meaning of the town name? I like to know about things like that."

"So do I." He glanced at me, smiling. "My understanding is that it is an Arabic word, like so many others that begin with 'al.' I was told that the name derives from 'al-Basit,' meaning 'the flatlands, the plains.'"

I looked out the window, and indeed there stretched out before us only great verdant carpets of agricultural fields, a few small farm buildings, and some slightly larger factories dedicated to small industry. Ernst continued to explain: "There are a few reasons why Albacete has been chosen as the headquarters."

I smiled as I waited for him to mention them, which I had the feeling he would do. His explanation of the name of the town reminded me so much of my Tío Julio and his natural tendency to enlighten that I began to feel more comfortable in his company. Ernst raised a thumb in the air as he began:

"First of all, the town is located centrally to the active fronts of the war. It is not far from the eastern ports, or Levantine ports, as they are called. And it has an airport with a concrete runway, a definite advantage. It has access to railways and highways. You see that we are now on the Carretera. And we are also in the middle of cultivated fields, which provide food for the army, though coffee and sugar are sometimes scarce."

"Yes, I have noticed that."

"One more thing about Albacete. . . ." He hesitated and lowered his voice. "There are supposedly fewer anarchists here, which puts Party officials more at ease."

I was not sure how to respond, sympathizing as I do with many anarchist views. I cleared my throat and turned to face the rear seat, as I noticed that the English soldier, David, was coughing almost constantly. "Are you all right, David?"

"Thank you. I hope to ease this cough—by spending my leave—close to the sea. Though the sea is, in a way—the reason for the cough." He paused and coughed again. "The ship I boarded at Marseille—to come to Spain—was torpedoed—and I nearly drowned."

"You were aboard the *Ciudad de Barcelona*?" I raised my voice in surprise.

"Both of us were!" He nodded toward Bernard, who showed prominent cheekbones and a mop of black hair. "I don't remember much—I think I lost consciousness—but I do remember—that some fishermen in the town of Malgrat—got me onto land—in a little boat."

"Oh, my goodness! You are both so fortunate! But are you saying that you were not the only volunteers aboard the *Ciudad de Barcelona*? The papers said that the ship was carrying food supplies and machinery, not much more."

"Quite the contrary," responded Bernard. "There were over two hundred of us. But we had to board in secret—pretend that we were French tourists."

"Yes, the French border—was sealed—because of the bloody—Non-Intervention Agreement," David said, "so we had to enter Spain by sea." He coughed and hacked and seemed short of breath, and I did not want to force him to speak.

"How about you, Bernard, how did you survive?"

"By a miracle," he answered, raising thick black eyebrows, emotion emanating from deep brown eyes. "I was luckily on the deck, and I only remember the huge explosion, and then flying across the water. I thought it was the end. I don't know how to swim. But I landed on a piece of floating wood and managed to hang on to it. I just hung on all afternoon and all that night. I could see other fellows being rescued in little boats, but I guess they didn't see me and I kept floating farther away from the shore. When it began to get light, a hydroplane somehow spotted me and swooped down. I couldn't tell if it was one of ours or one of theirs, but when they threw me a float, I just started to cry and put myself in their hands. It still feels like a dream."

"Oh, thank God it wasn't the fascists!" I exclaimed.

I looked out the window again and noticed that the landscape was evolving into something more resembling a desert or even a moonscape, reminiscent of the Insel-books of my childhood. Flat, cultivated fields gave way to hard ground and small hillocks spaced widely apart, punctuated by scrubby pine trees.

Suddenly Ernst pulled the auto off the road, braked the vehicle, and said, "Let's get out and have a look."

We all did so, and I gasped. Thrusting up into the cobalt blue sky was—a medieval castle!

"Another example of the Arabic contribution to Spain," announced Ernst.

Again, Ernst's way of explaining brought back memories of my Tío Julio and with it the promise of harmony among peoples, as Tío's explanations had done.

"The castle was built to protect the town of Almansa," he said, "where we will soon stop to refill the gasoline tank."

"Well then, I will surely feel safe and protected when we stop for gasoline," I commented, smiling up at Ernst.

"The castle is beautiful, but a castle will not stop the fascists," remarked David.

"Which is why we are all here, right?" responded Bernard, to which we all agreed.

We returned to the auto to proceed toward Almansa. I wanted to hear Ernst talk more, so I continued, in English, "And may we ask you for the origin of the town name, Comrade Ernest?"

"I am sorry to disappoint you, but scholars do not agree on the etymology. There is some dispute about the number of consonants in the Arabic root."

"Oh, similar to Hebrew," I commented, without thinking.

"And once we are in Valencian territory, you will notice many towns whose names begin with 'Ben.' I am sure you can imagine that this is a prefix before a family name. Be looking for signs of those towns and of course, Benissa itself. In this case, we have the children of Issa, whoever they were. . . ."

We stopped briefly in the charming town to replenish the gasoline and to use the bathrooms, which were surprisingly clean and well-equipped, at least the women's bathroom. I suggested to David that he buy a bottle of water to keep himself hydrated.

The journey continued through graceful plains and rolling hills, dotted with pretty little towns, almond and olive orchards, and sheep. Our next major objective would be the port city of Alicante, where we would stop to eat.

I was curious about Ernst's family and background. "Are your parents still living, Ernst?"

"My father died in 1922. He and my mother had already divorced, and he had married—a Protestant woman. My mother is still living and well, *Gott sei dank*. How about *your* parents?"

"Ach, my father died just this past January. He would probably still be alive today, at age eighty-five, if an automobile had not run him down in the streets of Berlin. He was still working, *schlepping schmatas* to some shop."

"Oh, I am so sorry." He paused. "He obviously meant very much to you."

"Oh, God, yes." I dropped my head for a moment, as the sorrow and pain at Papa's death welled up anew in my chest. Ernst put his hand on my arm and quickly withdrew it as I sighed and resumed, "My mother died of pneumonia nearly ten years ago. All my siblings are living, however, Gott sei dank, and two of them have children. I miss them so much." I tried to brighten my mood as I turned to face him. "And you? Do you have siblings?"

"Yes—my younger brother has two small children. They have emigrated to the Netherlands, where they think they will be safer." He paused for a moment and glanced at me. "Halevai."

I smiled to hear the familiar Yiddish expression after so many years.

"My sister is older than I. She converted and married a Protestant man, and they live in Heidelberg with their children," he went on. "I think they don't want to associate with the rest of the family."

"That is too bad. It is so lovely to be close to nieces and nephews, without the responsibilities of parenthood."

"Well, I hope to have children of my own someday."

This time I replied, "Halevai."

As we approached Alicante, the briny, fishy breeze blowing from the Mediterranean stirred my senses. It was going to be my first time on these shores except for the brief passage through Barcelona, and I longed to visit the sea.

"Will we actually get to the seashore?" David asked Ernst, anticipating my question and my wishes. I imagine he hoped for a positive impression, to erase the terrible ordeal he had been through.

"Unfortunately not," was the reply. "Headquarters has us assigned to a specific restaurant, close to the highway we will take to Benissa, and I will have to return to Albacete tonight, so there will be no time for us to be tourists."

What we saw of the city looked quite elegant, with beautiful buildings and tall palms. As in Albacete, we noticed workers constructing air-raid shelters under city squares. As a principal port, the city is very vulnerable, and its proximity to the seat of the government in Valencia makes it especially strategic.

The restaurant was large and nondescript, and the entrance was monitored by milicianos who examined our papers and our ration cards and inspected our vehicle before permitting us to enter the building. Once we were seated inside, Ernst explained that many of the women and children we saw were evacuees from Madrid who were now living in the Levantine city, under very poor conditions, subsidized by the government. I was glad to know that there was fresh fish available, and the two soldiers and I all agreed that we had been missing it and were looking forward to eating more of it. It was also pleasant to be served rice, and we remarked that it was good that the rice harvest was still occurring in Valencia, the rice-growing capital of Spain.

After eating and refilling the tank, we continued on the winding mountain road up the coast. Ernst anticipated my wishes to know why Benissa, a town that appeared so remote, at least from Albacete, had been chosen as a leave and convalescent center for our international soldiers. I laughed and asked him if he had been instructed to memorize these lists of factors that he communicated so readily.

"Oh, I just like doing this. This is how my mind works," he responded with a chuckle.

"We need more minds like yours. Shall I take notes?"

He laughed and again held up a thumb to begin enumerating: "So again, location, at the rear guard, sufficiently distant from the front lines. Next, the town is accessible via train, by highways, and by sea. There has been a front-line hospital there in the past. It is also in a rich agricultural area. And probably most importantly, the politics: Most of the people who live in and around the town tend to be politically on the left, socialists, though there are some holdovers from the pro-monarchic despots and the pro-Church activists who would probably like to return to power. But the SRI has a solid foothold there and there is also an active *Comité Antifascista*."

I applauded his performance, and he returned his right hand to the steering wheel with a big smile.

"I should also add that the center itself, since it is a former Franciscan monastery, is strategically located on a hilltop and is completely walled in."

"Those Franciscan brothers were not simply animal-loving pacifists," I commented. "They were also prepared for war."

"We can thank them for that," concluded Ernst. "And we are now arriving."

We approached the gate of the walls surrounding the convent-center, stopped, our papers were requested, and Ernst drove through the gate toward the center, built on sober, Renaissance lines and looking very solid and fortlike.

We gathered our equipment and entered the intake office, where I turned in the medical information for Bernard and David, and they showed their own identification. We were directed through the interior patio, where groups of men were gathered, some of them singing and playing guitars. Despite being bandaged and even with some missing limbs, most of them looked tanned and healthy and made room for the newcomers to take seats, which they did, setting down their valises.

Ernst soon appeared at my side, took my arm, and said, "Let me show you the way to the director's office, where you will be checking in. I will introduce you."

We entered the small office, probably a former monk's cell, and Ernst continued to speak German as he greeted the young man seated behind the desk, who was blond-haired and had deep-set, narrow eyes.

"Comrade Højland, salud! This is Comrade Klara Philipsborn. She has just come from Ocaña and will be looking after some of the men on leave." He pronounced the director's name in a way that brought back to me the sounds made by the many Danish-speaking people in Kiel, once part of Denmark.

"Egon Højland," responded the young man, smiling and extending his hand as he rose. He had some difficulty getting to his feet, and I realized that he had been injured.

"Salud, camarada," I began in Spanish, and then continued in German, "I am very happy to be here, and I know that the soldiers on leave are also happy to be in Benissa."

"Yes, this is the perfect location to heal and to rest from the terrible war," he responded, also in German. Then, in Spanish, he said, "Camarada Lucila, will you please show Camarada Clara to room one-seventeen?"

"I must leave now," interrupted Ernst, moving toward me. "I need to be in Albacete tonight."

"Oh, such a long journey," I replied, looking up at him. (Was that an appropriate response?)

"The full moon will guide me." He smiled. "No need to worry."

He seemed to understand how I was feeling—but how *was* I feeling? We walked out into the hallway.

"I would like to give you something that explains how my transport department fits in the organization of the Albacete base and where Benissa figures in the scheme." He pulled this paper out of his pocket and handed it to me.

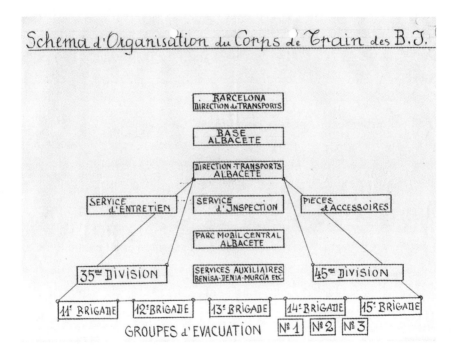

I took the paper and extended my other hand. "Thank you so much for a most enjoyable and educational ride."

He took my hand and held it for a moment, and his green eyes—yes, they were green—locked into mine. "It was truly my pleasure. It will not be my last trip here."

"Oh, I hope not." I realized that the woman called Lucila was also standing in the hallway, and I picked up my belongings as Ernst walked toward the patio, and I stood looking after him. Just before reaching the door, he turned to look back, and I quickly turned away and followed Lucila.

The room she led me to was apparently also a former monastic cell and reminded me of the room I had occupied at La Cabrera. I simply dropped all my things there without inspecting the facility and rushed outside to find a spot from which I could behold the sea and the pine-covered hillsides, splashed with moonlight. I drew in the air, fragrant with sea salt and herbs, clean, healthful. I imagined myself opening my arms and drifting upward toward the moon and then floating down to the sea, which rose to lift me and deposit me on the shore. My eyes closed and I felt the sea-green eyes of the driver from *Parc Mobil Central Albacete* shimmering against my cheeks. I cannot write anymore and will organize my belongings in the morning, but first I will tuck the little piece of paper into these pages.

BENISSA, Tuesday, 29 June 1937

A stellar way to begin the day: I was filling out a form to order medicines from the pharmacy of Jaume Giner in town when a volunteer from the main office stepped in to the supplies room. "Camarada Clara, you have a telephone call." I hurried down the hall to Comrade Egon's office, and when I picked up the receiver, the deep voice floated atop the static crackling of the telephone line:

"Buenos días, Camarada Clara"—and then, in German, "I am calling to wish you a happy birthday."

My mouth froze and I was unable to utter a single word, did not even know what language I should be speaking and could barely hold onto the receiver. "Oh . . . Comrade Ernst, thank you so much," I finally managed. "How kind of you to call."

"Not at all. Do you have plans to celebrate?"

"Oh no, there is no time." I tried to say something normal. "How are you?"

"I am also busy. How are our two brave soldiers doing?"

"Bernard and David? They have gravitated toward their respective language groups. David goes down to the beach at Calpe with his English-speaking comrades, and they play cards and splash in the water, which is only about knee-deep. Bernard exchanges a few words in Yiddish with the Polish comrades, but mostly he likes to sit in the shade and read. I took him to our little library, and he found a book of French poetry."

"What a nice thing for you to do. How lucky they are to have you!"

(What a sweet, kind thing to say!) "The patients have many things to make them happy here. Are you seeing a lot of wounded?"

"Not many. I am looking into other types of service right now. There seem to be plenty of drivers. But I hope to take a drive out to Benissa soon."

"That would be lovely. Thank you again for thinking of me."

"I have not been thinking of much else."

The connection abruptly terminated, and I put down the phone and moved outdoors into the gentle sunshine. I took a seat on a stone bench, and as my rational senses gradually returned and my heart rate normalized, something occurred to me. I realized that I must speak with Egon Højland privately.

I returned to his office and approached his desk, and addressed him in German: "Comrade Egon, I must ask you a question: How would an international volunteer know the birthdate of another volunteer?"

He looked at me for a moment, and then looked to one side. "I would say probably through some intelligence service or through the application papers, or perhaps through the Party. Is there some information that you need?"

"Ah—no, but thank you. I just need to understand the system a bit more," was my weak reply. For a few moments I had been feeling and reacting like an adolescent, and now I realized that I must assess this situation seriously. This charming young German-Jewish man, veteran of the Tank-Brigade and now a driver for the International Brigades, is interested enough in me to ascertain my birth information. Who knows what date he found—I have reported a variety of years—but whatever it was, he still felt compelled to telephone me. And he wants to see more of me. God knows I would like to see more of him!

But to return to war news, an issue of the CNT newspaper left near the wall calendar reports the alarming news that Andreu Nin, the director of the

CNT and founder of the POUM, has "disappeared," and people think he has been kidnapped by agents of Stalin. He was last seen alive on the Ramblas in Barcelona on the sixteenth of this month. Since then, all over the city, graffiti appear on walls demanding, "*On és Nin?*" (Where is Nin?). I am looking to find people from the local CNT, from whom I hope to learn more.

I was determined to get more information on the disturbing notice about Andreu Nin's supposed disappearance. So today in town—after visiting Jaume Giner's pharmacy, where I ordered pain medications and gauze—I found the Casa del Consell Municipal (City Council Building), a three-story, whitewashed structure whose balconies were draped with the colors of the Republic. The building also houses a Casa del Pueblo and the CNT. The Civil Guardsman at the door greeted me and let me in, probably because I was wearing my whites. Once inside, I asked about the CNT and was told that Councilor José Baidal, founder of the CNT in Benissa, could probably be found in an upstairs office. The office door was open and behind a desk sat a man in his mid-thirties, pounding on a typewriter. He motioned for me to take a seat, which I did. He wore a beret pulled toward one side of his head and had placed a lighted cigar in an ashtray by the typewriter. His shaggy eyebrows drew together in a frown as he engaged in a death-struggle with the innocent machine. "*Tanta paperassa* (So much paperwork)!" he growled as the type-bars jammed and he attempted to separate them, reaching inside the typewriter and struggling with the bars. On the wall I noticed a certificate from the Anti-Fascist Committee of the People's Front. Finally, he finished and greeted me in the Valencian tongue:

"*Bon dia*, Camarada."

I introduced myself in Spanish—I am just becoming accustomed to hearing *valencià* and do not yet feel comfortable using it—and then said, "I understand that you have brought the CNT to Benissa. I have been working at the Leave Center here for just a few weeks as a nurse."

"Ah, welcome." He nodded. "We are finally making good use of the Franciscan convento," he continued in a mixture of *valencià* and *castellà*, which is how the people here refer to the Spanish language. He retrieved his cigar and took a couple of puffs. The odor was not unpleasant.

I smiled and continued. "Yes. I heard recently from an article in the CNT paper that Andreu Nin has—disappeared."

He leaned forward with interest at these words.

"I hear that it is suspected to be the work of Stalin," I went on, "against the POUM and the CNT and against Trotsky. What can you tell me about it?"

"*Xe, chica*, these days more and more people who say they support the revolution and maybe quote a line from Trotsky are being accused of the worst—of being fascists."

I sighed and shook my head. (It was just as I feared.) "Ah, now I think I have a little better understanding of what happened in Barcelona in May."

"*Això mateix!*" Baidal affirmed. "Nothing pleases Franco's hard little heart more than to see the left fighting the left."

"So every time I hear someone saying that winning the war is the most important goal, I can think of that person as—"

"A potential enemy," he declared, finishing the dreaded thought for me as he sat back in his chair.

My stomach lurched and I looked down, still shaking my head. "This means that I—we—need to be very careful of what we say. *Gracies,* camarada," I managed—my first attempt at the local language. I rose to my feet and put out my hand, which he shook warmly after laying his cigar in the ashtray once again.

Now back at the center, the needs of the patients are reclaiming my attention, but I'm looking at everyone with slightly more open eyes—or at least I hope that my mind is a bit more open since my conversation with the cigar-puffing Councilor of Benissa.

BENISSA, *Thursday, 5 August 1937*

The oddly-shaped ambulance pulled up in front of the gates of the convento at about noon, papers were presented, and the vehicle was admitted to hospital grounds. I was standing in a shaded doorway with a volunteer and a patient, my heart hopping somewhere between my stomach and my mouth. The driver's side was facing away from me, so I had to wait even longer as he walked around the front of the auto to open the side doors, looking about as he did so, and smiling as he spotted me. An orderly and the volunteer Héctor began to assist the passengers—two of them strapped to stretchers and two in seats—in descending. Once he saw that the patients were attended to, Ernst walked toward me, and I somehow met him halfway, grateful to my buttery legs for propelling me there. We grasped each other's hands and smiled broadly and deeply into each other's eyes, uttering not a word.

"*Guten tag,*" greeted one of the passengers, interrupting the spell as he walked unsteadily from the ambulance, clutching the arm of the orderly. He was wearing fatigues with the insignia of a lieutenant sewn onto the shirt: two stripes and a red star. "I am told that I will be in good hands here with you, Camarada Klara. Right now, a warm bath and a comfortable bed will begin my healing regimen." He continued on slowly through the entry door and Ernst explained:

"You have just met Teniente-Comisario Hermann Mayer. He has fought on the fronts of Madrid, Jarama, Guadalajara, and most recently, Brunete, where he picked up a case of typhus."

"Oh, no!" I cried. "Conditions must have been filthy there. We have been keeping the hospital here clean and free of lice and promoting good hygiene. Teniente Mayer will probably have to be kept isolated," I went on, addressing the volunteer at my side, "and those who care for him must be sure to scrub thoroughly."

The two men who had come in on stretchers were placed on gurneys and wheeled in to their assigned beds. One had an amputated leg, and the other had an arm in a cast up to the shoulder and extending before him. I noted the telltale foul odor indicating that the "Spanish method" for compound fractures was in place, and I was not looking forward to being in close company with him.

"I am going to take care of the papers in the office," said Ernst, putting a hand on my arm, "and then I have some time before I leave for Albacete. Do you have some free moments to take a drive to the beach?"

"Ah, I will see if I can be relieved, and I will wait for you right here." I was not due for a break, so I enlisted Meta Müller, another nurse from Germany, by telling her that I would fill in for her tonight. I peeled off my whites, changed into alpargatas, splashed some water and cologne on my neck and arms, and stepped into the patio just as Ernst emerged from the north wing.

He had obviously never seen me in civilian clothes, and he hesitated a moment, his mouth forming a little "O!" I smiled at his response and headed toward the ambulance, which was fortunately parked in the shade of a palm tree.

"What sort of vehicle is this?" I asked Ernst as he started the motor and put the vehicle in gear. "It is shaped like my little dachshund, Lumpi!"

"Ha!" he chuckled. "It was donated to the Central Sanitaria Internacional (International Health Center) by New Zealand's Spanish Medical Aid Committee."

"Wonderful! Our bus was donated by the Spain-India Aid Committee, and I thought that was as exotic as we could get. So where is this New Zealand doggie taking us?"

"Have you been to Cala Els Pinets?"

"No, we usually take the patients to Calp, on the bus, which lets us off right at the beach."

"Well, Cala Pinets is closer but not as accessible. We will have to park at a distance, but I think you are capable of a little challenge."

"Ah, now I am intrigued. I hope the challenge is not too great."

"I will be with you if it is."

I had already begun to trust Ernst, and with that statement I relaxed in my seat, at the same time feeling drawn to his way of speaking and aroused by the responses of my body when near him. After about fifteen minutes of winding roads he pulled the auto over to a wide spot, and we got out. Across the way was what looked like a sheer drop to the Mediterranean. Once we had crossed to the other side, the challenge became obvious: a steep, narrow path twisted down around sharp-looking boulders and spindly pines before finally opening out to a tiny cove of blue-green water flanked by a pebble-covered beach.

I tightened the straps of my alpargatas as Ernst pulled a woolen blanket from the ambulance.

"I will go first, in case you slip," he said, reaching out a hand to me. Then, in a sort of sidelong scrabbling plunge accomplished with a lot of laughing and quite a bit of sliding, we reached the bottom in a cloud of dusty pebbles, both of us remaining upright.

"Are you all right?" he asked, still holding my hand.

"Of course! And now what?"

"How about this?" he asked softly, dropping the blanket and taking my other hand as he kissed me gently on the lips, for which I was more than ready. (Take it slowly, Klara!) I pulled away a bit and spread the blanket at the edge of the water. He drew off his boots, sat down on the blanket and put his feet in the water. It looked so inviting that I also untied my alpargatas and tossed them behind me, joining him on the blanket. The water was quite warm and lapped softly against my feet.

"I am so unused to the fact that there are no high tides," I remarked. "If this were the North Sea, this might be the hour when we would have to fly up the path or be swept away."

"That is true. But if I had to be swept away, I hope it would be with you, Klara."

I turned my face toward him, and we kissed again, this time for a long moment. He began caressing my feet as we looked out to sea at the shifting spectrum as it played from green to blue and back again. I slid my arm across his shoulders and played with his hair, which had grown a bit since the last time I saw him and curled around my fingers. I wanted to have him right there—we were alone, and it felt so right, but the pebbles had other plans and were beginning to make their presence felt sharply through the blanket.

Finally, it became too uncomfortable to remain seated and I stood up and stretched. Ernst stood and took my hands again.

"Klara, I want to take you back with me to Albacete the next time I come. Would you like that, and would you be able to get away?"

"Oh, yes," was all I could reply before backing away and adding, "but we had better start flying up that path. Gravity will not be in our favor this time."

We separated and dried our feet on the blanket and put on our footwear.

"This time you go first," he suggested. "If you slip I will catch you."

Halfway up the path I did slip and scraped my knee against a rock and cried out, "Ay!" I quickly recovered my footing despite the bleeding and the pain, and we completed the climb uneventfully. I took advantage of the kit in the ambulance to pour some hydrogen peroxide over the scrape and bandage it. All the way back to the convento-hospital, Ernst kept asking me "Are you all right?" I felt a caring that I had never known from a man, and it warmed my body and even lessened the pain.

We pulled into the parking area of the hospital, and after Ernst switched off the engine, he cleared his throat and asked, "Would you like to have a copy of a recent *Solidaridad Obrera*?"

"Oh, yes, I would." I did not expect such an offer. Is this an indication of his political views? I wondered. *SO* is definitely pro-Trotsky.

He reached into the pocket of the jacket that was hanging on the back of his seat, pulled out a plain envelope, and handed it to me. *He must trust me enough*, I thought. I so want to trust him.

I took the envelope, and we both got out of the vehicle. I wanted badly to kiss him again, but it was not possible, as he had to leave immediately for Albacete.

So I am on duty tonight, working Meta's shift, which is fine because I know I will not be able to sleep. I am with the new patient, Hermann Mayer, who is running a fever with a headache, which I am trying to calm. He has been thoroughly bathed and is gradually replacing the fluids he lost from vomiting and diarrhea, but the illness could still progress to the lungs. We are doing everything to save him from the horrible phases of typhus that lead to the end. He is sleeping now so I am able to write in my diary. His breathing is fitful, but I am calmed with the presence in my head of the blue-green swirl of the Mediterranean Sea and the kiss of promise that it witnessed.

BENISSA, *Friday, 6 August 1937*

Today I worked a double shift. After the night shift that I had filled in for Meta, I accompanied some convalescing German and Austrian soldiers to Calp, a lovely beach. We were taken in the roomy bus, and the "boys" brought playing cards from various regions and even a portable phonograph, a bottle of wine, bread, and cheese. There was no need to scramble down or clamber up a rocky embankment. The water was shallow and calm. I took the bandage off my knee for a while, but the salt water stung the wound, so I just sat in the sun and enjoyed a few rare moments of sunbathing while listening to fox-trots and tangos. I already miss Ernst. It feels like I am actually embarking on a relationship. I do hope that we agree politically, and the fact that he has given me a copy of *Solidaridad Obrera* bodes very well. How we might get on sexually, who knows, but he is so gentle and caring and intelligent that I am ready to try. So much can happen during wartime, so I am trying to enjoy each day, even the days I do not see him. It feels natural to be with him, almost like a brother—not that Artur and I ever had such a friendly relationship.

Our center for soldiers on leave is being converted to a full-fledged hospital and will have medical directors along with the administrative personnel. We will be extremely busy readying the convento to take on around 150 patients a day, some of them from nearby Dénia, which cannot accommodate any more patients. We will not be performing surgery as it will not be a field hospital but one of general treatment and convalescence. I am looking forward to this new status, as it is almost too easy simply to accompany the guitar-strumming and card-playing boys on leave before they return to risk their lives for democracy and progress. Comrade Mayer is a bit less feverish and may be recovering from the typhus. He will probably assume an administrative role once he feels completely well.

BENISSA, *Sunday, 22 August 1937*

I have had to wait until last night's appearance of the full moon and an automotive *panne* in order to consummate what I have been longing for since I heard those German R's uttering my name just two months ago in the dining room of the Gran Hotel in Albacete. In the transition process from leave center to hospital, Ernst had been bringing in busloads of patients and then needing to leave almost immediately. Furtive kisses in corridors, clasping of hands, and *adieu!* But yesterday afternoon he drove into the patio with whitish smoke pouring out of the exhaust of poor Lumpi, the name I have given the dachshund-shaped ambulance donated to our *Causa*. As soon as the patients were accommodated, Ernst rushed to the administrative office to see if there was a mechanic available. Unfortunately—fortunately for me—none would be available until today. Comrade Mayer did his best to search for help, to no avail. The solution:

"Comrade Liefmann will have to spend the night in the hospital until his vehicle has been restored to an adequate condition to return to Albacete. He may take a room in the wing of the soldiers on leave, in order to avoid patients who are contagious."

Ernst conveyed all this information to us in the dining room of the hospital, over a more delicious and varied than usual paella. I immediately knew what to do: I pulled a page from the little notepad that we use for ordering medications and wrote "Z-117"—the number of my room. As we left the dining room, I slipped it into his hand with a conspiratorial squeeze.

I had again been scheduled for the night shift, but persuaded two volunteers to replace me, claiming a headache. I bathed, shampooed my hair, applied generous drops of jasmine oil behind my ears and in the hollows of my arms and legs, and slid into bed at around eleven. By midnight the full moon had begun to send her furtive spies through my window when my door quietly opened. I sat up against the wall and pulled the sheet down, inviting the moonlight to reveal my body. He pulled the door closed and, whispering my name, began to take off his clothing. He extracted something from his pocket.

"Preservativo?" I whispered hoarsely.

"Yes!"

"Thank you," I whispered again and drew the sheet completely away as he knelt beside me on the bed, caressing my breasts and kissing my mouth. I rolled onto my back and pulled him to me, unable to wait any longer. Our lovemaking began gently and deliberately, but soon we lost control, and I had to force myself not to scream out, as my moans and my cries would have soared out of my window and across the patio to patients and staff, even to the collaborating moon. We finally collapsed, amid sobbing and gasping.

I woke alone with the first light—had not heard him leave. I know I did not dream it. When I was about to enter the office of the new Chief Medical Officer, Ernst passed by in the hallway and touched my back. I turned and said, "Good morning, Camarada Ernesto. Did you find someone to fix Lumpi?"

"Yes, someone is coming to replace the gasket, which had blown. I will be able to leave soon." Then, in a lower voice, moving closer, "But I wish I could make another break in it."

"Oh, I would not want you to injure your gasket," I remarked, placing a hand on his cheek, which bristled with a day-old beard. "Perhaps the next time you could bring more gaskets."

He took my hand and kissed it. "I will be saving all my gaskets for the next trip to Benissa."

"I look forward to it. 'Til next time, camarada." I hurried into the office to avoid doing something foolish, and Ernst continued walking toward the door.

So now that we are a hospital (Hospital Number Ten), we have a Chief Medical Officer. His name is Leo Samet and he is a young (not quite twenty-nine) doctor from Poland. Jewish. Studied medicine in Prague and came to Spain only in January as an emergency paramedic. He was injured at the battle of Brunete and I think his post here in Benissa is part of his recovery. His Spanish is very limited, and I have resorted to Yiddish, or what I manage to express in Yiddish, to communicate with him. He had called me in to his office today to ask about the status of Hermann Mayer's typhus, which seems to be in remission:

"*Vos hat ir geton tsu heyln Khaver Hermann fun di tifus* (What did you do to cure Comrade Hermann of the typhus)?" he asked, placing a pad of paper before him to note down any miracle I might have performed. He asked this in an earnest tone, raising his eyebrows and peering at me above his glasses.

"*Ikh hub gurnisht geton* (I didn't do anything)," I replied, truthfully, "just kept him clean, hydrated, and isolated. I think that he must have entered the battlefield in a very healthy condition, in his favor when he fell ill."

"Well, whatever you have done, I hope you can keep doing it," he concluded. "Good work, camarada Klara."

I left his office pleased and sailed through today's routine, also hoping that I can indeed keep doing what I have been doing, especially what I did last night.

ALBACETE, *Friday, 10 September 1937*

I am writing these words in my diary, which is open in my lap, in the lobby of the elegant Hotel Regina, waiting to return to Benissa after twenty-four hours of bliss. But I shall save the details for later.

We have a new doctor-nurse team at Benissa: Dr. Hugo K. and his wife Dina, both from Austria. Dr. K. also arrived as a typhus patient—he probably picked up the disease in Málaga, where he was working with the Thirteenth International Brigade. Comrade Leo Samet introduced us and described me to Hugo as an expert at curing typhus, which I vehemently denied. Hugo and Dina came to us from Murcia, whose hospital housed many refugees, many of whom had typhus and typhoid fever. They both seem like charming, delightful people, and I look forward to knowing them better.

And good news came in the form of a twenty-four-hour leave granted me by Comrade Leo and the administrative office. Ernst was due to bring in patients from Albacete yesterday around noon. Egon informed me that I should take advantage of Ernst's return trip and my free day in order to determine which patients now located in Albacete should be brought to Benissa. I had to restrain myself from displaying the glee with which I received that notice from Comrade Egon.

Lumpi rolled smoothly into the patio at around ten thirty, exhibiting no signs of its earlier troubles and shooting out no visible exhaust. I escorted the new patients to the medical office to be registered, and Ernst reported to Administration. I was eager to see how he would respond to Egon's plan. I waited in the hallway after orderlies had taken patients to their rooms. As he emerged from the administrative office, he looked around until he spotted me and walked toward me, smiling. I met him in the middle, grasped his arm, and simply said, "I am just going to pack a bag."

"The nights are getting chilly in La Mancha," he warned, still smiling.

"I am not worried about that." I hurried off to gather my things.

By eleven thirty we were aboard the ambulance. We got the gasoline tank and the radiator filled in Alicante and began the northwesterly journey toward Albacete and the Castilian *meseta* (plateau). Our conversation was awkward at first, focusing on the landscape. The terrain began to look brown and bare in comparison with the fertile green Mediterranean hillsides. I decided to talk about the new medical team:

"We have a new medical couple at the hospital, Hugo and Dina, both from Vienna. They seem very nice."

"Ah yes, I think I know who you are talking about," he responded. "The K's. Backgrounds very different. Dina's family was very poor. Father sickly."

"But Ernst, how do you know all this?"

He fell silent for a moment, then put his hand on my leg. (Electricity through my body!) "All right . . . I think I can tell you . . . I am now a driver for the SIM, the *Servicio de Inteligencia Militar* (Military Intelligence Service). The Service was declared official early in August by Indalecio Prieto, the Minister of National Defense."

I turned in the seat to look at Ernst, who suddenly appeared to me as a different person.

"The SIM was recruiting and screening new members, and they especially wanted Germans. I was already being trained for the SIM back in June. They thought I would be in an ideal position as a driver from Albacete. And I took advantage of my contacts in the Service to find everything I could about you. I knew you were from Germany, but I wanted to make sure that you were not from the Gestapo."

"Oh, so is that how you knew when my birthday was?"

"Ah, yes."

The thought of Ernst being involved in espionage added a curtain of mystery that intensified my desire for him.

"What is the purpose of the SIM?" I asked.

"It is mainly to keep watch over the internationals in Spain. Prieto is suspicious of the rivalry among some of the international groups. He is also hunting for 'fifth columnists' and even looking for Soviet agents."

"So do you think I am a fifth columnist or a Soviet agent, Ernst?"

"Oh, Klara, no, no!" he responded. "But I am beginning to be suspicious of the Service itself. Scarcely a month old, they are already starting to mention Trotskyites and anarchists as possible 'enemies.'"

I recalled my conversation with José Baidal, and my throat tightened before I asked him the essential question:

"Ernst, do you think that it is more important to win the war or to accomplish the revolution?"

He hesitated a moment as he maneuvered a mountain curve: "I think that in order to really 'win' the war we must fulfill the ideological phase; in other words, win the hearts and minds of the people. So much more important than the military victory. What do you think?"

"I agree completely!" I almost shouted, feeling overjoyed that he had passed some sort of test.

We both fell silent for a while, and I enjoyed looking out of the window at the crops that were ready to be harvested, especially the grapes, hanging heavy and promising on the vines. As two o'clock approached, I was starting to feel hungry. Ernst must have anticipated my wishes, and suggested, "Let's stop to eat in Almansa. Do you remember the castle?"

"I do, and I would like to have a better look at it if possible."

We entered the town and drove toward the castle until we found a suitable-looking restaurant that advertised "*Comida típica manchega.*" I pulled a white gown out of my bag and put it on over my dress but kept my alpargatas on. The interior of the restaurant was simple but charming, and I noticed first that the bathroom was *anständig*, as dear Mama would have said (clean and decent), my main criterion for eating anywhere.

A teenaged boy, younger than military age, approached our table and recited the brief menu. We both decided to order a *pisto manchego* (vegetable stew of La Mancha) and the lamb chops *a la brasa* (olivewood-grilled) sounded delicious.

"Would you like to try our local *garnacha*?" the boy asked. "It has won prizes."

"That sounds wonderful," I said. "When is the grape harvest? Those grapes look as if they are saying, 'Pick us! Pick us!'"

"The harvest is next week," he answered, his slightly pockmarked face brightening. "My sisters and I will be picking too."

The boy returned in a moment with an unlabeled bottle, saying, "Gift of the house. You are internationals, right?"

"Yes, indeed," responded Ernst, "but we do not need any gifts. It is a gift for us to join with the Spanish people in your fight against fascism."

The boy thanked us and left the wine. Ernst poured some in each of our glasses, and it gurgled musically as it exited the confines of the bottle. The color was a deep, purplish red, and if deep purplish red has a flavor, this wine had it: dark, rich, mature, fragrant, serious. The boy soon returned with two individual red clay dishes (made from the Castilian soil, evidently) each filled with a rainbow of stewed vegetables: the pisto manchego. The flavors had amalgamated somewhat, but I was still able to note two kinds of sweet pepper, green and red, eggplant, tomatoes, courgettes, onions, and garlic.

Dipping bread into the mixture enhanced the experience, both in taste and texture.

"I think I could eat just this forever," I remarked, as I pushed the half-eaten dish aside to take another sip of wine.

"Smell that lamb grilling?" asked Ernst. "I am going to enjoy that maybe even more than the pisto."

With that the lamb chops made their entrance, perfectly grilled and seasoned, and I was glad that I hadn't eaten more of the pisto. We had slowed down the eating pace when the cook, a man of about sixty, emerged from the kitchen, wiping his hands on his apron. His gray hair bristled out from each side of his head.

"Did you enjoy the food, camaradas? And how about our garnacha? It is the high climate that produces the finest wines."

I nodded. "We certainly did enjoy the food and are still enjoying your garnacha."

He came closer to the table. "Permit me to show you why you are so welcome here. My name is José Ramón Fernández, and this is my grandson Gregorio." He squeezed the boy's shoulder and pulled a newspaper clipping out of his apron pocket as he continued, "This article came out in yesterday's *Defensor de Albacete*. It reports that members of the International Brigades have acknowledged the children of the soldiers of our town, Almansa, who have given their lives to defend the Republic."

He laid the clipping on the table between us. I pointed out the words as I read aloud—"We give thanks to the brave internationals for this proof of their love toward our children who are grieving over the loss of their parents—a proof that is lovingly recognized by the anti-fascists of the world"—and immediately burst into tears. Ernst put his arm around me, and José Ramón patted my shoulder.

"Please keep the clipping as this gift of thanks from Almansa to you, camaradas. And there is no charge for today's meal."

I have gratefully kept the clipping. Tears are springing into my eyes at this new reminder of the generous spirit and the sacrifice of the Spanish people.

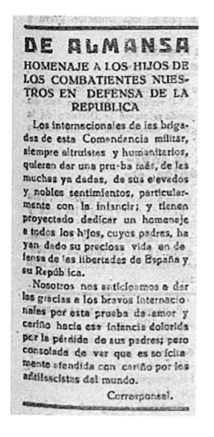

DE ALMANSA

HOMENAJE A LOS HIJOS DE LOS COMBATIENTES NUESTROS EN DEFENSA DE LA REPUBLICA

Los internacionales de les brigadas de esta Comandancia militar, siempre altruistas y humanitarios, quieren dar una prueba más, de las muchas ya dadas, de sus elevados y nobles sentimientos, particularmente con la infancia; y tienen proyectado dedicar un homenaje a todos los hijos, cuyos padres, han yan dado su preciosa vida en defensa de las libertades de España y su República.

Nosotros nos anticipamos a dar las gracias a los bravos Internacionales por esta prueba de amor y cariño hacia esa infancia dolorida por la pérdida de sus padres; pero consolada de ver que es solícitamente atendida con cariño por los antifascistas del mundo.

Corresponsal.

We returned to the bathrooms, and I splashed cold water on my tear-streaked face and rinsed my mouth, and on exiting the bathroom I noticed that Ernst was slipping a bill under one of the plates. I quickly did the same, and then we left the restaurant in silence. I took off my white gown and tossed it into the back seat as we climbed back into the ambulance.

"I think it is time for a siesta after this meal and these emotions," I suggested, "and you must be ready for some rest after having done so much driving today."

"Indeed, let us find a place in the shade of the castle." We drove to the eastern side of the looming stronghold to the end of a little side road that was completely tree-shaded, rolled down the windows to let in the cool breeze and moved to the back seat. We immediately put our arms around each other and began kissing, gratefully and tenderly. Our caresses became more urgent until we had satisfied each other, after which we sank into a sweet sleep.

"Do we know where we are staying tonight?" I asked once we had awakened and returned to the road.

"I think the Hotel Regina would be the best, right on the Paseo de la República. It is mostly used by the air squadrons. I have to return the ambulance to the Auto-Park, so you can go and register, and I will come back after leaving the vehicle and picking up a few things from my room. Can you wait for me in the bar?"

"I hope it will be all right to wait in the bar. How modern is Albacete?" Some bars in Spain are still off-limits to women, and though progress has been made since the institution of the Second Republic, I am never sure how smaller towns regard "free" women.

"You will be fine, I am sure. I will find you, no matter where you are."

We pulled up in front of the hotel, its balustrades eerily illuminated by the protective blue lights of Albacete. Not as ornate as the Gran Hotel, the Regina is elegant, modern and classical at the same time, if possible.

"Oh, I didn't expect anything so beautiful!" I exclaimed.

Ernst chuckled, retorting, "Those were exactly my thoughts when I met you."

I squeezed his arm, laughing; then I slipped on my white gown, climbed down from the ambulance, gathered my bag, and closed the auto door behind me. The thin cotton gown kept me from the cooling air of the meseta as I approached the hotel. Two men in uniforms held the heavy, bronze door of the hotel open for me, and I thanked them and made for the front desk which was attended by an elderly woman wearing thick glasses. I could not identify her accent. I presented my documents and requested a room for the night, telling her, "I am going to be meeting—a friend. Is there someplace we might sit and order some tea?"

"You may wait in the bar," she replied, handing me a key to a room on the second floor (which the Spanish call *el primer piso*). "There are small tables suitable for women, and I am sure you can order tea there."

Suitable for women? I repeated silently, thinking, We are not free yet! But all I said was, "Oh, thank you, camarada," and I was indeed genuinely grateful that I had passed this small barrier.

I walked through the lobby toward the mahogany staircase, brushing past fragments of conversations in several languages. I climbed the stairs to the second floor and opened the door to Room 108. The room was not very large, with a double bed, an armoire, a night stand with a basin and a pitcher, and a bedside table with a small lamp. A couple of chairs and a small desk. I lowered the heavy wooden blinds and switched the lamp on, and it glowed amber-hued. Then I entered the bathroom, ran some water in the sink, and combed my hair with my wet hands, allowing it to spring to life. Back in the room, I opened my bag and pulled out a dark red or maroon dress, whose rich color resembled the garnacha wine we had enjoyed earlier. I put the dress on and in the slightly tarnished mirror of the armoire, I observed quite a bit of décolleté. *Clarita!* I daubed a drop of jasmine oil between my breasts and threw a light woven silk shawl over my shoulders. I left the lamp lit, took the copy of Agatha Christie's *Murder in Mesopotamia* that I had borrowed from the hospital library at Benissa, locked the door, dropped the key into my pocketbook and headed down the stairs.

The bar was just to the right of the lobby, and there were indeed small round tables in the main area. At the actual bar, men were seated on stools, many of them in military uniforms and most of them speaking French and smoking. I took a seat at a table from which I could see the door and was soon approached by a plumpish young woman with straight black hair and very white skin. "*¿Qué ba tomá, camará?*" she asked—Andalusian accent.

I ordered some tea with milk, opened the book, and began to read. The pot of tea soon arrived, along with a cup emblazoned with the name of the hotel. The milk in the silver pitcher was condensed, as fresh milk is reserved for children and for hospital patients, but it nevertheless added a rich flavor to the tea. After about twenty minutes, Ernst entered the room. He was dressed in civilian clothes and wearing a beret, and he carried a small valise. *A man that handsome is looking for* me? I thought, feeling beautiful myself and important. I straightened my body and leaned back a bit in my chair. He looked around the room, and I reached out a hand toward him as he spotted me and took the seat opposite mine.

"That tea looks good," he said, "but I am going to order something more . . . serious."

The young woman soon approached: "For the *señó*?"

"A cognac, please. May I have a Caballero*?*"

"Yes, of course."

Ernst glanced at my book: "What are you reading?"

"A mystery," I responded. "And I suspect that I am becoming a part of your mystery. Do you plan to investigate me and report me to the SIM?" I laughed. I closed the book to look at him. He was staring at my breasts.

"Only if you promise to investigate me," he replied, leaning over the table toward me. The cognac arrived, and he inhaled its vapors before swirling it in the glass and sipping it. "And God knows I would like to be investigating you tonight."

"Be careful of what you might find in your investigation," I warned mockingly.

"The first thing I will investigate is that dress," he murmured, setting down his glass. "It is the color of the wine we drank today. You look delicious—I would love to taste you."

I smiled. "Do you recognize anyone in this hotel?"

"I don't think so. They are mostly French aviators, the squadron organized by André Malraux. Their dominion is the air—mine is the land."

"Oh, Malraux, the writer. I have never read his books. And I am also earthbound."

Ernst drained his glass. "And how far from Planet Earth is the room you reserved for us tonight?"

I simply looked toward the staircase, gathered my handbag, and stood up. Ernst pulled a bill out of his pocket and left it on the table. We walked in silence toward the stairs and to the second floor. The room glowed golden, softly illuminated by the little lamp. I used the bathroom first and took off my underwear, without taking off my dress.

Ernst used the bathroom next, and soon emerged holding in his hand the little package containing a contraceptive *preservativo*, which he set down on the bedside table. He then lay down on the bed on his back, hands clasped behind his head, and asked playfully, "Will you please investigate me now, Camarada Clara, in your *garnacha* dress?"

The dress stayed on me while Ernst investigated me, tasted me, and allowed me to crown him with the convenient *preservativo* as we discovered new pleasures before finally creeping under the blankets for a light, tender sleep.

Morning sounds woke us, the percussive din from the streets. Workers rebuilding their city after the bombings. We stretched and opened the blinds, revealing delivery vehicles and women carrying baskets. Ernst explained his next assignment: "I must pick up some soldiers from the training base at Tarazona and take them to Benissa for a few days' leave. Why don't you relax here at the hotel, and I will pick you up on the way to Benissa?"

"That sounds perfect."

We finally descended to the lobby, showered and dressed. A cup of café con leche sits on my table as Ernst has departed for Tarazona, while now I fill these pages with an account of my twenty-four hours of delight.

BENISSA, *Saturday, 23 October 1937*

It was not even necessary to wait for someone to post it to the "wall newspapers." The disaster is on everyone's lips: Franco and the IV Brigade of Navarra have moved into the last Republican strongholds of Avilés and Gijón. Asturias, valiant, brave Asturias, after nearly five hundred days of resistance, has finally fallen, and with it, the Northern Front. I have such tender feelings about Asturias, without ever having been there. Perhaps it is because of María Josefa of the Ocaña Penal, who taught me so much about humanism and humanity, or possibly even our Madrid sereno, Antón, who helped me to understand the plight of the miners.

The ominous news was delivered yesterday afternoon by Commissar

Hermann Mayer at a general gathering at the hospital, also attended by Ernst, whom I had not seen since my twenty-four hour leave over a month ago. We sat close together, and I longed to bring him to my room, but he had to return almost immediately to Albacete. I say "ominous" because of Hermann's comment:

"Now that the northern phase of the uprising has been completed, Franco can now turn toward advancing on—the Mediterranean." He paused to allow that phrase to sink in. That is *us*! I grasped Ernst's arm at that chilling statement, and he put his hand over mine. I felt his protection, but who will protect us all against the constant march of Franco, with his superior firepower and his host of Nazis and Italian fascists?

Today's issue of *Solidaridad Obrera* carried a report on the visit of President Companys of the *Generalitat* of Catalunya and his associates to Madrid, together with President Negrín and his entourage from Valencia. They arrived in the early hours and were received by military and political brass. Both presidents delivered radio speeches, lauding the broken and starved Madrid in its resistance to the enemy and declaring it the "spiritual capital of Spain." I just wonder what is behind this move. Perhaps this excerpt from the Catalan president's speech is an indication: "We must hit hard in the rear guard, strengthening its virtues and completely eradicating differences and disagreements . . . There is but one way to attain peace: by winning the war."

It makes me feel ill to consider the possible meaning of these statements: The loss of the Northern Front forces us to concentrate on local conditions, and the discord that now characterizes the local "rear guard" (the left—again, that is *us*) must be eliminated. Another way of interpreting the speech is that the very discord on the left is what has caused the loss at the front. And the last phrase, given either one of the meanings of the first phrase, is therefore an impossibility. The revolution has obviously not been attained. It certainly has not been possible to eliminate the discord on the left, which grows stronger and deadlier. I am feeling endangered myself, along with my like-minded comrades: *On és Nin?* My words will remain with me on these pages or be destroyed.

BENISSA, *Thursday, 28 October 1937*

Another shift in the order of things: the Spanish government is moving its seat from Valencia to Barcelona. This in the midst of a torrential rainstorm and rising rivers, as the enemy pushes eastward through Aragón. With the move, the government hopes to be able to utilize the war industry still standing in Catalunya. Franco's campaign has gained important arms factories in the Basque region and of course in Asturias.

In my personal and professional life comes a change I am looking forward to: on Saturday I am going to be registering at Albacete and establishing residence there, still as a part of the SSI system. My role will be expanded, as I will be translating for some of the doctors and also teaching some Spanish classes.

I am also looking forward to the trip to Albacete, in an ambulance carrying soldiers returning to base from leave and a couple of colleagues, with my lover at the wheel. But I will miss the mild Mediterranean climate, especially as winter approaches.

VII

ALBACETE, *Saturday, 30 October 1937*

I did not think I would be happy to be part of any governmental system, particularly one engaged in warfare, but I have been made to feel welcome and appreciated here, having just arrived. Dr. Oskar Telge himself, the Chief Medical Officer, welcomed the "new generation" of workers. He is tall and pale, with high cheekbones and a rather pointed nose, and spoke in a fairly relaxed manner, considering his many responsibilities and the petty rivalries I hear about between Spanish and international officials. He offered a working definition of the SSI as an "anti-fascist organization active from the front to the rear guard, and an expression of international solidarity, particularly that of doctors, with the Spanish people."

I will be working in the main *Ambulatorio* (out-patient clinic) two to three days per week, alternating with duty in the base hospital, which will add a couple of pesetas to my salary. I am sharing a room with Meta Müller, and we are housed in a sort of barracks at the bullring, built in the "Moorish" style of Madrid's Las Ventas. Ernst and I have not been able to enjoy any time alone. He dropped me off last when bringing the soldiers back to base, and we were able to do no more than hug and kiss briefly. Though I am already very busy, I long for more intimate moments with him.

ALBACETE, *Friday, 12 November 1937*

I am finally back in Albacete after five days' sick leave. A combination of the unheated rooms in our barracks, walking through the streets to the office and to the hospital in the icy windy weather, and contact with ill patients, quickly sparked respiratory infections both in me and later in Meta. When I developed a high fever and a hacking cough, I thought of Mama and how easily respiratory infections developed into pneumonia with her, and I realized that I was too weak to work. Fortunately, I was assigned on Tuesday of last week to the hospital at Benissa, where I was transported along with a wounded Greek soldier. Equally fortunate was the fact that it was Ernst who drove us there, though we two patients rode in the rear of the ambulance, equipped with a steam-delivering device that brought much relief. I was reminded of the steam treatment dear Tío Julio and Asun prepared for Mama in Seville, and I slept during most of the trip, calmed by healing steam and pleasant thoughts.

What a delight to be once more on the shores of the Mediterranean! Its warmer nights and pine-scented air brought relief to my lungs. I arrived there on November 2 and noticed immediately that Dina, the wife of Hugo K., is about six months pregnant. Her skin glowed, and she looked healthier than she had when I last saw her.

"Dina, you are very brave to have a baby in these times," I began.

"Yes, you probably think I am crazy, but I told Hugo, 'In case something happens to you, I want to have your baby.'"

I tried to imagine what that was like and thought that she must love him very much. Do I feel that way about Ernst? I am really not sure.

My barracks-mate Meta was admitted at Benissa on November 5, with quite a few others, both ill and wounded. As we all began to recover, we celebrated with a musical performance using instruments donated to the hospital (guitars, a piano, and a violin). I do not find words to describe the collectively composed polyglot *opera buffa* created by the Belgian, German, Greek, and American patients, but it brought laughter to the staff and to the other patients and probably hastened our own healing. What ensured my recovery was the fact that Ernst arrived at Benissa on November 7, too late to return to Albacete but in time to be warmly—or, better said, hotly—received by me all night in my room on the last opportunity before returning to these shared chilly bullring quarters.

Here is the official list of those hospitalized just in the past month, my name included:

ALBACETE, *Thursday, 9 December 1937*

I am feeling more comfortable in Albacete. A recent article in *El Defensor* referred to the town as "the Babel of La Mancha," and I think that is probably one of the aspects that make me feel most at home. As an example of the linguistic mix, in hospitals and even at training grounds and in surgery, the lingua franca for many of the internationals is Yiddish!

The only drawback to my comfort is the brutal cold I must endure—though it is, of course, nothing in comparison with what our soldiers face in the icy trenches. I have been imagining the possibility of Ernst and me renting a room together. I occasionally see adverts in the papers and on the bulletin boards and I am planning to speak to the Base Commander about it. I am becoming better known since I have expanded my translating and teaching activities, which encourages me to seek new possibilities of resolving my living and my loving situation.

Working in the Ambulatorio is a recently arrived woman known as "Melitta Gruber." She appeared jittery and wary in the first days she was here, but happy to finally be in Spain. She works in the card-indexing department, the *Kartothek*, and often enters and leaves the office with a Captain Hermann Endler. She seemed in need of company, and I was drawn to begin speaking to her almost immediately—and I soon asked if she would like to have tea with me. About my age, she has a broad, calm forehead, thin lips, and dark eyes. Prefers to be called "Mela." Even when she smiles, there is a look of sadness about her, a vulnerability that appeals to my protective instincts.

"How did you learn Spanish so well?" she asked me as we took a table—still wearing our coats, even though we had chosen the warmest corner of the SSI cantina, closest to the kitchen.

"I have been living here since 1930. I was working at the Medical School in Madrid when Franco's putsch happened in July of 1936. I signed up right away with the Fifth Regiment."

"Ah, so you missed the Nazi takeover in . . . You are from Germany, right?"

"Yes, from Kiel, but my family has been living in Berlin since I was a little girl. Not many of us are left there. And you? Oh, and shall we have the same kind of tea? What do you like?"

"I would prefer *früchtetee* (fruit tea), if they have it here."

"How about mint tea with honey?"

"That sounds lovely."

We ordered a pot of tea and some madeleines, and Mela continued, "I was born in Bukovina, officially a part of the Austro-Hungarian Empire, but I have been living in Vienna."

"Oh, did you come to Spain directly from Vienna? I can't imagine how you could have done that."

"No, you are right . . . I could not. I have been living in Switzerland, in Chur, near Zurich. But I kept my connections with the anti-fascists in Austria. So many wanted to volunteer in Spain but could not do so directly."

"So how did you stay safe?"

The tea and biscuits arrived, and she waited until the boy who was serving us was well out of earshot. I realized that she still fears being spied upon and I felt compassion for her, but then remembered that I may not be any safer than she is.

"Well, it depends on what you call 'safe.' I had to use a false name while in

Chur"—she looked about her, leaned in toward me, and lowered her voice—
"'Emma Bachmayer,' and as such I arranged the passage to Spain for many
Austrian anti-fascists. But there was always someone in Austria who betrayed
me, and they kept finding me. I have lost count of the times I have been arrested."

"Oh, that is terrible." I poured the tea, which looked thoroughly steeped,
and the stimulating fragrance of the dried mint rose with the steam. "You are
lucky to be alive—and lucky to be in Spain, despite the war," I added, hoping
to encourage her decision to come here.

She stirred some honey into her teacup and took a sip. "It is precisely the
war that brings me here. The last time I heard that they were after me, I was
determined not to get arrested again, and I was able to take the same route
I had been arranging for others. Yes, I am lucky to be alive and to be here to
fight fascism and anti-Semitism, even if it is by filling out and sorting index
cards." She dipped her madeleine into the tea and lowered her voice again.
"And my real name is not even 'Gruber.' I am also known as Melitta Ernst, the
name of my ex-husband."

"And 'Gruber'?"

"Oh, I was born 'Melanie Grünberg.'" She pushed back a lock of her dark
hair, and her delicate skin began to flush a bit with the hot tea. "And at least
now we—I—have a safe and warm place to live."

"Warm? You live in a warm place?" I opened my eyes widely and leaned
toward her. "I am staying at the bullring and must do all I can not to catch
pneumonia."

"Oh yes. Norbert and I are renting a room in one of the private homes that
the government has taken over."

"Norbert?"

"Oh, that is his real name—I mean the Captain, who uses the name
'Hermann Endler.' His real name is Norbert—or Nathan—Badian. His
brother, Siegfried, is also here in Spain. He is a dentist and offering his services—dentists are so badly needed here. We applied for local housing with
the Base Commander as soon as we arrived."

"That is a wonderful idea." I added, "I have been thinking of doing that with my—friend, a driver at the Auto-Park." My heart began to beat rapidly at the thought of actually living together with Ernst.

"Ah, yes, do it!" she said, smiling.

When we were done, I paid for the tea and the biscuits, and we hugged tentatively—she is not yet acclimated to the Spanish ways. We wrapped ourselves in our coats, scarves, and hats once more, and I thanked her earnestly for the idea that I hope to act on soon.

ALBACETE, *Sunday, 12 December 1937*

An all-Jewish company has just been formed as a subgroup of the Dombrowski (XIII) Brigade, part of the Palafox Battalion, with its many Polish volunteers. They have named the new group the Botwin Company in honor of Naftali Botwin, a Polish Jew executed in 1925 for killing a Polish policeman who had infiltrated the Communist Party and had been informing on its members. From speaking with comrades who are strict adherents to the Party, I have been getting mixed responses to this news.

Ernst and I attended a meeting at which the new group was announced, and several of us met afterwards at a café. We were soon joined at our table by Benno, an Austrian worker from the Ambulatorio.

"Who needs a *Jewish* company?" began Benno. "Judaism is a religion," he added, "and we as Communists recognize organized religion as the enemy of progress."

"Being Jewish is more—or maybe even less—than a religion," I interjected. "What danger do people who call themselves Jews pose to the Party? Being Jewish is certainly not a nationality, which is why I am not a Zionist. And I am not particularly religious either."

"But did these Botwin people come to Spain because they are Jews?" Benno queried.

I leaned toward Benno as I asked pointedly, "Did *you* come here because you are a Jew?"

"Well, no, I came to fight fascism."

At that moment Ernst intervened, also leaning in, "Would you have come to Spain to fight fascism if you were not a Jew?"

"How can I answer that question?" Benno responded, leaning back and raising his arms. "According to Janek Barwinski, the slogan of the Botwins will be 'For our freedom and for your freedom.' How dare Jews separate themselves this way from other anti-fascists?"

"Separate? I see it as quite the opposite of separation," I responded.

"Yes," agreed Ernst, "isn't that the meaning of the word 'and'? Doesn't that slogan join us, join *us* to *you all*?" He squeezed my hand under the table as he said this, and I turned toward him and pressed my knee into his leg.

"I will think about that," conceded Benno, "and I wish you a good day." He nodded before getting up from the table, wrapping his scarf around his throat, and making his way through the door and out to the cold and rainy street.

I was glad to see him go because I could not wait to tell Ernst my plan: "Ernst, I had an appointment this morning with Doctor Telge."

"What are you up to now, *Klärchen*?"

I took a sip of my café con leche before continuing. "I found out recently from an office worker that it is possible to rent rooms in private homes taken over by the government, and I have put in a request to do just that. Telge agreed to pass my request along to the Belgian Base Commander, Captain Jean Schalbroeck. What do you think?"

"I think you are brilliant, and I do hope you were able to convince the Comrade Base Commander." He slid his hand across my thigh, murmuring, "And I wish we had a room to go to right now."

"So do I, but now I must rush off to the hospital," I said, standing and pulling my scarf around me.

"And I must return an ambulance to the Auto-Park. Of course, I will help you pay for the room," he offered, also rising and donning his camel's hair coat and his Russian fur *ushanka* hat. He looked so young and handsome, and I suddenly wondered if he was seeing other women. But I cannot let myself think like that. Above all, I am feeling lucky, at my age, to be entering into a relationship with such a kind and fine man.

I stayed warm during my shift by rubbing our warriors' frostbitten feet and hands in attempts to forestall amputation, a simple act that many Spanish surgeons are encouraging—in conflict with the French doctors, who are too ready with the saw. Patients responded to my cheerful attitude, and their limbs warmed under my touch. Ah, the power of love!

ALBACETE, *Wednesday, 15 December 1937*

My faith in bureaucracy is restored (if indeed I ever had such faith)! This notice was in my in-box at the Ambulatorio this morning and authorizes me to rent a room in town. Ernst came by to drive me and some patients to a hospital a few kilometers away, and I gave him the news as soon as I climbed into the ambulance.

"The room will be in your name, Klara," Ernst began. "How shall we deal with this?"

"I don't think it should be a problem. You are free to move out of your quarters, aren't you?"

"Yes, of course, though I will have to inform the SIM. And I will probably have to give your name."

"Then it is entirely up to you, Ernst," I concluded. "Is that a problem for you?"

"Well, no," he admitted.

Does he really want to do this? I wondered.

As if in answer to my doubts, Ernst took my hand and kissed it, as he murmured, almost moaning, "I want to be with you, *Klärle*."

I almost wept at his sincerity, and to think that he actually did want me, but I returned to the moment at hand to explain, "All these housing units are part of properties requisitioned from fascists who supported the uprising. I think the Republic will be happy to receive a little more income."

"Ha, yes!" He laughed gently, and we kissed and hugged before I slid down

from the ambulance and returned to my icy taurine abode for what I hope is
one of the last times.

ALBACETE, Saturday, 18 December 1937

The first snows have begun to fall, and as winter begins, there also has begun a
battle on a new front: Teruel, a city south of Zaragoza, near the Aragón front.
But there is a happy note:

Success! We have found our love-nest: a large room, including kitchen
privileges, in the home of a former mayor of Albacete, Manuel Falcó Reig.
Falcó was killed as Republican forces retook the town after it had been taken
over by "nationalist" sympathizers for the first seven days of the fascist coup.
His home was later requisitioned by the Republic. It feels somewhat strange
to be occupying a house bearing such a history. My qualms are assuaged by
the fact that the house is on Calle Ramón y Cajal, which connects me to my
days in Madrid.

After we looked at the house this afternoon, Ernst revealed an unexpected
piece of news: he will be taking the train on Monday for Barcelona on a two-
day assignment for the SIM as the service takes part in the recently activated
Tribunales de Espionaje y Alta Traición (Tribunals for Espionage and High

Treason). They will be presided over by military magistrates, and Ernst has not given me any more details about the nature of the tribunals (or his role in them, for that matter). At least we will have one night together in the mayor's house at number 6 Calle Ramón y Cajal, though I feel that I have been robbed of time together that we so well deserve.

ALBACETE, Monday, 20 December 1937

Ernst left early this morning for the train station and what will be a lengthy journey to Barcelona, via Valencia. It felt comfortably domestic to share café con leche, toast, and *membrillo* (quince preserves) before sunrise from the utilitarian tableware furnished in what we have already begun to call the "mayor's kitchen." Last night was one of the sweetest of my life. I admit that the drafty bullring stalls and even the freezing, starving citizens of Madrid and the soldiers dying at the front vanished from my consciousness as we embraced all night between layers of thick, warm quilts and eiderdown comforters.

Yesterday after we took possession of the room, Ernst transported some newly arrived Brigaders to an outlying training area and I enjoyed playing my new role of *hausfrau* as I took my basket and a sufficient number of ration coupons to the warehouse where food is distributed, called here the *Capilla Salamanca*.

I wanted very much to replicate Mama's healing and nutritious chicken soup, and I think I came close to succeeding. Although chickens are quite high-priced and not covered by my coupons, I thought it would be a bargain in the long term to make a large pot of soup, serve the meat separately, and especially to render the fat (yes, schmaltz!) and keep it to spread on bread. (Unfortunately, I have not found rye bread here.) I was able to find an onion and some carrots, and the kitchen is already equipped with olive oil and salt. I wasn't sure how I would thicken the soup until I spotted brown rice, much cheaper than white, and I remembered that Gina had always cooked it and repeatedly lectured all of us who would listen about how much more nourishing it was than white rice. Coffee was very expensive so I just bought a small amount, and since fresh milk is not available, I bought a can of condensed milk, which we enjoyed for breakfast.

After dinner, Ernst unwrapped the surprise he had brought: a bottle of sparkling Codorniu wine, from Sant Sadurní D'Anoia, in Catalunya, but available right here in Albacete at Ros y García on the Avenida 14 de Abril. We enjoyed a glass seated in front of the wood-burning stove as the ferocious wind threatened to break into our idyll, but we ignored its threats as we began to kiss and move toward the bedroom.

I had been careful not to ask Ernst about his SIM assignment in Barcelona. I find myself attracted to a certain air of mystery about him, and it feels so good that I am able to maintain a separate identity, which he respects. Does the fact that Ernst and I enjoy being together and yet are content to spend time apart mean that this is love? No matter what the correct appellation, and despite the pain and misery I witness each day in my work, I feel a fulfillment in my life that I have never experienced.

As if in response to my trust, just before falling asleep after a brief lovemaking, Ernst confessed, "Klärle, I am thinking of resigning from my position with the SIM."

"Oh, I understand. Have you thought of what you will do? And what the response will be to your resignation?" I remembered that he had mentioned his mistrust of the organization even when he had first joined them and I was concerned for him, but I am still learning to trust him.

"Of course, I want to stay in Spain. I cannot go back to Germany. There are other positions available at the Auto-Park. Perhaps just maintenance of the vehicles. I have repaired tanks, and our tanks have been badly damaged at Teruel. What their response will be—I just cannot think of that."

We drifted off to sleep without resolving that issue.

VIII

ALBACETE, *Friday, 24 December 1937*

Ernst has not returned from Barcelona! He was due in last night, and I woke with a start this morning in a cold and empty bed. I somehow got through a day of work in the hospital—no out-patient duty today—feeling sick and terribly anxious. I did not talk to anyone there. After I left the building I took a bus to Calle Zapateros and the Auto-Park and encountered a young man called Julius whom I knew to be friendly with Ernst. He was doing paperwork, seated at a desk inside the warehouse, his small frame bundled up against the cold. He looked up, smiling, as he saw me come in.

"Good morning, camarada. What have you done with our Comrade Liefmann?" he asked, cheerily.

These words made me feel even worse and I thought I would faint. I leaned on the desk, my legs shaking. "Julius, I came here to ask you if you have seen him. He didn't come home last night."

"He hasn't come here either, Klara. I thought he may be on a long assignment or maybe he took the week off to sit by the fire with you."

"No . . ."—I tried to steady my trembling voice—"he would have told me if he were planning to stay longer in Barcelona. I haven't seen him since Monday morning." I did not mention that Ernst had intended to resign from his work with the SIM. To whom would I tell that? I am afraid to confide in anyone in a position of leadership, all of whom are connected to the Komintern and hence to Stalin, especially Political Commissar André Marty, with his suspicion of any possible dissidence. I am sure that Ernst would not have expressed his personal feelings to this young, newly arrived Austrian who is so lighthearted and does not even take the war seriously.

I don't remember leaving the Auto-Park warehouse. I took a bus home to see if perhaps he had come back, but there was no sign of him. I forced myself to heat some of the soup and eat some bread and cheese and am now seated at the kitchen table. I just dozed off, and I startle awake with every creak of the house in the wind. If he is not back by morning, I will return to the Auto-Park and then go to work at the hospital where I can be of some use.

ALBACETE, *Sunday, 26 December 1937*

Today I am so worried about Ernst that I barely have room in my heart for the joy I should be feeling about the war news, an official victory: Republican forces have held off the "nationalists" at Teruel, while the coldest winter on record in Spain is claiming lives that bullets and bombs have spared. How long will this last, against the overwhelming air and land power that the fascists will surely summon up? Only today matters.

The Party is calling for mass street demonstrations while I receive men—and too many boys—with recently amputated toes, feet, legs, fingers, and hands, and who of course cannot march in the streets. Franco has had to turn from his offensive in Guadalajara to stand up to our troops in Teruel, and so far, the surprise element is working in our favor.

I returned alone tonight, and leafing through today's *Frente Rojo*, my anxiety over Ernst's absence is eased somewhat at the tributes to these two beautiful Roses that appear on page six:

Rosa Luxemburg is named "figure of the week" as an international revolutionary hero and a great writer and Marxist, though oddly not as a founder of the German Communist Party, which disappoints me. It feels like an abyss between these times and the years I devoted to Rosa's personality and her writings. What would she be doing and how would she be treated if she had not been murdered in 1919? Would her name be on a file in the office of the Tribunal of Espionage and High Treason?

The other Rose, Rosario Sánchez, also has a deep personal meaning for me, since I cared for her as that shattered right hand was amputated in the basement of the hospital at La Cabrera, and during her recovery. She lives today and is honored by our heroic poet from Valencia, Miguel Hernández.

Nuestra figura semanal

Rosa Luxemburgo

ROSA Luxemburgo es una de las más grandes figuras del movimiento revolucionario internacional. A su nombre va asociada una de las épocas más heroicas de la revolución proletaria: el alzamiento espartaquista de Berlín.

Rosa Luxemburgo era, a la par que una luchadora infatigable, una gran escritora e investigadora de la doctrina marxista, con cuya interpretación enriqueció la obra histórica de los grandes maestros.

Nace en polaca. Estudiando, en Zurich, se incorpora el movimiento socialista. En 1893 funda, con su paisano Leo Jogiche, el Partido Socialdemócrata de Polonia y Lituania. Al poco tiempo de esto, participa activamente en la labor de propaganda y agitación desarrollada en el centro de Europa, sin romper por esto su contacto con el movimiento revolucionario polaco. En la revolución rusa del año 1, combate con gran entusiasmo, siendo encarcelada. Uno de esos más famosos folletos agota con el título «Reformas Sociales o Revolución», siendo su obra científica más importante «La acumulación del capital», publicada en 1912.

Durante un movimiento huelguístico, la soldadesca germana la asesinó, privando al proletariado internacional de uno de sus más heroicos y abnegados dirigentes revolucionarios.

Rosario Dinamitera

Rosario Dinamitera

I will hold the image of these two brave women as I attempt to sleep tonight, hoping that Ernst will return to me.

ALBACETE, Monday, 3 January 1938

It is now two weeks since Ernst's disappearance. I cannot call it anything else. Almost as painful as his absence is the fact that I do not know to whom to turn, whom to ask. I often notice posts in the newspapers about missing persons, but those notices are nearly always placed by family members, which of course I am not. Sometimes I feel desperate enough to paint my plea on the walls of Albacete, similar to the *"On és Nin?"* messages that appeared around Barcelona when Andreu Nin was taken. Could I write *"On és/Dónde está/Wo ist/Where is/Où est/ Где находится/היפֿא Liefmann"*? He is not well-known enough, and I would probably be arrested for defacing public property. The city is completely buried in white now, and fierce winds hurl the stinging snow in my face.

A new regulation has been introduced: the Spanish Communist Party has just decreed that all foreigners who are members in their respective countries must apply for membership to the Spanish Party. The notice came to my attention this morning as I was standing in front of a wall newspaper alongside the American, George Chaikin, one of the Abraham Lincoln Battalion volunteers who also works in the Ambulatorio with me. I was contemplating putting up a notice about Ernst, when George addressed me in his peculiar language mixture: "*Gib a kuk* (look at that), camarada, the Central Committee is trying to make us internationals Spanish. What *cojones!* (balls). Aren't we *Communisti* enough for Spain? I am a Party member in my country, *¿y tú?*"

I was surprised at the boldness of his question, and I assumed it was either part of the reputed Yankee familiarity or informality or of stories I have heard about George as being combative, a quality I rather admire. He pointed to items on the board, favoring his right arm, as he is still recovering from a badly fractured collarbone, consequence of a wound he received at the Battle of Brunete. He was dressed in a uniform that did not resemble any others I had seen. I asked him about it.

"Oh," he said, laughing, "I got this at the Army Surplus Store before I left Jersey. No one here seems to mind that it is from another war."

I had never heard of the "Army Surplus Store" but thought it was a good idea. I turned my attention to the notice, which was posted in French.

"You probably have the German one in your in-box," George suggested.

I had not even looked at my box when I arrived in the morning, but indeed there were copies of the notice in German and in Spanish.

"Are you going to apply, George?"

"Do I have a choice? Either that or *adiós, España*, I suppose. But I am here to defeat fascism, and I think I have a better opportunity to do it here. God knows I have had no luck on the streets of Trenton. How about you, camarada? We need more strong women like you in the fight." His deep-set black eyes, shaded by black eyebrows, penetrated my gaze, belying his casual conversation.

"Yes, I will apply, though I already consider myself a member." Then I decided to take advantage of the opportunity to ask him another question, and lowered my voice: "George, what do you know about the SIM?

"The SIM? *Nu*," he began, scratching his cheek with his good hand, "I know that they have become completely independent of the Republic and are carrying out orders from the Kremlin and have formed their own tribunals to go after anarchists and Trotskyites, and, well, freethinkers in general. I hear stories about torture and summary executions."

Just what I did not want to hear! I stammered something and backed away to allow him to leave. As I walked down the hall to translate for a German patient, I considered that the possibility of officially becoming a member of the Spanish Communist Party might give me access to information about Ernst, and I am determined to request an application.

After leaving the Ambulatorio I put in a couple of hours with the patients, treating more men wounded by machine gun fire and especially men with gangrene or the so-called "trench foot" caused by the horrible, record-breaking cold that besieges Teruel. Loyalist forces still hold the upper hand there. One of the reasons is the fact that the textile industry within Republican territory is still strong, and while Franco's forces are stronger within northern areas devoted more to heavy industry, their uniforms are not adequate against the temperatures that have reached minus eighteen degrees. I am feeling proud to have had a garment manufacturer as a father.

ALBACETE, Thursday, 20 January 1938

The war grows even more brutal unless it is just my reaction to events. After a month of Republican control of the provincial capital, Teruel, the fascists have launched an offensive on the city, backed up by German and Italian air power. The Loyalist government had begun to return the area to normal, restoring mail delivery, initiating radio broadcasts, delivering supplies, and rebuilding destroyed structures, but we are again on the defensive. The Republican taking of Teruel had been a brilliant strategy to distract Franco from yet another attack on Madrid, brave, stalwart Madrid, but the "nationalists" are drawing on infinite resources, in open defiance of the "Non-Intervention Agreement." New and more brazen bombings have occurred in the past few days, probably the worst of which was yesterday's attack on Barcelona, in the center of town, at noontime, by Italian aviation. One hundred seventy deaths were recorded, including many children, on their way home from school for the midday meal.

News from SSI Headquarters is that our organization will become a subsection of the *Inspección General* and will bear the new name of *Ayuda Médica Extranjera* (Foreign Medical Aid). Most importantly, our entire base is to be relocated to Barcelona. I am not certain when this will take place.

I have still not heard anything about Ernst, and aside from occasional torturous thoughts that he may have gone off with another woman, my deepest fear—far more torturous—is that he has met some horrible fate. Each night I dream he comes back, and I wake up many times with my heart pounding. My visits to the Auto-Park are received with the same shaking of heads and what I perceive is the wish that I would just stop bothering them.

ALBACETE, Tuesday, 8 February 1938

The latest carload of convalescents arriving from Benissa brought some happy news: Dina and Hugo's baby, Anita, was born last Thursday. I think of Dina's decision to bear Hugo's child during these tragic times: the choice of a free-thinking woman, to be admired and perhaps emulated.

ALBACETE, Wednesday, 23 February 1938

Teruel is lost! Evidently Franco's generals resorted to some of the tactics employed by the Republican Army to gain control of the city, namely surrounding vulnerable forces, with the addition of calling in the overwhelming air power of their Fascist and Nazi allies. From Aragón, Franco will now continue to advance eastward, and we must prepare for that reality.

ALBACETE, Sunday, 13 March 1938

Anschluss! The German word is echoing off the walls of hospital rooms, corridors, and offices, pronounced in various accents. Contrary to his promises (what else is new?), and to forestall an imminent Austrian referendum, Hitler has invaded Austria and made it a part of Nazi Germany! As soon as I heard this term, late yesterday evening, I sought out Mela and we agreed to meet together with her companion, Norbert. I thought we could speak more privately in the "mayor's house," so I invited them for tea. Norbert asked if he could bring his brother, Siegfried, and of course I accepted. Since I have no time to cook I just bought some raisins and almonds and a few hazelnuts and four dried figs at the Capilla Salamanca, and a bottle of sweet wine (*moscatel*) at Ros y García.

My three guests arrived at about five o'clock. The weather is warming slightly, but I had built a fire in the stove against the evening chill, and on the kitchen table I had placed a colorful tablecloth and napkins I found in a drawer. I had also found some dried berries at the market with which to brew some früchtetee, remembering that Mela had wanted it when we met for tea in the cantina.

Norbert and Siegfried, about ten years apart, have almost identically kind faces—younger brother Siegfried has a very broad forehead that reminds me of Einstein's. They asked me about Ernst, and I had to fight back tears as I explained that I had not heard from him since he had left for Barcelona on assignment in December, without revealing the exact nature of the assignment. They sighed and shook their heads and murmured expressions of sympathy. I was glad that no one said, "He will no doubt return soon," because I am gradually becoming reconciled to the possibility that he will indeed never return. He even appears less in my dreams.

I had found some lovely blue-and-white ceramic bowls in a cupboard and filled them with the raisins and almonds.

"I am so sorry I do not have a more elaborate spread to offer you," I began, and was assured by all three, "Please do not worry—this looks wonderful."

"When I was at the Medical School in Madrid the students called this food '*músicos*'—'musicians'—though I am not sure why. The advantage is that you do not need cutlery to enjoy it."

"Which is probably why it is called 'músicos,'" suggested Siegfried, "because you use your hands."

"Then it should be called '*masajistas*' (masseurs), shouldn't it?" Norbert said, and we all laughed and began to relax.

I had purchased six glazed clay glasses at a ceramics shop near Base Headquarters, and I decided to open the bottle of moscatel and propose a toast, which they all echoed, joining glasses with a dull earthen clink.

I took a sip of the delicious, almost edible sweet wine and then addressed all three: "So what do you know about this Anschluss? How are people receiving it?"

"Well, of course, annexing Austria goes completely against the Treaty of Versailles," began Norbert, flinging one hand into the air, "but since when does that *meshugginer* respect treaties?"

"If you want something, just take it! Raw materials, industry, currency reserves, hydroelectric resources, are all needed by Germany!" exclaimed Siegfried.

"Yes, to continue to aid Franco in his fascist conquest," I added.

"But I think it was Göring who really pressed for annexation, as the only implementation of Hitler's Four-Year Plan," suggested Norbert.

"Yes. Hitler made a threatening speech in February, the Austrians set up a referendum on independence, and now we know the results. The Wehrmacht marched in yesterday morning, crossing the border at his birthplace, Braunau am Inn," Mela said with a growl of disgust.

"Oh!" I almost shouted. "I read an article about five years ago about Hitler's *gemütlich* relationship with his *gemütlich* birth town. It was in the Seville *ABC*, from the days when Seville was called 'Sevilla la roja'! There are pictures of him in *lederhosen!*"

"*Feh!*" exclaimed Siegfried.

"Please, no!" added Norbert, shaking his head in disgust.

We all fell silent for a moment. Mela's head was bent, her eyes downcast. "I have received a call early this morning, from colleagues in Austria," she began, her soft voice quivering. "Jews were forced to their knees and made to scrub away the pro-independence slogans that had been painted on the streets of Vienna. Jewish shops have been plundered, and Jews were driven out and chased down the streets. And this is not just by the Wehrmacht. I am referring to the local Austrians!"

"Gottenyu!" I gasped.

Siegfried then refilled our glasses and raised his: "To freedom!"

We eagerly followed suit and drained our glasses.

"I wish I could go back to Austria and help get them all out," declared Mela, almost tearfully. Norbert put his arm around her.

"*Schatzi*, you would reach out to the whole world if you could. And so would I. You must take care of yourself here, where you are safe and where it may be possible to defeat fascism."

Safe here? Defeat fascism? We all nibbled on the músicos, and I considered expressing my doubts and fears, but then realized that I had in my—I should say, the mayor's home—three people whose land had just been invaded by the same madman who had taken mine. I felt encouraged to voice my views.

"I think, I hope, that we are in a position to be able to defeat fascism by educating others in the principles in which we all believe."

"Yes, not by war," offered Siegfried.

"Right!" I agreed. "How can we hope for an enlightened populace if everyone is killed or maimed, never able to emerge from a state of ignorance, illiteracy, and greed?"

The March wind began to lash against the house. "How about a pot of früchtetee?" I suggested.

"Oh, I would love that," responded Mela, and the men agreed.

"We can use these same glasses, can't we, Klara?" asked Norbert.

"Certainly! I appreciate that!" I responded.

The dried fruit yielded a delicious tea, and we all added a bit of honey. As we hugged good-bye, the three thanked me for the invitation, and I wished peace to them and to our world at war.

ALBACETE, Friday, 25 March 1938

This afternoon I received a telephone call from Gina, who had some exciting news: She, Artur and the three girls are vacating their home in Denmark and leaving for England. On Wednesday, March 30, they will board the SS *Paris* in Southampton for New York!

"Wonderful! Where will you stay?"

"We will spend some time with the Benjamin Liebowitz family in New York City. I don't know if you remember Ben. A physicist friend of Leo Szilard's."

"Yes, I think I do. Where will you go after New York?"

"We will all board a Greyhound bus and head westward. Artur has been promised a job at a hospital in Denver, Colorado, and the girls and I will continue on to Berkeley, in California."

"And how are the girls? Nora must be about ten by now."

"Yes, she is. And Renate is fourteen and Ellen is sixteen. They are looking forward to the voyage, though they will miss their Danish friends."

"Ah, well, please send my love to them all and to Artur."

"I will. You should also come to America. Why do you stay in that horrible war?"

I felt as if I needed to come to the defense of my commitment to Spain and felt terribly misunderstood by my sister-in-law. I tried to remain calm as I explained to her, "Of course it is horrible. When was there a war that was not horrible? But I am working against fascism, even against Hitler, if you can believe that. If we stop Franco, Hitler will realize that he cannot conquer all of Europe."

"Halevai, Klara," responded Gina. "I must go and finish packing."

"I wish you a safe voyage."

Would I want to go to America? The *goldene medina* and all? With all the horrors of war and fascism and my love torn from me, I still would not trade what I have here in this land of the generous, self-sacrificing Spanish people.

ALBACETE, Friday, 15 April 1938

The news tore into Base Headquarters late this afternoon like a surgical saw, negating yesterday's celebration of the seventh anniversary of the founding of the Second Republic: Franco's Navarra troops have reached the Mediterranean Sea, at Vinaròs, about halfway between Valencia and Barcelona, as the culmination of the Aragón Offensive, accelerated after the fall of Teruel. Spain is effectively sliced in two. Dismantling of our base and total evacuation will begin immediately, and everything and everyone will be transferred to Barcelona. Evacuation of patients, equipment, and even prisoners will be accomplished by train, lorries, and ambulances, via Valencia.

We have also gotten word through intelligence that Franco, instead of continuing north into Barcelona, which would probably fall quickly, bringing an end to the war, plans to plunge south through the Maestrazgo, the wild mountain region to the north of Valencia, intent on destroying the city on the Turia River. This will buy us a bit of time before setting out on the journey but in the long run will prolong the war, at a human cost that is barely imaginable. Unfortunately, the moon is full, and we are all aware of the dangers of being bombed in transit, so time will be spent preparing.

My memories of Albacete will linger with me forever, I am sure, between the treasured days and nights of love with Ernst and the grief at his disappearance that still claws at my heart.

IX

BARCELONA, Saturday, 30 April 1938

After two weeks of frantic organizing and uprooting and two days of creeping in our motley caravan across the darkened plains of Castile, pausing in Valencia and scanning the skies for airplanes, we have all safely crossed enemy territory. We followed the contours of the Mediterranean Sea to arrive at Barcelona, still proudly majestic as it rebuilds from the ruthless bombings. Only this morning, the *Aviazione Legionaria delle Balleari,* the Italian air force stationed in Mallorca, bombed the Port of Barcelona, killing an estimated forty people.

The new Ayuda Médica Extranjera headquarters is located at the Rambla de Catalunya, number 126, at the top of the Ramblas, the lovely promenade so characteristic of Catalan cities, which in Barcelona thrusts up into the city from the port. The building is a pleasure to behold. It was constructed in 1903, designed by architect Josep Puig i Cadafalch, and I must say that I cannot conjure up a term to describe the style, at once modern and ancient, which the Spanish call *plateresco,* with its galleries and windows adorned with images of stellar artists, including Beethoven and even Wagner! And on the Ronda de Sant Pere, off the Plaça de Catalunya, in a beautiful bookshop called Llibreria Catalònia, I found this lovely volume for my latest tagebuch.

Simultaneously to my move from Albacete, the American surgeon Dr. Edward Barsky has replaced Dr. Oskar Telge as Chief Medical Officer. I barely glimpsed Dr. Barsky in Albacete, as he was dedicated to creating *ex nihilo* entire hospitals all over Spain, and then he went back to America to elicit aid for Spain, returning to Barcelona last month. I do hope to meet him here.

I have been assigned to more administrative-clerical tasks in Barcelona and will probably be spending more time in an office than in hospital. I hope I can be useful in both settings. This afternoon I was handed a list of personnel, and I was pleased to see that Norbert heads the list as captain, assigned his pseudonym of "Hermann Endler." Mela ("Melitta Gruber," number 25) is also included in the administrative department, in charge of the Kartothek. It will also be entertaining to be in the same office with George Chaikin (number 16), God forbid the atmosphere becomes too quiet and peaceful. I am number 21 on the list.

```
              Administradores   y personal administrativo. †2)        8 41

  1. Endler Hermann      administrador       austriaco
     capitan
  2. Hauptreif Albert        "              aleman
     Teniente
  3. Stuart Henri            "              francés
     Teniente
  4. Wagner Erwin    Sargento   "           americano
  5. Gimeno Jaime    Soldado    "           espanol
  6. Munoz Manuel       "       "             "
  7. Barr Hermann       "       "           americano
  8. Savinet Pierre     "       "           francés
  9. Segall Maurice   Teniente "            polaco
 10. Plaza Augustin     "       "           americano


 11. Kluster Werner  Sargento  ayuda administrador    aleman
 12. Vignatelli       Soldado    "         "          italiano
     Libero
 13. Marjues Garcia     "        "         "          americano
     Rafael
 13./a. Germain Raymond "        "         "          francés
 13./b. ZIPSER JACK     "        "         "          polaco

 14. Haberlin Maria          secretaria              yugoslava
 15. Valbuena Casto  Soldado  "                      espanol
 16. Chaikin Georges  Sarg.   "                      amerikano
 17. Rubint Wladislaw Soldado "                      hungaro
 18. Barat Pedro      "       "                      espanol
 19. Martin Emile L. Capitan  "                      frances
 20. Hunziker Albert Alferez  "                      suizo
 21. Clara Philipsborn        "                      alemana
 22./a. Albertini Enrique     "                      italiano

 22. Rytiewski Johann soldado  kartothek             aleman
 23. Bakran Victor            "    "                 yugoslavo
 24. Berger Zenno    Sargento "    "                 austriaco
 25. Gruber Melitta          . "                       "
 26. Galeani Germaine         "                      italiana
 27. Carmen Alarcon           "                      espanol
 28. Berta Müller             "                      alemana
 29z


 29. Buss Fritz     Sargento  tresorero             aleman
 30. Santiago Cobos Teniente    "                   hungaro
 31. Herzfeld Eugen Alferez     "                     "
                                    ./.
```

Dr. Barsky and his American assistant, Mildred Rackley, have taken charge of setting up the various hospitals and moving the patients in. We five women administrators have been put up in the Hotel Majestic Inglaterra, on the Passeig de Gràcia, not far from headquarters. I am sharing one room with Berta Müller, whom I am just getting to know. Our room is occasionally cleaned by the overworked staff, and I am glad I have brought my own soap. The food is tolerable. Some celebrity international journalists can be glimpsed here and sometimes heard in boisterous arguments.

The city is bravely preparing for tomorrow's May Day, and I wonder if Franco has special plans to interfere with the celebrations. I have also pledged to myself to learn Catalan.

BARCELONA, *Wednesday, 4 May 1938*

The reports circulated on May Day celebrated the resistance of Loyalist troops to the fascist attempts to penetrate the Maestrazgo, southward toward Valencia. Actual good news accompanying the expected patriotic slogans.

Yesterday I received a notice that I was to report to Dr. Barsky's office this morning to receive instructions on my assignment for an indefinite period: preliminary screening of potential blood donors for the Transfusion Service, headed and pioneered by Dr. Frederic Durán i Jordà. It was a pleasant walk from the Majestic to headquarters on the Rambla de Catalunya, and on my way I took my time to listen to snatches of conversation in Catalan, most of which I did not understand. I was looking forward to meeting Dr. Barsky but instead was greeted—in German—by his secretary, Mildred Rackley.

Mildred smiled in a friendly manner, displaying large teeth, which I have come to associate with Americans, and offered me a seat beside the large desk, which was covered in papers. "*Entschuldigung* (Sorry)," she began. "I just arrived this morning, and Dr. Barsky likes to have all his papers within reach, even if he can't see them."

"Oh, do not worry, camarada." It was eerie to hear the German language, spoken with what sounded like a Hamburg accent—my Ernst!—issuing from the mouth of this very American-looking young woman. She explained that she had indeed studied art in Hamburg.

"So what may I do to help the Cause at the Transfusion Service?" I asked. "I am somewhat familiar with the procedure since I worked with some of Dr. Bethune's colleagues in Ocaña."

"Yes, we know that." She smiled again and pushed back a lock of thick and glossy light brown hair, which she wore pulled to one side over her broad forehead. "Doctor Bethune visited Dr. Durán's facility late in 1936 and learned much from his methods. The Center, Hospital Number 18, is now centrally located on Carrer de Mallorca, 216. You will be doing the intake interviews there. The hospital and Dr. Durán's staff have been broadcasting appeals for donors over the radio and even at concerts."

"What kinds of incentives are being offered? It was so difficult to receive blood donations in Madrid and Ocaña."

"Well, thanks to Dr. Durán, the method of collection has improved considerably. The 'direct method' is no longer being used, donors' veins are not being opened any more, and, best of all, donors are being rewarded with hot meals following donations, since they fast before donating."

"Wonderful! It is good to know these details when I am interviewing people."

"Yes." She smiled again. "And it will be helpful if you are able to speak Catalan. We know that you speak German, Spanish, French, English, and some Italian, but we weren't sure if you speak Catalan. We have a questionnaire in Catalan that you may use to ask the questions."

"And I hope I understand the answers!" This time I smiled. "I am somewhat familiar with the language from the time I spent in Benissa. But I would like to have someone read the form aloud to me in Catalan so that I can hear how it should sound."

"An excellent idea. We will get someone from Dr. Durán's staff to spend some time with you."

Mildred stood and offered her hand, shaking mine brusquely. She is tall and athletic-looking, more robust in appearance than most European women. I suppose it is also an American look.

"Thank you for coming in, Camarada Klara."

"My pleasure, indeed. Thank you for this helpful information."

BARCELONA, Saturday, 7 May 1938

This morning I gave myself an hour to walk from the Majestic to Hospital Number 18 on the Carrer de Mallorca for my eleven o'clock appointment with Dr. Durán's assistant, Alfred Benlloch. I crossed the Ramblas and was soon on the carrer, featuring many elegant buildings of four to five stories. Street life was active, with workers completing the dismantling of badly bombed buildings.

Once in the hospital, a young female volunteer showed me into a small office off the admissions office, and soon the very young and energetic Alfred Benlloch entered, vigorously shaking my hand to welcome me. On the wall was a colorful poster calling on citizens to donate blood for the war effort. He had prepared and copied the questionnaire for prospective blood donors, in Catalan. He first asked me to read it to myself to see how much I understood, and then to ask him about anything I did not understand. I thought that was a brilliant way to proceed. But I was embarrassed to find a word in the very first question that I did not understand:

"I think I understand everything except a word in the first question, *vegada*." (The question was *Has donat alguna vegada?*)

"Oh, of course, it is the same as '*vez*' in Castilian."

"Ah!" I laughed. "In other words, 'Have you donated before?'"

"Right! So now I will read the questions and you can repeat." He began reading slowly and carefully and I imitated him as well as I could.

After the fourth question—"Are you over eighteen years old?"—I asked him, "Is there a maximum age to donate?"

"Well, not really, but if people seem weak or infirm, we discourage it."

We reached the question asking if the person weighed over fifty kilos and I asked him if there was a maximum weight.

"We have not set a number, and with the war and the food shortages, we do not expect many donors who are overweight."

We both nodded sadly at that idea.

"You are sounding good, and I think the people will understand you perfectly," he stated. "Now I would like to show you my laboratory where we analyze the blood," he offered proudly.

The site was truly impressive and immaculate looking. Assistants in white coats were at work mixing donated blood with citric preservative and anticoagulants in differently sized conical glass vessels.

"What a beautiful laboratory!" I exclaimed.

Alfred looked so pleased at my praise that I asked him, "What is your role in this laboratory?"

"Dr. Durán gave me three days to set it up, when we first heard that we were moving here. He put equipment at my disposal and offered any assistance that I required." He smiled broadly, and I realized how accomplished he is at his young age. "With Dr. Durán's method we are now able to send thirty-five liters of blood weekly to hospitals three hundred kilometers from here."

"So where did you study—Camarada Alfred?" I did not know what sort of title he bore, and I am still cognizant of the standards of equality implemented by the Republic.

"I studied with a private teacher and then entered the Liceo Francés. I completed my baccalaureate, but the war started before I was able to enter university."

"With your experience here, you could probably teach some classes."

"My work here is important, and I am content that I am able to participate this way."

A wise youth from whom I can learn much!

BARCELONA, *Wednesday, 18 May 1938*

Bombing, bombing, bombing—three days and three nights of bombing! The main target was the port and the ships anchored there, beginning on Thursday. I was just about to get out of bed, and Berta was still asleep when the huge explosion shook our room and rattled the windows. Berta leaped out of bed, screaming, in Latvian, "*Cukas, cukas* (Pigs, pigs)*!*" and I told her, also shouting, probably in German, "Just get dressed in case we have to run out!"

Once it was quiet and we were dressed and a little calmer, we went downstairs to get the news. We did not learn details right away, but what people were saying is that this was the hour in which the trading business was conducted on the piers, and that the bombing was aimed to kill a maximum number of people. By now I have been informed at Headquarters that Thursday's bombing struck the ship *Ciudad de Sevilla*, moored at the Moll Nou (New Dock), killing more than fifty people and partially sinking the ship itself.

When I arrived at Hospital Number 18 on the Carrer de Mallorca, I still felt disoriented, with my hearing affected. It calmed me somewhat to speak quietly and encouragingly to prospective donors and to concentrate on getting all their information correctly. After the first two interviews, Alfred Benlloch burst into my little office, looking flushed and enthusiastic.

"They are bombing us at night, despite our anti-aircraft guns," he began excitedly. "Why is that? Because we are looking for the aviation with lights. And then they bomb the lights and our anti-aircraft weapons to boot. Why can't we detect them by using sound instead of light? We calculate where they are by measuring their speed, and then—¡pim! ¡pam! ¡pum!—we shoot them down!"

He aimed at the ceiling like a child with a toy gun and I almost laughed at his eagerness.

"Bravo!" I exclaimed.

Who knows how long it will take before Alfred finds the proper authorities to submit his ideas and then to implement them. Especially given his age—he is just twenty!—and his lack of military experience, I cannot imagine anyone taking him seriously.

VIC, *Thursday, 19 May 1938*

An unexpected assignment and from a valued source: Early this morning I received a message from Mildred Rackley that I was to report immediately to Dr. Edward Barsky for a temporary mission. I presented myself at once and was greeted by a tall, energetic man with a somewhat British appearance, angular facial structure, and a slight moustache.

Dr. Barsky's desk was still covered with papers, but he quickly located the one he was looking for, after inviting me to sit. He began in a quite adequate German, "Thank you so much for volunteering for the cause of Spain, *Kameridin* Klara."

"It is I who should thank you, Comrade Dr. Barsky," I responded in English. "I am in Spain since 1930 and have already experienced monarchy, dictatorship, the promise of democracy, and incipient fascism. Our American comrades are much appreciated for your sacrifices."

Waving the paper, he said, "We have recently received this memo from Dr. Eloesser, head of the American Hospital at Vic, a mountain town about seventy kilometers north of here. He is extremely alarmed at the number of typhus cases reported there, even among those who have been inoculated. Scandalous, don't you think?"

"It certainly is."

He laid the paper back down among the jumble on his desk and began to shuffle through the other papers. He finally sat back in his chair and clasped his hands behind his head, grinning apologetically. "Well, I can't find it now, but we received a report from Dr. Leo Samet, who was at Benissa before evacuation. He remembered you as having been successful in curing cases of typhus there."

I felt my face flush and started to disclaim any credit for curing typhus but decided to defer to this man in whom the Spanish government and the Brigades had placed their trust.

"We are sending you to Vic for a few days to gain your perspective on what may be an epidemic. We have sent Dr. Glaser, a German doctor, to replace Dr. Eloesser as head, and we would like you to work in the office with him, as there are a number of international patients as well as staff, and your language abilities are needed."

"Certainly, Doctor. When would you like me to be there?"

"There is a train at three twenty p.m. from the Plaça de Catalunya. You will be met at Vic at five o'clock."

And indeed, the trip was that precise, and at the same time enjoyable, despite the very high military presence, especially traveling through the town of Granollers, which features weapons construction and electrical plants. The landscape, moving through the Osona region, was almost alpine, showing off green meadows and striking rocky mountain formations, and pleasing the eyes with wildflowers of all colors. How I love this land!

Three wounded men were picked up at one of the last stops, and we were met at the station by an earnest, bearded, British volunteer called George. Once all were loaded into the ambulance, George drove us here, to Via 28 and the simply constructed building which formerly housed the convent of the Carmelite Sisters of Charity. On the way he explained, in the fragmented lingua franca of the international volunteers, the various ways of referring to the hospital: L'Hospital Internacional de Vic, American Hospital Number One, Military Hospital of the International Brigades, or Military Clinic of the International Brigades. George pointed out the office of Dr. Willy (Wilhelm) Glaser, where I was to report, and then he strode briskly down the hall toward the front steps.

The percussive clash of Dr. Glaser's typing reached me as I approached his open door. He beckoned for me to take a seat, which I did, placing my medical bag and satchel on the floor beside the chair. His light-colored hair stood stiffly, aiming out in various directions. Without introducing himself or offering any sort of preface, he suddenly raised his head and asked, in German, "How do you say 'essential' in Spanish?"

Startled, I replied, "'*Imprescindible*,' Doctor." He obviously knew who I was. He couldn't say 'hello' first? Was this a test?

He typed for a minute or so more, and then ripped the paper noisily out of the typewriter, still looking at the paper: "Well, I guess you know why you are here. I hope you have not drunk any water. If you open a tap, you will notice that the water is purple. This is because they have used an additive—"

"Potassium permanganate?" I cut in.

"Yes," he answered.

"I was told that the problem here was typhus," I said. "But if there is a problem with the water, perhaps what you have here is typhoid fever, rather than typhus, or in addition to typhus. What is the source of the water here?"

"Ha, you should say 'sources'! The water system inherited from the Carmelite nuns was a labyrinth, and who knows how they survived it. Some of the water came from the convent gardens, and then, less than a month after the hospital was established, there was a sewage overflow."

So they have sent me here to stem a sewage overflow and a typhoid epidemic, which they call typhus, I thought, dismayed. Out loud I asked, "So what are you doing for drinking water? Of course, Franco has taken over the hydro-electric projects of the Pyrenees—"

"We are still bringing water in from the mountains," he interrupted.

"And how are you delivering it for consumption?" I asked.

"We use an existing cistern."

"Has the cistern been analyzed for contaminants?"

"I am not sure," he admitted. "They had a Catalan bacteriologist here and I think he approved it."

"Well, perhaps you should add chlorine to the mountain water. I have read about the typhoid epidemic of 1914 and I know that even bottled water made people sick," I said—and then, as an afterthought: "Has anyone suspected sabotage?"

"Sabotage? Ridiculous!" he snorted. He then stood up and gestured toward his desk, abruptly changing the subject. "You will be using this office space, as long as I am not here. All written reports that are not in French or Italian need to be translated to Spanish. Oh, and you will sleep in the women's dormitory. It is quite decent and safe. In fact, my daughter even sleeps there."

I picked up my things. Dr. Glaser walked into the hallway with me and pointed to the left, toward what was evidently the women's dormitory, then returned to the office and closed the door.

The room was spacious and well-ventilated. I found a cot that I assumed I was to use, just as a woman in nurse's uniform entered and introduced herself, in an understandable Spanish, obviously expecting my company, "Salud, Camarada Clara, my name is Ray Harris. I am a nurse from New York."

I thought it would be easier to communicate in English, so I switched to that language to ask, "How long have you been in Spain?" I sat down on the cot and patted it, inviting her to sit.

"Since January of last year." She turned to face me. "I am a part of Dr. Barsky's team, so I have worked at various locations. I checked in at Albacete and worked at Villa Paz, Córdoba, and Colmenar. Since the evacuation I have been working at Mataró and am helping out here in Vic for a short time."

She was dark-skinned and rather plump, with close-cropped dark, curly hair. Her accent in English did not sound like that of other Americans I have met, and I asked about her background.

"I grew up in Canada, but I was born in Russia."

"Ah, perhaps that is why your diction in English is so clear." We both laughed.

"My father teaches at Hebrew school, but don't ask me about my Hebrew diction."

"Ha, don't worry about that! I am more interested in the water supplies. What do you know?"

"Well, I haven't been here long, but I do know that we must be very careful. And I heard stories when I arrived."

"What kind of stories?"

Ray lowered her voice and her eyes darted toward the door. "Sabotage. Medical supplies have been delivered with vials that have been emptied."

"Gottenyu! That certainly sounds like sabotage to me," I said. Recalling Dr. Glaser's recent response, my curiosity was aroused.

"That could happen at any point during the delivery process," she continued, "but right here in town we sometimes wake up to see swastikas painted on the walls. We scrub them off, but they often reappear the next morning."

"The fifth column is everywhere," I said, probably unnecessarily, shaking my head. Ray stood to leave, and we hugged and promised to get together soon. "You must also meet Erika Glaser," she added.

"Related to the doctor?"

"Yes, his sixteen-year-old daughter. Though you would never know it."

I wondered about that statement as Ray left the room.

Supper was served at about nine o'clock. As I entered the dining area, I noticed Ray Harris beckoning to me. By her side stood a very young and tall girl with shoulder-length brownish hair, smiling pleasantly. Ray introduced Erika Glaser to me as "the most patient and hard-working among us," and Erika greeted me with a friendly *"Hallo!"* and hugged and kissed me, Spanish style.

The fare was tortilla española with a local rustic bread called *pa de pagès,* which I wanted to devour in its entirety as the variegated crust crunched between my teeth and the slightly sour hint of the *molla,* or interior of the bread, demanded further acquaintance. To drink, we were given gaseosa, which I sniffed and in which I did catch a whiff of chlorine.

After supper, Ray suggested, "Let's go out for a ciggie."

"I don't smoke," I replied, "but I'll step outside with you two."

We moved out to the quiet stairway and sat on the steps in the spring evening, which was quickly ushering in a cover of purplish clouds. It was Erika who pulled a packet of Mexican cigarettes, *Delicados,* out of her bag.

"These are a parting gift from Dr. Eloesser. He regularly received them in the post, along with chocolates from San Francisco. I do miss him. He was so kind and even allowed me to watch him in surgery and explained as he went along. I was taller than he, which did not seem to bother him." She lit cigarettes—exotically oval-shaped—for herself and Ray, blowing out clouds of rather fragrant smoke.

I asked Erika about her background.

"I was born in Pommern, but we have been living in Spain since before the war." She spoke English with a decided German accent—I can now detect it! "My mother ran the Pensión Vienesa in Madrid, across from the Palace Hotel."

"Ah, I know it well—Calle Cortes, right?"

"Yes, and I worked at the university for a while, but since the war broke out, we have been moving as my father gets different assignments."

The conversation was interrupted as an ambulance pulled up and George assisted the stretcher-bearers in transferring two wounded men into the hospital, glancing over his shoulder at Ray as he entered the building. Ray and Erica rushed in with them and I returned to the dormitory, suddenly exhausted.

I had been warned about cold nights but was not prepared to be awakened by the chill at what must have been three o'clock. I wrapped a blanket around myself and made my way down the hall, looking for the linen room. As I opened the door, the hall light illuminated the spectacle within of what Shakespeare dubbed the "beast with two backs," in the form of Ray Harris and George, the British ambulance driver, moaning and writhing on a tiny army cot. I don't even think they heard me as I closed the door and returned to the dormitory to add these lines to my diary.

VIC, *Saturday, 21 May 1938*

The dormitory was empty when I woke this morning. I visited several patients ill with typhoid fever, none with typhus. Alois, a thirty-five-year-old Czech volunteer, presented an extremely enlarged spleen, along with anemia. He was very confused, and I supposed that his brain was probably infected, showing him to be in the terminal stages of this terrible, preventable disease.

As I descended the front stairs to get some air, two women workers were scrubbing the steps and singing a beautiful Catalan song. I smiled and nodded to them when suddenly a woman appeared in the doorway, shouting, red-faced, in a German-accented Castilian, "You are supposed to be working! No one is paying you to sing!"

I was so ashamed that an obvious countrywoman of mine was behaving in such a rude and disagreeable way toward members of the host nation that I simply shook my head at her, and when she returned to the building, I told the workers that their song was lovely and attempted the Catalan saying "*Qui canta sos mals espanta*"—"Singing drives away one's ills."

I will be returning to Barcelona early tomorrow morning, and Ray and Erika invited me to have a meal in town and had arranged to take breaks in their shifts. Fortunately, tomatoes were available from somewhere warmer, and we were able to enjoy *pa amb tomaquet*, grilled bread rubbed with tomatoes, Catalan style. While we were tasting the house red wine I said, "There was such a rude woman this morning—German accent—she scolded workers who were singing as they washed the steps."

"Oh dear," conceded Erika, dropping her head, "I'm afraid that sounds like my mother."

"Oh, sweetheart," I murmured, grasping her arm, "I am so sorry. I had no idea."

Ray put a hand to her mouth, stifling a laugh. "It is not your fault, Claire. Marie-Thérèse has a—difficult time—with other people."

"Yes, she does," admitted Erika. "With me as well."

"In that case, I am still sorry," I said, putting my arm around the girl.

"Why don't we get someone to take our picture outside," suggested Ray, after we had paid. "I have my camera with me."

We stepped out into the narrow medieval Vic streets just as two British soldiers came along and offered to snap a photo of us. I will save a space to paste the picture once Ray sends it to me.

We strolled awhile, pretending to be tourists, and then returned to the hospital and to more wounded. I told Ray that I was going to go to the linen room for another blanket for the cold night ahead, saying pointedly, "Better do this now, while the room is clear, eh, Ray?"

She blushed red, and I squeezed her arm: "You are lucky—enjoy!"

I do not think I have contributed anything of any import to the American Hospital Number One or to stemming the terrible forward march of typhoid fever or of typhus, but I have made two lovely friends, along with my share of faux pas.

BARCELONA, Wednesday, 25 May 1938

This day began with a horrible bombing. Staff and even potential donors at the hospital breathlessly related the details: The principal target was the beautiful Mediterranean city of Alicante (memories of palm trees, briny fragrances, salty fried fish, Ernst!), specifically its Central Market. The market was packed with people, a fact considered by the Italian pilots of the Savoia S-79 *Sparviero*

(Sparrowhawk) airplanes that took off from their base in occupied Mallorca at eight in the morning. They dropped ninety huge bombs over the city, just one phase of the fascists' ruthless attempt to terrorize and demoralize civilian populations all along the Mediterranean coast as they push toward Valencia. The reports say that the sirens did not sound, so people did not reach those *refugios* that we had seen on our way to Benissa. The result was over three hundred dead.

Alfred Benlloch displayed his clear reasoning: "The bombers flew in over land, not from the sea. The antiaircraft sensors point toward the sea. That must be changed!"

When I returned to the hotel, I found a message that had been left for me: The SIM has ordered my presence at their offices on Puerta del Ángel, number 24, on Friday, 27 May, at noon. My hands turned to cloth on reading the notice. They may have news about Ernst! I will probably dream about him tonight, and I hope the dream is a sweet one.

BARCELONA, Friday, 27 May 1938

It is not midnight, the hour I usually write in this diary, but rather about three o'clock in the afternoon. I am sitting in the sun, at a table in the sand on the Barceloneta. On my table, alongside my diary, is a glass of *vino blanco dorado de Gandesa*. Within the range of my vision stands a sign indicating that there is a refugio nearby. Except for the possibility of being bombed at any moment, I feel relatively safe. To explain:

I had asked for the day's leave, considering my appointment with the SIM. I hardly slept last night, going over in my mind what could possibly happen and imagining multiple scenarios solving the mystery of Ernst's disappearance. I dressed in my whites, which gives me a sense of professionalism. I entered the building at Puerta del Ángel, number 24, at about a quarter to twelve. My hands fluttered like captive birds and my heart was pounding in my throat. I searched for some sign on the main floor indicating SIM offices but found nothing, so I climbed the stairs to the next floor. As I walked along a hallway, a door opened and a dark-skinned, Spanish-looking man stepped out. Receding hairline, lips pursed in a half-smile.

"Camarada 'Pilizbó'?"

"Yes, Clara Philipsborn," I replied, relieved, and offered my hand, which he took briefly and rather limply.

"Grimau," he responded, opened the door more widely, and stepped aside. The room was small and windowless. On the wall hung portraits of Lenin and Stalin, Lenin's slightly askew. Behind a desk that was bare save a cardboard folder and an ashtray sat a pale, thin man, wearing rimless eyeglasses and a plain gray shirt. The man called "Grimau," wearing a similar shirt, took a seat along the wall. The man behind the desk remained seated, pronounced his name, "Kurt Laube," and gestured toward the chair facing the desk:

"*Nehmen Sie platz, Frau Philipsborn* (Have a seat, Mrs. Philipsborn)," he said, using the formal terminology.

I sat down as Laube opened the folder, glanced briefly at it, and pinned his gaze on me over his spectacles:

"So you are born in Kiel?"

"Yes, but I have lived most of my life in Berlin." I wondered if this was a friendly conversation and decided to continue with, "And you?"

He nodded as he leaned back in his chair: "I was born in Rathenow, near Berlin, but I have lived most of my life in Nowawes."

"Oh," I brightened, "my brother and his family settled there, before emigrating—"

"Yes, to Denmark," he concluded.

(*Ah, so he knows that,* I thought.)

He turned a sheet in the folder over, then looked up. "Now we must ask you, Frau Philipsborn, if you are acquainted with a man called . . . Ernst Liefmann."

I sat up straighter as my heartbeat clutched my throat. "Yes, I am, but I have not seen him since December—is he all right?"

"We will ask the questions, Frau Philipsborn. Do you know his occupation?"

"He came to Spain with a Tank-Brigade," I began, sitting back in the chair, "and later worked as a driver for—for your organization, the SIM."

"That is what he told you?"

The chill in his voice froze my face. But I leaned forward to defend Ernst, to defend myself:

"That is what I *know* because he drove me and many patients and other medical staff. I also visited the Auto-Park in Albacete, and he was known there."

He continued, as if he had not heard me, "What was your relationship with Ernst Liefmann?"

I realized that he knew this already, so I just confirmed: "We were— are— close friends—and we shared a rented room in Albacete, with the permission of Base Commander Schalbroeck."

Laube removed his glasses as he gestured toward me, raising his voice slightly: "This permission was given to *you*, was it not? Not to Herrn Liefmann."

"Yes, that is true."

"And you invited Herrn Liefmann to . . . live with you?"

"Yes, I did."

Laube paused and replaced and adjusted his glasses. His thin lips twitched in what may have been intended as a smile. "So—if you knew him so well, you must have known . . . that he was a *hochstapler*!"

"Hochstapler!" I gasped. "A confidence man, swindler? Absolutely not." I swallowed and struggled to avoid weeping. "He is a kind, honest, gentle man."

"Quite the contrary," exclaimed Laube triumphantly, tapping the folder. "What he admitted to us is that he stole weapons from the Army of the Republic and sold them to the fascists."

"Not possible! I would have known if he were doing such a terrible thing. Ernst is as loyal an anti-fascist as I!"

"Ah, and that brings us to your situation, Frau Philipsborn. Herr Liefmann knew where we could find you." He looked down at the papers in the folder, nodding his head.

"My situation? What about my situation?" I began to raise my voice. I did not expect that I would be the topic of this meeting and was now completely disconcerted.

Laube reached into a drawer and pulled out another folder, setting it on top of the first one. "We have reports about your connections to the German Embassy in Madrid. And about your association with—'circles hostile to the Republic.'"

"The German Embassy? Of course I had connections with the German Embassy. I was—I am—a German national living and working in Spain, and I had to visit the Embassy to renew my visa." I was aware of my voice becoming shrill but could do nothing to control it.

Again, he seemed not to have heard what I said. "And your connections with enemies of the Republic?"

"Never! Not knowingly, at least. I was employed by the university, where all sorts of people came through."

"And your attendance at meetings where the ideas of Trotsky were promoted? Can you deny that?"

"I was interested in all possibilities for preventing a fascist takeover in Spain. I worked with students and wanted to be able to discuss matters with them."

Laube closed the folder and leaned back a bit in his chair. "Well, no matter. We cannot dispute the authority of the source of this information." He paused: "Comandante Carlos himself."

"¡Hijo de puta!" I shouted, jumping to my feet and knocking my chair over. Grimau also rose and took a step toward me, holding out his hands as if to restrain me. Fearing that he might touch me, I righted my chair and sat down again, gasping in rage. I took advantage of the fact that both men seemed utterly unprepared for that outburst, to control my breathing and my voice.

"Let me explain," I began. "I met Vittorio Vidali on only two or three occasions, at the Hospital Obrero on Calle Maudes." I thought for a moment, trying to recall the details, now minus the vodka-drenched fog. "Our conversation was on general topics. He did ask me if I had contact with Germans in Spain." Words echoed in my mind: 'Do you have German friends, Tedeschina? Are there others here?' Why would he suggest that I had Nazi connections? Oh, it was obvious. All right. It was now or never. I swallowed and looked Laube straight in his pale blue eyes. "Comandante Carlos did not know . . . that I am . . . a Jew."

Laube's jaw dropped, and he gasped. His pale skin reddened. He pushed his chair back.

"W-well, we will be watching you," he stammered. "Oh, and your application for membership in the Communist Party of Spain has been rejected. Here is the notice." He shoved a paper toward me, which I stuffed into my pocketbook, my hands shaking uncontrollably. "You may go now."

Grimau took a step toward Laube with a puzzled expression, and I realized that he had probably not understood a word of what we were saying, except for my shouted curse. My legs felt like jelly as I gathered up my pocketbook and stood to leave. What words of parting does one utter in such a situation? The two of them were just standing and looking at each other in a state of suspended animation, and I think I must have flown out of the room and down the stairs, since I certainly do not remember going through the door.

Along with a few bomb craters and chunks of building material partially blocking the sidewalks, the streets of Barcelona welcomed me back to the most normal place in the world. Gentle, pastel colors, elegant buildings, sweet air, children at play. My legs commanded me to move, move, move toward the sea, find a quiet place, and take stock of what had happened—what it means in my life. So I started along Puerta del Ángel (the Angel's Gate) until I reached the Barceloneta. Evidence of bombing was everywhere, but there were people sitting and lying in the sand on blankets and beach chairs—children playing in the water—cafés right on the waterfront. I walked to the water's edge, pulled off my shoes, and let the tiny waves splash on my feet. These same blue-green waters that witnessed Ernst's and my first kiss. Our Mediterranean! *Mare Nostrum,* as the Romans called it. I put my shoes back on and turned back and found this table and was soon approached by a teenaged boy in a white jacket:

"*Què t'agradaria, camarada* (What would you like, Comrade)?" (Yes, 'camarada,' not 'Frau Pilizbó'!)

"*Un vi blanc, si te plau* (A white wine, please)."

"*Ara mateix* (Right away), camarada."

And then, the reckoning: Why did the SIM call me in? They obviously have done something with Ernst and wanted to use that information to get me to admit to something. They said that he had "confessed" to crimes. Gottenyu— they must have tortured him. What horrendous things could they have done to make him confess to crimes he obviously did not commit? And why would they have taken him in? Because of me?

The boy has just brought my wine and it is glorious, in harmony with the sun's kind caresses on my face. I wanted that warmth on my feet again, so I looked around surreptitiously, pushed off my shoes, and dug my toes into the sand. Delicious!

So Ernst is either in prison or they have killed him. Agents of our Republic, agents of the Communist Party. My Party, the Party of Rosa Luxemburg! Yes, they were after *me*. It is because of *me* that he was taken in and maybe killed. And why? Was it all because of what Carlos reported—that I had connections to the embassy? Is that why he supplied me with the vodka? I was so thrilled that Comandante Carlos wanted to be with me. Ha! He just wanted information from the German nurse and then—another function of the vodka—he raped me! How stupid I was! I feel like shouting "hijo de puta" again, but I do not want to frighten these people who are enjoying the warm spring sunshine.

Worst of all—dare I ask myself? If he had known I was a Jew, would he even have attempted to get information from me? Probably not. And all because I have been trying to hide my identity since I arrived in Spain. But just now, at the Angel's Gate, my revealing that I am Jewish may have saved my life. Otherwise, I might not be savoring the fragrant wine, the kindly sun, and the sparkling Catalan language here on the Barceloneta, but would instead be languishing in a cell in the basement of Puerta del Ángel, 24. How can I forgive myself for causing the death of an innocent man, a man I loved? It is worse than if I had committed a medical error and lost a patient. How can I atone for this sin?

But am I judging myself too harshly? I wish I could speak to another Jew about this dilemma, which is spiritual rather than political.

I look around me now at these people—my comrades. I have chosen to live in your land and to serve your Republic. I am at this moment feeling love for you all and gratitude for your accepting me. But—do you know that I am a Jew? Would that change anything? I now think of Uncle Julius and his need to hide who he was. I will never know all his reasons.

I am soon going to head back up the Ramblas, and perhaps while walking or in a dream tonight or as I awake tomorrow, a way to assuage my terrible guilt will come to me.

BARCELONA, *Saturday, 28 May 1938*

Who knew that help would come through food! I returned to the hotel at about seven o'clock yesterday and was so exhausted that I just dropped onto the bed and slept for about three hours. I awoke in the dark and at first did not realize where I was. Berta was not there. My body felt different, and my head felt like someone else's—I am not sure whose. I bathed and dressed. Then I realized I had not eaten anything, sustained only by that glass of wine. Suddenly I felt like having something hot and something sweet, not necessarily in the same dish. I went downstairs and took a seat at the bar. I did not want to sit with anyone I knew or at a table by myself. I did not want to be alone with me, the me who had caused Ernst's death. I greeted the bartender, an elderly man whom I assumed was Catalan. He was smoking and in fact everyone seated at the bar seemed to be smoking, which somehow comforted me, as I was now enveloped in a cloud. Perhaps it would carry me away, leaving all my iniquities on the ground. I asked the bartender if he had any kind of food that was sweet.

"You are fortunate, camarada. Tonight we have *mel i mató*."

"Mel i mató? What is that?"

"A typical Catalan dessert: honey and cheese, a soft, fresh cheese."

"Oh, that sounds like what I want. How is it served?"

"Let me show you." He opened the door of the refrigerator behind him and pulled out a water glass filled with white cheese, through which peeked the amber swirls of honey. Atop the cheese reposed what looked like white petals.

"And what are those?" I asked, pointing to the petals.

"*Tarongina.*"

"Tarongina? What is that?"

"Azahar," chimed in the man seated at my left, in Castilian.

"Azahar!" I exclaimed joyfully. "From Seville?"

"*No, xiqueta, és de València—València la lliure* (No, girl, it is from Valencia—*free* Valencia)!" answered the bartender.

(Of course, not from Seville, my Sevilla la roja, now occupied—and violated—by the monster Queipo de Llano.)

"This is what I must have—please." It must have sounded strange because I got some odd looks but did not care. "And—do you have any fruit tea?"

"I think we can make what you like, xiqueta," the bartender assured me, placing before me the glass filled with mel i mató on a saucer with a teaspoon, flanked by a tissue-paper napkin advertising "Hotel Majestic" in red letters.

I first plucked from the glass a single petal of the azahar and rolled it around in my mouth with eyes closed. I now understand how Christians feel when they are taking communion: they are literally *in-corporating* (bringing into their bodies) the essence of another being, which they believe to be holy. The azahar transported me to my first trip to Seville and to my feeling of living or having lived in every layer of the culture of Spain along with its human inhabitants. Something I never felt while living in Germany. Where *do* I come from? Where is my home?

I opened my eyes and dipped the spoon into the glass and took the first bite, though I really should not say "bite" because I did not need to bite the food, just draw it into my mouth with my lips and press it against my palate with my tongue. The cheese was not salted, so there were no feelings of aggression that salt sometimes suggests to me. It comforted me as mother's milk comforts an infant, and the honey took me to the world of bees and flowers and sunshine, a world without war, before men had even invented war.

A young waiter approached from the kitchen, carrying a silver teapot and a teacup on a tray.

"Could I have some honey for this tea?" I asked. Honey—the sweetness of a world at peace.

"Right away, camarada."

After he left, I practiced the word for honey, "*mel,*" with eyes closed, dropping the back of my tongue to produce the typically Catalan sound of the "L," and then suddenly opened my eyes: "Mel—Mela—Melanie—Melitta!" I exclaimed aloud, knowing whom I would be looking for today.

Upon returning to my room around midnight, I greeted Berta, brushed my teeth, and put on a soft white cotton nightgown. My bed felt soft and welcoming, and as I closed my eyes, I felt surrounded by the soft gray cloud and nourished and rocked to sleep by the words "mel i mató."

This morning as soon as I arrived at my little office at Hospital number 18, I telephoned Headquarters and left a message for "Melitta Gruber" to telephone me. I also telephoned the Bristol Hotel, where I believed she and Norbert are staying, and left the same message. Around two hours later I was called to the telephone.

"Good morning, Klara." Mela's voice sounded clear and musical despite the imperfect telephone lines (at one kilometer's distance!). "*Nu, was geht* (So, what's happening)?"

I hesitated, as we had not spoken much since arriving in Barcelona from Albacete, but her tone encouraged me. "Would you have some time today to talk to me in private? I am having some problems and just need to talk to someone I can trust."

"Oh, of course. Where would you like to meet? I will be free at three o'clock."

Where could we meet where no one could listen to our conversation? I thought of the Spanish expression "*Las paredes oyen*"—"Walls have ears." Of course! In the open air—the air does not have ears, or walls.

"There is a little park on the Passeig de Gràcia, just across from the Avinguda del Catorze d'Abril—you know, the wide street that crosses the city diagonally. Can we meet there, in the park, at three thirty?"

"All right, I will meet you there."

As I interviewed prospective blood donors, I tried very hard to concentrate on the people and their responses to me, and not to think about what had happened yesterday—was it only yesterday?—or to think about what I might say to Mela and what she could possibly say to me.

I arrived at the park, called the Jardinets de Gràcia, at a little before three thirty and gazed at everything that was green and at the fountain that was spraying bravely heavenward as if this were a normal day in a normal, peaceful city. Children played in the open spaces and hid behind banana trees, shouting and laughing. The green tones and the babbling of the fountain and of the children were collaborating to calm my spirits. But when Mela arrived and reached out to hug me, I burst into tears and clung to her, sobbing.

"Come, sit." She took my arm, and we moved to a bench that faced the fountain. Mela silently waited for me to collect myself.

"Oy, Mela, I think I have killed Ernst!" I immediately regretted beginning in such a melodramatic and perhaps frightening way and began weeping again.

"How is that possible? What happened?"

I pulled out a handkerchief and wiped my eyes and blew my nose. "When he left Albacete, he told me he was coming to Barcelona on an 'assignment' for the SIM. He did not say anything more about this assignment, and I did not ask him anything. As you know, I have not seen him since."

"Yes, so how can you say that you killed him?"

"Well, the SIM called me in to their office yesterday. A German agent talked to me, and there was a Spanish man there as well. At first they tried to make me comfortable but soon they told me that they had taken Ernst in and that he had 'confessed' to some terrible crimes against the Republic and the Loyalist Army. He had also told them where I was. And the reason they had picked him up"—I began sobbing again—"is that they had a file on me."

"On you?"

"Yes. This report said that I had contacts with the German government, which of course I did, because I came to Spain in 1930 and had to report regularly to the embassy in Madrid to renew my visa."

"Right—I understand."

"But then the report went on to say that I was involved 'in circles that have hostile attitudes toward the Republic.'"

Mela gasped.

I continued, breathlessly, "When Ernst and I took a room together, they found out about our relationship, and they thought they could find out more about me by taking him in, which was easy because he was already working for them, and they tricked him into taking a train to Barcelona by fabricating an assignment for him. They must have tortured him, and I imagine that people say anything that the torturers want them to say if the torture is severe enough."

"But how did they get that crazy story about you?"

"That is the worst part." I paused and looked at the water in the fountain and made myself take a breath. "When I was in Madrid, a man who is very important in the Party and the Fifth Regiment came into our hospital. He was seeing an Italian woman photographer who worked there, and I think he came to visit her and maybe another woman who was there as well. A short time after we were introduced, he invited me to share a bottle of vodka in a hospital room that was unoccupied."

"Vodka?"

"Yes, vodka—I had never had vodka before. He kept refilling my glass, and he was asking me whether I had German friends or family here in Spain. I think he asked me other things too, but I don't really remember because I was becoming so confused from the vodka. He was putting his hands on me, and I think he kissed me, and"—I began yet again to sob—"I woke up on a bed—in the middle of the night—with my *gatkes* on the floor. He must have raped me."

"Gottenyu!" exclaimed Mela. "But how did that information about you get into a file with the SIM?"

I swallowed and wiped my face again. "Mela, that man—was Comandante Carlos! I was so taken to think that such an important person was interested in me that I willingly met him in that room and drank all that vodka. I answered all the questions he asked me, but what I did not tell him was . . . that I am Jewish!"

"You were not obligated to tell him that, Klara."

"No, I was not obligated, but if I had told him, I am sure he would not have asked me all those questions about Germany. And he would not have to invent the other nonsense about associating with enemies of the Republic." I rushed to finish, before I could explode into weeping again: "He would not have anything to report to the SIM, and the SIM would not have suspected Ernst, and they would not have taken him in, and he would be here with me today!"

We both fell silent for a moment; then Mela placed her hand firmly on my arm: "Look, Klara, I am sure you have your reasons for not telling the world that you are Jewish. We are certainly not obligated to do so. Every day it becomes more dangerous for Jews in our countries."

"True," I admitted. "And God knows that Jews are not the most welcome people in Spain."

"So have you told anyone here that you are Jewish?"

"A few people."

"And what was the response?"

"I don't think anyone was terribly shocked. But I was definitely not about to tell the head of the Quinto Regimiento that I am a Jew."

"There, you see? And do you think most people even know what it means to be a Jew?"

"Ha! I am sometimes not sure myself! In Germany, we look different from the majority of Germans—you as well in Austria?"

"Yes, definitely."

"And here in Spain, we look like everyone else. So when I first arrived, I decided that being Jewish or not was a matter of choice."

"Hmmm, maybe so. But do you think we would be here in Spain, fighting fascism, if we were not Jewish?"

"Ah, I had conversations on that topic, when the Botwin Battalion was first formed." I paused to think and then continued, "And now it occurs to me that Vittorio Vidali's decision to create a file about me was just a part of his role with his faction of the Party. The fact that I came from Germany was ammunition enough for him to go about his devious campaign and carry it to its absurd conclusion, no matter what my religion." I stood and stretched, feeling suddenly strong and free. "Shall we go back? I'll walk you to your hotel."

Mela stood and I hugged her tightly.

"You are wonderful. Thank you so much for being such a good friend and confidante."

"I am glad that I was free to talk," she answered simply.

This day has certainly ended differently from the day before. I am feeling grateful for the true friendship of a kind and generous woman and strengthened in my anti-fascism, despite the rejection by my own party.

I now feel strong enough to paste here the list of people whose applications for Party membership were not accepted. It is interesting to see that George Chaikin was also rejected. A small consolation for me is the fact that my name is spelled so abominably and that I am listed as Spanish. Do you even know who I am, dear comrades?

BARCELONA, *Monday, 30 May 1938*

I am trying to make the best of what has happened today. Early this morning, about eight o'clock, as I was getting ready to go to the hospital, a boy from the hotel desk brought me a message that I was to report to Dr. Barsky's office immediately. I kept my whites on and walked quickly to AME headquarters. Dr. Barsky was not there, but Mildred Rackley greeted me with a solemn expression and closed the office door as I took a seat. Her look froze my face, and my heart grasped my throat as I waited for what she might say.

"Comrade Philipsborn, we have received word that you have come under surveillance by the SIM."

I felt my body stiffen, my fingertips numb.

She went on, opening a folder on the desk, her large teeth now menacing behind pulled- back lips. "A person in these circumstances is not qualified to perform service to the Ayuda Médica Extranjera. Even though we have been receiving positive reports about your work, information such as this"—she tapped the paper within the folder—"requires us to discontinue your service with us."

I leaned forward toward Mildred, placing a hand on the desk and trying to control my emotions and to steady my voice. "Comrade, I am aware of that report, and I assure you that it is based on completely false information. Can you please investigate it?"

"We have indeed investigated it thoroughly and the source is unimpeachable. We have also received notice that your application for membership to the Communist Party of Spain has been rejected. This decision is—final," she announced, snapping the folder shut, adding, "Of course we can also no longer support your stay at the hotel. We ask that you vacate the premises by Sunday, June fifth."

I sat back in silence, unable to look her in the face—that open, American face. I could only see the inverted V eyebrows and feel the hot, sweaty hands of "the unimpeachable" comandante on my throat, now gripped by a rage that threatened to leap forth in the strongest curse I could hurl in a language I do not even possess. But I then remembered who I am and that I deserve respect. I swallowed. The image dissipated, the rage abated, and I somehow found the strength to rise to my feet and declare, "Thank you, camarada. Let me remind you that I am a good Communist and have always been loyal to the Spanish Republic. I will comply with AME regulations and discontinue all connections with this service by Sunday. Salud."

I walked out, leaving the office door open, rapidly left the building, driven as if propelled, and crossed the diagonal Avinguda del Catorze d'Abril until I reached the Jardinets. I took a seat on the bench where Mela and I had had the conversation that had allowed me to think more clearly. I let the musical splashing of the fountain relax the muscles of my throat. But then I began blaming myself again for having been so weak and vulnerable in the face of the attentions of an important man.

I suddenly felt a need for movement and stood and began to pace slowly along the path on the edge of the garden. I felt utterly alone, isolated from everyone around me. I simply placed one foot in front of the other. My only thought was that my life was a failure. I have committed acts that caused my life to fail. I told myself to keep walking. Then a Hebrew word entered my head, echoing the shushing sounds of the fountain: *Ashamnu:* the recitation of sins, each one beginning with a letter of the word, Ashamnu, "We are guilty." I turned and reversed my direction. "We commit ourselves to recognizing that our failures are self-destructive." When I reached the spot at which I had started, I moved closer to the fountain and began to circle it in a narrower path.

My mind peppered me with questions: Have I destroyed myself? Oh women, oh sisters, is it our destiny to behave this way? We have been considered lesser beings since Adam's rib. But aren't we the strong ones? Do we not bear the weight of children unborn and the pain as we birth them? Was I thinking that I could raise my status through the favors of a demigod of the Communist Party?

Thinking? What thinking? There was nothing rational about my agreeing to meet in Room 18 of the Hospital Obrero with the most powerful man in the Fifth Regiment. I was simply playing a role inherited from generations of our mothers and our grandmothers. So now what to do?

I reversed my direction again, circling so closely to the fountain that I felt the mist of its spray cooling my face and my neck. My breathing deepened, and I opened my arms as I kept walking. I must counsel myself, just as another wise woman counseled me only a few days ago. Camarada Klara the Wise is counseling Clarita the vilde chaye to forgive herself for reenacting a badly written drama. And I should perhaps even forgive all those who preceded me, all who are to follow.

The thoughts, the words quieted down, and I heard only the water, knew only the forgiveness. I sat on the edge of the fountain and dipped my hand into the water. Goldfish swam close to my fingers and darted away. Two little girls approached the fountain and began to splash each other, laughing, and scampered away. I wanted to run with them and splash them, but I stood and began walking back toward the hotel.

It will be all right.

BARCELONA, Tuesday, 31 May 1938

I woke this morning and took a hot shower and shampooed my hair, hoping that the stream of warm water would force the tangles out of my mind so that I could organize my affairs. But as I entered the lobby, agitated conversations were taking place. There has been another devastating bombing, this time in Granollers, the small city about thirty kilometers to the northeast of here. My train had passed through there traveling to and from Vic! It was attacked this morning by five airplanes departing from the Italian base at Mallorca. The aviation was reported both as Savoia-Marchetti and as Junkers. They dropped around sixty bombs, along with incendiary devices. Though the targets were presumably munitions and electricity plants, civilian deaths are being estimated at over two hundred. I have also heard rumors today that the initial target was Barcelona itself but that the aircraft were repelled by our antiaircraft guns (Alfred's work?).

I sat for a moment in the lobby, deciding on my next actions. I will need to make living arrangements, I realized. I cannot return to Germany. Can I emigrate to England? Perhaps someone in the Mond family can help me. My nephews are there, and I could stay with one of them. But I love Spain and I still feel like a Spaniard, despite what has been done to me here, despite the war. I should be able to find work. And how to keep working for the revolution?

I picked up a copy of today's *Vanguardia* from a table and turned to the announcements for *huéspedes* (lodgers). An advert titled *"Bonita habitac"* immediately caught my eye. The address is centrally located, includes kitchen privileges, and if the need arises, I will be close to Headquarters (on the very Ramblas!). I decided to don my whites and even carry my medical bag.

I arrived at the building in fifteen minutes, climbed the two flights, and knocked at the door. The flat was clean and airy. The lady renting the room, a widow named Beatriu Blanc, was impressed with my credentials, which I framed with the necessary omissions. She asked me why I needed a room since I was working for the AME, and I told her I needed a quiet place to study and write.

"It will be quiet enough for you here, dear, unless the fascists come to bomb us."

We agreed on a monthly fee, and I will be moving in on Friday. The building looks solidly built and is not far from a refugio in case the *Aviazione Legionaria* does come back to bomb us. Let the bombs fall where they may, I feel unbelievably lucky.

I had saved the *Vanguardia* page, and I ordered a cup of tea at a café on the Rambla and searched for the *Enseñanza* (Lessons) section. There on the *same page* as the housing notices were two adverts placed by the Liceu Dalmau and its "Institut Linguaphone." The fascinating prospect of multiple languages (even Esperanto!) being taught under one roof must have been directed to me. I left the tea half-finished and covered the short distance to the Carrer de València and the elegantly curvaceous brick building. As I waited to be seen, I studied a photograph on the wall of the Institute's director, Delfí Dalmau. It displayed a bespectacled and bearded young man with a serious expression and a thick crown of hair.

I was received by a middle-aged woman in a gray suit wearing similar eyeglasses as were depicted on the director's portrait. She addressed me in Catalan, and I began my introduction in that language, continued in Castilian, and ended in German, with a few French and English phrases inserted for good measure. When the Catalan woman and the Frenchman, who entered the room as I was speaking, asked me about my experience in teaching adults, I mentioned my short-lived classes at Albacete and emphasized what I had done at Ocaña. I described my method of using *Der Struwwelpeter* as a German textbook. I also told them that I had studied Spanish in Berlin at the Berlitz School.

"Oh, camarada, you are the perfect person for this organization," exclaimed the woman.

I became so enthused that I almost forgot to ask about the pay for teachers, and the lovely thing is that they pay *per language*. No politics were mentioned, and I did not see any telltale portraits on the walls, save that of the founder of the Liceu.

I returned to the hotel and notified them at the desk that I would be moving out on Friday.

BARCELONA, Tuesday, 7 June 1938

"*Incipit vita nova.*"

My new life has begun with the new month and warmer days, and I am feeling more at peace and personally respected. Yesterday I met with the founder and director of the Liceu, Dr. Delfí Dalmau, and what a fascinating hour I spent with this most interesting man. Dalmau was born in Catalunya but received his degree in Argentina and was exposed to many languages and cultures there, not to mention right here in Barcelona.

The teaching method used at the Liceu is called the "direct method": the learner is addressed in the language he or she is learning, much as we experienced in the Berlitz school in Berlin and as I attempted to use in Ocaña. A tool that Dalmau says he initiated is that of making recordings of native speakers for the learners to be able to hear and imitate the authentic sounds of the language. He asked if I would be willing to record some literary passages in German, and I am very keen to do this.

I have always relied on my language abilities in my work, as a means to accomplish my professional goals, but now in this new setting, language itself is the goal, is the subject and the object. It changes my perspective entirely. I am feeling grateful for this gift, which I don't think I ever fully appreciated.

As I was about to leave the Liceu this afternoon, I received a telephone call from Mela.

"Klara, how are you?" Her voice sounded worried.

"I am fine, Mela. I am enjoying this new job and my lovely apartment on the Ramblas."

"I am so glad." She then lowered her voice: "Klara, I have intercepted a message sent to AME Headquarters from Dr. Glaser in Vic, which mentions you."

"Oh! Could you please read it to me?"

She read the message: "Since the departure of Comrade Lieutenant Linick we need, for the director's office, a comrade who speaks perfect Spanish and some foreign languages, and we therefore ask you to send us, if possible, Comrade Clara Philipsborn."

"Oh my goodness, what are they going to do with that?"

"I have no idea. But I have to hang up—I must not be seen with this document."

"Oh, of course. Thank you so much for letting me know."

Now, back in my room, I am wondering: Will the AME try to contact me and send me to Vic again? If they do, will I go? Give up this most promising job at the Liceu and my room? I can only wait and see. If I am not notified, it will mean that they are not going to honor this request. And if they do contact me and ask me to go to Vic, I think I should require some sort of retraction, or at least an apology for having dismissed me. And if I go to Vic, I will have to work under Dr. Glaser, despite his unpleasant nature, and perhaps even collaborate with the dreadful Marie-Thérèse. It would be lovely to see Erika again, though. At least I think I have an advantage with the position I am in now.

BARCELONA, Tuesday, 26 July 1938

From an existence steeped in politics and lively and often bitter discussions, alternating with blood, bandages, ether, and morphine, my daily activities now take place in the rarefied atmosphere of dictionaries, polite conversations, and theories of language, interrupted occasionally and violently by bombs dropped on a civilian population by would-be invaders. The building on the Carrer de València shakes, windows sometimes crack, heart rates accelerate, but soon conversations and lessons resume. The progress of the war and fear of a complete fascist takeover are topics that are rarely mentioned at the Liceu Dalmau. I fill this newly created vacuum in my life by reading *Solidaridad Obrera* or *La Vanguardia* and listening in to conversations that are guaranteed to occur daily in cafés on practically any street. I received no word from headquarters regarding an assignment in Vic, so I have dismissed that possibility.

The word "Ebro" ("*Ebre*" in Catalan) has provided the dominant sound on Barcelona streets today, uttered with tones of optimism that I have not heard for a long time. In order to stem Franco's march toward Valencia, a plan to distract him northward and westward was initiated yesterday morning as Republican troops crossed the Ebro River into enemy-held Tarragona, a move for which the fascists were evidently completely unprepared. The crossing occurred at several points along the curve of the river, accomplished by rafts, tanks (across pontoon bridges), and even individual swimmers.

The appellation of the newest addition to the Army of the Republic is very sad for me to contemplate: "*La Quinta del Biberón*"—that is, the "Baby-Bottle Draft," formed by seventeen- and eighteen-year-old boys. Federica Montseny is said to have coined the term, on hearing that President Azaña had decreed that boys born in 1920 were to be added to the list of draftees. That is the year that Putzi was born! I witnessed his birth—and now babies of his age will be trained to kill and will be dying for the Republic and for land and freedom.

THURSDAY, 22 September 1938

NEGRIN ANUNCIA LA RETIRADA DE VOLUNTARIOS

Ginebra, 21. — (Urgente). — Esta tarde, ha hecho uso de la palabra ante la Asamblea de la Sociedad de las Naciones, el Presidente del Consejo español, Dr. Negrín, quien ha justificado la proposición de que sean retirados de España, todos los evoluntarios extranjeros y anuncia que el Gobierno español, ha decidido ordenar la retirada de todos los voluntarios extranjeros, incluso los naturalizados españoles, alistados desde el principio de la guerra civil. Además, el Dr. Negrín, ha pedido el nombramiento inmediato de una Comisión internacional, encargada de controlar dicha retirada. — Fabra.

Outrage!! All I can feel is outrage! Dr. Negrín, practically a colleague, disciple of Ramón y Cajal, has attempted not only political suicide, but with his absurd decision he is determined to take all of Spain down with him. The outcome of his ill-fated move to cross the Ebro should have been enough. Though it distracted Franco momentarily from his advance on Valencia, it brought down upon our troops the might of Franco, his Nazi and fascist allies, and their superior weaponry.

As if the war maps and the bombings and the tears of loved ones did not cry "defeat" loudly enough, President Dr. Negrín's address, delivered yesterday in Geneva to the League of Nations, imagines that the enemy actually has not only a heart but a sense of fairness and logic. His proposed solution? End all foreign intervention in Spain and dismiss all foreign volunteers, including those who acquired Spanish citizenship at the war's beginning. What is he expecting? That Hitler and Mussolini and Stalin should telephone him and say, "Fine, Juanito, we will all go home tomorrow. A pity about what we did to your country and oh, a pity about all that gold you gave us Russians in exchange for our antiquated weapons"?

I will translate a passage from his speech, which was translated into

Spanish from French and appears on page one of *Solidaridad Obrera*: "Once foreign intervention in Spain has been eliminated, I can guarantee that a policy of national conciliation, directed firmly and energetically by a governing Authority, would allow all Spaniards to forget these years of suffering and cruelty and to quickly reestablish peace within Spain's borders."

What a completely unbelievable, unreasonable statement! If I could respond to him and to his absurd proposal, it would be like this:

Dear Dr. Negrín:

Do you expect that the criminals Hitler and Mussolini, who violated the policy of non-intervention from the outset of Franco's military coup, will now miraculously withdraw from Spain, just because you say it might bring peace to do so? Do you believe that the League of Nations, powerless to prevent Germany's invasion of Austria and Czechoslovakia and Mussolini's invasion of Ethiopia, has the authority to reinforce your utopian fantasy? And can all Spaniards simply "forget" all the suffering we have endured just because you "guarantee" it will happen?

Salud y República,

Clara Philipsborn Mond

I did not go to work at the Liceu today. I drifted from café to café, returning over and over again to Negrín's speech. People were dumbstruck. I am dumbstruck. My throat is swollen with rage, and I am completely bewildered. What is my status? I do not have a document that is worth the paper it is printed on. My passport calls me German, Hitler's government says I am stateless, and the Communist Party of Spain says I am Spanish. I am no longer permitted to work for the Ayuda Médica Extranjera, so I cannot even attend to the wounds of the newly recruited hordes of brave Spanish boys whose bodies will be torn apart by the fascists, laughing as they drop yet more bombs on towns and cities with an impunity now guaranteed by the president of our government, who would expel those who came to aid us. Could I set up a clinic in the streets or in a shelter? I would have to look for other medical people who are at liberty. Remain in Barcelona and teach languages? Since when do fascist governments tolerate speakers of other languages, except as spies? Is exile open to me? The French border is largely sealed off, and I would probably have to find a way to walk across. Mexico is welcoming Spanish exiles, as are some South American countries. Perhaps a ship will sail from one of the few remaining free ports, such as Alicante. But how long will Alicante remain free? Ships even sail occasionally from Barcelona, under threat of bombing. I could be safe in England. Linguaphone has schools in London. The Mond and Mathias families could help me. But how to get there? Perhaps I could use a passport of one of my Mond cousins in Seville, though I do not trust their politics, with all their blessings from His Holiness, and they might even turn me in. Perhaps the SIM will relent, as Kurt Laube seemed to backtrack about my German connections when I told him I was Jewish. They might provide me a way out of Spain—or they might show me the same fate they showed Ernst. In my medical bag I still have my Fifth Regiment-issued Astra 400 38 "La Puro," and I still know how to use it.

I must stop writing now. I am not making much sense. I am feeling completely abandoned, with no one to turn to. Shall I return to the SIM tomorrow—or to AME headquarters to speak with former colleagues or other stateless Jews and anti-fascists? Should I head for the border, for the port, if things seem quiet, or simply report to the Institut? I think it is best to close my diary now and bundle it up with its three comrades in a safe place in my room on the Rambla de Catalunya. Tomorrow I shall seek a safe place for myself. *Die gedanken sind frei.*

AFTERWORD

Thus ends Klara's diary, but not her story. Recent information has turned up evidence that the historical Klara, again falsifying her age and even her name, did manage to come up with some documents and flee fascist Spain for England – where she was not welcomed (as an "enemy alien" and as a Communist). She escaped to the relative freedom of the Americas — possibly Venezuela, where her trail fades away.

The history books can tell us about the fates of others in this story. For more stories about Klara and her compatriots, go to https://www.judith berlowitzauthor.com/blog

IMAGE CREDITS

p. 16: Sevilla, Reales Alcázares, Patio del yeso https://en.todocoleccion.net/postcards-andalusia/bonita-postal-sevilla-real-alcazar-patio-yeso~x26410937

p. 34: Julius Mond. Photo property of Francisco Alba Riesco, with his permission

p. 37: Gerda Philipsborn, Günther Berendt and "Lumpi." Photo property of Gerry Brent, Z"L, with his permission

p. 38: Ellen Philipsborn. Photo property of Shawna Kim Kent, with her permission

p. 44: Ida Mond Philipsborn, obituary. *Berliner Tageblatt*, 5 Nov 1927, p. 10 http://zefys.staatsbibliothek-berlin.de/list/title/zdb/27646518/

p. 44: Ida Mond Philipsborn & Clara Philipsborn, Bavarian Alps, ca. 1915 http://www.dannen.com/lostlove/, With permission of the author

p. 52: Clara with nieces, Opel. Photo property of Shawna Kim Kent, with her permission

P. 67: Madrid, Las Ventas. *ABC* 28 Nov 1930. Hemeroteca Digital, Biblioteca Nacional de España https://www.abc.es/archivo/periodicos/

p. 74: Madrid, collapsed building, 26 Alonso Cano St. *ABC* 13 Nov 1930. Hemeroteca Digital, Biblioteca Nacional de España https://www.abc.es/archivo/periodicos/

p. 80: Madrid, Residencia de Señoritas, snowball, Herminia & Pilar. Property of Dr. Rosa Peraita, with her permission

p. 85: Madrid, Republic wins election, *El Heraldo de Madrid*, 13 Apr 1931. Hemeroteca Digital, Biblioteca Nacional de España http://hemerotecadigital. bne.es/details.vm?q=id:0000384902&lang=es

p. 101: Ellen, Renate, Nora Philipsborn, Denmark, ca. 1931. Photo property of Shawna Kim Kent, with her permission

p. 110: Preservativos, ad for condoms, *El Socialista*, 8 Nov 1932 http://archivo. fpabloiglesias.es/index.php?r=hemeroteca/ElSocialista

p. 117: Nazi May Day. *Berliner Tageblatt.* http://zefys.staatsbibliothek-berlin. de/list/title/zdb/27646518/-/1933

p. 118: María Dolores Heraso Romero de Mond, Obituary. Sevilla, *ABC,* 16 Aug 1933, p. 36. Hemeroteca Digital, Biblioteca Nacional de España https:// www.abc.es/archivo/periodicos/abc-sevilla-19331213-6.html

p. 133: ¡Mujer! *El socialista,* 16 Nov 1933, p. 1. Fundación Pablo Iglesias http:// archivo.fpabloiglesias.es/

p. 141:   Nuremberg Laws racial chart. https://encyclopedia.ushmm.org/ content/en/article/the-nuremberg-race-laws

p. 171: Hospital Obrero de Maudes https://urbancidades.wordpress. com/2016/06/06/hospital-de-jornaleros-san-francisco-de-paula/

p. 174: Caricature of Comandante Carlos: With kind permission of Biblioteca Virtual de Prensa Histórica, Gobierno de España, Ministerio de Cultura y Deporte

p. 180: Clara's ID card, Fifth Regiment. With kind permission of España. Ministerio de Educación, Cultura y Deporte, Centro Documental de la Memoria Histórica, ES.37274

p. 197: Julio Mond Kaiser obit, *ABC,* 10 Oct 1936. Hemeroteca Digital, Biblioteca Nacional de España https://www.abc.es/archivo/periodicos/

p. 202: Madrid, Women on the metro. *ABC,* 10 Nov 1936, p. 6. Hemeroteca Digital, Biblioteca Nacional de España https://www.abc.es/archivo/periodicos/

p. 207: Jacob Philipsborn. Photo property of Shawna Kim Kent, with her permission

p. 247: Auto Park Train Corps. *RGASPI,* Fond 545, Opis 2, Delo 216, IMG0033 http://sovdoc.rusarchives.ru/sections/organizations//cards/220852

p. 264: Almansa a los BBII. *Defensor de Albacete,* 9 sep 1937, p. 3. Biblioteca Digital de Albacete "Tomás Navarro Tomás": http://pandora.dipualba.es/ results.vm?q=parent:0000000720&lang=es&view=main

p. 275: Liste des Camarades…Blessés…. *RGASPI* Fond 545, Opis 3, Delo 695, p. 73 http://sovdoc.rusarchives.ru/sections/organizations//cards/220852

p. 281: Albacete, Permission to live in town. *RGASPI,* Fond 545, Opis 2, Delo 63, IMG 293 http://sovdoc.rusarchives.ru/sections/organizations//cards/220852

p. 289: Rosa Luxemburgo. *Frente Rojo,* 26 Dec 1937 p. 6, Biblioteca Nacional de España, Hemeroteca Digital http://hemerotecadigital.bne.es/details. vm?q=id:0000189234&lang=es

p. 289: Rosario Dinamitera, *Frente Rojo,* 26 Dec 1937 p. 6, Biblioteca Nacional de España, Hemeroteca Digital http://hemerotecadigital.bne.es/details. vm?q=id:0000189234&lang=es

p. 302: Administradores. *RGASPI,* Fond 545, Opis 3, Delo 669, p. 3 http:// sovdoc.rusarchives.ru/sections/organizations//cards/220852

p. 315: Vich, Clara with Erika Glaser and Ray Harris. Photo by Fredericka Martin. Fredericka Martin Papers, ALBA 001, Tamiment Library and Robert F. Wagner Labor Archives, New York University, with permission

p. 328: Lista de los solicitantes. *RGASPI,* Fond 545, Opis 3, Delo 669 http:// sovdoc.rusarchives.ru/sections/organizations//cards/220852

p. 336: Negrín anuncia retirada. *Solidaridad obrera*, 22 Sep 1938 www.hemerotecadigitalbne.es

ACKNOWLEDGMENTS

To those who have been more helpful than they can imagine, including institutions kindly granting permission to reproduce images, and individuals offering support for Klara's journey, so far from home:

Dr. Werner Abel, Francisco Javier Alba Riesco, Eduardo Albaladejo and El Boletín, Dr. Rina Benmayor, Biblioteca Nacional de España, Pilar Bonet Rosado, Gerry Brent Z"L, Centro Documental de la Memoria Histórica, Harriet Chaikin Coyne, Eliza Chaikin Kenan, Dr. Nicholas Coni, Gene Dannen, Steven Frank and the United States Holocaust Memorial Museum, Anthony L. Geist, Joshua Goode, Dr. Helen Graham, Caitlin Hamilton Summie, Raymond Meyer Hoff, Libby Jordan, Dr. Gerdien Jonker, Shawna Kim Kent, Krissa Lagos and She Writes Press, Juan Miguel León Moriche, Lucia Liss, Robert Llopis i Sendra, Rob MacDonald and Solidarity Park, Patricia Martínez de Vicente, Julian Robert Mathias, Armando Mauleón Cangas, Golda van der Meer and Editorial Mozaika, Peter Mond, 4th Baron Melchett Z"L, Linda Joy Myers, Mark Newman, Dr. María Rosa Peraita Adrados, Thomas D. Philipsborn, Félix Población Bernardo and Diario del Aire, Kate Jessica Raphael, Eulalia Ramírez Nueda and GEFREMA, RGASPI, Dr. Sergio Riesco Roche, Daniel Sánchez, the Tamiment Library and Robert F. Wagner Labor Archives, Armand Volkas, Peter Verburgh, Nancy Wallach, Alan Warren, Lauren Wise and She Writes Press, and Ana Zamora.

Especially acknowledging Brooke Warner and her life-changing gift to women writers, She Writes Press, my husband, Cy, first editor, inspiring writer, fellow traveler, and the rest of my loving and patient family, including the Philipsborns scattered worldwide.

ABOUT THE AUTHOR

© Victoria Mauleón

Los Angeles–born author Judith Berlowitz had just retired from her Spanish-teaching position at Oakland's Mills College when her genealogical research uncovered a Gestapo record mentioning a relative, Clara Philipsborn, who was the only woman anti-fascist volunteer in the Spanish Civil War from the German state of Schleswig-Holstein. The few details of the report led to more research, which led to *Home So Far Away*. In addition to her career teaching Spanish and world cultures, and a stint as a tour guide, Judith is a card-carrying translator and has published in the field of ethnomusicology (Sephardic balladry), oral history, and Jewish identity. She sang for years with the Oakland Symphony Chorus and is now a member of the San Francisco Bach Choir. She lives in San Francisco with her husband, not far from her three daughters and three grandsons.

SELECTED TITLES FROM SHE WRITES PRESS

She Writes Press is an independent publishing company founded to serve women writers everywhere. Visit us at www.shewritespress.com.

An Address in Amsterdam by Mary Dingee Fillmore. $16.95, 978-1-63152-133-1
After facing relentless danger and escalating raids for 18 months, Rachel Klein—a well-behaved young Jewish woman who transformed herself into a courier for the underground when the Nazis invaded her country—persuades her parents to hide with her in a dank basement, where much is revealed.

Expect Deception by JoAnn Ainsworth. $16.95, 978-1-63152-060-0
When the US government recruits Livvy Delacourt and a team of fellow psychics to find Nazi spies on the East Coast during WWII, she must sharpen her skills quickly—or risk dying.

Portrait of a Woman in White by Susan Winkler. $16.95, 978-1-938314-83-4
When the Nazis steal a Matisse portrait from the eccentric, art-loving Rosenswigs, the Parisian family is thrust into the tumult of war and separation, their fates intertwined with that of their beloved portrait.

The Sweetness by Sande Boritz Berger. $16.95, 978-1-63152-907-8
A compelling and powerful story of two girls—cousins living on separate continents—whose strikingly different lives are forever changed when the Nazis invade Vilna, Lithuania.

In the Shadow of Lies: A Mystery Novel by M. A. Adler. $16.95, 978-1-938314-82-7
As World War II comes to a close, homicide detective Oliver Wright returns home—only to find himself caught up in the investigation of a complicated murder case rife with racial tensions.

Tasa's Song by Linda Kass. $16.95, 978-1-63152-064-8
From a peaceful village in eastern Poland to a partitioned post-war Vienna, from a promising childhood to a year living underground, *Tasa's Song* celebrates the bonds of love, the power of memory, the solace of music, and the enduring strength of the human spirit.